Dolphi
The Dolphin Man

GRAHAM R. LOWE

TRAFFORD

• Canada • UK • Ireland • USA •

Note for Librarians: A cataloguing record for this book is available
from Library and Archives Canada at www.collectionscanada.
ca/amicus/index-e.html
ISBN 1-4120-9009-1

*Printed in Victoria, BC, Canada. Printed on paper with minimum
30% recycled fibre.*
*Trafford's print shop runs on "green energy" from solar, wind and
other environmentally-friendly power sources.*

Offices in Canada, USA, Ireland and UK

Book sales for North America and international:
Trafford Publishing, 6E–2333 Government St.,
Victoria, BC V8T 4P4 CANADA
phone 250 383 6864 (toll-free 1 888 232 4444)
fax 250 383 6804; email to orders@trafford.com
Book sales in Europe:
Trafford Publishing (UK) Limited, 9 Park End Street, 2nd Floor
Oxford, UK OX1 1HH UNITED KINGDOM
phone +44 (0)1865 722 113 (local rate 0845 230 9601)
facsimile +44 (0)1865 722 868; info.uk@trafford.com
Order online at:
trafford.com/06-0765

10 9 8 7 6 5 4 3 2

ACKNOWLEDGEMENTS

I would like to thank friends and family for all their support and dedication. I would also like to thank all the teachers who have helped me through life to make me a successful person. Thanks everyone, I couldn't have made it without you.

Special thanks go to Ric O' Barry for inspiring my dedication to and passion for dolphins. Dolphins have brought me this far and I shall one day make a big difference in this world for them.

Finally, thanks to everyone for purchasing this novel. This is an adventure story that is not for the faint of heart and should be read with a clear and open mind.

I hope you will all enjoy reading this story as much as I enjoyed writing it.

For my granny, Lovey Lowe, in South Africa

With the exception of actual agencies and organizations mentioned in the story, the characters and facility names are fictitious. Any similarities to actual persons living or dead are purely and entirely coincidental.

TABLE OF CONTENTS

Prologue

_____

IN THE YEAR 2046, a war, that had thrown the whole world into chaos for many years, was about to come to a conclusion. A time travel device had been developed by a group of soldiers who wanted to head into the past to locate and obtain a weapon of great power and potential. The soldiers' motives for obtaining the weapon are unknown. While the soldiers were having a final briefing before undertaking this trip back in time, a small group of rebels, their enemies, infiltrated the base and used the time travel device themselves. Enraged at this action, the soldiers travel back in time to pursue their enemies and find the weapon that could change history. Where did they go? They traveled to the point in time in the past where a certain series of events occurred that lead to this war and when the powerful weapon first appeared. That is where this story begins.

CHAPTER 1

What a Great Way to Start the Day

---

*"Things often never change when you go off to work.
But the one thing that can change, is attitude."*
—Graham Lowe

IT WAS SUNRISE on the morning of Friday April 23, 1999. The first sound that Dr. Steele Monroe Jay heard that morning was the loud beeping of his radio. He tried to slap it missing a few times but he eventually mashed that button. He saw that it was 6:00 a.m. He slowly got out of bed, stretched, yawned and scratched his fingers through his messy brown hair. Dr. Jay is a thirty-nine year old marine mammal veterinarian working for the Marine Research Institute labs on the outskirts of Miami. At five feet ten inches, and weighing one hundred and sixty pounds, he is in pretty good shape and proud of it. He lives in the North Miami district and is married to the beautiful blond haired, Jennifer and is the father of three teenage boys, Mike, Walter and Sid.

Dr. Jay didn't feel like going to work, but everyone feels that way, some mornings. Generally, he enjoyed his job. He didn't know it, but today, was going to be a day he would never forget. He went to the kitchen to make himself some coffee. As he entered the kitchen, he stepped in something that made him slip and fall to the floor. *That* woke him up. He could now see that there was a huge mess on the floor. Somebody had trashed the kitchen. "This is a disaster…" he said assessing the situation. A dog was in the kitchen, sniffing around. "Squall," Dr. Jay said to the dog, "why didn't you wake us up when our home was being invaded?" Squall was the Jay family's dog; a male border-collie. "Oh, how could I forget, you're getting old and are developing hearing problems. Wake up everybody!" he yelled as he began looking around the rest of the house. He could see that someone had broken in. Some paintings and curios were missing.

"Oh my god," said Jennifer as she noticed the mess in the kitchen.

"I need some coffee," said Dr. Jay feeling frustrated. Before he could even get to the cupboard, he could see what looked like dirt all over the floor. He saw the red coffee can lying on the floor, empty. "Look at that," said Dr. Jay. "The coffee is all over the floor. What am I supposed to drink now?" he said beginning to feel depressed.

"Milk or juice," said Jennifer. As she went over to the fridge, she too slipped in the liquid on the floor. Dr. Jay helped pick her up.

"You're stepping in it," said Dr. Jay. Jennifer turned and saw the milk and orange juice on the floor. "I slipped in that too," he added. He then saw that garbage had been poured into the sink. "These weirdoes have gone too far!" said Dr. Jay going over to the telephone. It had not been stolen and was still working. He called the police and reported the incident. Dr. Jay groaned as he sat down at the kitchen table. Within half an hour, a female officer, who identified herself as Officer Monica Roans, arrived to take the report. Officer Roans said, "hmm... it looks like whoever did this *is* a real weirdo."

"I can't believe that there was a robbery at our house and we all slept through it. Our coffee machine was stolen too, but I do have a cappuccino machine in my office at work that I just took in yesterday. At least that wasn't stolen... I am dying for a coffee. You wouldn't happen to have one on you by any chance?"

"You'll live," said the officer.

"You can dust for fingerprints all over my house if you want," said Dr. Jay as he walked in the direction of his bedroom.

"Don't worry sir," the officer said. "Let's hope that this psychowhack turns up soon."

"... Psychowhack?" asked Dr. Jay.

"Never mind," she replied.

As Dr. Jay passed Jennifer in the hall, she said, "you go get dressed for work. I'll start to get this mess cleaned up and see what I can throw together for breakfast."

CHAPTER 2

A Plan is Born

"One idea, with the proper thinking, planning and
ethical flexibility can change the world."
—Graham Lowe

O N A DOCK, not far from the Marine Research Institute Labs where Dr. Jay works, four men were talking. Three of the men, Jack Degrasso, Robert Pines and Drake Evans, worked for the fourth man named Mr. Jem. Mr. Jem is the president of the M.R.I.L. He wasn't a very social man and most of the time he spoke only when it was necessary. He had the build of a strong man, but was of average height. He had brown hair with some gray ones struggling to take over his head.

"Beautiful morning, isn't it sir?" Robert asked.

"Did you bring us out here for something?" asked Jack. Mr. Jem yawned out at the ocean.

"I've been thinking…" Mr. Jem spoke. "We need to come up with something that'll blow everyone's minds away."

"Uh… I think I know," said Drake. Drake was reading an old book that had once been a best seller, 'The Creature from the Black Lagoon'.

"Yes?" asked Mr. Jem listening to what Drake had to say.

"Oh, it's nothing," said Drake. "I just thought of this idea, but now I'm getting way ahead—"

"Just spit it out," interrupted Mr. Jem.

"Alright," said Drake. "I have read most of this book and this

Black Lagoon creature is pretty fascinating. I wonder if such creatures would be possible to create. I have heard a lot lately about scientists mapping the genetic information of the human genome and that kind of stuff."

"What?" asked Mr. Jem.

"A half human-animal thing," said Drake. "I was just pondering about the possibilities of creating a creature with the mix of two species like a werewolf for example... "

"Drake," said Jack, "you're daydreaming. Don't waste the boss' time." Jack was the youngest of the three.

"Yeah," said Robert, "you must have spent too much time reading that nonsense."

"I don't want to think of it as nonsense, you picture book reader," Drake grinned. He then returned to reading his book. Robert, quietly giggling to himself, grabbed Drake's book and threw it over the dock and into the water.

"That was my book!" said Drake. "That was a birthday present!"

"Hey," said Robert, "just wanted to wake you up to reality."

"You're not in reality either, Erik the Red," Drake mocked, making fun of the red beard and mustache on Robert's face.

"That does it," said Robert as he ran his fingers through Drake's hair and rubbed it all around messing it up. Drake then did the same to Robert's hair and began shoving it all around. The two began to wrestle all around the dock in a friendly manner.

"Leave him alone Drakey," said Jack.

"So you're sticking up for mister garbage-face are you?" asked Robert.

"No way," said Jack. Robert then made a quick swipe with his hand through Jack's hair. "Why you... !" Jack said as he joined in the pathetic hair wrestling. The three men were good friends. They had a good relationship with each other and they enjoyed working for Mr. Jem. Drake worked at the front desk, Jack worked as a lab technician and Robert was a personal assistant to Mr. Jem. They also did special jobs for Mr. Jem.

"Stop it, you bunch of ladies!" yelled Mr. Jem. Everyone stopped and faced Mr. Jem with wacky hairstyles. "You know," he said, "now that you've mentioned it, Drake, that's not a bad idea for starters. I've noticed you reading that book. The subject you just spoke about is one I am interested in. Maybe something like that *could* be possible. I think I have something that might be of interest. Locked up in my safe, I have a… chemical that… could do something. I brought you three out here because I wanted to talk to you about it. It's an amber color and it was used for experimentation that I was involved in a long time ago."

"What color is amber?" asked Drake.

"It's the yellowish portion on a traffic light," Mr. Jem answered.

"Oh."

"Anyway," Mr. Jem continued, "this chemical is something that I feel is very important. It came from my old job years ago. If you want to talk about science, you're speaking to the right guy. I got fired because everyone thought I was responsible for poisoning someone with this."

"You mean you've tested it on people?" asked Drake.

"No," said Mr. Jem. "Someone drank the stuff by accident."

"Oh my," said Drake getting interested. "Who was this guy?"

"… Somebody," Mr. Jem replied with a sigh. "All I did was study animal facts about crabs and dolphins and so on. That's why I became such a good marine life scientist. I then went on to build the Marine Research Institute Lab along with help from you guys. But now, things… are getting boring lately."

"Tell us more about this chemical," said Drake.

"It is not a good story," said Mr. Jem feeling angry. "The lab where I had been working has been closed down for years now. I had taken some of the mutagen because I really believed I could do something with it in the future. I had no job and also, I wanted my wife and child…" Mr. Jem was quiet for a moment. He turned away from everyone.

"Mr. Jem?" asked Drake.

Mr. Jem put his hand on his chin. After a few seconds, he turned around facing the three men. "Hmph," said Mr. Jem, "what does it matter anyway?"

"Fine," said Jack.

"What I'd like to know is, what does this mutagen do?" asked Robert.

"It was developed to basically cause a fast mutation of a living organism," said Mr. Jem.

"Cool," said Jack.

"How are you going to do this mutation stuff?" asked Drake. "How will you create that kind of a creature I thought up?"

"Let me guess," said Robert. "You get a gun that fires a needle with that junk in it!"

"Don't call it junk!" barked Mr. Jem. "You are correct, but something is missing from this chemical and I would like to find out what is required for it to work properly. This person I knew spent his life developing it, but died before it could be perfected. The only thing I can think of is to… add blood from an animal. I predict that if you were to combine the substance with the blood of an animal and inject it into a human, voila! Well at least that's what I think. Also, about the person that it killed, he had a cup of coffee and he was working on something that he couldn't take his eyes off. The coffee and the mutagen were right next to each other. He just happened to pick up the wrong one and accidentally drank the mutagen. When he swallowed it and realized it wasn't his coffee, he spat out what he could, but it was too late. I was in the room with him when this happened. His body had begun to deform and he looked like the Elephant Man. Then suddenly, he dropped dead."

"Geeze…" thought Drake.

"Huh…" thought Jack.

"Poor guy," said Robert.

"I quickly locked the chemical in the safe because I knew that it mustn't fall into the hands of the wrong people," said Mr. Jem. "This was top secret work and the man who created this stuff would have wanted it hidden."

"Was this guy important?" asked Drake.

"… Of course he was," said Mr. Jem. "I knew him very well."

"So are we really going to try that stuff even though it was a failure?" asked Drake.

"Of course we will," said Mr. Jem. "And don't call it a failure."

"Sorry, sir," Drake replied. "How long ago was this incident with the guy who drank this stuff and died?"

"Many years," said Mr. Jem. "I have been working for years in secret to perfect this chemical. I am ready to try combining some animal blood with that mutation molecule."

"Is that what it was really called?" asked Robert.

"That's what I call it," said Mr. Jem. "It mutated that guy's internal organs. Maybe some blood needs to be added, some DNA.

I need to experiment with it. I can't just keep this stuff forever. It needs to be put to use… for *his* sake. His legacy is in *my* hands now." Mr. Jem bowed his head. Drake, who had noticed Mr. Jem's sad expression, took Jack and Robert off to one side.

"You know," Drake whispered to his buddies, "if we can help him with this, he just might be a little happier." Drake walked over to Mr. Jem, got in front of him, stuck his arms out to the side as if about to give him a big hug, and then spoke, "no problem, Mr. Jem!" He then signaled for his buddies to come over. They all got together with Drake. "We would be happy, very happy, to help you with anything that you may need for this little experiment. We are so eager to help a man like you who grieves over such a tragic event." Mr. Jem then, with a little effort, managed a smile.

"You really care, don't you?" he asked. "Okay, I'll go for it. But, what creature should I take blood from?"

"An alligator," said Drake.

"Too dangerous," Mr. Jem said.

"A bird," said Jack.

"Too difficult to catch."

"An ant," said Robert. Drake and Jack both turned towards Robert.

"An ant?" Drake and Jack spoke in unison.

"Yeah," said Robert. "I've always wanted to know what a gigantic ant, crushing cities, would look like."

"Oh bug off," said Drake. "Get it? *Bug* off?"

"Why you…" said Robert as he went back to messing up Drake's hair. They all began wrestling again. Mr. Jem turned his head away from the clowns, sighed and stared out at the ocean again. He then saw something that caught his eye. It was leaping out in the distance of the ocean and it was getting closer. It leaped again getting closer still. He made out what it was; it was a bottlenose dolphin. As it leaped, it was jerking its head left and right as if something inside its head was hurting it. "Hey!" yelled Mr. Jem as he waved his arm behind him to get the attention of his friends. They stopped wrestling and walked over to Mr. Jem. They straightened out their hair and looked in Mr. Jem's direction. "There," said Mr. Jem pointing. "*That's* the target."

"Look," said Drake, "a dolphin. It's coming closer to the shore."

"Why can't we get a specimen from one of the dolphins back at the Institute?" asked Jack.

"Because," Drake explained, "if someone sees us trying to obtain one, they might start asking questions. Well Jack, you know what you have to do now."

"Oh no," Jack groaned, "why me?"

Robert spoke, "because you're the one who works with the dolphins, you're the youngest of us, dolphins love to play with kids and therefore—"

Drake laughed out loud as if it was the funniest thing he had ever heard.

"Hey!" Jack yelled as he shoved Robert with both hands. Robert giggled at Jack's reaction. "I may be the youngest of you all, but twenty-five years old is not a child. Fine, I'll do it. I've got a needle and syringe that I can use to take the blood."

"You just so happened to have one on you?" Robert asked.

"I had just got my stuff ready for work, when Mr. Jem brought us out here," Jack replied. "I'll... wait a minute... Mr. Jem, do you intend on *mutating* that dolphin?"

"No, no," Mr. Jem replied. "I just need the blood. Besides, if it became like the black lagoon creature, I wouldn't want it to go loose. I don't even have the stuff that does the mutating with me right now."

"Of course," Jack said.

"Try whistling to it and see if it will come," said Robert. He then winked his eye to Drake. "We will stand by on shore if there is a problem," At that point, Robert and Drake were standing behind Jack. Robert had his hand behind Jack's back and Drake did the same. "You're probably going to get wet doing this," said Robert smiling, "so you might as well take a... SWIM!" Drake and Robert both pushed Jack off the dock and Jack yelled as he was falling. There was a loud splash and Drake, Robert and Mr. Jem all began laughing. The water level was a little shallow, but there was enough for Jack to land in without hitting the bottom. Jack then stood up and wiped his face. He raised his fist to Robert and Drake and yelled, "you vicious... sharks!" He turned to see that the dolphin was getting closer. Jack started to wade towards the dolphin. He started to splash the water with his hand and whistle. The dolphin came in closer jerking its head every two to three seconds.

"We should get in there and help him out," said Drake to Robert. "This could be tricky with the way that dolphin is moving." Robert and Drake ran along the dock back to land and then went down to the water and began to wade in. The dolphin slowly swam right up to Jack. "Hey there…" Jack spoke as he attempted to put his hand on the dolphins head. Just as he touched it, he got a shock. "Yow!" Jack yelled as he fell into the water. Drake and Robert hurried over and helped Jack up.

"What happened?" asked Drake.

"… I don't know," Jack replied. "… Huh, must have been the static electricity from all that hair wrestling." Jack looked at the dolphin that was still there. "You all right?" asked Jack as he touched the dolphins head again. He got a shock again which put him back into the water. "What the hell?" wondered Jack.

Drake then touched the dolphin's head. He too got electrocuted.

"Damn!" said Drake.

"Hey!" yelled Mr. Jem on the shore. You're meant to get its blood! This isn't a $wim-with-the-dolphins program!"

"There's something going on with this dolphin!" yelled Jack.

"Just do it!" yelled Mr. Jem. Just then the dolphin's head started to glow with a white light.

"What in the name… ?" wondered Drake. The dolphin's brain was visible with the white glow.

"Mr. Jem!" yelled Robert. "I don't think this is an ordinary dolphin here! It does not even try and leave when this shock thing…" The dolphin's mouth then slowly opened.

"I better get this over with quick!" said Jack. He took out the needle. "Hold that creature, you guys," he said as he went for the dolphin's tail fluke. He carefully stuck the needle into the tail fluke and began to take the blood. The dolphin screamed and suddenly, Drake and Robert were catapulted away from the dolphin.

"Did it!" said Jack. As Jack was taking the needle out, the dolphin's tail jerked and the needle made a big scratch. The tail then whacked Jack and he got stunned but managed to hold onto the blood specimen. Some blood was trailing as the dolphin swam away. Jack rubbed his side where the tail had hit him and waded up to his companions.

"Are you guys okay?!" Jack asked.

"Yeah," said Drake. Jack noticed the trail of blood from the dolphin.

"Damn, I got the blood sample alright," said Jack. "But I ended up INJURING the poor thing! If it shows up at the M.R.I.L, don't mention a word about this!" The men were arguing about the staff of the M.R.I.L finding this dolphin and learning about the mysterious thing it did. Their arms were flailing around in the chatter. "Well *something* got in its head!" yelled Robert.

On the shore, Mr. Jem got angry seeing the men argue. He saw what had happened to the dolphin, but it didn't even phase him.

"You guys got the sample yet?!" yelled Mr. Jem.

"Yes!" yelled Jack.

"Then let's go back to the M.R.I.L! I'll show you guys the mutagen I have!"

"The staff are never going to believe this when we tell them..." Drake said to Jack and Robert as they left the water.

"Maybe we shouldn't tell them," said Jack. "This could be important. Looks pretty exciting to me. Wonder if anyone else will encounter that dolphin?"

CHAPTER 3

Off to the Office

"Good morning! And in case I don't see you,
good afternoon, good evening and good night!"
— Jim Carrey
Taken from the movie: "The Truman Show"

"WAIT UNTIL I get my hands on whoever messed up my house," said Dr. Jay as he ate the breakfast Jennifer had prepared. "What a story I am going to tell the guys at work. Wake up early, see my house robbed, and now I'll probably have a long day at work doing nothing but paper work and bottle-feeding octopuses. Nothing interesting happened during the week and there's nothing special scheduled for next week."

After he finished his toast, he put his head down on the table. Jennifer came over and started to massage his back.

"We'll handle this mess later," she said. "Try not to let it bother you. You'll have the weekend to rest."

"You're right," said Dr. Jay. "Besides, I really do enjoy my job." He then looked at his watch.

"Oh no! Now I'm late!" he said. "I've got to get to work!" He got out of his chair and gave Jennifer a kiss. "I love you honey!" he said. "Bye Mike! Bye Sid! Bye Walter! Make sure you get to school on time!" He ran out the door and went over to the garage. He got in his car and drove out of the driveway. Dr. Jay drove a blue colored Chrysler Convertible. He was glad to see it was still there.

Dr. Jay had a desire to help the animals of the ocean. He grew up enjoying marine life and felt he could make a big difference for them one day. He became a marine veterinarian to help realize that dream. He was not just a vet however; he was also a safety inspector for the M.R.I.L facility. He was determined to make sure there would not be any accidents that could cause harm to marine mammals or the people who were just as committed to helping marine life as he was.

"What a beautiful day!" Dr. Jay said. "Maybe things are looking up. My job can be so boring sometimes. But, I have to help treat the ocean creatures suffering from poisoning by dioxins and all that crap that people keep dumping. Dolphins... dying these days from very bad or careless people... whalers, commercial fishermen... . My duty is pretty simple, I have to help the creatures who are sick or injured, so I'm working for a good cause. I'm going to try to feel more optimistic today. I won't let a stupid house burglary stand in my way..." Dr. Jay was coming up to a traffic light. As he approached, it started to turn from amber to red. "... or a red traffic light," he added. Dr. Jay sometimes had a habit of talking to himself when he felt nervous, upset or just plain excited. He looked left and right down the other street and saw the cars passing in front of him.

"Maybe I'll play some music," Dr. Jay thought. He could see a cassette tape sticking out of the deck. He pushed it in and it played. Dr. Jay then heard a man say, "doe!" and a high pitched voice that sounded like a Chipmunk character replied, "money?"

"No."

"Biscuits?"

"No!"

"Let's see now, bread?"

"ALVIN!"

Dr. Jay then stopped the tape. "What is this?" he thought. He took it out and looked at it. "Sing with Children: The Chipmunks?! Sid!" What Dr. Jay heard was from the song, 'Do-Re-Mi' from: 'The Sound of Music'. The tape dated back to 1984. Dr. Jay's youngest son, Sid, listened to The Chipmunks as he drove him to school sometimes.

The traffic light was still red and it was beginning to make Dr. Jay impatient. "A minute has already passed!" he yelled to the light. "This is going to make me even later for work!" Just then, he heard a screeching sound from behind. "Huh?" he wondered as he looked behind him. "What is this?"

He saw a black colored vehicle that looked like an armored van used to transport money. It was swaying towards him. Behind it, there were three police vehicles chasing it. It wasn't slowing down. When Dr. Jay realized the van was coming at him at a dangerous speed, he had to think quickly. He put his foot on the pedal and quickly took off going through the red light. As he drove though the intersection, a car on the right screeched its brakes as it tried not to hit him. Luckily, there was no collision as Dr. Jay swerved away and got back on the road. There was no safe place to pull over. He saw the black van getting closer to him. It then drove along side him. He shouted to the dark, tinted windows of the van, "what is your problem, you wacko?! You almost got me killed!" The passenger side window of the van rolled down and Dr. Jay could see a figure wearing some kind of cloak. The figure made an inhuman, growling sound and showed a large set of teeth! They were canine teeth and looked very sharp. Dr. Jay gasped and yelled, "I'm out of here!" He tried to find a way to get out of the car chase. He tried slowing down to let the police get past him. Unfortunately, the three police cars pursuing the van had blocked off the lanes. To make matters worse, before Dr. Jay knew it, it was just him, the black van and the police on the road; no one else. The police were acting as a barrier. There was no way to get behind them. The rear window of the van opened and a red, shiny, basketball sized orb, that looked like it was made out of crystal, hovered outside the window. It was making this electrical sound and it started to glow. It began to flow with electricity and then instantly shot a bolt of lightning in front of one of the police cars. An explosion was heard and the spot where it hit became a large hole in the road, forcing one car to come screeching to a halt. "What in the name… ?!" Dr. Jay yelled in shock. The police car's windows opened and the cops were hanging out shooting their pistols at the strange car. Dr. Jay tried to speed away from the van that was next to him to get away from this pursuit. He had no such luck. "Father of three, dead in a police chase shootout," thought Dr. Jay. Just then he noticed the strange car had this yellow basketball sized orb sticking out of its window. "Now what?" asked Dr. Jay. The yellow orb had this aura glowing around it and then a second later, a police pistol flew towards the orb and clung to it. Dr. Jay looked behind and saw that the guns of the police officers were slipping out of their hands and flying right into the car of the strangers. "Who are these guys?" wondered Dr. Jay. "What the hell's going on?" He suddenly felt his car slowly jerking left towards the van. He tried to turn his steering wheel all the way to the right, but he couldn't turn right at all! Whatever that yellow orb was, it was pulling his car like a giant magnet. He looked ahead and saw that he was coming to an intersection. The light up ahead was red. The magnetism suddenly stopped and Dr. Jay had control over his car again. As he came to the intersection, he swerved to the right to dodge the cars that were coming towards him and went through the intersection. Several cars collided making a huge traffic jam. After he was a safe distance away from the collisions, he stopped his car and looked behind him once more. He saw the black van had stopped short of the mangled cars in the intersection. It then shot several bolts of lightning setting the police cruisers' front hoods on fire. The van did a sharp left turn and drove off in the other direction. The police got out of their burning cars quickly and were yelling "move!" and "run!" and so on. The police ran from their vehicles which suddenly exploded. Dr. Jay was confused and shocked. He watched the fire for a moment, but then he took a deep breath and drove off feeling that he had had enough excitement this morning.

CHAPTER 4

_____

A Mystery Occurs

_____

"Anything suspicious is worth investigating."
— Graham Lowe

WHEN MR. JEM and his three close assistants arrived at the M.R.I.L, they went up to Mr. Jem's office and seated themselves at his desk. Jack went to get a test tube at Mr. Jem's request. The office was roomy and fancy. It had a big rectangular window behind the desk that looked out on the ocean. The office also had a back room that contained a dining table, a mini bar and other things. Mr. Jem had gone to the back room to fetch the mutagen that he had talked about earlier. He returned to his assistants and sat down at the desk. Jack then returned with the test tube. He sat down and handed it to Mr. Jem along with the vial containing the dolphin blood he had taken earlier. Mr. Jem poured the blood into the test tube first and filled it about halfway. He then added the amber colored mutagen and when they mixed together, the substances began to bubble and started to fizz towards the top. It settled down and the color of it was now orange. Drake, Jack and Robert's eyes were wide open in amazement.

"This looks interesting," thought Mr. Jem. "Now, all I need is a test subject. But that will have to wait for later. You three go dry yourselves off and get to your posts."

"Okay!" said Drake.

"Thanks for showing us that," said Jack.

"Hope it works, Mr. Jem," said Robert.

Mr. Jem had thought about of putting it into the city's reservoir, but that would make his experiment go out of control in the city and he only wanted one person injected with it for a little experiment. (If his experiment was put into the water and everybody turned into dolphins, that would be rather unusual.)

* * *

Meanwhile, Dr. Jay drove into the parking lot.

He drove into a spot 100 meters away from the building. "Made it!" he said as he parked his car and got out. He looked at his watch. "Damn," he muttered, realizing he was late.

He walked inside the M.R.I.L getting ready to check in. There were potted plants and pictures of coral reefs and marine creatures on the walls inside the lobby. It made for a relaxing atmosphere. Dr. Jay had been working at the facility for almost a year now. The building was built right next to the ocean allowing the staff to operate in a number of areas including making a quick response to whale stranding reports. Dr. Jay went to the front desk and started to check in.

"Good morning," he said to the guy on duty. "Sorry I'm late. I kind of lost track of time when my house got robbed and weird things started happening."

"Uh huh," the desk manager replied. He rarely showed any interest. He then began to look though a directory. "Let's see now… Dr. Steele M. Jay…" He then frowned. "This is the third time this week you've shown up late. No one else here has had this many lates before. Looks like something needs to be done. I have to report this. He picked up the phone and called Dr. Jay's supervisor. After a brief chat, he informed Dr. Jay that he would have to stay late tonight to close this place up for the weekend.

"Oh thanks, I *really* needed that!" Dr. Jay spoke sarcastically as he banged his hand on the desk.

"Don't give me crap now, okay?" asked the desk manager. The man at the front desk was about an inch taller than Dr. Jay. He had black hair. He was wearing a white shirt with no tie and was wearing a chain necklace with something hanging from it lying on his chest. It was a shark in a curved position and it was wearing sunglasses. It was the icon of the sports equipment company called Maui and sons.

Dr. Jay looked at the desk manager. "Hey, I know you. You're Draco, one of Mr. Jem's assistants."

"It's Drake!" he angrily corrected. Dr. Jay then walked away.

"Lousy S.O.B," he muttered.

"What did you say?!" Drake shouted.

"I said, I think I see a bee," Dr. Jay lied. "You know, buzzzzz!"

"Well, fine then," said Drake. "Hope it does not sting you!"

"Sure," said Dr. Jay thinking of Drake as an S.O.B. Drake was a tough man and had a serious face most of the time. He turned the other way.

"Yeah right," Drake said to himself, knowing he had been insulted. "There hasn't been a single bee in here since—" At that moment, his phone rang. A few moments later, he went to the loud speaker.

"Dr. Jay to the dolphin medical pen. I repeat, Dr. Jay to the dolphin medical pen. Actually, get your BUTT over there right now, 'cause it's an emergency! They have been waiting for you for a while because of your late arrival that I just wrote down in the book along with the rest of your lates."

"What the?" Dr. Jay thought. He turned to see Drake on the loudspeaker. "Actually," said Dr. Jay, "I said you *are* a lousy S.O.B!" He ran over and grabbed the mike Drake was talking into. They began wrestling over it. "You ever hear the expression, 'slow and steady will win the race?'" Drake asked. "Well I don't believe in it, and you lost, you three legged tortoise!" The microphone flew out of their hands and went up to the speaker where the sound was coming out. There was a loud, painful shriek over the whole building and everyone in the lobby covered their ears including the ones who were fighting over the mike. Dr. Jay and Drake stared murderously into each other's eyes for a little. Dr. Jay then said, "whatever," and walked off. Drake picked up the mike and said, *"sorry about that, everyone. Return to your activities."*

* * *

Dr. Jay calmed down and went to the dolphin medical pen area that was just past the shark den. The dolphin medical pen was actually a room that was much like a boathouse with sliding doors that opened out to the ocean. Dr. Jay went into the room and got his coat and equipment out of the locker. A technician approached him.

"What happened?" asked Dr. Jay grumbling about the task Drake had given him later in the afternoon. "Another sea urchin damaged?"

"Where have you been?" asked the technician. "We have been waiting for you for over twenty minutes."

"Sorry, Henry," Dr. Jay replied. Henry Guy was Dr. Jay's best friend at the institute. His job was to make sure the proper equipment was available to the researchers, especially for serious emergencies.

"We need you over here," Henry said. They saw a dolphin that was very weak. "There's a tiny blood spot and a scratch line on her tail fluke and it's about the size of a needle point."

"You're right, Henry," said Dr. Jay noticing the red scratch mark. "It looks like she's lost a lot of blood from that scratch." He looked at the mark on the dolphin's tail fluke. "This scratch looks like an injection needle's point. I think somebody must have taken a blood sample without proper procedure. Was it an accident? Anybody here do this?"

"No," Henry replied. "We found her outside near the shore this morning."

"Who would want to steal blood from a harmless animal I wonder?" asked Dr. Jay. "It's seems strange, but it fits in with the bad day I have been having. First my house is robbed, then I'm late for work, then there was this bank truck being chased by the police that had strange people who sounded like Godzilla who got me caught up in a car chase and almost got me killed and stuff, then the desk manager called the boss who has made me stay here late tonight to close this place up and—" Just then, he heard the dolphin squeak and whine and then suddenly she was not moving. "The dolphin is flat lining!" someone yelled. "She is not moving a muscle!"

Dr. Jay went over and monitored the dolphin. He could see Jack, one of Mr. Jem's assistants. "Did you keep water over her Jack?" asked Dr. Jay.

"Yes!" said Jack. "There are no life signs!" Dr. Jay put his hand on the dolphin's side and he could not feel a heartbeat. He then put his hand on the dolphin's head. "Yow!" yelped Dr. Jay as he got a shock. The dolphin's melon began to glow white. "What the hell?" thought Dr. Jay. After the glow stopped, the life monitor suddenly kicked in. "Her life signs are stable?" asked Jack puzzled as he checked the life sign monitor.

Dr. Jay curiously put his hand on the dolphin's head again and once again, he felt a shock.

"What's going on here?" asked Dr. Jay. "I got shocked!" Jack put his hand on the dolphin's head and got a shock too. "Ouch!" he yelped. The melon of the dolphin began to glow white again. "Not again…" Jack said, remembering the incident with the dolphin earlier in the morning.

"What was that?" Dr. Jay asked.

"Nothing!" Just then, the lights in the room started to dim. The life sign monitor started going haywire. The wave line started to make a funny pattern and the cardio monitor was reading 400, 800, 999, 100, etc. The dolphin then screamed. Suddenly, the life sign monitor exploded. At the same time, Dr. Jay, Henry and Jack were knocked to the ground, covering their ears at the sound of the scream. All the lights in the room then went out, leaving the room pitch black. The dolphin stopped screaming when the white light in its head started to move towards its' mouth. The mouth opened and the white energy shot out and started to bounce around the room!

Everyone was screaming and trying to protect themselves as the energy ball bounced everywhere knocking things over. "Keep filming!" yelled somebody as a researcher with a camera tried to catch the action. The energy ball bounced off a wall and into a working computer. Then in a flash, the lights came back on.

Jack made a fist and somebody held him back as he went for the dolphin. "That dolphin tried to destroy everything!" yelled Jack.

"Hey! Hey! Hey!" yelled Dr. Jay. "Don't blame the dolphin! Everybody just calm down and relax now that it's over. Whatever that was, I don't think it was the dolphin's fault." Everybody was staring at Dr. Jay. "Look, those of you who don't need to be here, get out of here." Everyone, except Henry and Jack left in a hurry. "I'm going to check that computer for viruses." Dr. Jay walked up to the computer and moved the mouse around and clicked several buttons to check for viruses. "Nothing…" said Dr. Jay. He then clicked on the 'My computer' icon and checked the system status. "Whoa!" said Dr. Jay noticing something. "The processor speed on this computer is 5000mhz, there is 500 gigabytes of disk space, 3 gigahertz of RAM, these readings can't be right…" Dr. Jay then played a sound clip on the computer. "The sound is perfectly clear!" he added. Henry walked over to Dr. Jay.

"This computer used to have tons of problems and low performance before," said Henry.

"I don't like what that white stuff was doing," said Dr. Jay. "It could be dangerous. I don't know what the hell that was."

"I've never seen anything like that before," said Henry.

"Hey Jack," Dr. Jay asked. "Do you know something about this?"

"No," said Jack. "I have never seen this dolphin before. I'm just nervous about this mysterious thing, this… enigma."

"Whatever," Dr. Jay said. "How's that dolphin by the way?"

"She… looks fine," Henry spoke.

Dr. Jay took a deep breath and said, "Henry, run a series of tests on that blood drained dolphin and make sure she's healthy. We've also got to figure out what the hell just happened. I've got to make a phone call to my wife. Call me if anything else happens. For now, quarantine that computer. Keep it tucked away in a storage closet or something."

"Okay," said Henry. "Let's get this girl back to normal again as soon as possible." Jack then rubbed the dolphin's head. He got no shock this time. The dolphin seemed calm and assured. "The shock is gone," Jack said. The dolphin then jerked and bit Jack's hand. "Argh!" yelled Jack. "That peace loving creature bit me!"

"You had best give her some room," said Henry.

"Whatever," said Jack. "What just happened was freaky and I hope that does not happen again. In fact, could we smash that computer into pieces right now?"

"No, this could be interesting," said Dr. Jay. "We should get some professionals to look at this later on. By the way," he added as he put his hand on his head, "that scream gave me a headache."

"Me too," said Henry.

"Me too," said Jack. "And I feel sick."

"Huh?" Dr. Jay wondered. "I'm feeling sick too…" Their headaches then got worse.

"Oh…" groaned Henry. "I'm losing my strength!"

"What the… !" Dr. Jay gasped as he dropped to his knees. Henry and Jack dropped to the floor moaning. "What is… wrong with… me… ?" Dr. Jay whispered as he collapsed to the floor. Suddenly, all three of them were unconscious.

CHAPTER 5

More Trouble Occurs

"Be prepared."
— Boy Scout motto

D R. JAY SLOWLY opened his eyes. He found himself lying on
a bed. "Are you alright?" asked a voice. There was a doctor
looking down at him. "You lost consciousness from that loud noise.
It knocked you and two others out," he said. "The other two have
already recovered."

Dr. Jay groaned. "Has anything serious happened to me, Doctor?" he asked as he crawled out of the bed. "No," the doctor replied. "But you've been out for an hour and a half. It is now 10:30
A.M." Dr. Jay noticed that he was in the infirmary. "I heard that
there were strange things happening in the dolphin medical pen,"
the doctor added.

"Yeah," Dr. Jay replied. "Some power failure and a weird ...
thing."

"Oh, there was a power failure alright," the doctor said. "One
and a half hours ago, a power failure didn't just happen in the medical pen, it happened throughout the entire building."

"Oh my," Dr. Jay said. "I should get going to my office right
now."

"Come back if any problems persist," said the doctor.

Dr. Jay left the Infirmary and found himself in the corridor leading to the offices. "God damn!" said Dr. Jay, thinking about the
mysterious incident that had happened in the dolphin pen.

There were two walkways on the floor above him connected by several bridges. On the upper right level of the walkway, stood Mr. Jem and Robert looking down on Dr. Jay.

"Who is that down there?" asked Mr. Jem.

"I think that's Dr. Jay," said Robert. "He's a marine mammal veterinarian and a safety inspector. He is one of the individuals who lost consciousness from the mysterious, loud noise down in the dolphin medical pen."

"Maybe we can test this on somebody here who wants to be someone different, something extraordinary," Mr. Jem said. "I want to find out if this stuff is truly effective." Mr. Jem was thinking about experimenting on someone in the facility. The thought of creating something fascinating was exciting him.

"Are you sure you want to do this, Mr. Jem?" Robert asked. "How about we arrange for a professional medical staff and a volunteer at some place instead?"

"Shut it," Mr. Jem said as he stuck his hand close to Robert's mouth. "I thought I told you dummies before, that this stuff is TOP… SECRET. It's my decision."

"Whatever you say," said Robert. "Right now, Drake is down at the front desk, Jack's working on a room to house your experiment, and I'm here. I just got a call from Drake and one of the things he told me, is that Dr. Jay's supervisor has ordered him to stay late tonight and close the place up."

"Close the place up, you say?" Mr. Jem asked. "Maybe testing this on him would be… ah, I don't know. By the way," he added, "is there any more information on what happened in the medical pen earlier?"

"A technician caught the strange event happening on videotape," Robert answered.

"I would like to see this tape," said Mr. Jem. He then whispered, "in any case, when it's lunch break, I want you, Drake and Jack to go find some computers for our project."

"We don't have any new ones in stock," said Robert.

"I know," Mr. Jem said. "Just *find* some other computers in this place and take them to the new room.

"I'll do that," Robert said.

Down below, Dr. Jay heard the voices above. "Test what?" he thought, "and on me?" He could hear them talking, but could not really make out what was being discussed. He found the elevator and went in. He selected the second floor and it took him up. "He's coming," said Mr. Jem. "Let's return to my office. Also, make me a gin and tonic."

"Yes sir," said Robert. They both moved into Mr. Jem's office.

When Dr. Jay came out of the elevator, it was quiet.

"What the heck was Mr. Jem talking about?" thought Dr. Jay, "a project? Huh, must be something new and I'll be part of it maybe. I could use a new job challenge with more pizzazz. Dr. Jay walked towards his office passing by other people going to their offices. He opened the door and got seated at his desk. His office was small, and had a few things that offices usually have; a paperweight, a holder for pencils, etc.

"Nothing in here appears to be stolen. That's a good sign," Dr. Jay said. "I better call my family and tell them about this night work thing." He sat in his chair and dialed his house.

After a few rings the answering machine came on and he heard his own voice.

After the message and the beep, he spoke. "Hello honey. It's Steele and I'm working late tonight. Send the kids to bed before I get home. I'm closing the place up for the weekend. Lot's of strange stuff has happened today. I wanted some more excitement in my job, but I didn't expect something that could cause harm to this place. I'll tell you about it all later. It's getting to be a pretty crazy day today. I will be home very late, okay? Right-oh, bye-bye!"

He hung up the phone and started to work on some reports but found he could not concentrate.

"Alright now," Dr. Jay said to himself. "The type of dolphin that had its blood drained was a bottlenose dolphin. If that dolphin were Flipper, we would be popular for doctoring him up. If it was that dolphin and we at M.R.I.L were making him all better, I would probably be on television or in National Geographic magazine or something like that. That would be cool. But it's unbelievable how something white and freaky came out of that dolphin's head and bounced around into one of the computers. So..." He sighed and said, "I've got to stop talking to myself like this."

Sometimes, Dr. Jay was informed that there were people who owned dolphins that had suffered an illness or an injury and he had to go over to take the report. To his surprise however, he had done very little for the dolphins and most of the time, he was in conversation with the owner. Dr. Jay once suggested that pen conditions should be improved and dolphin show routines be reduced, but found himself being told that he was there strictly to tend to the dolphins health, not to tell people how to do their jobs and it was none of his business. Dr. Jay had wanted to say something, but heeded the warning that what the owner said was right. It had bothered him and he found himself thinking about it now.

Dr. Jay got up out of his chair and left his office to look around for any problems. He helped participate in the clean up in the dolphin medical pen for a little while. He was told that tests had been conducted on the sick dolphin. She was back to normal and ready for release. Dr. Jay took the liberty of putting an identification tag on the dolphin's dorsal fin. It read, 'M.R.I.L 037' and had some contact information on it. The dolphin was then loaded into a special stretcher and was carried outside by a group of people.

Two hours had passed and it was 12:30. Dr. Jay returned to his office.

"I'm thirsty," he said. "I think I'll go power up this new cappuccino machine and have a drink."

He walked over to the shelf. He activated his cappuccino machine and put a cup in place. When the coffee was ready, he returned to his desk. He was about to take a sip, when the phone started to ring. Dr. Jay picked up the phone and set his drink on the table in front of him. "This is Dr. Jay," he answered.

"Hey Dr. Jay buddy, this is Henry. Just to inform you, we have successfully released that dolphin back into the wild."

"Thanks," replied Dr. Jay.

"Oh, and by the way," said Henry, *"earlier this morning, before you got here, I overheard one of Mr. Jem's conversations. I couldn't make out what he was saying, but he said something about dolphin D.N.A and something about the creature from the black lagoon. Do you know anything about it?"*

"Hmm… sounds very fishy…" thought Dr. Jay. "I wonder… could Mr. Jem and his men have anything to do with that weak dolphin that you guys found?"

"Well," said Henry, *"I doubt it. But Mr. Jem sure is acting strange lately. I feel like the whole day is starting to go sour."*

"Maybe Mr. Jem has an idea for a new kind of addition to this facility," said Dr. Jay. "I also overheard him talking about something. It's all imagination and creativity. Usually, things do not work out the way you think they are going to work. Maybe that's his problem."

"Maybe you are right," said Henry. *"In any case, if you're hungry, why don't you go get some food at that new place in the neighborhood."*

"You mean the Denny's?" Dr. Jay asked.

"Yes."

"Now listen, I know it's a pretty weird day today, but—" Dr. Jay suddenly heard an explosion over the phone that made him jump and made some of his desk accessories jiggle a bit. The vibration also knocked his drink off the table and it spilled all over his lap. "What the hell was that?!" Dr. Jay asked Henry, panicking.

"It sounded like it came from the dolphin medical pen!" said Henry. *"I'm going over there right now!"*

"I'm on my way!" said Dr. Jay as he hung up the phone. He looked down and saw his pants were soaked. "Dammit!" he yelled. "Haven't I suffered enough today?!" He took some tissues and tried to dry off his pants. "I better get down there immediately. It can't be… can it?" he thought. "Could that computer with the white enigma in it have anything do with this? I just bet it does. I better get out my pad and pen and inspect damages there."

He took out the note-pad and a pen and left his office to head over to the dolphin medical pen. He ran from his office, got into the elevator and went down.

When he looked up, he saw some bubble gum stuck on the ceiling of the elevator. For fun, he wrote down, <u>Report bubble gum stickers</u> (people who stick gum on places like the elevator ceiling) <u>to the disciplinary committee.</u>

When he left the elevator, he headed towards the lobby and saw other people running in his direction. Dr. Jay pushed his way through the crowd of people as he entered the medical pen. There was smoke everywhere and it was difficult to see anything. "Help me!" a voice yelled out. Suddenly, a figure ran out of the smoke. It was Jack, running for his life. As he ran out, Dr. Jay yelled out, "is anybody else in there?!" but got no answer. As the smoke started to clear, he could see that a large hole had been made in a wall. He then caught a glimpse of something. There was someone else inside the room running out through the hole. The only thing that Dr. Jay could see was what looked like an orange lizard tail with black stripes disappearing through the hole in the wall. "Hey!" Dr. Jay yelled. "Come back here!" He ran over to the hole and looked outside. He could see nothing. "Come back here, you vandal!" he yelled. "It's your own grave you're digging!" The suspect was out of sight. "He sure got away pretty quick," he thought. He looked back into the room. The whole place had been vandalized!

"What… what happened to the dolphin medical pen?!" Dr. Jay gasped.

Some of the computers had been smashed into splinters and everything was a mess.

Dolphin pen is vandalized was the next thing that Dr. Jay wrote down in his notepad. Big hole in the wall, 5 Computers destroyed, Significant damages.

"I better find Henry," Dr. Jay said to himself. He left the dolphin pen and went back to the lobby. Henry was running towards Dr. Jay with some security guards. Dr. Jay ran up to Henry as the security guards went into the pen. "Hey, Henry!" yelled Dr. Jay. "Something has—"

"I know!" interrupted Henry. "Somebody just wrecked the dolphin pen. Some of us saw the ones who did it."

"Was it that damn freaky white enigma thingy that happened earlier?" Dr. Jay asked.

"You are not going to believe this…" said Henry. "Jack just passed me and said that he was being attacked by a group of… dinosaurs!"

Dr. Jay was silent for a moment. "I thought I saw a tail," said Dr. Jay. "But it must have been my imagination. Do you know who it was really?"

"This isn't a joke Dr. Jay," said Henry. "Jack's eyes were full of fear. He wouldn't lie. He said a bunch of big ass lizards were trying to destroy the computers."

"What about that computer that was quarantined?" asked Dr. Jay.

"We better find out," said Henry. As Henry and Dr. Jay went back into the room, they went to the closet and opened the door. It was still there, untouched.

"Looks like they didn't go near here," Dr. Jay said. "I wonder if this particular computer is what they were after."

"Maybe," Henry replied. "This is awful… and just when we finally got everything cleaned up!"

"Let's get back to the lobby," Dr. Jay said. As they made their way back out, they faced a group of frightened and curious people.

"Everyone stay back!" Dr. Jay shouted. "Okay, anyone here see what those things were?"

"Yeah," someone said, "five different colored monsters that looked like dinosaurs or something."

"You mean people wearing costumes?" asked Dr. Jay.

"Nope, they appeared to be reptilian-like people with sharp teeth and claws. They were all wearing brown cloaks that kept their faces hidden, but their teeth were showing and by what I saw, they were all canine." Dr. Jay then thought about what the guy had just said. He remembered seeing something cloaked, with a large mouth and sharp teeth. "Those things," the witness continued, "seemed to be attacking only the equipment and had no interest in tearing up people. Jack witnessed it all and managed to get away. He said he's going up to Mr. Jem's office. Each of those lizards was a different color as I had observed. Orange, green, white, red and yellow."

"Um," Dr. Jay interrupted, "have you…" He then faced everyone and got their attention. "Has anyone here seen a black colored bank truck or anything else like that on the grounds recently?" The group of people thought to themselves and then somebody spoke out, "I think so… Why, yes I did. I saw one pass by about an hour ago. Why do you ask?"

"Well…" Dr. Jay said, remembering the black vehicle that was being chased by police; the one that got him caught up in a crazy car chase. "I think the… vandals may have used that to cover their tracks or something," Dr. Jay said.

"I've got to go check out the damage," Henry said. "And by the way, what happened to your pants?"

"Don't ask," Dr. Jay replied. Henry hurried through the door to the medical pen. Dr. Jay went to the restroom and used the automatic hand dryer to try and dry his pants.

"… Damn," Dr. Jay thought as he left the washroom. "I wonder what the hell's going on? Are we talking about Godzilla's spawn or something here? Dinosaurs are extinct and everybody knows that. It could have been a bunch of costumed vandals."

Dr. Jay decided to go through a pair of doors that said on them: RESTRICTED TO STAFF PERSONNEL ONLY. He was authorized to search the maintenance area which kept the whole building powered and active. The walls were made of big, grey bricks. "Boy," he thought, "everything's going crazy around here." The hall was quiet and the silence comforted him. As he walked down the hall, he saw a sign on a door saying, 'Do not enter! Keep out by order of the facility's President.' Dr. Jay looked puzzled. "Keep out by order of... Mr. Jem?" he thought. He then heard some kind of a buzzing noise coming from the knob of the door. He also saw there was some kind of plastic covering on the knob and a little 'Danger, high voltage' sign. "High voltage... ?" he thought. "Is this for real?" Suspiciously, he took a quarter out of his pocket, opened the covering on the knob and dropped the quarter onto it. A spark flashed and the coin went flying.

"Whoa!" said Dr. Jay as the coin just missed him. "God, everything's going crazy around here... Didn't I just say that already? If anything else goes crazy around here, I'm going to snap. I wonder why Mr. Jem doesn't want anybody in that room? Maybe it's a new project. But why the security?" He then heard his stomach growl. "I better get out of here, get something to eat, and clear my head." He grabbed his quarter, went out the door back to the lobby and went out to get some lunch.

CHAPTER 6

A Further Investigation

"They say curiosity killed the cat, but when I became curious
about marine mammals and learned more about them in a
particular situation involving man, it felt painful for me. It
changed the way I thought about dolphins, but I'm still alive."
— Graham Lowe

AFTER DR. JAY had his lunch, he returned to the institute. He liked the food at the place he went to, but the coffee he had there wasn't to his liking. He spotted a soft drink vendor. He put a one-dollar bill in the paper money slot and pressed a button for a Coke. Nothing happened. He pressed other selections including the button to return the money, but still, nothing happened. He then banged on the machine. "Stupid piece of crap!" he yelled. He went over to the front desk. Drake was there and he saw Dr. Jay's reaction as the machine ate his money. Drake was laughing as Dr. Jay approached him. "Hello, Drake," Dr. Jay said.

"Why don't you just kick it and see if it will work," Drake joked.

"Ha, ha, laugh it up," Dr. Jay said. "Look, just pass me a piece of paper so I can indicate that the machine is out of order." As Drake handed out a piece, Dr. Jay wrote, 'This machine is out of order because it's a stupid piece of junk'.

"Maybe you can fix that," Dr. Jay said.

"How?"

"By shaking it so it will fall on your face, flattening you as a result, and then everyone will call you 'pancake man' for the rest of your life," Dr. Jay replied, as he took a piece of scotch tape. "Now we're even." He headed off to attach the message to the machine. Drake made a fist in anger, but then he sighed as he saw a couple of people walking towards him. He prepared to greet them.

* * *

Dr. Jay went to the dolphin medical pen and saw that there were people cleaning up the mess. The hole that had been made in the wall was being covered up with a blue tarp on both sides. He could see his friend Henry participating in the cleanup.

"Hey, Henry," Dr. Jay said.

"Oh, hey there," Henry replied.

"Wow, what a mess," Dr. Jay said observing. The whole room looked like it hadn't been visited for a hundred years. There was dust, debris and stuff turned over. "This is insanity," Dr. Jay said to Henry. "Who would do this to us and why?"

"I wouldn't know," Henry replied.

"You guys said it was a bunch of colored dinosaurs that did it," Dr. Jay said. "I think what you guys saw may have been costumes."

Henry laughed. "I think you're right. That's what I'm thinking too." Both of them started to laugh. "Why the hell are we laughing anyway?" Dr. Jay said, still laughing. "We could have been killed by that enigma thing."

"Of course," Henry said. "So you call it that? An enigma?"

"That's what Jack called it earlier," Dr. Jay said. "That word fits it perfectly. How are you feeling after waking from that noise that rendered us unconscious?"

"I feel fine," Henry replied. "The doctor said there weren't any problems with me and Jack, so we got back to work."

Suddenly, Drake entered the room. "Hide me," Dr. Jay said as he went behind Henry. "That guy is really ticking me off today." Drake walked up to someone in the room. Dr. Jay saw it was Jack. "Mr. Jem wants us," Drake said.

"Right now?" Jack asked. Drake nodded his head and the two of them left.

"So," Henry said, "about that enigma in the computer, I'll package it up and send it on Monday to the computer company for analysis."

"Okay," Dr. Jay said. "I hope we get rich and famous if it's something remarkable."

"Yeah, but I'm scared of what it has done today," Henry said.

"I know," said Dr. Jay, "I'm scared too. I hope that, and the vandalism with the explosion doesn't happen again."

"Well, I'll be heading home right now," said Henry.

"Okay, have a great weekend," Dr. Jay said.

"You too."

It was getting late in the afternoon. Dr. Jay went back to his office and finished up some paper work.

* * *

Inside Mr. Jem's office, he and his men were having a discussion over the plans of his experiment. "Listen up Drake and Jack," Mr. Jem said, "I want you to go down to the lab and set things up. Drake, prepare the big glass container for holding the specimen. Jack, I want you to go fill the pool with water. There is a pump that you can use. Robert, you must get some computers and set them up in the lab. Most of the people are starting to go home, so you shouldn't have any trouble. I want you all to be quick in doing it."

The three all agreed on their jobs. "Now don't be surprised if this doesn't work," said Mr. Jem, "but when I mixed those two substances together as I showed you guys earlier, it looks like it could do something. I feel like this could work. Now move out."

"We will not fail you, sir!" the three men spoke.

"Ah, ah, ah!" said Mr. Jem. "You're in my office, and in my office you say... "

"Sorry, we won't fail you, Mr. Jem!" the men spoke correctly.

* * *

As people were starting to leave, Drake and Jack were working hard to prepare the lab for the experiment.

Dr. Jay went down to the dolphin medical pen one more time and gave one last inspection of the room. There was nobody there. "Well," Dr. Jay said to himself, "the day is finally over and I am

glad that I survived all the crazy stuff that has happened." He then
noticed that a few pieces of paper were lying on the ground behind
a set of desks. He went over and bent down on his knees to gather
them together. As he was about to get up, he noticed that somebody
had come into the room. He could see Robert, one of Mr. Jem's
assistants, looking around. His back was now turned to Dr. Jay
and he hadn't noticed him as he entered. Somehow, Robert looked
guilty and furtive. Dr. Jay decided to stay hidden to see what Robert
was about to do. Robert went over to a closet and opened it. After
looking inside, he grabbed a computer and began to take it out. Dr.
Jay realized it was the computer that contained the white enigma.
"You're heavy!" said Robert as he lifted the computer and began to
walk out. He then left the room.

"I better find out where he is taking that computer..." Dr. Jay
thought as he walked over to the door. He went back out into the
lobby. He could see Robert taking the computer into the restricted
hallway. Dr. Jay ran over to the door and caught it just before it was
about to shut. He peeked inside and saw Robert standing at a door.
Dr. Jay went in and crept slowly along the wall on his left side. He
could see that Robert was standing at the door saying 'Do not enter!
Keep out by order of the facility's president.' Dr. Jay noticed a gap
on the left side of the hall. He slowly walked into it and watched
from in there.

"Hey guys," said Robert, "It's me, Robert. This computer is
heavy so could someone please open the door?"

"What's the password?" asked a familiar voice on the other
side.

"What? We didn't arrange for a password, stop messing around!"
Robert said.

"Password confirmed," the voice replied. "Anybody around?"

Dr. Jay kept out of sight as Robert began looking. "Everything
is quiet, Drake," said Robert, "now open the door! I can't hold this
thing much longer!" The door opened. Dr. Jay could see Jack and
Drake inside. "Come right in and put it over there," said Drake. The
door closed. "Drake... Jack... and Robert," Dr. Jay thought. "Mr.
Jem's three subordinates. I wonder what they are up to? I wish I
could tell Henry that the computer has been taken, but he's already
gone home. I think I'll ask Mr. Jem about that room. But for now,
it's time to close the place up." He walked back towards the lobby

and went back to closing up. Dr. Jay, however, didn't notice a security camera that had been monitoring the hallway. Mr. Jem had a video screen in his office that monitored security. "Well, well," Mr. Jem said recognizing the figure. "What the hell do you think *you're* doing... Dr. Jay?"

CHAPTER 7

The Experiment Begins

"Be aware of the situation you are in.
Things could get complicated without a warning."
— Graham Lowe

DARKNESS FILLED THE skies at 11:00 pm. Inside Mr. Jem's office, Drake, Robert and Jack were standing at his desk. "Listen up, you three," Mr. Jem said. "I have chosen a target for experimenting the mutagen and DNA. Take a look at this footage that a security camera caught near the restricted room earlier." Mr. Jem played the footage. It showed Robert carrying a computer and walking funny. Drake laughed. "Ha, ha, ha! You look so funny wobbling like that!" he joked.

"Shut up, it was heavy," Robert said.

"Where did you get that one?" Jack asked.

"I found it in a closet inside the dolphin medical pen that had been attacked twice today." Suddenly, Jack was silent. "… What?" Robert asked.

"That computer—"

"Pay attention!" Mr. Jem said. Everyone faced the monitor and they saw a man hiding in a gap in the wall and then reappearing to examine the door. Mr. Jem stopped the tape and then zoomed in on the man's face.

"Somebody was following me?!" Robert asked. Drake then recognized who the man was.

"Hey…" Drake said. "That's the guy who's closing the place up

— the guy who argued with me earlier — the guy who called me, 'Pancake man!'"

Jack and Robert laughed. "Pancake man?!"

"That's enough," Drake said. "He was hoping the vending machine would squash me someday. That man is... Doctor Steele Monroe Jay!"

"Yes," Mr. Jem said.

"I hope he didn't see too much," Robert said.

"He probably didn't," Mr. Jem said, "but let's *allow* him to. For tonight, we experiment on him..." A crash of thunder sounded outside and it began to rain. Mr. Jem then leaned forward and said, "... and it has to be tonight."

"But I know that guy," Jack said. "We work together. I couldn't betray his trust."

"No?" Mr. Jem asked. "Then perhaps *you* would like to be the test subject then."

"Uh, no, that's okay," Jack said.

"I have a plan to execute this experiment," said Mr. Jem. "I will stay here. One of you will drop down through the trap door to the secret lab and land in the pool that is now full of water."

"Not me!" Jack said. "I've been shoved off a dock into the water and I've been rendered unconscious today, not to mention the freaks that bombed the medical pen and caused about $7,000 damage in equipment with me in the same room. No more surprises."

"I'll do it," Robert said.

"Okay," Mr. Jem said. "When you get down there, get out of the pool and unlock the door. Leave it wide open. I will call Dr. Jay's office and tell him to make sure all the doors in the hallway restricted to staff only are locked. Then—"

"Then we slam the door, jump on him and inject this stuff into him and watch the sparks fly!" Robert interrupted.

Mr. Jem banged his hand on the desk. "Don't interrupt me!" he shouted. Robert kept quiet. "I have a gun that marine biologists use to collect blubber samples from large whales," Mr. Jem continued as he picked up the gun. He removed the blubber collection device and took out what looked like a tranquilizer needle. It contained the mutagen and the dolphin blood. He loaded it into the gun and passed it to Jack. "Use this as a means of firing the substance into him," said Mr. Jem, "but don't let him see any of you, not even one glimpse. I'd like him to think you guys had turned in for the night. If you think he suspects you, retreat to my office and fire the needle into him when I give you the signal."

"Mr. Jem," said Jack, "the firing velocity of this gun is very powerful and is meant to puncture a great whale's layer of blubber. This has never been tested on a human being before."

"Then I'll do it," Drake said as he grabbed the gun.

"Goody," Mr. Jem said. "Robert, get down there. Stand back while I activate this trap door." Mr. Jem pressed a button and suddenly, a flap in the floor opened. "I was intending on using this as an emergency exit in case of some, well, serious emergency. Don't be afraid of it, Robert. It will be fun, just like a water slide."

"Okay," Robert said as he stared at the hole. "… Tallyho," he said as he jumped into it. "Whoa!" he shouted as he slid down the chute.

"That's done," Mr. Jem said. "Now to call Dr. Jay… "

* * *

Inside his office, Dr. Jay felt everything was done. "I'm tired," he thought. "Lazy weekend, here I—" His phone started ringing. He picked it up and said, "hello? … Hey, Mr. Jem. Everything's all closed up, so… You want me to check the doors of the restricted hallway to see if they're locked and then report to you?" He sighed as said, "fine, I'll do that. See you soon." He hung up the phone and left his office.

Drake and Jack opened Mr. Jem's office door slightly and peeked out to see that Dr. Jay was heading off to where Mr. Jem had wanted him to go. They saw him head down to the first floor. They hurried down the stairs and went in the direction of the lobby. The corridor was dark. When they got to the lobby, they peeked around the corner and saw Dr. Jay. They hid their heads just as Dr. Jay turned around. "Somebody following me… ?" thought Dr. Jay. "… Nah," he said, thinking everything was all right. "Guess it was nothing…" Just then, a guard passed by.

"Dr. Jay?" asked the guard.

"Yes?"

"You the one who is responsible for closing up the place for the weekend?"

"Yes."

"Two of us will take turns guarding that hole in the wall for the weekend. The tarp should work fine until the workmen come by to fix it. Hopefully, everything will be back to normal on Monday." The guard then walked away towards the dolphin medical pen. "Now who would make a hole in the wall like that... ?" the guard questioned himself as he went through the door to the room.

As Dr. Jay traveled down the restricted hall, he turned each handle on every door to see if they were locked. He then noticed a door that was open. "Hmm... this door is not locked," Dr. Jay thought, "in fact, it's wide open." He was about to shut it, when he noticed the sign on the door, 'Do not enter! Keep out by order of the facility's President.' It was the same door he had seen earlier that made his quarter fly, and the same place where he saw Robert take the computer that held the white enigma. "I know I shouldn't, but what the hell, I'll just look around quickly." He went in leaving the door open. From the lobby, Drake and Jack were peeking through the doors and saw Dr. Jay go in. "Let's go," Drake said. They slowly crept towards the room. As they approached the door, they peeked inside and saw Dr. Jay inside the room looking around. "Gee," said Dr. Jay wandering around. "I wonder what gets done here?" He saw lots of stuff from the dolphin pen, like computers, lamps, and work chairs. "One of the computers came from the dolphin medical pen of course," said Dr. Jay recognizing things.

"Mr. Jem's guys must have taken this stuff... I wonder where that computer with the white enigma could be?"

Drake and Jack turned away. "What the hell is he talking about?" Drake whispered. "I'll tell you later," Jack replied. Suddenly, they heard a door open further down the hall. They turned and saw Robert, soaking wet, slowly walking towards them. Jack approached him and whispered, "why did you take that computer from the cupboard in the medical pen?"

"I thought that computer was an unused extra," Robert replied.

"Shh..." whispered Drake. They continued watching Dr. Jay search the place. Dr. Jay saw a rectangular glass box standing vertically on its side. It was filled with water with bubbles coming out of the bottom and heading straight to the surface. The container had some sort of breathing apparatus inside.

"Strange," Dr. Jay thought to himself as he examined the thing.

He noticed the pool nearby. "A swimming pool… Certainly this must be a type of research lab. The floor seems wet. Has somebody been swimming here? Maybe these computers will tell me something about this place…" Dr. Jay sat down and powered on one of the computers. After ten seconds, it was ready.

Drake took out the gun and pointed it at Dr. Jay and was about to fire. Dr. Jay saw the computer starting to glow a bright white color. "What?!" Dr. Jay wondered as he got out of his chair. The light blinded Drake so he couldn't pull the trigger. The light then faded. "Oh god," Dr. Jay gasped. "This must be the computer with that enigma in it…" He faced the computer. "Uh… whatever you are, if you have any voice or mode of communication, speak to me." Nothing happened. He opened a word processor and typed, 'If you can communicate, tell me who you are'. A moment passed by. Suddenly, some text magically appeared on the screen. It said, 'AN ENIGMA, AM I?'

"What the… ?" thought Dr. Jay. He typed, 'what are you? Who are you, and how did you know I referred to you as that?' Suddenly, the whole computer powered off. "What?" he thought. "I didn't even… Maybe it's time I reported to Mr. Jem." Drake was peeking from the corner of the door.

"Guys," Drake whispered, "I think it's time for plan B."

"Right on," Robert replied. As they ran off, their footsteps made a noise. "Who's there?!" Dr. Jay shouted in shock. "Did somebody follow me or see me in here?" he wondered. He went out into the hallway and looked both ways. Everything was quiet. He then thought, "not enough coffee today. I'm getting so tired. I better get out of here right now." He turned off the lights in the room and closed the door. His hand was still on the door knob and as the door shut, he felt an electric shock. "Ow! Stupid high voltage security!" he shouted. He then noticed the covering for the knob. He closed it over the knob and looked below to see there was a keyhole. "Maybe a key is needed to deactivate that thing," he thought. He hurried back towards the lobby. Suddenly, he slipped and fell backwards. "Ow! What the… ?" As he got up, he could feel that the ground was wet. He was confused. It had not been wet when he came down a few minutes before. He went through the doors back into the lobby. He could see a guard wandering around. "Excuse me!" said Dr. Jay. "Did you see anybody come out of this hall?"

"I didn't see anything," said the guard.

* * *

Mr. Jem's subordinates were soon back in Mr. Jem's office.

"Mr. Jem," said Drake, "he is coming up here to your office. He got into the lab and explored a bit. Now he's coming up here, so it's time for plan B. Besides, espionage isn't really my style."

"I thought not," Mr. Jem said.

"This plan better work," said Robert.

"Get into hiding," said Mr. Jem. "Go into the shadows next to the door and… "

A minute or two later, Dr. Jay knocked on the door. There was no answer. Dr. Jay then twisted the knob and found it was locked.

"He's not here," Dr. Jay thought. "I better get out of here and get some sleep." Just then, as Dr. Jay was about to walk away, the door opened by itself.

"What the…? Hello?" he asked as he walked in. "Mr. Jem? Are you in here?"

As he walked in further, Jack, who was hiding in the shadows, snuck by Dr. Jay and went out. He grabbed the door, thought in his mind, "Dr. Jay, forgive me," and then slammed the door and quickly locked it.

Dr. Jay almost jumped out of his shoes as the door slammed. He spun around quickly. He saw the door was slammed shut. He ran over and tried to open it.

"Hey!" yelled Dr. Jay, "who locked me in? Hey!" He then turned around. "Mr. Jem?" he called, "are you in here?" As he walked forward to Mr. Jem's desk, he could see there was a lamp shining on some papers. "What's this?" Dr. Jay thought as he read through the papers. He could see that there were plans of the hidden lab he had entered. He saw the words, 'use dolphin blood and mutagen together, inject into living specimen, create creature from the black lagoon.' "Creature from the… Damn! I knew something was going on here! So he is trying something crazy and not even informing anyone about it. I'd better inform security." Dr. Jay went back over to the door and tried to get out. "Why won't this door open?" he thought, struggling to try and open it. He heard a noise behind him.

Turning around, he saw Mr. Jem at his desk. "You didn't read any-thing in these papers, did you?" asked Mr. Jem.

"Oh!" Dr. Jay exclaimed in reaction. "You scared me. Look, enough with the mystery. I wanted to give you my report." He walked up to Mr. Jem's desk. "The dolphin medical pen has been cleaned up and everything is secure. Things have been a bit weird today, and now I want to get the hell out of here and go home to sleep." Mr. Jem was not going to let him do that however. He was now in the position of distracting the subject.

"I heard about the dolphin who tried to destroy everything with its mind," said Mr. Jem. "In fact, take a look at this footage," He put in a tape and played it. It showed total darkness and something that looked like a strobe of light bouncing everywhere. "Whatever that was, it caused a lot of damage," Dr. Jay said. "It entered that computer and then everything stopped."

"And then you followed someone who took it," Mr. Jem added. Dr. Jay was becoming nervous. "You going into places without my permission?" Mr. Jem asked.

"Well…" said Dr. Jay, "I… uh… "

"So…" Mr. Jem interrupted, "you know about our secret labora-tory…"

"I do now," said Dr. Jay. "You should not be making labs with-out informing me and everyone else and I don't like what you are researching. I'll admit that I read those papers on your desk. What's this nonsense about D.N.A and the creature from the black lagoon? I'm calling security and I'm showing them this evidence."

He then saw something on Mr. Jem's desk. It was a wood carv-ing of a turtle. "That turtle…" Dr. Jay thought. "May I look at that?" Mr. Jem nodded. Dr. Jay grabbed it with one hand and looked under it, there was masking tape and black permanent marker writing that read, 'Property of the Jay family.'

"That's *my* carving!" said Dr. Jay. "You mean *you* robbed my house?"

"Oh," said Mr. Jem realizing something, "your house was bro-ken into last night?"

"Yes," Dr. Jay spoke, "you didn't know about that?"

"Of course not," Mr. Jem replied, "Seriously, I thought it was a gift that Drake gave me." Near the door, Drake was hiding in the shadows. He could see Dr. Jay right over the trap door. "Why do you rob people's homes?" asked Dr. Jay.

"Hey, my three close friends must have done this," Mr. Jem said, "I had no involvement. It was a random attack. They're just a bunch of silly clowns who like to do stupid things. They were out partying and they must have done some neighborhood exploring."

"That's your explanation?" Dr. Jay asked. "Well, that *stupid thing* is over the line."

"Just forget about that and listen to what I have to say," Mr. Jem said. "We put all our sweat and blood every day into helping sick and injured creatures. We all have to find some kind of humor in a place where we work to save nature. You have been having a very bad day today, haven't you?"

"Damn right," said Dr. Jay. "But robbing people's homes is not what I call humor! You have a responsibility to manage this facility to help improve the ocean environment."

"Don't be naïve," Mr. Jem said. "My management in this institute is only a secondary interest. Today is a special day for this experiment I am conducting."

"You mean, *illegal, unauthorized* experiment," Dr. Jay said.

"I've always found this job boring," Mr. Jem said, "but I just locked that thought away. Now, I need more than just this job of running a marine research facility, okay? I mean, I want more!"

"Oh, shut up already!" said Dr. Jay. "I don't give a damn about how boring you find this! Did you take that dolphin's blood?"

"Boy, you're smart!" said Mr. Jem. "But it was Jack who did that."

"Jack?!" Dr. Jay asked. "Jack Degrasso who works in the medical pen?! He unintentionally takes things from my house and doesn't even *know* he's in *my* house? Now, he harms a dolphin for a stupid blood sample? He's a bright guy, why would he do that?"

"How should I know?" Mr. Jem asked. "Even famous people like Michael Jackson do stupid or weird things sometimes. Everybody does."

"What about those unidentified people who wrecked the dolphin pen earlier?" Dr. Jay asked. "Do you know anything about that?"

"That's a different story," said Mr. Jem. "What happened was unexpected. It's as if somebody knew about our plan. Jack claimed he was nearly killed. And that 'white enigma' that people referred to it as, that bounced into a computer, that could have been an alien from outer space for all I care. Maybe I could utilize it for something."

"Have you created your 'Black Lagoon' creature yet, Dr. Frankenstein?" asked Dr. Jay. "I mean, something like that is not possible and you are not going to create that thing. You should be ashamed of yourself for trying to mutate a dolphin that has done no harm to humans."

"Oh, I'm not mutating a dolphin," said Mr. Jem. "Because you found out about this, I'm going to mutate *you*."

"Oh really?" asked Dr. Jay. "Well you'll never take me alive, you… you… mutant creating weirdo!"

"Of course I will," said Mr. Jem. Drake was still standing in the shadows pointing the gun at Dr. Jay's right arm, waiting for the signal.

"There is one last thing I would like to say before we call it a night," said Mr. Jem. Drake's finger was right on the trigger. "Oh boy…" Drake thought in his mind. "This is it… the moment of truth…"

"… You're fired," Mr. Jem spoke deeply as he moved his finger in a downward motion. Drake squeezed the trigger, the gun fired and the needle shot right into Dr. Jay's right arm. Dr. Jay let out a loud scream. "What the hell?!" he shouted as he turned around. "Who's there?!" he yelled, trying to make out the shadowy figure. Mr. Jem flicked a switch that opened the trap door. As Dr. Jay felt himself begin to fall, he grabbed the ledge with his left hand and then with his right. He was holding on tight, not knowing what was happening. Mr. Jem ran around to the hole and put his foot on Dr. Jay's left hand. Mr. Jem said, "I'm sorry about this, but I can assure you, I'm only human." Mr. Jem then put his foot on Dr. Jay's face and pushed hard. Dr. Jay fell down the chute.

"Ah!" he yelled as he zipped down the chute like he was going down a slide. He looked in horror at the needle in his arm. He could see an orange liquid slowly draining out into his blood system. Before he knew it, he found himself sinking underwater in the pool in the secret lab. He struggled to swim up to the surface. He used his left hand and tried to find the needle. The last bit of the substance entered his blood stream as he finally managed to pull out the needle which then sank to the bottom of the pool.

"Oh my god!" said Dr. Jay as he rose to the surface. "How did I get here? What..?" The effect of the injection suddenly hit him with a sharp pain. "Guah!" he moaned. "What… is this injection doing to me?!" He felt his heart rate shoot up to three times the normal speed. He tried to swim out of the pool. By the time he got to the edge of the pool, he had started to mutate. "ARGH!" he yelled. "Somebody help me! Help! I can't… breathe! I feel like… my insides are… ripping apart!" He was twisting and jerking around. He saw his skin beginning to turn gray and he could feel something shoot out of his back and rip right though the back of his shirt. Then all his clothing began to rip apart. Dr. Jay screamed at the top of his lungs. As he tried to get out, he felt his stomach burning and his face changing shape. Dr. Jay's whole body was in agony. He didn't know what to do. "Nooo!!!" he cried. He lost his strength and collapsed with half his body out of the pool. "God… help me…" he gasped. He then passed out thinking he was dead.

* * *

Meanwhile, Mr. Jem and his three assistants were running towards the elevator. "Good work, boys!" said Mr. Jem as they went in. "I would sure like to see if he has become something unique." Mr. Jem took some gum that he had been chewing out of his mouth and threw it up to the ceiling. It hit the grid and it fell down. The three men looked at each other and Drake immediately picked up the gum. He looked at Robert and then signaled him to pick him up so that he could be lifted up to the grid on the ceiling. He stuck the gum in one of the holes of the grid next to the few other pieces of colored gum.

"… Nice shot, Mr. Jem," said Drake. They got out of the elevator and went down the corridor towards the lobby. "We must hurry!" said Mr. Jem. "I don't know if my experiment worked or not, but we have to hurry and find out." As they went into the lobby, it was almost completely dark. They found the restricted hall and went in. They came to the door of the lab. "Remember to use the key," Mr. Jem said. Drake took out the key to the room and put it in the keyhole. There was a click and the electric buzzing noise stopped. "Let's keep our fingers crossed," said Mr. Jem. As the cover on the knob was opened, Drake turned the knob, opened the door and everyone went in. They turned on the lights and saw at the pool's edge, a human-like figure with dolphin skin, a dolphin head and a dorsal fin. It was unconscious.

"Wow!" said Jack.

"Look at the size of him!" said Drake.

"It's a human that looks like a dolphin!" said Robert. "Let's check if he's breathing!" They went over and felt the dolphin figure's neck. There was a pulse. There was also some slow breathing from the blowhole on the back of its head.

"It worked!" Mr. Jem said, astounded. "The effects are… are… greater than I expected! Come on guys! Lift him out and put him in that container." The trio pulled the mutant dolphin figure out of the pool. "Yiee, this guy weighs a ton!" Drake said. He went up a ladder, carrying Dr. Jay's mutated body by the armpits while Robert held the feet and Jack held the ladder. "YEOW! I know what you mean!" Robert said.

"Hey, stop complaining!" Mr. Jem said. As Drake managed to get to the top, he jerked the mutant animal into the container and faced him upright. Drake put the breathing apparatus around the blowhole and then they were done.

"Mission accomplished guys!" said Mr. Jem. "Everyone, thanks for helping me with my experiment… It really works…" he said, looking at the mutant. "I wonder," he said quietly to himself, "if I can make more of these… "

"Huh?" Drake asked. "What did you say?"

"It doesn't matter," said Mr. Jem. "Let's just leave him here for tonight."

"Okay," said Drake. "Nobody's going to come tomorrow because it's the weekend. That means we will have the time to research this thing." He faced the container and said, "you deserve this for hoping a vending machine would crush me!" he shouted. "And can you believe it?" he asked Jack. "This is the same guy whose house we robbed last night. What a coincidence!"

"I overheard him talking to Mr. Jem," Jack said, not sounding very happy. "How did we end up as *his* place? I didn't want to do anything to his house."

"Come on guys," said Mr. Jem. "Let's go. We will celebrate tomorrow." Mr. Jem, Drake and Robert were about to leave the room, when they stopped and turned to see Jack staring into the glass container at the mutated Dr. Jay with the bubbles rising around him. Jack felt saddened. "… I'm… so sorry…" Jack said. Drake and Robert watched Jack staring at someone he had known so well, become something completely unnatural. They suddenly felt sorry too. They walked over to Jack. "What are you two doing?" Mr. Jem asked. "Let's go, now!" Drake and Robert didn't listen to him. Drake put his hand on Jack's shoulder and Robert did the same on Jack's other shoulder. "Hey," Drake said, trying to cheer him up. "He could have gotten us arrested if we let him get away. I know you were friends with him, but now, things are going to change around here."

"Did we really have to do this?" Jack asked.

"I know," Robert said. "I don't think it was a good idea breaking into his house as well as doing this to him, now that I think about it. I worry about his family."

"… We didn't break into his house," Jack said reflecting on the night before. "We saw the door of that house wide open when we were out partying. I remember seeing flashlights flickering in the window. It looked like a robbery was in progress. You guys got curious and went inside, playing G.I Joe or something. I followed you and noticed that, paintings and stuff were taken down. When you thought you heard the intruders coming, both of you grabbed some things and ran out. You passed me something and convinced me to run. Somebody else was already in there and we took advantage."

"You're right," Robert said. "What were we thinking?"

Mr. Jem was staring at his subordinates who were feeling guilty for what they had done. It made him mad, not just the fact that they were feeling bad for Dr. Jay, but also the fact that they had disobeyed an order from their superior. His three close friends had never ignored or disobeyed him before. It made him very angry. "Hey!" Mr. Jem shouted. Everyone turned to Mr. Jem. He took a deep breath and said, "look, I'm sorry about this too, Jack. At least he's not dead. We'll set things up so that he will be in a happy environment and you will be able to talk to him about whatever. It's very late. Let's all go home and hit the sack. We'll discuss things in the morning, okay?" After a moment, Jack faced Mr. Jem, nodded his head and walked towards the exit without saying a word. As everyone left the room, Mr. Jem turned the lights out, closed the door, and locked it.

CHAPTER 8

Birth of a Dolphin Man

"Constructing a novel is much like a jigsaw puzzle,
only a novel has no cardboard pieces and no complete picture to
follow, but a puzzle of words and a picture in my mind. The pieces
fit to create plots and when the puzzle is complete, not just worlds,
but universes can be created."
—Graham Lowe

DR. JAY WAS floating inside the container, still unconscious with the breathing apparatus wrapped around his head. His clothing had ripped to shreds during his mutation and he was now completely naked. He was no longer human.

Inside the room, the computer that contained the white enigma suddenly powered itself on and a message appeared on the screen. It said: I SHALL NOW TRANSFER MYSELF INTO THE NEW SPECIES' HEAD AND ESCAPE. That message then disappeared and the computer typed up another message for the newly mutated Dr. Jay to read. The computer suddenly started glowing. The glow started to emerge from the computer and flow through the computer wires. It slowly flowed through the wires on the ground towards the outlet in the wall. It looked as if the mysterious enigma was moving itself. It then appeared in a different set of wires that were suspended above the container holding Dr. Jay. As soon as it was above the container's opening on the top, it stopped. Suddenly, the wire started to catch fire. First, there was a flame. Then, it started to sizzle and sparks began flying. Finally, the wire broke in half and the two ends fell and touched the water in the container. The water became electrified and the enigma shot out and went onto Dr. Jay's head. Electricity was bouncing everywhere in the container as the enigma flowed into Dr. Jay's head through his ears. It was going right inside his head! After it finished 'transferring' itself, the electricity stopped. Dr. Jay's eyes were still shut, but he was conscious. All he saw was darkness, but even though his eyes were closed, he also saw something else. He saw what looked like neon-white colored bubbles floating around him.

"Mmm..." Dr. Jay groaned. "What... is... this...? Where... am... I... now?" He slowly reached out and felt the glass in front of him. He began to kick and punch the glass in order to break free. As his eyes opened slightly, he felt a stinging feeling. Everything he could see was a blur.

* * *

Meanwhile, back at Dr. Jay's house, the children were getting ready for bed. Jennifer walked into Walter's room. She saw him at his desk working on something. "Mom?" Walter asked as he took a glance at her and then went back to whatever he was doing. "Why is dad not home yet?"

"He left a message earlier saying that he had been directed to... Walter, stop playing with that thing for a second!" she said. Walter looked up. "... He's closing up the Institute for the weekend. He will probably be quite late."

"Okay," Walter said. Walter at age 14 was fanatical about science. His room contained a bookshelf of science books, a desk with gimmicks strewn about and a poster of Albert Einstein above his bed. When his mom walked into his room, he was busy working on an invention . There was a box, a wire and a plastic suit. His ambition was to create something that would allow the user to disguise himself as another person using photo rendering technology. He was aware that such a design was sophisticated, but he was persistent about what he was doing. He thought to himself that, one day, just like the Wright brother's airplane, his work would amount to something.

As Jennifer was about to head to her room, she passed Mike and Sid, her two other sons.

Mike asked her the same question Walter asked.

"It's nothing," said Jennifer. "Steele is just coming home late. He had to close up the Institute for the weekend."

"Mom," Mike said with a grin, "call him dad, honey, dear or Dr. Jay. Call him anything, but not Steele. I don't think that is a real first name. I think it sounds like a nickname you'd give to a guy working the smelter."

"He was named after his grandfather, Stanley Steele Jay," Jennifer said. "His mother liked that name. It sounded strong and powerful to her. Soon, the name stuck."

"Whatever you say," Mike said. "I'm too tired to argue about anything right now. Good night mom."

"Good night," Jennifer replied as Mike walked away. Mike at 16 was the oldest of the three children. He was interested in martial arts and along with his brothers had been attending Tae-Kwon-Do classes. It was one of the few things he was good at.

"I bet daddy has seen a lot of dolphins today mom," said Sid. Sid, the youngest at 12, loved dolphins. One day, he wanted to have his very own dolphin and name it, Dolphi. He made the name up himself by taking the word 'dolphin', removing the 'n', and making the 'i' sound like 'eye'.

"I am sure you will get to see the dolphins again soon, sweety," said Jennifer. "Now, you best be off to bed." She gave Sid a kiss and they walked away to their rooms.

* * *

Back in the lab, Dr. Jay was still trying to break the container's glass barrier. He kept kicking and kicking. Finally, a few cracks formed and they got bigger. He gave the glass one final blow with both of his legs and the glass shattered. The water gushed out and so did poor Dr. Jay. He landed on the floor and then slowly got up onto his knees. He looked at his hands. They didn't look like his normal hands. They looked gray and had something that looked like webbing in between the fingers. "Oh man…" he said softly. "What… have they done to me? What… have they done to my body?"

"Hello, my creature from the Black Lagoon!" said a voice that came over the loudspeaker.

"Mr. Jem…" thought Dr. Jay.

"How did you wake up so quickly?" asked Mr. Jem. *"It doesn't matter anyway. You can't talk to me. Have you looked at yourself in the mirror yet?"* Dr. Jay struggled to get up on his legs. When he got up, he turned around to find a mirror. He was shocked when he saw his new body. His head looked like that of a dolphin. His body still had its human shape, but it was hairless. The skin was mostly grey, but the chest and belly area was a white-ish color. His feet had three toes with large webbing in between. He was a half-human and half-bottlenose dolphin creature!

"AAAHHH!!!" he yelled. "What the hell have you DONE to me?!"

"I thank you so much for participating in my little experiment," said Mr. Jem. *"I bet I can make many other half human and half animal creatures possible. I always wondered if this mutagen had an interesting effect."* Dr. Jay looked up and saw a camera pointed at him. *"Ha, ha, it's alive!"* said Mr. Jem sounding like Doctor Frankenstein. *"You can't escape. That door has a ten digit number set. You should stay in the water if you don't want to dehydrate. Please cooperate with us in future experiments because I want to learn more about what I have just created. Adios!"* Mr. Jem went off the speaker.

"Mr. Jeeeeem!!!" Dr. Jay yelled with rage as he ran to where the camera was. It was out of reach, but he saw a ladder nearby. He grabbed it and threw it at the camera. The ladder flew fast and hard and the camera shattered from the impact. He then went silent and looked at himself again. "So that's what my boss was talking about... Creature from the black lagoon, dolphin D.N.A, and testing it on someone... It was me... They've tested it on me and now I'm no longer human... I'm no longer human..." he repeated, bowing his head down. He sat on the ground and put his hands on his eyes and sat there crying. "No..." he said softly to himself. After a minute, he got up and looked back at the mirror. He was horrified at the sight of what he had become. He began to remember his knowledge of dolphins. "If I am like a dolphin, then I must have a dolphin's abilities," he thought. "I should keep my skin moist every once in a while." He just stood there looking in the mirror at his cold, naked body. He was a mutant dolphin alright. He walked right up to the mirror and looked at his eyes. "They're still human," he thought, "but the eye color is black. I've never seen a black eye color. I've also noticed that there is a change in my voice. I'm also a few inches taller and still pretty fit looking. Mr. Jem is not going to get away with this." Dr. Jay felt he was going crazy. He was thinking about a name for his new form. "Maybe I should go with a name that suits my new body," he thought. "I've seen it happen with others on cartoon shows like the Teenage Mutant Ninja Turtles and The X-Men for example. My name should be… Greyguy… nope… Flipperman… heh, heh, good one, but no… What is a good name? D-o-l-p-h-i-n… Dol-fine… Doll…" He then thought about the dolphin that Sid had wanted. "Oh, what was that name that Sid had spoken of about a dolphin he wanted?" After a brief moment, he then said, "… Dolph-eye… Dolphi, that's the name! That sounds like a good name he came up with, Dolphi: D-o-l-p-h-i. I am a dolphin… mutant… no, a dolphin… creature, thing, monster… good god, no. I'll think up something later."

Dr. Jay, who now called himself Dolphi, had walked over to the pool and noticed his ripped clothes at the bottom. He jumped into the pool and grabbed the clothes. The water he was in felt so good to his skin, but cold. He swam up to the surface so fast, he jumped out of the water like a dolphin. "Yikes!" he yelped as he landed on the floor with a thud. "Ouch! Man, I guess I'm a dolphin and that's what dolphin's do, but wow! I can't believe how fast I just swam! I feel so much stronger! Before that quick dip, I felt a little dry. Now I feel so refreshed! My skin feels so smooth! I… gotta shut up. I shouldn't be wasting my time here any longer. I better find my car keys and get out of here as quickly as possible." He was searching the pockets for the car keys. "Come on," he said trying to find the car keys. "Keys, keys, keys…" He found them. "Good," he said. He took one last look at the mirror. He felt sad, but he made a bit of a smile to see his teeth.

"Wow," he said. "I must have about eighty-eight to a hundred sharp teeth in this strange mouth of mine. I'm going to bust out of here and try to make the best of this bad situation." He looked away from the mirror and tried to run over to the door. But then, he slipped on a puddle on the floor and fell on his back. "Oww!" he cried. He rubbed his back and felt something. He could feel that had a dorsal fin. "Man that hurt! My feet are slippery." He tried to dry his feet off with his breath, but no breath came out of his mouth. Instead, the air came out of his head. He felt the back of his head and found a hole. "I have a blowhole, huh?" he thought. "I guess my life has changed forever." He got up and ran over to the door. The door was locked. He looked at the number pad. Ten digits had to be entered. "How am I supposed to know the code?" he wondered. As he turned around, he saw a computer powered on. He walked over to it. He saw a message up on the screen. It said: I NEED YOU TO ESCAPE. SIT DOWN AND FACE THIS COMPUTER AND CLOSE YOUR EYES. THINK ABOUT TRYING TO HACK THE COMPUTER WITH YOUR MIND. YOU WILL THEN ENTER A VIRTUAL ENVIRONMENT. SELECT THE CORRECT ORDER OF NUMBERS TO OPEN THE DOOR.

"What the?" Dolphi thought. "Who typed this up? This sounds weird, but I guess I have no other choice." He sat in the chair and closed his eyes. He then immediately felt a jolt inside his head. It happened very quickly and it made him yelp. He heard a voice in his head say, "accessing computer network array." He was then able to see what looked like a computer silicon world. He felt like he was flying across computer circuits and going into cracks that led to other places. "Whoa!" he shouted. "What the blazes?!" He could not control his flight. He was then directed to this one little interface. There was a bunch of numbers showing from 0 to 9 and a code entry box.

"Uh, hello?!" Dolphi called out. "Who's doing this?!" There was no response. He turned back to the green, glowing interface. "So, now what?" he thought. When he turned around, he could see a funny spiked ball floating in the air. He wondered if he could swim over to it. He then started to move. As he got closer, he heard a female voice in his head say, "access code."

"Can you acknowledge me?" Dolphi asked. Once again there was no answer. When he touched the ball, it changed shape. It began to wash over his head. It made Dolphi nervous. He suddenly saw a loading screen. It said, 'scanning' and a meter went to 100%. He saw details on the numbers that looked something like this: 0: 90-100% 1: 20% 2: 40-60% 3: 10% 4: 0% 5: 70-80% 6: 30% 7: 0% 8: 50% 9: 0%. Dolphi had no idea what this was at first, but then, he began to think about it. "Maybe if I input the numbers in order of percentage…" he thought. The stuff that was on his head suddenly left off him. It went back into its spiked ball form. Dolphi turned and swam back over to the interface. A little red flashing box saying, 'memory' suddenly popped up. Dolphi touched it and a screen popped up showing him the numbers that had been scanned. After looking over the numbers, he tried to find a way to input them. The numbers from 0 to 9 had boxes around them. He lifted his hand and when his finger was over the number 3, the box was highlighted. He touched the number and it was entered. He entered the numbers in order of percentage and input the code: 3162825500. Green colored text then popped up saying, 'Access Granted' and white text underneath the green text saying, 'Opening Doors'.

"Okay, uh…" Dolphi said. "Could I get out of here please?" There was a green light in one of the circuit board-like walls that lit up. It was drawing a line made of light in a direction past the number interface. Dolphi swam along, following the light. The line then took him to another weird shape and a voice said, "exit." When Dolphi touched the shape, he began to fly backwards really fast. It was like an extreme roller-coaster ride going backwards. It made his adrenaline rush. There was a flash of light and Dolphi fell off his chair, opened his eyes and found he was back to reality. He lay there breathing heavily. The experience felt so chilling, he just lay there and wet himself. He looked over to the door. It was open. "What… just happened?!" he thought, thinking about the virtual world. "What… was *that* all about? Is this part of my mutation? It better not be. I… I gotta get out of here!"

He quickly stood up, grabbed the car keys and ran out of the room, confused, afraid and soaked in his own urine. He slammed into the wall on the other side of the hall and fell down. He got up again and ran down the hall trying to find an emergency exit. He found one and pushed himself into it. As the door burst open, he ran outside. It was raining very hard. He dropped on all fours. He could feel the rain falling on him. "Ahh…" he sighed. The rain was not only soothing to his skin, but it was also cleaning him up from the accident he had. He suddenly heard an explosion. The sound was loud and he felt it make his head tingle. "What was that?" he wondered. "That sounded like it came from around the building in the parking lot." He ran alongside the building. After he made his way around, he saw a badly wreaked car on fire. His was the only car in that particular parking lot that night. "My car… !" he gasped. He saw the fire blazing. He watched as the rain slowly extinguished it. As he went over to the destroyed car, he looked at the license plate number. M75*JRN was what it said on it. It was definitely his car. He turned to look at the building. "Mr. Jem!" he yelled. "I'll be back sometime, you hear me?!" He then saw the front doors of the facility open. The security guards must have taken notice. Dolphi ran away as fast as he could. "I better find my way home," he said to himself. He looked at the car keys and saw a small picture of his family. He took out the picture and looked at his keys again. He threw them at the wrecked vehicle knowing that they were useless. He left the parking lot and ran down the street in the pouring rain. It was dark and scary and he didn't understand what had happened to him back in the lab with the computer. When he closed his eyes, he saw the rain drops making an image in his head. He was so terrified, he wasn't aware of what it was.

* * *

He seemed to be walking for quite a long time down the lonely road. After walking for an hour, he got close to the city of Miami and traffic was starting to get active. He then ran quickly to find the nearest alley. He soon found one. Just when he thought he was safe, he crashed into somebody and they both fell down.

"Hey!" the figure yelled. He glanced at Dolphi as they got up. "Ah!" he gasped looking at Dolphi's shadowy figure. "Who are you?!" Dolphi saw the guy take out something rectangular from his pocket. He pressed something and a blade popped up. It was a switchblade.

"Oh, great," Dolphi thought. "Look, I'm sorry. I didn't mean–"

"What the hell are *you*?!" the angry man asked loudly. "I'm gonna kill you, you freak!" He started to lunge at Dolphi. Dolphi ran out of the alleyway and ran down the street as fast as he could. Some people gasped and quickly jumped out of the way as Dolphi ran past them. He came up to a road and a car stopped in front of him. Dolphi jumped and rolled over the hood of the car. The dorsal fin on his back went into the hood making a dent. Inside the car, the passenger asked the driver, "what was that?"

"It looked like some sort of a giant Flipper dolphin," the driver replied.

"Maybe I won't drink so much next time."

Dolphi looked behind him to see that the armed man was still chasing him. He then ducked into another alley. He was breathing hard and the alley was pitch black. He could not see a thing. The man appeared at the entrance to the alley way.

"No!" said Dolphi pleading. "Please don't hurt me!"

"You're freaking me out," said the man. "You charge into my turf and run into me with that crazy get-up of yours and think you can get away with it? Die, you freak!" As the man attempted to stab the knife into Dolphi, Dolphi grabbed his wrist with one hand and squeezed it. "Agh!" the man groaned. Dolphi's grip felt very strong. "Let go!" the man yelled. "Let go!"

Dolphi was panicking so much, he didn't realize that he had picked the man up and thrown him to the end of the alley. Dolphi couldn't believe his strength and neither did the attacker. The man got back up on his feet. He turned to see a vehicle back up in front of him. The rear of the vehicle opened and somebody grabbed the man before he or Dolphi could make out who it was. The man was yanked into the car and he dropped his knife. The car drove off. Dolphi walked over to the knife on the ground. He picked it up and walked up to the end of the alleyway. He looked in the direction the car had gone. It was sitting there, some 30 meters away. The door of the car opened and the man was thrown out. He got up and scrambled away. The car then drove off.

Dolphi was feeling cold and tired and scared. He looked through the alley. There was no one else there. At the corner, he could see some flattened cardboard boxes.

"Ohh..." Dolphi moaned mercifully. "I wish I was home..." Whoever his saviors were, he thanked them in his mind. He was suddenly so tired he felt he couldn't move on. He decided to use the cardboard boxes to make himself something to sleep on and to block others from seeing him. Dolphi found it impossible to fall asleep. He lay awake for a long time thinking about his new body, his new form and his new life. He had become something different from everybody else. He wasn't sure how he could live the rest of his life. "I've gotta fall asleep," he moaned in fear, "I've gotta think, I gotta relax, I..." He shut his eyes tight and tried to go to sleep. When he did close his eyes, he could see the raindrops making some kind of image in his head. The hazy white color of the surroundings was pretty. It calmed him down and and soon, he fell asleep.

Unknown to Dolphi, there was somebody at the end of the alleyway watching him. Whoever it was, it was wearing a cloak with a hood. The figure slowly walked towards Dolphi and looked at him for a minute. The figure then took off his cloak and, aware that Dolphi was asleep, placed it over him as a blanket. The figure then took off leaving Dolphi all alone...

CHAPTER 9

The Creator's Past

*"From the past to the present, our experiences in life
shape our personalities for the future."*
—Graham Lowe

B ACK AT THE M.R.I.L, Mr. Jem was in his office sitting in his chair
facing the window. The rain was pouring down the window. He
was very quiet. He just stared out the window feeling amazed at
how successfully his experiment had worked. His subordinates had
gone home and he had just got back from meeting with the security
guards who had informed him about the car that had exploded out
in the parking lot. Before Drake left, Mr. Jem had ordered him to
blow up the car that belonged to Dr. Jay by doing something to the
gas tank. Drake then had to convince the security guards that, that
was his car that exploded and that it was an act of vandalism (by the
same people who bombed the dolphin medical pen). Before that, he
had driven his own car around the side of the building.

Mr. Jem continued to stare out his office window without showing any emotion. The rain pouring down outside reminded him of
another rainy night. A night when his life was changed forever. He
shut his eyes and remembered back to when he was ten years old;
back to events that led to Dr. Jay's mutation.

* * *

The night was dark and rainy, he was next to a building that had a sign saying it was a rescue shelter. He was banging hard on the metal door. "Open up!" he cried in distress. "Please open up! Give me sanctuary!" The door opened and a middle aged man appeared. The man gasped as he saw what looked like blood on the boy's sweater. "Oh my! Where are your parents, young man?" he asked.

The boy explained to the man that he was in a car with his parents driving home after seeing some play that had bored him. The rain was pouring hard and his father who was driving was arguing with his mother about how boring he found the play as well. The hard pouring rain made it difficult to see. There was another car coming in their direction and they were slightly over the centre line. His father's head was turned to his wife and when she saw that he was almost about to hit the other car, she yelled, "look out!" The father turned his car away and due to the slippery conditions, he lost control and drove through a corner railing and went down a rocky slope. The car began rolling. After rolling over and over the car slammed up against a tree. The frightened boy slowly got up and crawled to the front calling for his mom and dad. They were lying motionless and he shook them to see if they would respond. There was no response from either of them. He then saw the front of the car was on fire. There was a loud bang and the fire got bigger. The fire made his parents visible. He could see blood on their faces and he realized that the car was upside down. He screamed for his parents to wake up, but they still didn't respond. He wasn't bleeding, but he had gotten his parents' blood on him while he was shaking them. He crawled to one of the car doors and tried to open it. It didn't open. He could see that the fire was beginning to get inside the car. He kept trying to open the door. He then made out the door lock. He pulled it up and tried to open the door again. This time, it opened. He crawled out and stood back from the car yelling to his parents that the car was on fire. He couldn't understand why the rain wasn't putting it out. Suddenly, the car exploded in a ball of fire. The boy screamed as the car was destroyed along with his parents. He scrambled up the hill and ran along the road to find help.

The man was horrified by the boy's story. "Uh... hold on a minute," the man said. He turned around and disappeared into the building. "Nurse?" he called. "Nurse?!" The boy waited for a minute. The man came back. "I'm sorry," the man said, "all of our beds are full. You must find another place to stay." The man told the boy

about the location of another shelter. The directions confused the
boy as he was not familiar with the roads. The man closed the door
in his face. The boy banged on the door again. "Please!" he cried, "I
don't know how to get there! Please give me a place to stay!" When
no one came he finally gave up and ran off sobbing. He walked for
several city blocks trying to find some other place, but everything
was closed and traffic was rare. After wandering for a while, he collapsed on the sidewalk and lay silent. A few minutes later, a man
wearing a trench coat and carrying an umbrella came walking down
the sidewalk. He saw the boy lying on the ground and hurried over
to him.

"Are you alright?" he asked. The boy slowly got up. "My goodness!" the man said looking at the bloodstain on the boy's sweater.
"Let's get you to the hospital immediately!" The man grabbed the
boy's hand and walked him a few blocks to where his car was. He
placed the boy in the car and got in with him. There was a driver up
front. "Get to the nearest hospital immediately!" the boy's rescuer
said.

"Yes sir!" the driver replied as he drove off.

"What is your name, little boy?" the man asked.

"... James," the boy said through his sobs. "James Harland."

"What happened to you?"

"... I just got into a terrible car accident," James cried. "... My
parents... they..." he then passed out.

* * *

Mr. Jem now remembered a few months later. After he had his
unfortunate accident and the loss of his parents, he was sent to the
orphanage. Before he was known as Mr. Jem, he went by his first
name, James. He was sad to have no parents, but he didn't really
miss them. Mr. and Mrs. Harland's relationship with each other had
been unsteady and they had had arguments all the time. Their last
argument had put an end to them. James hated them for not caring
for each other or for him, but he hadn't wished for them to die.

One day, James was told that there were people who might want
to adopt him. At first, he wasn't looking forward to it. After many
couples had visited, it was driving James crazy and he didn't know
what to do. There was even one couple that wanted him to help

with farm work! James thought, that'll be the day! He was then told that there was one more couple to see. Their names were Richard Orville Jem and his wife, Casynthia (kah-sin-thee-ah). When James saw the man named Richard, he recognized him immediately. It was the same man who had found him on the streets the night of his accident. James asked why did they want him. He was told that after trying for some time, the Jems couldn't have children of their own due to infertility. Also, in James' record, it said that he was a bright child. Richard felt that this was a boy who wanted to learn unique things and the education the orphanage was offering, was not challenging enough for him. The Jems felt this boy was the right one for them and they would care for him. They promised him he would learn all kinds of things. James had accepted them willingly.

* * *

After James had been adopted, his name had become James Richwood Jem. He then thought ahead to when he was a teenager. One of the things that had interested him was martial arts. He was sitting at a table drinking a beverage. He was wearing a Karate uniform. His belt color was brown. He was being approached by another man in a Karate uniform. This man was the instructor who had been hired for private lessons.

"You have worked hard building knowledge and strength throughout your life," the instructor said. "I am most pleased with your progress. There is something that Dr. Richard Jem would like to bring to your attention. Since he has adopted you as his son, he wishes for you to be part of one of his most important research projects in his Special Projects Center." James knew that his adoptive father was a scientist, but he didn't know exactly what he did.

"What sort of project?" James asked as he sipped his drink.

"It is top secret and even I am not allowed to know what goes on. It's very rare for people to get in that place. He would gladly appreciate your involvement. You would be very surprised at what he has in there."

"Sounds interesting. I wonder what kind of research is so top secret? I would do anything for my father, for he has done so much for me."

"That is a very wise choice. You have shown honor throughout your training. You have flourished with great effort. For that, I will present to you, your chance to earn your first degree black belt." James put down his drink, got out of the chair and faced the instructor. He was holding a small wooden box. James stared at the box for a short while. He then raised his hand, made a loud cry, swung his hand down on the box and broke it with a Karate chop. Inside was a black colored belt. "Congratulations," his instructor said.

"They better not call me J.J. when I'm there," James said with a determined look on his face.

* * *

As the years went by, James studied a range of topics such as marine wildlife and genetics, his new father's favorite. James felt that he was finally living a perfect life. But one day, there was a turning point. His adoptive mother Casynthia had come down with cancer. She wasn't getting any better and Richard knew that one day soon, she would pass away. Saddened by this, he was prompted to try to find some way to rid her of her disease. But it was too late for Casynthia. She passed away one rainy afternoon. After her funeral, Richard vowed never to rest until he found a way to combat the cancer disease. James felt his new father's sorrow and wanted to help him find a cure. Richard believed that genetics, being his favorite interest, would be the answer. James also insisted that he help out with the research as well. Richard had a secret laboratory where he did most of his studies. He was the laboratory's Director and he wanted his research to be secretive because he didn't want to be pestered by Government officials. It was his belief that the Government would interfere with his research.

One day, in Richard's personal laboratory, he and his staff developed an amber colored substance. Richard took a sample of cancer cells, added the substance and checked it under the microscope. He could see that the cells were disintegrating. James was in the same room with him.

"James!" Richard called. "Something's happening with these cancer cells!" James hurried over and looked into the microscope. He was in awe of what was happening. Richard then went to pour himself a cup of coffee. "It appears the cells are being devoured," James said. James decided to prick his finger and put some of his blood on a slide with the substance. When he looked under the microscope, he could see the experimental substance was doing something to the blood cells.

"Hey, dad!" James called. Richard came over and set his coffee down next to a small glass jar containing the substance. "I just put some of my blood with this stuff and it's causing the blood to mutate into something grotesque," James told his father. He moved away to let his father see.

Richard scratched the back of his head in curiosity. "I don't understand. The substance is not only eliminating cancer cells, it's causing normal blood cells to mutate without any control. My staff told me they had created a new RNA structure and augmented the fastest reproductive genes to it. That's all they did. The structure is not complete yet and there are still plenty of gaps to fill. This isn't a cancer cure, but perhaps this will do something else." As James went to get a Band-Aid for the finger he pricked, Richard was still looking into the microscope. He was wearing a pair of gloves and he tried to reach for his coffee. He instead grabbed the jar containing the substance. James turned and he noticed his father drinking the wrong stuff. "DAD!" James yelled. It was too late. Richard had gulped some of it down and when he realized that it wasn't his coffee, he jerked back from the microscope and looked at what he was holding. He quickly put down the jar and felt his stomach starting to burn. What happened next was horrible, his body was beginning to deform. James was standing there, watching in horror as his father mutated into something horrible. "Oh my god!" James yelled panicking. Richard fell to the floor and stopped moving. James checked to see if there was a pulse. There was none. Richard was dead. James turned and saw somebody else was in the room. It was one of Richard's staff members. He was wearing a lab coat and his head was completely bald. James was standing over Richard's body and he was too petrified to say anything.

"What happened here?" the man asked. "What did you do to him?!" He ran off before James had a chance to say something. It was too late and it ended up looking like it was his fault. James was thinking what to do now. He looked at the jar containing the substance. He grabbed it, put the lid on to seal it and went over to the safe. He knew the code, so he opened it, placed the jar inside, left the room and ran back to his living quarters.

* * *

It was as if history was repeating itself. James had lost both his real and his adoptive parents. Since the laboratory was secret, the staff could not report this to the police. It was an order Richard had given in case an accident causing death occurred in the laboratory. The bald man who walked into the room and saw Richard lying at James' feet, was the Assistant Director. Mr. Jem remembered something that had happened a little later on. The Assistant Director named Wilkes was making a speech to everyone at the lab about the loss of Dr. Richard Jem. He was standing on a podium and talking into a microphone. Everyone was seated in the auditorium. James was sitting next to a brown haired woman that he had gotten to know during his time in the laboratory, her name was Sophie and she had also worked in the lab. They both liked each other a lot. James had explained to her what happened to Richard Jem and how Wilkes thought James had murdered him. She believed him. Wilkes motioned to James. "James Richwood Jem," he said. James stood up. "You were at the scene when Dr. Jem, your father died suspiciously. Is there anything you can say in your defense?"

"Of course," James said. "It was an accident. He mistakenly drank a substance he had developed, instead of his coffee. I had nothing to do with his death. End of discussion."

"It doesn't matter if you did or didn't," Wilkes said. "We have lost an important man and we will have to figure out what to do with this experiment we worked so hard on. I don't think there is any place for you here."

James frowned. "Am I being fired? Then I'm getting out of here!" He began to walk towards the door leading out of the room. Sophie went after him. Just before James was about to walk out, a strange man walked up to the podium, grabbed the microphone and shoved Wilkes out of the way. "Hey, what are you doing?!" Wilkes shouted. "Alright, nobody move!" the man shouted as he showed a badge. "FBI! You are all under arrest!" That was the cue for the S.W.A.T units to charge through the windows as they descended from their cables. Panic erupted. People were running in all directions. James and Sophie ran out the door together. "Let's head for my father's personal lab!" he said. "There's a secret emergency exit there!" They ran through the hallways until they came to the door.

It was locked. James then stood back and made a hard kick to the door. It burst open and they went inside. "It's behind that large cupboard!" James said. "There's a button behind it on the left side. You find it Sophie. There's something I need to get." As Sophie searched for the button, James went to the safe. He turned the knob in the correct sequence and opened it. He grabbed the jar containing the substance. Sophie found the button and pressed it. Some kind of device made the cupboard move to the side. A passageway was revealed and they went into it. The cupboard then closed behind them.

* * *

After the raid, the entire place was shut down. Most of the staff were charged for unlicensed genetic research. However, the authorities didn't find anything of major interest to them. The laboratory was independent. Since there was no record of people checking in, James and Sophie managed to get away unsuspected. James had received money in his father's Will. There was nothing in it that would make authorities suspect James was involved in illegal research and they never came after him.

He had become a grown man now and he wasn't alone. It was time for him to pop the big question to Sophie. They soon married. One day, they had a child of their own. It was a boy and they named him Aaron. They lived a happy marriage for a while. When Aaron was six years old, the family had gone to the graveyard where James' father had been buried. They found the gravestone and next to it was the grave of Richard's wife, Casynthia. Richard had asked in his will to be buried next to her.

"We are here to remember a man who saved my life after I was in a terrible accident," James said. "He raised me, because I was all alone after my real parents died and he had no children of his own. He wanted to raise me to become somebody. He and Casynthia brought me into their lives and turned me into a very strong man. After losing his beloved wife to cancer, he did everything he could to find a cure. Instead, he came up with a mutagen that took his life. Richard was a great man and he will always be my hero. Thanks to you, father, I have a wife and son. You have lost everything, but I promise you that your research will not have been in vain. I have kept the jar containing the mutagen. It's all that's left now. I will now show my wife and son what is left of your facility. Rest in peace."

* * *

James and his family entered the laboratory through the same passage that he and Sophie had used to escape before. Everything had been boxed up. The Jems were up on a walkway and a large vat of chemicals with its roof open was down below. "This place brings back memories," James said.

"Sure does," Sophie replied. "We should have suspected that there was a mole or two in this place."

Aaron had brought a dinosaur toy with him. He moved the toy around and growled to make the sound effects. "Could you be quiet, Aaron?" asked James. "This is a place daddy used to work at and he wants to share this moment with you." Aaron then stopped growling and he didn't say anything.

As Aaron was growing up, he was acting strangely. He didn't seem to behave like normal children. He would jump up and down and would talk senselessly to himself for example. He couldn't make any friends at school. James and Sophie felt their son had a mental disability. The Jem family walked across the walkway until they were directly over the vats.

"You must have been very disappointed at having all of the blame being put on you for what happened to Richard," Sophie said.

"Yes," said James. "But I have you and Aaron now. I can move on in life."

Suddenly, a voice had shouted out. "You three!" someone yelled. The Jem family turned to see who was there. Two men had approached them. One had long, messy, brown hair and the other was bald. "This is a restricted area," said the bald man. He looked closely at James' face. "Ah, James Jem," he said. James recognized the bald man.

"Wilkes?" James asked. "What are *you* doing here?"

"I should be asking you that question," Wilkes replied. "We saw you enter the facility. My friend here has a small problem and he found this to be a perfect opportunity."

"Yeah," the brown haired man said. "You're father lost everything including his life because of you."

"That's not true," said James. "It was an accident and I did nothing!"

"Richard was like a father to all of us," the brown haired man said. "In fact, he was the only family we ever had. The only family *I* ever had. We have been left with nothing now and it's all thanks to you!"

"Uh, Norton," Wilkes said, "he's got a wife and child, I don't think this is the right time to—" Too late. Norton suddenly pulled out a gun.

"No!" Sophie cried. She jumped in front of James with her hands out, pleading for Norton to stop. Suddenly, it all happened so fast. Norton squeezed the trigger and a loud bang followed. Aaron screamed like a little girl and covered his ears at the sound of the gunshot. "No!" cried James. He then turned and picked up Aaron and tried to run. The gun then fired again and hit James in his lower back. James then jerked and Aaron flew out of his arms. James fell and hit the ground.

"Daddyyyyyy!!!" Aaron screamed. His voice was cut short when the sound of a splash was heard. James lay motionless on the floor.

"You killed them all, you STUPID IDIOT!" Wilkes yelled. "This was not part of the plan. What the hell got into your mind?! Let's get out of here!" Both of them ran away as quickly as they came.

James slowly opened his eyes and struggled to get up. He reached back behind him to feel where the bullet hit him. He felt something behind him sticking out of his pants. He pulled out the object and looked at it. It was the holy bible and it had blocked the bullet. He had taken it with him to his father's grave. He then got up and looked around. Aaron was nowhere in sight. "Aaron?!" James called out. There was no answer. He looked over the railing to see if he fell down. He could see bubbles popping up in the chemical vat down below. James' eyes and mouth were wide open. All he saw was the toy dinosaur that Aaron had, slowly sinking in the vat of chemicals. Its head disappeared beneath it. "No..." James said in a horrified voice. "No, no, Jesus Christ, NO!" he yelled. He then looked at his wife lying on the ground. She had been shot right in the head. He bent down and felt her neck. There was no pulse. "Oh my god, Sophie… ! This… this can't be happening!" He then lifted his head up high. "NOOOO!!!"

* * *

The memory echoed away and Mr. Jem's eyes shot open. At the same time, he gasped and breathed heavily. He saw that he was in his office. He must have drifted into a dream and had a nightmare. He put his hand on his face and wiped the sweat off. He then turned to face his desk. He opened a drawer and pulled out something. It was the bible with the bullet still lodged in it. He had kept it after the unforeseen incident.

There was so much tragedy in his past. He lost his parents and adoptive father to accidents, his adoptive mother to cancer, and now he lost his wife and son to an armed gunman. He felt like he should have used his martial arts to take down the gunman when he had the chance. Or he shouldn't have had the bible in the back of his pants and should have died along with his family. He had had thoughts of suicide, but he had decided to live because his wife had given her life for his. He had moved elsewhere and using the remaining money he had, he decided to build an institute for researching marine life where he could try to live happily, the Marine Research Institute Labs. He also wanted that to be his home, just like Richard Jem's laboratory. Richard had decent houses to live in, but the laboratory was his life and his real home.

During the construction of the M.R.I.L, there were three people who had taken a great interest in the facility. Drake Evans, Jack Degrasso and Robert Pines were a trio hunting for jobs together. They had seen the facility being built and met Mr. Jem asking him if there were any positions for them. Mr. Jem seemed to like their eagerness. He told them he'd think about it. He had soon gotten to know that the three were very spirited. Mr. Jem was thankful for the arrival of his three new friends and they got along well. However, Mr. Jem's painful memories couldn't leave his head. He didn't want to tell his friends about all the darkness in his past because he wanted to try to put most of it behind him. The only thing he wanted to do, was to make his father proud of him. The mutagen that killed his father was his legacy and one day, he planned to fulfill that legacy. He intended to learn whatever it was capable of. That day was today.

Mr. Jem sighed. "So your work really is something, father..." Mr. Jem spoke quietly to his father's spirit. He then put the bible back in his drawer, got out of his chair and went to his bedroom.

CHAPTER 10

The First Dream of the Dolphin Man

"Dream manfully and nobly, and thy dreams shall be prophets."
—Statesman Edward Bulwer-Lytton

DOLPHI WAS FAST asleep in the alley where he had taken shelter after his escape from the M.R.I.L. He lay on the flattened cardboard boxes with the rain pouring down on him. As the night went on, he had begun to drift into a dream. "Mmm..." he hummed softly. He found himself on a white field that looked like he was on top of the clouds. The sky was black and hazy. He began walking and soon came across a cloudy bump. Just ahead, a ghostly human figure slowly materialized into view. Dolphi froze. An old woman wearing a silky robe appeared in front of him.

"Who... are you?" asked Dolphi.

"You don't recognize me?" the woman asked.

Dolphi's expression changed as he remembered something. "No way..." he said. "Are you... my grandmother?"

"Yes, my boy," she replied.

"... Is... this for real?" Dolphi asked as he sat down on the cloudy bump.

"Let's just say we're communicating to each other from different realms," she said as she sat down with him.

"Different realms?" Dolphi asked. "Am I dead?"

"No," she chuckled.

"But, two years ago..."

"Yes, I passed away." Dolphi's grandmother had passed away

two years ago. He and his parents were deeply saddened. Dolphi knew that she had died because of old age, but it was still difficult to accept that she was gone. She was a special person in his life and it took a while to get over such a loss. Dolphi couldn't let such an emotional blow bring him down. Now, it appeared, she was right there in front of him.

"Something terrible has happened to me," Dolphi said.

"I know what has happened," she said. "You got into some serious trouble and ended up being mutated."

"I know," said Dolphi. "But I don't understand. Why did this mutant dolphin thing have to happen to me? Is Mr. Jem planning on making more creatures like me? *Will* there be anyone else like me… in the future?"

"You are asking so many questions to the wrong person," Dolphi's grandmother said. "It's something you should find out yourself."

"Mr. Jem, my own boss, turned me into something that I am not," said Dolphi. "I will make him pay for this."

"You started by running away."

"I know, I know I ran away, but I was frightened by what was happening to me. I suppose I should find a way to get Mr. Jem arrested for making me into a monster."

"You don't look like a monster," she replied, "you look like a cute dolphin who can do anything."

Dolphi sighed. "I should not have been so curious about that lab. I should have instead ran out the door, gone to a payphone and called the police. I feel so stupid. What are my wife and kids going to say about me?"

"Calm down," Dolphi's grandmother assured him. "I'm sure you will be able to explain things to them. Now, I want to talk to you while we have this opportunity."

"Okay, so what do you want me to do?" Dolphi asked, "become the Miami Dolphin's next mascot?"

"No, no!" she laughed. "Do you still have an extreme passion for marine mammals?"

"Of course."

"Can you imagine encountering a dolphin as you are? Dolphins would be baffled with curiosity, wondering who and what you are.

They probably wouldn't know if they were encountering a man or dolphin."

Dolphi almost smirked at that. "Cute... I'll keep that in mind. Listen, I wanted to ask you something. I somehow had the ability to dive into a computer world. Do you know anything about that?"

She paused for a few seconds. "I wouldn't know for sure," she said. "However, it appears to me that there is something in your head that is allowing our communication to be possible."

Dolphi suddenly felt his head hurt a little. "Something's happening to me," he said. When Dolphi slowly blinked, he thought he saw something. He then shut his eyes and saw some kind of image appear. He saw a dark and silent world. He then saw a figure coming up a hill into view. Dolphi saw that the individual was some kind of half-human, half-cheetah! It was naked apart from a dirty shirt covering its chest, a pair of gloves on its hands and a pair of strange anklets on its feet. It wore a specially designed helmet and it had a wicked gun in its hand. Just then, a human figure ambushed the cheetah from behind and they both began to wrestle. Dolphi then saw colorful gunfire in the distance. He could see a whole bunch of figures charging and firing at each other. Some were animal figures like Dolphi, others were human. Some had been shot and others got beaten or clawed to death. The world then disappeared and Dolphi opened his eyes. "Whoa. I just saw a world where humans and these, animal-like monsters like myself are fighting each other."

"You're right," said Dolphi's grandmother. "But, as a note, you shouldn't judge yourself as a monster."

"That felt so real. What was that?"

"In heaven, you get all the answers," she said. "But those answers are not for mortal men to hear."

"What? I don't understand."

"However, I can tell you that what you experienced was a foretelling of the future."

"A foretelling... of the future...?" Dolphi asked, confused. "I'm capable of that?"

"You shouldn't be," she replied.

Dolphi felt nervous. "What is wrong with me... other than my mutated form?"

"I'm afraid I can't say. Sorry I can't be of any help."

"... Okaaaay... What about what I saw?"

"Perhaps your boss is responsible for creating some kind of war between man and mutated animals," she replied.

"A war?"

"It could happen. You will find out for yourself someday. Listen, our time here is about to come to an end. Good luck and remember I will always be with you and your family." Dolphi wanted to give her a hug, but when he reached an arm to her, his hand went through her like she wasn't there. She slowly faded away and the dream ended.

* * *

Dolphi woke up. He opened his eyes and saw it was morning. He then shut his eyes and groaned. He felt cold, wet, tired and very hungry. He stretched out and yawned.

"Oh god..." he moaned as he sat up. "I cannot believe I slept on the streets like a homeless bum... What's this thing?" he wondered as he looked at what was on him. He saw that something had been placed on him while he was asleep. At first, it looked like a blanket, but as Dolphi studied it, he realized it was intended to be worn. It was a cloak that looked like it was made out of a potato sack material. "Who was here last night?" Dolphi thought. He put the cloak on and lay on his side looking up at the sky. The rain last night made him feel refreshed. The sun was now shining brightly. To Dolphi, it hadn't felt too bad sleeping in an alley with rain covering him to moisten his skin. The alley wasn't that dirty but it felt different waking up here than at home. He lay on the soaked cardboard in thought. "What a crazy dream. A war involving mutant animals like me? Strange... I've got to find out what this means someday... "

CHAPTER 11

The Experiment Goes Further

"At his best, man is the noblest of all animals;
separated from law and justice he is the worst."
—Aristotle

MR. JEM WOKE up at 6:00 am that morning. The excitement of creating a mutant was probably the reason he was up that early. Unaware that his creation had escaped, he hurried on down to the lab to see if it was doing anything. (He knew that the security camera for the room had been smashed by Dolphi, and so he hadn't seen him escape.) When he was inside the hallway where the lab was, he could see an open door. With a look of concern, he ran over and looked inside. He saw the glass holding container was destroyed. Broken glass was strewn about and water was all over the floor. The creature he had created was nowhere in sight. "Dr. Jay?" Mr. Jem called. "Come out, come out, wherever you are!" He searched everywhere in the room and looked in the swimming pool. When he realized his mutant wasn't there, Mr. Jem cursed out loud and kicked a chair in anger. He left the room and went towards the lobby in a huff. Before he went through the doors, he heard voices on the other side.

"Listen, Robert," said a voice, "when Drake gets here, I will discuss what we should do about Mr. Jem." That was Jack talking. "Ah, here he comes." Mr. Jem opened one of the doors slightly and saw Drake walk in through the front doors. When the three met, they began to talk.

"Okay, we're all here," Jack said.

"Did you see Mr. Jem?" asked Drake.

"No, he's probably still sleeping."

"Alright, so what's the idea?" asked Robert.

"I was thinking last night," Jack said. "I feel like Mr. Jem has created a monster and he might create more of those things."

"Is that bad?" asked Robert.

"Maybe. I think we should report this to the police as soon as we can. We helped Mr. Jem with this illegal experiment and I don't want to get into any further trouble."

"But he, or I, helped make only one mutant," Drake said. "Why are you so concerned that we are going to get into trouble?"

Jack hesitated. "I just... don't want to get involved in anything like that again. Mr. Jem might ask us to help him make another mutant. If we make more of those unnatural creatures for him, they might create terrible problems. I think we should call the police and inform them of last night's events. Now, who's with me?" Everyone was thinking for a moment.

"You know, I think you're right about creating monsters for a mad scientist and not being aware of your conscience," Drake said.

"I opened that door for the helpless veterinarian to get curious and wander into the lab," Robert said. "Well, the injection was supposed to happen there, but I contributed to the experiment. I guess something needs to be done."

"Alright," Jack said. "Mr. Jem has been a good friend to us, but now, we must do the right thing."

Mr. Jem could not believe this! His own friends were going to betray him! He was thinking about what should be done to stop them.

"Wait, I wonder how we are going to prove to the police that there's been an illegal mutation?" Drake asked.

"I was about to get to that," said Jack. "We should get Dr. Jay out of that place. If we can convince him that we are sorry for what we have done and get him out of there, we can prove the mutant part and then," Jack sighed, "testify in court about this and hopefully, Mr. Jem gets the worse sentence and we will probably receive lesser charges for being accessories before the fact. I'll go get the key for that door to the lab." The key was hidden somewhere in the shark den nearby. When Jack came out with it, everyone headed to the doors where Mr. Jem was listening in. He hid where the doors would open and cover him from view. The three men went through the doors and went down the hall without seeing Mr. Jem. When they got to the lab, they saw the door was open. "It's open?" Drake asked. "Mr. Jem, are you in there? Uh, how's that dolphin guy doing?" When they walked into the room, they saw the broken container.

"God..." Robert said.

"... dammit." Jack finished.

"Is he in the pool?" Drake asked. They went over to look into the water. "He's not there. Now what?" Suddenly, Mr. Jem was outside in the hall. He quietly pushed the door closed. Everyone turned around. "Hello?!" Drake called. "Is someone out there?!" There was no reply. He went over to the door. "Great, we can't get out without that ten digit number code. Does anybody remember it?"

"Yeah, I think I remember part of it," Robert said.

With the three men locked in the room, it bought Mr. Jem some time to make a plan. He snuck out into the lobby and went to the shark den...

As the minutes passed, the trio in the lab were figuring out the numbers.

"Let's see, 316282... what was the rest?" asked Robert.

"You opened the door last night," Drake said, "how could you forget?" They began arguing. Just then, a phone in the room began ringing. Jack went to get it.

"Uh, hello?" Jack asked.

"Good morning, is that you Jack?" asked Mr. Jem's voice.

"Oh, Mr. Jem! The door to the lab has closed on us and we've forgotten the code. Can you get us out?"

"I see. I was looking for you guys. You showed up on time, but when I saw you weren't in the lobby, I had a hunch you were in the lab. Luckily I have it written down in my office. I'll just need to get it out. When you get out, I want you three to come up to my office and report to me about how the test subject is doing. Then, we have a drink to celebrate."

Mr. Jem told Jack the code and hung up the phone immediately.

"Mr. Jem?" Jack asked. When there was no reply, he hung up the phone and ran to the door and put in the numbers. The door opened. "Alright," Jack said. "Mr. Jem said we should go up and report to him about the mutant and then have something to drink as a celebration. We should probably go with the flow and snitch on him later."

They headed up to Mr. Jem's office and went inside. "Hello, my friends," Mr. Jem said as he sat at his desk. "Let's celebrate! Tell me, how is our mutant doing?"

"Uh, I don't know how to say it," Drake said, "but Dr. Jay has escaped."

Mr. Jem pretended as if he didn't know. "You better not be messing with me," he said unhappily.

"Of course not," Drake replied. "He must have gotten out somehow."

"Damn it!" Mr. Jem yelled as he pounded his fist on the desk. "How the hell did he know the numbers on that door lock?! He's probably trying to find his way home now!" He then took a deep breath and said, "we should have gotten better restraining equipment. It doesn't matter if he's gone," he said calmly, "at least the experiment worked. Come on, maybe if we drink this delicious orange juice, it will make me feel better. Let's go into the dining room. I know you normally serve the drinks for me Robert and we celebrate with champagne, but I want to reward you three with something delicious to help you wake up to the morning." As everyone went in and sat down at the dining room table, Mr. Jem came out with the drinks. He gave everyone a wine glass with orange juice in it. He then sat down at the head of the table.

"I thank you all for helping my experiment become a success. Combining the dolphin blood with the mutagen worked pretty well."

Playing along, the three said, "you are welcome, Mr. Jem!" They raised their drinks up in the air. They then drank their wine glasses down. "Mr. Jem," said Drake, "this drink tastes excellent! A little sour, but excellent!"

"Thank you," Mr. Jem replied, "I prepared it myself. Listen up everyone, last night, I saw on the security camera that Dr. Jay woke up and busted out of that container. I guess it just wasn't strong enough to hold him. He smashed the camera and so I couldn't see him escape." The three men were starting to feel a little ill.

"Anyway, did you rig his car like I asked you to?" Mr. Jem asked.

"Of course," Drake said.

"Wasn't he supposed to dehydrate if he left the water?" asked Jack.

"In case you didn't notice, it was raining last night," said Mr. Jem. "As a dolphin, he must keep his skin moist. Besides, he'd probably be okay for a few hours out of the water."

"Is it just me, or is it this juice?" asked Jack. "I'm feeling a little sick."

"Yeah," said Drake.

"Uh huh, this drink is making me feel funny," said Robert.

"Well," Mr. Jem said with a grin, "what I gave you was Sunny Delight, made with oranges grown right here in Florida. It contains vitamins C and B1 with a splash of shark D.N.A and the mutagen combined…"

"What?!" the men yelled. They dropped their glasses and the liquid spilled all over the table. They felt their tampered drinks give them immense pain. They grabbed their stomachs as their heads fell down on the table.

"What, you thought you'd rat me out and make me take the fall for it?!" Mr. Jem asked displeased. His three men were drooling and grunting with pain. "Now, it seems you guys are paying the ultimate price for breaking your loyalty to me!"

"Oh god… !" Jack moaned.

"What have… you done?!" Robert screamed.

"The pain, the PAIN!" Drake yelled in agony.

"I want you three to continue working for me…" Mr. Jem continued. Their forms suddenly began changing. Muscles were expanding, clothes were ripping and new body parts were growing. It looked so horrifying, even Mr. Jem himself felt nervous as it reminded him of his father's horrible fate. "… Only this time, you'll be serving me like loyal dogs, or in this case, sharks. Will you accept this offer?" The three men collapsed onto the floor. "It's growing… dark… !" Drake whimpered. They all then passed out.

"I'm glad you all agree," Mr. Jem said smugly. "I will make sure you don't remember me doing this to you when you all wake up. You will call me your 'master'… and I will dominate you!" He chuckled to himself at the sight of his new creations. He had turned Drake into a great white shark, Robert into a hammerhead shark and Jack into a thresher shark. "I suppose Jack was right," Mr. Jem said, "you guys really *are* 'vicious sharks'." He then made maniacal laughter.

* * *

Sid was the first to wake up in the Jay family's house. He headed straight for the kitchen and made himself some cereal. He went into an adjoining family room and turned the television on to watch Saturday morning cartoons. He had the volume up quite loud and Jennifer who was still asleep had woken to the noise. This had happened on a lot of Saturdays. Jennifer groaned and said, "honey, please tell Sid to turn the volume down." There was no response. She was unaware that her husband was not in bed with her. "Come on, wake up. It's your turn to tell him. I told him last time." When there was no reply again, she got a little angry. "Honey, I said wake…" She rolled over to the other side of the bed and suddenly realized Dr. Jay wasn't there. "… up?" she finished. She crawled out of bed and walked into the bathroom. "Steele?" she called. He wasn't there either. "Okay…" She went into the kitchen and saw Sid sitting on the couch. "Sid," she said.

"Oh, sorry mom," Sid replied as he went to turn the volume down.

"No, I'm not talking about that, have you seen your dad?"

"No, I just got up."

"Where is he?" she thought as she went outside to the garage. She looked in and around the garage and didn't see Dr. Jay or his car. "Great, something's got to give!" she said frustrated. She went back inside and went to Walter's room. "Walter, we've got a problem," she said. Walter crawled out of bed half asleep. "I want you to meet me in the foyer after I get Mike up."

As soon as everyone assembled, Jennifer said, "boys, I want you all to search different parts of the house and then we meet up in the front foyer." Mike searched the bathrooms, Walter searched outside in the backyard, Sid looked downstairs and Jennifer looked around the rest of the house. They were all calling for their father. They later met in the front foyer. Everyone said that they could not find their father. "Maybe if I check phone messages," Jennifer said. She went to the kitchen phone and played back the answering machine. There was nothing new. She then called his office number and waited. After many rings, there was no answer. She went back to the foyer. "I feel so scared," Jennifer said. "He said he had to close up work, but surely it didn't take him all night."

"I was thinking," Mike said, "... nah, dad couldn't have gone to a bar and got drunk and had to stay at a hotel. He doesn't do that kind of thing."

"Well, it's not like him to not come home after work, and not to call." Jennifer said. "Let's get dressed and head to the M.R.I.L. He might have had an accident or something." Everyone got ready and headed out to the garage where Jennifer's minivan was parked. They drove off to search for their missing dad.

CHAPTER 12

Homeward Bound

"Not until we are lost do we begin to understand ourselves."
—American Author Henry David Thoreau

DOLPHI WAS WATCHING the people walking by, out on the city streets, from his position in the alley. He couldn't let anyone see him. Bringing unwanted attention could attract the police and result in something unpleasant happening to him. Unfortunately, the only way he could get out of the alley was by going out onto the sidewalk.

"Damn," Dolphi thought as he heard his stomach growl, "I am starving. I've got to find a place where there will be food."

The hooded cloak he was wearing covered his whole body, but even so, his appearance would be suspicious. He took two long soaked pieces of cardboard. He carried one under each arm to block off his sides making himself look like he was a homeless bum. He was still clutching the keychain picture of his family. "I hope this is good enough cover," he thought. He felt his breathing was being restricted. "Oh, right." He ripped a hole in the backside of the hood so that his blowhole was clear. Dolphi left the alleyway and began to walk up the street.

He was looking for a place he could eat. He turned a corner and there was a woman and a boy coming in his direction. They looked at him oddly as they passed him by. Dolphi suddenly sneezed and a spray quickly shot out from his blowhole. "Cool!" the boy said. Dolphi turned and noticed the boy looking at him. The mother then put her hand on the boy's shoulder and moved along, knowing that Dolphi, the mysterious stranger, was none of their business. Dolphi walked up the street and turned another corner. People were giving Dolphi's unusual appearance a very strange look, but then moved along without saying anything.

He soon came upon a seafood restaurant. He had no money on him and he couldn't just walk inside. So, he quickly went into the alleyway beside the building. When he got to the end, he peeked around the corner and saw a man facing the other way putting a loaded garbage bag into a dumpster. The man then disappeared into an open back door. Dolphi dropped the soaked cardboard as it was completely useless now. He walked up to the door and looked inside.

He could see boxes and fish lying on packs of ice. There wasn't anyone in sight. "Well lucky me!" Dolphi thought seeing his advantage. "I better make this fast." He went for some Red Snapper. "These should suit my appetite nicely." He took one and put it near his mouth. "Wait," he thought, "what am I doing? I'm going to eat raw fish and swallow it whole? … Oh, what the heck!" He put the fish in his mouth and gulped it down. "Ack!" he choked. "I guess I'm not used to such an eating method." He picked up more fish and began stuffing them into his mouth and gulping it down. "Mmm…" he hummed as he felt his tummy filling up. "Now that was good. I suppose it takes a few tries to learn how to gulp down your food if you're a mutant dolphin or something. Now I'm getting used to it. This fish also tastes pretty good. It's like eating sushi or something." He noticed a sink in the room. He walked up to the tap and took a sip of the water and found it was fresh water. He then put his head right under the tap and gulped down the water. After gulping down about a gallon, he took his head out from under the tap.

"Much better," he thought feeling replenished. He suddenly heard footsteps coming from within the building. "I better get going," Dolphi thought as he dashed out the door taking one last handful of fish.

Someone walked into the back room and looked at the open door. "Who's banging about in here?!" asked a man as he entered. "What the… ?" He noticed some fish missing. He ran over to the door and looked out. There was nobody there. "What happened to some of the fish?" he asked himself, "and who left the water running?" Someone else walked into the room. "What's up?" the second man asked.

"Damn thieves," said the first man. "Somebody snuck in and stole some fresh Snappers."

"Well, don't just stand there, find who ever broke in."

Dolphi went down the other side of the restaurant and just before he was about to go out onto the sidewalk, he peeked around the corner and saw there was a police cruiser stationed just meters away and there was an officer inside. Dolphi walked backwards into the back lot and could see that there was a fence that he could jump over. It led into residential backyards. Suddenly, he felt something grab at his hood and a voice called out, "hey, you!" from behind. Dolphi's hood was pulled down and that made him turn around instantly. He saw the two men from the restaurant facing him. The first man had brown hair and wore an apron. The other was a younger man who wore restaurant staff clothing. "What is *this*?!" the younger man asked, looking at Dolphi's dolphin head.

"I was hungry," Dolphi replied calmly. He then ran for the fence. "Stop!" the older man yelled. As Dolphi was grabbed, he turned and threw the handful of fish he had into the older man's face. Dolphi then pushed him off, making him fell down hard. The younger man ran up to his friend to help him up. Dolphi then leaped over the fence and began running through the yard to the other side.

"Call the police!" the older man yelled to the young man.

Dolphi continued jumping over other fences keeping close to the houses so that if anybody was looking out of their homes, he could hide below the windows. He was thinking of getting out to the ocean and swimming home, but he didn't live near the ocean and the vegetation at the end of the yards was too thick to pass through. After running through fifteen yards, he felt very hot and tired. When he came across the fence into the next yard, he saw it had a swimming pool. "Water…" Dolphi thought. "I've got to cool down…" He took off his cloak and jumped into the pool and went under water. He felt the water cool him down. He then swam up fast and made a tremendous leap out of the water. "Whoa!" he said as he came splashing down.

Meanwhile, a young girl inside the house happened to look outside.

"Mommy," said the girl, "there's a dolphin in our swimming pool."

"Oh, really?" asked the mother, not believing, as she looked outside. Dolphi leaped and did a somersault in the air. The mother's eyes widened. "That dolphin... looks like a human!" she said. The father of the family then walked into the room. "What are you two looking at?" he asked as he looked outside. "What on earth... ?" the father asked as he saw the gray figure climbing out of the pool. "We've got a dolphin... with arms and legs playing in our swimming pool?"

Dolphi looked at the house. He could see that the little girl and her parents were looking at him.

"Uh-oh!" Dolphi thought as he ran over to his cloak. He put it on and ran towards the next fence. "I blew it!" he thought as he jumped over. "They are probably going to call the cops on me!"

"Looks like I better call the police," said the man inside the house. As he was about to call the police, he stopped. "Wait, was that thing breaching out of the water?"

"He sure was," the man's daughter said.

"Interesting..." the father thought. He faced the phone again and instead of dialing 911, he dialed a different number.

Dolphi jumped over more fences. He felt tired of running and thought that people inside their homes might be noticing him, but he couldn't give up. He ran past a barking dog that was tied up outside. "I bet the whole nation will be out to get me sooner or later," he thought as he panted hard. He was glad that the dog was tied up.

As Dolphi jumped over the next fence, he saw an old woman sitting in a wheelchair outside on a porch. He went up to the side of the porch and observed her. She was sitting there motionless, staring out into the yard. Suddenly, her wheelchair moved forward unexpectedly. Dolphi saw that she was about to go forward and fall down the porch steps! Seeing this, Dolphi immediately dashed up to the porch. The wheelchair went down the first step and the woman was ejected from her seat. The woman gasped and Dolphi ran up in front of her and caught her before she hit the ground. "I've got you!" he said.

The old woman felt relieved. "Hello?" she asked as if not being able to see her rescuer.

"You were nearly injured," Dolphi said. He then carried her back up the porch and placed her back in the wheelchair. "Now, there is no need for alarm. I'm just trying to find my way home."

"Thank you so much," the old lady said. Dolphi felt a little relieved when he realized that she was blind so she was unaware of his appearance, but even so, he felt sorry for her condition.

"Don't worry," Dolphi assured her, "I am not a house breaker or an escaped convict or something."

"I believe you. If you were a criminal, you'd probably do nothing for a damsel in distress."

"You said it," Dolphi grinned. "So, you don't know how to get to the ocean, do you?"

"If you listen, you can hear the waves crashing just beyond the trees. I have a son who told me that he can get to the beach by crossing at the roundabout in the road and going through an opening in the foliage just around the corner. You go through it and there is a shady spot where the sand starts. It's lovely and it's only a minute away. My son likes that spot when he wants shade after a swim on the beach."

"Thanks, I'll keep that in mind," said Dolphi.

"One more thing," the old lady said. "You sound like a dolphin." Dolphi smiled and made sleepy eyes. He then started to giggle thinking about it. His giggle sounded very dolphin-like. He covered his snout with his hand so as not to give himself away. "That sounds cute," the old woman giggled.

"Uhh... I meant to laugh like that if you think I'm a dolphin," Dolphi said.

"Fine," the old lady said, still giggling. "Perhaps you should move along now. Once again, thanks for saving me from a terrifying fall."

"My pleasure," Dolphi replied. "Farewell!" He went to the other side of the yard. "That was way too close," Dolphi thought. "But still, I helped someone who could not look after herself."

Dolphi came to a high wall that he couldn't get over. He ran alongside the old lady's house and looked around for any people passing by. He felt very nervous about being caught. He had already attracted the attention of the two seafood restaurant workers and a family who owned a pool. He was aware that going home on his usual route that he took to work was like trying to look down an alligator's mouth with a lit match. He would have to go through the city of Miami. Right now, he was in a neighborhood outside of the city. "This is so risky," Dolphi thought feeling nervous. He stepped out on the driveway of the house next to him. "Ow!" he yelped, "Ow! Ow! Ow! This driveway is hot!" He hid beside the house again. The sun felt really hot today. Dolphi took one last look around and ran as fast as he could to get across the street. The road also felt hot. He hopped on one foot and then the other as he ran across the roundabout.

"Ow! Ow! Ow!" he yelled. After he made it to the other side, he found the opening in the foliage and went in. After passing through, he found he was stepping on sand. He could see large palm trees and the ocean. He was feeling very hot. He then knew that the cloak was wearing him down. He took it off and looked around. He could see a stream of water running out to the ocean. He suddenly noticed a few people walking along the beach from the right. Dolphi immediately ran back into the bushes. The people didn't walk in his direction, but he had to be careful. When he turned his head, he saw a pond that was formed by the stream. It didn't look very scummy, so he decided to hop in. The water felt cool and comforting. "That road was so hot," he thought. "I better rest here for now. I can't risk getting spotted again."

He lay in the pond and looked at his reflection. "What a great day I am having so far, breaking into a restaurant, stealing fish and making so much of a commotion... what an ordeal!" He looked at the small picture of his family that he still held on to. He still felt uneasy about his mutation. Dolphi closed his eyes and soon started to cry tears of sorrow. "What is my family going to think of me?" he thought. "I hope I can find them and tell them I am their father." He lay under the water with his blowhole above the surface. He then took a quiet nap hoping that everything would turn out okay.

CHAPTER 13

Finding Dolphi

"There is nothing to fear but fear itself."
—President Franklin Delano Roosevelt

WHEN THE JAY family drove into the parking lot at the M.R.I.L,
they saw the burnt car.

"Look!" Mike pointed to the wreck. "I wonder what happened
there?" Jennifer parked the car and everyone got out. They walked
around the wreck, studying it and came to a shocking conclusion.
"It's dad's car!" Mike exclaimed.

"Oh my god..." Jennifer panicked. "Did somebody blow him
up?!" Mike examined the driver's seat. "I don't see any charred
remains or anything," he said.

"Somebody made sure he couldn't get home?" Sid asked.

"I think so. I have a bad feeling about this... Let's go inside the
building." Mike walked up to the building's entrance and tried to
open one of the doors, but found it was locked. "Predictable," said
Mike.

"He must be in there," Jennifer said still worrying. "How can we
get in?"

"Maybe there's a back door," said Walter.

"Let's go look for one," said Mike. Walter and Sid went over to
the right side of the building. Mike saw the uneasiness in his mother
and patted her on the back. "I'm sure dad's here," he told her. "Let's
not give up hope too soon."

Jennifer sighed. "You're right, sweety."

"Hey, Mike!" Sid called. "Come check this out!"

Mike ran over and saw Sid pointing to the ground. Mike saw footprints, but not normal, human footprints. "It looks like somebody had walked out here wearing flippers," Mike said.

"Well," Walter said, "I haven't ever seen any flippers with such short webbing. And if anybody *was* wearing flippers, that person had walked out of this emergency exit," Walter studied the direction of the footprints, "and headed straight for the parking lot and not the ocean... "

"That's curious," Mike said. He saw the door did not have a handle or knob to open it. "Come on," he said, "let's head back towards the front."

They went back to the front and saw their mother was holding onto something.

"I just found dad's keys shining on the ground," she said. "The family picture on here is gone... "

"Did he take it with him?" Mike asked. "He must have. It also doesn't look like there are any keys on here to open the facility."

"We didn't check to see if anybody's inside," Jennifer then remembered. She walked up to the entrance and knocked on the door. "Anybody inside?!" she called. Nobody came. "There's usually security guards watching the place," she said.

"I'll go check around the other side of the building." Mike said. He went over and traveled up the other side. He noticed there was a blue tarp on the side of the wall held in place by ropes. As he pulled on it, he could see a hole in the wall. There was another tarp in the way. Mike pushed that aside and went through. He found himself inside the dolphin medical pen. He didn't see anybody around. "Dad?" Mike called out, "It's me, Mike! Are you here?" There was no answer, so he went out the door and found himself in the lobby. He could see his family outside pondering and trying to open the doors. Mike then ran up to the entrance and pushed the bar on one of the doors and it opened. Everyone went inside. "How did you get in, Mike?" asked Jennifer.

"Some hole in the wall," replied Mike. "Now, let's find dad."

"Let's split up and search different areas," Jennifer suggested. "Except for you, Sid. You stay with Mike so you don't get lost."

Everyone began to call out for their father and for anyone else who was in the building. Jennifer decided to go to up her husband's office to see if he was there. The keys that she had found in the parking lot had the key to open the office door.

Walter went into the shark den. He looked around the room and saw lots of fish tanks containing different specimens. In the middle of the room, there was a swimming pool sized tank filled with murky water. He noticed stairs next to the tank going down. He went down and saw the side of the tank could be seen through, except visibility was restricted because of the murky water.

The whole family had visited the facility many times in the past, so everyone knew their way around.

"I don't think dad's down here," Walter thought. He went back up the stairs. One of Walter's shoelaces had come undone and before he made it to the top, he tripped on his shoelace and fell on a nearby push utility cart. The cart moved a little as Walter used it to prevent his fall. A wheel on the cart had rolled over a tile on the floor in the corner of the room and pushed it up on an angle. As Walter bent down to fix his shoelace, he noticed the tile sticking up. He removed it and he could see a key and a piece of paper. He saw writing on the paper. It read: OUR LITTLE SECRET, 3162825500. "Our little secret?" thought Walter. He suddenly heard a noise behind him that made him nervous. He turned and saw the water in the tank swirl. "Probably one of the lab creatures," he thought.

Mike and Sid decided to go through the 'authorized personnel only' doors. They continued calling for their father but still had no luck. They soon came upon the door leading to the lab where their father had been mutated. They looked to the left and saw a large crack in the wall across from the door. "This doesn't look right, does it?" Sid asked Mike.

"It sure doesn't," Mike replied. The crack they saw had been made by Dolphi who slammed into the wall in panic and confusion after he escaped.

Sid looked at the door opposite the crack. "Keep out by order of the facility's president," he read. He walked over to the door and saw the doorknob with the plastic cover and the high voltage sign. "I think this door may be hiding something," Sid said. "That sign over the knob is probably fake." Sid opened the plastic cover.

Mike felt nervous. "I wouldn't do that if I were…" Sid touched the handle and he received a shock. He yelped and fell backwards.

"… you!" Mike finished as he quickly bent down to help Sid up. "Are you okay?" Mike asked.

"Ouch," Sid rubbed his hand. "I guess I was fooled." The two then heard doors open down the hall. They turned and saw Walter.

"Guys?" Walter shouted. "Any sign of dad?" He jogged over to his brothers.

"I take it that you haven't either?" Mike asked.

"Not even one security guard. I have a hunch that something's really off."

"Yeah," Sid agreed, "like this suspicious crack in the wall opposite this electrified door."

"Perhaps this key I found fits into this door," said Walter. He inserted the key into the slot and turned it. There was a click and Walter slowly reached for the handle heeding the warning of the high voltage. Sid cringed, fearing that Walter would also get a shock. However, he didn't. He opened the door and said, "strange, I've never seen a door with this kind of security here." He looked inside and could see that there were no lights on. When he found the light switch and turned it on, he saw what looked like blood on the ground. Everyone gasped.

"Sid, don't look," Mike said as he covered Sid's eyes. "Walter, go get mom and bring her here right away."

"Yes," Walter said as he ran back towards the lobby. "I think I'll go return this key," he thought.

"Listen," Mike told Sid, "just stare at that big crack in the wall. I'm going to look inside and see what has happened."

Mike walked into the room and examined the blood on the floor. It looked like two people had been killed and dragged into the pool. The water in the pool was red and he noticed two dreaded objects floating on the surface. Mike gulped hard and looked at the bodies. He went for something long to reach the bodies and dragged them in. When he examined them, he saw they were security guards who were missing a lot of flesh. Mike turned his head and saw Sid standing in the room looking at the bodies with a blank look on his face. "Hey, what did I tell you to do?!" Mike angrily asked him.

"I'm sorry," Sid explained, "but I just couldn't wait out there thinking of the possibility that, dad is in here and he's dead. Besides, I've seen both Terminator movies and I can tolerate this a little."

"I don't care. You should not disobey me, especially when we are in a serious situation here."

"I know. Neither of those two are dad, are they?"

"No, they're the security guards. No wonder we couldn't find them. But, this is gross! Most of their flesh has been ripped apart! It looks like they've been attacked by..." Mike studied some flesh and saw large teeth marks and jaw patterns in the shape of... "... Sharks?" Sid asked.

"Impossible," Mike said. "Judging from the blood on the floor near the pool, these guys were killed there. Sharks don't just jump out of a pool, attack them and drag them in. A person must have murdered them with a gun or something and fed them to the sharks. Say... *are* there any sharks in that pool?" As he walked around the pool and looked in the bloody water, he couldn't see anything in it. "There's not a single living thing in that pool," Mike said. "Now, I am getting really scared... "

"Perhaps they were killed elsewhere and their corpses were dragged here," Sid suggested.

"It would be extremely risky to take a shark's meal and put it in a different location," Mike replied.

"I wonder what this place is anyway?" Sid asked. Just then, Walter, and Jennifer walked into the room. When their mother saw the blood, she was shocked.

"It's not dad," Mike said. "These two were the security guards that had been watching the place."

"Oh my god!" Jennifer shouted. "Murder! My poor husband, where are you?!"

Mike suddenly spotted something against a wall. "Look!" he said. He saw what looked like ripped clothing. "These are the clothes dad wore when he left for work yesterday! Now I *really* have a bad feeling about this..." Jennifer went up to the ripped clothing, picked it up and held it close to her. She felt like she was about to cry. "Where is he?" she asked desperately.

Walter noticed a number pad next to the door. "I wonder what this is for?" he thought. He saw there were computers and medical equipment in the room. He went up to the computers and powered them on. "Maybe somebody was working on these computers and there might be something that can tell us where dad is," Walter said. When he had a computer loaded up, Walter immediately began clicking around, searching for something that had anything to do with his father.

Meanwhile, Mr. Jem had been watching everybody go into the secret lab on the security camera in his office. He headed down and entered the shark den and whistled. "Come, my babies!" he called into the tank.

Walter soon found something of interest on the computer. "I think I've got something!" he said. Everyone looked at the screen.

"It looks like somebody is creating something weird," Walter said as he read the document. "Something about a chemical substance that creates a hybrid form of two species when mixed with the blood of a... desired animal and injected into a... human test subject?" Walter felt extremely puzzled. He continued scrolling down. "Let's see, a successful 'mutant animal' with a human form and... cetacean features was created last night and the test subject's name is..." Suddenly, everyone was in shock when Walter read his father's full name out loud. "... Dr. Steele Monroe Jay! What on earth is THIS for crying out loud?!"

Suddenly, a voice spoke from the door, "let's just say that he's found his place in history!"

Everyone turned to see Mr. Jem standing in the door.

"You!" Mike shouted. "You're Mr. Jem, the president of this place! You better tell us what has happened to our father, or we will—"

"What," Mr. Jem asked sarcastically, "you'd kick my butt? I knew you'd put up a fight. But right now, I don't feel like fighting. Instead, let me introduce you to my pets who will do that for me. Come!" he called.

Three figures walked into the room. Everyone's eyes and mouths opened wide when they saw three big mutant sharks standing side by side.

"What... what are you... you... things?!" Jennifer asked nervously.

"This is Chewer, Slice and I appropriately named the biggest one, Jaws," Mr. Jem said pointing to each one. Chewer was a hammerhead shark with brown colored skin, Slice was a thresher shark with yellow skin and Jaws was the worst of them; a great white shark with navy blue skin. Their abdomens were a whitish color. Their naked bodies stood from six and a half to seven feet tall, they had large, buff muscles, big mouths with lots of razor sharp teeth and they all had long, sleek, shark tails coming out behind them.

"Oh my god!" Sid gasped. "It's a trio of Street Sharks!"

"This is the next level of mutation," Mr. Jem said.

"Where's our father?" Mike asked.

"Yeah, where's my daddy?" Sid asked.

"First, I'd like to ask you how did you get in here?" Mr. Jem asked.

"You forgot to lock the door," Walter lied.

"Oh come now, you expect me to believe that? I saw you on the surveillance camera open the door with a key."

"Okay, you got me. Now, where's our father, Dr. Jay?"

"Oh, you must be his family," Mr. Jem said. "I don't know where he is, but we were trying some experiments and he decided he wanted to be a dolphin, so we made him into one.

"That's a lie!" Mike said angrily. "What happened to our dad last night? He never came home!"

"He's just like my buddies here," said Mr. Jem, "only he's a dolphin."

"Why you… !" growled Jennifer. "How dare you experiment on my husband!"

One of the mutant sharks suddenly spoke. "Hello, pretty lady," Jaws said in a deep voice. "You and your babies would look very tasty if we put you on a barbecue and charbroiled you, with a pinch of salt… "

"What do you mean?" Sid asked. "You three are standing right next to a human, aren't you? Why aren't you attacking him?"

"Because he's been very good to us," Chewer said. "We thought about attacking him when we first saw him, but he showed us he was on our side when he gave us something good to eat."

"You mean those… !" Jennifer gasped as she pointed to the dead security guards behind her.

The sharks showed Jennifer and the boys their bloody teeth and growled as a response. The horror was too much for Jennifer to bear. She suddenly fainted. She fell backwards and the boys caught her before she landed. "Mom!" Mike shouted, "please wake up!" He shook her, but she did not respond.

"So you really turned our dad into a mutant dolphin?" Walter asked Mr. Jem. "Do you know what he looks like?"

"He looks like these mutant sharks here," said Mr. Jem, "only, without the tail. That's right, kiddies! These aren't costumes, it's their real forms!"

It was now Slice's turn to speak. "Yeah, and those two humans tasted good to our smooth, tummy rubbin' lovin' bellies," he chuckled as he rubbed his stomach.

"I think your skin would feel like uncomfortable, scratchy leather," said Sid.

"Why you little…" Slice growled. "Hey boss, do you want us to eat their mommy in front of their eyes?"

"No," Mr. Jem quickly said, "spare her. I have… other plans for her. Anyway, I don't have time for you children. I am telling the truth about your father's whereabouts. I don't know where he has run off to. He's probably trying to run all the way home. He could have gotten into big trouble with the police and they had to open fire or something."

"*You're* going to be in big trouble with the police!" said Mike. "You must have blown up dad's car to prevent him from getting home in the first place."

"Bingo."

"What the hell have you got up your sleeves anyway? How did you create these things?"

"To be honest with you, none of this mutation stuff was planned. As crazy as it may seem, something good might come out of this."

"Yeah," said Chewer. "Our boss here recently introduced us to the shark den. We swim with the ordinary sharks and they seem quite astounded at our sharky appearances. You know, I'm thinking we should go shopping for some hot pants and…" Jaws gave Chewer a light punch in the side. "I'm just kidding guys!"

"Those things know human language…" said Walter. "They must have been human before, weren't they?"

"Shut up," said Mr. Jem, "that's irrelevant. I'm out of here. I'm going to work some more on your natural habitat, guys." Mr. Jem was about to leave when he noticed some severed wires above the room. "What happened up there I wonder? You kids haven't been fooling around with the wiring have you?"

"You think we can jump that high?" Sid asked sarcastically.

"Enough!" Mr. Jem said, "dinner is served, my loyal shark men.

Get them." He walked out of the room and closed the door behind him.

"Mmm... lunch!" said Jaws.

"Come on guys!" said Mike. "We've got to get out of here!" They got in fighting positions. "Come on, mom!" yelled Mike. "Wake up!" She still didn't move. Slice and Chewer ran up to a computer chair and picked it up. "Watch what our mouths can do," Chewer said. They put their mouths over the back support and seat and with great jaw power, they bit two chunks out of it and spat out the pieces to intimidate the children. "I can't believe those things are real!" said Sid. The sharks formed a circle around the kids and made snapping sounds with their mouths. "You're next on our menu!" Jaws growled.

"Take this!" Sid yelled as he ran towards Slice.

"Don't!" Mike yelled. As Sid approached Slice, he slid right under his legs just as Slice bent forward to try and bite him. Sid came up behind him and let out a "HIYAA!" yell as he jumped and kicked him in the backside of his tail. "Ow!" Slice yelled. Slice then swooshed his tail along the ground and tripped Sid. As Sid fell down, Slice picked him up by the legs. "AHH!" Sid yelled. "Get this guy off me!"

"Sid!" yelled Mike.

"Don't try to do anything funny or else I bite the kids head off!" said Slice. "Now stay still and let my friends eat you. If you do, they will finish you quick and painless by biting off your head."

"Over our dead bodies, you shark freaks!" yelled Mike.

"Freaks?" Jaws said angrily. "FREAKS?!" They ran at Mike and Walter yelling a battle cry.

Mike and Walter both dodged to the side and stuck one of their legs out just as the two sharks approached. They managed to trip them and both mutants flew into each other. As they made contact, their open mouths interlocked with each other and they got stuck. They struggled trying to free themselves.

"Don't eat me!" Sid pleaded, still hanging from Slice.

"I bet you taste like chicken, kid," Slice grinned, fixated on Sid's face. He then licked Sid's cheek with his big fat tongue. A large amount of saliva covered half of Sid's face.

Mike and Walter ran up to Slice and quickly tickled his armpits.

Slice burst out laughing and he dropped Sid. Walter caught him and then Mike and Walter kicked Slice in the stomach at the same time. Slice fell to the floor, landing right on the fin on his back.

"OOOWWW!!!" Slice screamed. "Help me, you idiots!"

"Are you all right?" Walter asked, helping Sid up.

"Yeah, but he got drool all over me!" replied Sid. "We have to get out of here! Mom, please wake up!"

"Forget her!" Mike said as they ran to the door. "I know, I don't want to leave her here, but we should save ourselves. We can't just drag her out without those guys catching up to us." As they tried to open the door, they realized it was locked.

Jaws and Chewer finally got their mouths out of the interlocked state. "Yuck!" said Chewer.

"How do we open this?" Mike asked. Walter saw the number pad on the door and realized something. "The number I have!" Walter said.

"Come on!" Jaws growled, "let's get them!" Slice got up and they all ran at the boys. Mike looked beside him and saw a ladder to his right that was standing up against the wall. As the sharks approached, Mike grabbed the ladder and lifted it onto its side, making it a horizontal barrier. The sharks clashed with the ladder and the boys were pressed against the wall. While Mike tried to push them back, Walter had taken out the little piece of paper he found with a number on it. He input the number as quickly as he could. The sharks now had their mouths on the ladder and they began to break it.

"Hurry, Walter!" Mike yelled. Walter input the last digits and he turned the door knob. The door opened and the boys rushed out as the ladder was ripped to pieces. Mike slammed the door shut. "Let's head to the emergency exit down this way!" Mike said.

"After them!" Chewer said.

"Yes, but the boss said we should use the numbers that he taught us instead of bashing this door down," Jaws said.

The boys came to the emergency exit and pushed on it. It didn't open! "I don't get this!" Sid said.

"Never mind, let's get over to the entrance!" cried Mike.

As Chewer finished keying in the numbers, he opened the door and the three sharks ran out. They looked both ways and saw the children running in their direction. The children slowed when they saw the sharks in their path. The sharks suddenly came running at them. They jumped at the boys in a flying motion; mouths open as if they were trying to tackle them in mid air.

"Down!" Mike yelled. The boys quickly ducked as the sharks flew over them and came crashing down on the floor. The boys continued running to the lobby.

"I sure hope we can get out of here alive!" said Sid.

"Hurry," Mike said, "we're almost there!"

The sharks got up and turned around. As slice turned, part of his tail slapped in Chewer's face. "Watch it!" Chewer said.

"Sorry, Chewey!" Slice replied.

"Chewey?"

"They're getting away!" Jaws yelled as he ran up the hallway.

The boys had made it into the lobby and headed for the doors that led outside.

"What about mom?" Sid asked.

"We can't turn back!" Mike replied. "Into the car!"

Back inside, Mr. Jem came out of the shark den as he heard the loud footsteps of the sharks entering the lobby. Slice had approached the entrance doors first. "Guys!" Mr. Jem yelled. "Do not go outside!" Jaws and Chewer heard him and stopped, but Slice had already gone out.

The boys had piled into the minivan and Mike was in the driver's seat. "It's a good thing mom left the keys in the ignition," Mike said as he turned on the car.

Suddenly, the boys felt the car bang hard. Mike turned and saw Slice biting into the door. Mike quickly put the pedal to the metal and started steering left and right to shake the shark off. Slice let go and the car raced out of the parking lot. Mr. Jem ran up to Slice.

"Are you trying to get me into trouble?!" he yelled. "Get back inside!" He banged his fist on Slice's head and Slice made a quiet whimpering noise as he ran back into the building. The boys drove quickly down the road away from the building.

"Mike," Walter said, "you're driving too fast!"

"Well as long as we are away from a great white shark, a hammerhead shark, and a... what was that third thing that was biting at us just now?" asked Mike.

"I think I recognized that third guy's form as a... thresher shark," said Walter.

"Okay," said Mike. "As long we are away from those freaks, we can finally take a deep breath. We better find a police officer that can help us."

"I'm scared!" said Sid.

"I know…" said Walter.

As Mike drove along, he began searching for someone who could help. Mike didn't have much driving experience as he wasn't particularly interested in cars. However, he was in control of the vehicle and was driving along well. Soon, Mike spotted a police cruiser stopped at the side of the road.

Mike pulled over to the side of the road near the cruiser and got out. He started to wave his arms. The officer got out of his vehicle. The officer was a big man with grey hair and a white mustache. "Officer!" Mike called. "I need your help!"

"What can I do?" asked the cop. "Is there a problem?" Mike noticed he had a strong southern accent.

"Do you know about the Marine Research Institute Lab?" asked Mike.

"Maybe I do. Why? Where are yer parents, young man?"

"It's a long story. We escaped from these mean-looking shark guys and our mom was left behind in some laboratory at M.R.I.L."

"Shark guys? Laboratory? Have you been watching too much Dr. Frankenstein or somethin'?"

"The M.R.I.L's president turned our father into some kind of… dolphin mutant who is wandering around somewhere."

The officer's expression changed. "What? Hold on a sec. If you's talkin' about sharks, then what is this dolphin thing all about?"

"I don't know," said Mike. "Except my dad's a mutant dolphin thing right now."

"A mutant dolphin?" asked the cop. "As in a guy with the head of a dolphin, those fishy creatures?"

"Mammals."

"Sorry."

"Do you know something?"

"Well, we got a report from a couple of restaurant staff that there's this guy who has the facial features of a dolphin. They claimed he broke into the back of the 'Fish n' Chips Away!' restaurant, stole some of their food and retreated into people's backyards."

Mike's eyes widened. "That could be him. But please don't hurt him if you guys find him. He wouldn't hurt anybody unless you did something to him and had to act in self defense."

"Right, what's yer name by the way?" the cop asked.

"Oh, I forgot. My name is Mike Jay. In that car are my brothers, Walter and Sid. We can tell you what has happened to us. Mike walked over to the car and told his brothers to come out.

As the officer approached the vehicle, something caught his eye. "Whoa!" he said in shocked amazement. He noticed the teeth marks in the car door. "It looks like you boys have been in a shootout or somethin'."

"Not a shootout," said Mike, "but something worse." Mike then explained his story.

* * *

Mr. Jem and his shark mutants were in the shark den. He was very furious at how they had failed to kill the children. "I can't believe you let those brats get away!" Mr. Jem yelled.

"We're sorry," Jaws said. "We underestimated them."

"As for you, Slice, you left a mark on that car that those kids can explain to the police!"

"We won't let anything like that happen again," Slice said.

"You better not," Mr. Jem said. "Now, I want you three to stay in this room and don't come out until I say otherwise. Understood?"

"Yes, boss," the three sharks said in a glum mood.

CHAPTER 14

A Friend is Made

"A hero is a man who does what he can."
—French Novelist Romain Rolland

DOLPHI SLOWLY OPENED his eyes as he woke up from his nap. He felt sick and dizzy. He yawned, stretching his mouth wide open. "I feel so groggy..." he thought. He got up and climbed out of the pond and went into the bushes. He walked up to the road and looked out at the neighborhood around him. It was quiet. A car was approaching so Dolphi backed up and watched it circle around the roundabout and go the other way. He hoped that the vehicle was his family's minivan, but it wasn't. Dolphi felt the silence around him once again. The neighborhood felt a little like a ghost town to Dolphi. He could still hear the ceaseless drone of traffic in the distance over the houses and birds singing around him. It was peaceful. It was quiet. Dolphi was smiling. He then felt the need to urinate. He walked over to a spot in the bushes. He hummed as if he was singing to the peaceful rhythm of the nature around him to try and feel better about himself. As he looked down, he saw something was missing. "Oh my god," he thought in shock, "where's my... ?" He then remembered that male dolphins hid their genitalia behind a slit on their bodies. Dolphi then pushed his out and then began to urinate. "Ah, there it is," he thought. He examined it and saw that it looked just like a dolphin's. He then finished doing his business. "I should stay here for now and get going when it gets dark," he said to himself. He suddenly realized he was hungry. "Now I wish I hadn't thrown that fish into that guy's face," he thought.

Dolphi heard somebody coming. He immediately dashed into the bushes away from the pond and lay down flat. He lifted his head a little and saw a man approach in the pathway entrance. The man was wearing a long sleeved, white and red striped shirt. He wore tan colored cloth pants and had a hat with a strap to keep it held on his head. It had a large rim around it to keep the sun off his head and neck.

The man stopped and took off his hat and shirt. His skin was a slight pinkish color and he had white hair on his head. He then took off his pants and there was a bathing suit underneath. Dolphi tried not to look so as not to invade the man's privacy. The man then went into the bushes towards the pond. Dolphi then realized that he had left his cloak over there. "Damn," he thought.

As the man approached the pond, he noticed the cloak lying on the ground. He turned his head around to see if anyone was nearby. "Anybody here?" he called. Of course, Dolphi decided not to answer. The man focused on the cloak again, studying it. "Cool," he said. He then went into the pond, lay down in the water and began relaxing. "Ahh... now this feels great," the man said. "So nice to cool off after all that fishing today."

Dolphi thought about the old woman whom he had saved, saying that her son liked to come to that spot. Perhaps this man was her son. Dolphi wondered how long the man was going to be there. As the man was relaxing, he heard a rustling noise in the bushes. He turned his head and looked, but saw nothing and continued to relax. Suddenly, there was a splashing noise and when the man turned, he saw an alligator right next to him! The man screamed and the gator rushed at him, jaws open. Dolphi heard the man and quickly jumped to his feet. Dolphi ran through the bushes and jumped into the pond. He could see the man had his hands on the gator's mouth, trying to keep it from biting him. Dolphi ran through the water to the gator and grabbed it by the tail. He pulled it away from the man and threw it behind himself. Dolphi went for his cloak and turned around after grabbing it. The gator ran at Dolphi and just as it came within range, Dolphi threw the cloak over its face. Dolphi grabbed the gator and lifted it out of the water. The creature had to be at least six feet in length from head to tail. Right after lifting it up, Dolphi threw it into the bushes. "Get out of here!" Dolphi yelled at the reptile. "Scram!" The alligator scurried away into the bushes with the cloak still attached to its face.

The man got up on his feet and Dolphi turned to look at him.

"Are you okay?" Dolphi asked.

The man felt very scared when the gator attacked him, but when he saw Dolphi's form, he felt a little relieved but a little nervous.

"Gee, thanks for helping me," the man said. "I thought I was about to be his lunch."

"Yeah, you're very lucky that I was here to save you."

"Yes indeed. Now, I have heard of good Samaritans, but I have never seen anything like this; a two legged dolphin coming to my rescue. Are you supposed to be some kind of restaurant mascot, or maybe, a costumed vigilante?"

"No, not exactly."

"Oh, wait a minute, you must be the guy who's been gallivanting in other people's backyards, right?" the man asked as he studied Dolphi's body.

"How do you know about that?"

"While I was out, I heard a radio report that a dolphin guy was wandering around somewhere and police are looking for him. You must have been very brave to do all that backyard jumping."

"So, you're not afraid of me?"

"Of course not! That's got to be a costume you're wearing."

"Well, let me be honest, it's not. This is my real form." Just then, a ringing sound came from the man's pants.

"Oh, that's my phone," the man said as he ran over to his clothes. He took the phone out of the pants pocket.

"If it's the police looking for me, tell them I'm not here," Dolphi said. The man answered the phone. "Hello?" he asked. Dolphi thought it was going to be the police. He had thoughts that the man was an undercover cop, so he backed off a bit.

"Hi, I'm doing okay," the man said, "except for an unexpected encounter."

"Who is it?" Dolphi asked concerned. Dolphi would have run away if anything went wrong.

"Hold on," said the man. He motioned to Dolphi. "It's my mother. Happy now, blubberface?" He then went back to his phone. Dolphi turned his back and tried to shut out his laughter.

"So how are you doing?" the man continued. His expression soon changed. "… Hold on, you fell out of your chair and you got saved by someone? … A dolphin-like voice?" He took a glance at Dolphi. "Maybe you can tell me about it later," he continued. "I'll be home soon. Love you, bye!" He then put the phone back in his pocket.

"Tell me, where do you live?" Dolphi asked.

"Right over there, beyond those trees" the man said pointing. Dolphi then realized that, that was the house where he had saved someone from a terrible fall.

"The old lady!" Dolphi said.

"Yes," the man said. "Oh boy, thanks a million."

"No problem. But, how did she manage to call you if she is blind?"

"Well, she is always near a phone in case of some serious emergency. She's not completely blind, she can make out the phone and call me using the speed dial. So, you told me you are a real creature?"

"Long story, I just need to find my way home."

"You're at the perfect spot. Just go down there and out to the ocean."

Dolphi almost laughed. "Uh, no. I'm not *from* the ocean. I used to be a human."

"Oh, that's kinda cool. I want to help you any way I can."

"If you want to help me, then the best thing for you is to go home."

"Do you want to come to my house?"

"I'm sorry," said Dolphi. "That would be nice, but I think I should stay here. I can't trust anyone because people may think I'm some monster and then try to hurt me."

"You're no monster," said the man. He put his hand on Dolphi's stomach and began to tickle him. Dolphi laughed hard and took the guy's hand off him. "That tickles!" laughed Dolphi. The man put his other hand on Dolphi's stomach and rubbed it.

"You feel like a real dolphin, man." Dolphi hummed as he felt the man's hand give a good sensation. "Aww… you're changing color." Dolphi looked down at his stomach. "My tummy's turning pink. I have learned that dolphin's tummies are pink when they are sexually stimulated. I think you better stop before I get overexcited."

"Okay."

"And speaking of my tummy, I'm hungry."

"Oh, I think I can help you with that. I was fishing today and I caught lots of fish, but they're very small. The bucket's around the corner." They went over to where the bucket was and Dolphi looked inside. "That's a lot," he said.

"I thought about keeping them," the man said, "but maybe they're too small. You can eat them, if you want." Dolphi grabbed some fish and swallowed them down in one gulp. "Whoa!" the man said astonished. "That's an interesting eating method."

"Sure is."

"Oh, I forgot to ask what your name is."

"My name is, well, I call myself, Dolphi."

"That is a very interesting name. My name is Regan, Regan Markinson. I'll check back with you later."

"I would like to ask you something," Dolphi said. "What is with the hat with the large rim on it? It looks like a sombrero."

"I have a case of albinism," Regan explained as he went over to grab his clothes. "My skin is allergic to the sun and I can get sunburn within 10 minutes. It helps keep the sun off my face and neck. A long sleeve shirt and long pants help as well. Someday, I'll move out of this place and get to somewhere more comfortable." Dolphi finished eating the fish. He then noticed something about the man's hands. "Your hands are bleeding," Dolphi said.

Regan looked at his hands and noticed the blood. "Yeah, that gator had sunk a few of its teeth into my hands as I tried to fend it off. I'll bandage it up when I get home."

"Another reminder," Dolphi said, "maybe you should not bathe in this pond anymore as it has now become a gator's territory. I'll continue to use this as a hideout, but I'll be very cautious from now on. I had fallen asleep here and I am very lucky not to have ended up as a reptile's snack."

"I'll remember that," Regan said. "Once again, thank you for saving me. I'll see you later. Bye!" Regan put his hat back on and walked off.

"One last thing!" Dolphi called. Regan turned to Dolphi. "Don't call me, 'blubberface'."

Regan smiled and made an 'O' shape with his hand to indicate 'Okay' and continued on to his house.

Dolphi went back through the opening in the bushes. He took a deep breath and sighed, feeling glad that Regan wasn't a bad person. He was impressed that he had managed to save Regan's life from an alligator attack and also his mother from a fall that could have shattered her frail body. It felt good for Dolphi to make a friend who understood him.

"Maybe I should walk around for a bit," Dolphi thought, "I need some exercise." He then sighed as he realized, "that alligator took off with my cloak and now I'm naked again. Guess there's nothing I can do about it."

He walked along the path to where he could see the beach and the ocean. When he looked around, he saw nobody. He set foot on the beach and felt the warm sun on his skin.

He turned and saw someone way in the distance, but the figure was walking away behind a rocky corner. Dolphi ran over to the water and ran right in. It felt good feeling the salt water around his body. He then opened his eyes under water and felt a little sting which then went away. "My eyes don't sting as much," he thought. He could feel a chemical in his eyes that was leaking out of a duct. It was soothing his eyes from the salt water. "This is a new feeling for me," he thought.

He swam out and looked around underwater. He thought about all the educational facts on dolphins that he had learned in his past life. Realizing he had a blowhole on his head, he put it above the water. He began to breathe in and out while most of his head was under water. It was like a snorkel only he didn't have one. "I feel pretty strong in this form of mine," he thought. He took a deep breath and dove down. He swam at a fast speed moving his legs vertically together just like a dolphin's tail. He then swam up to the surface and breached out of the water. He leaped to about ten feet and then crashed back down. "This is incredible!" Dolphi thought with exhilaration. "I cannot believe that I'm actually doing this!" He began to explore as he traveled out into the ocean. Dolphi was impressed that he was still holding his breath under water. He could hold it for quite some time. "I wonder what I can find around here?" he thought as he swam high and low.

CHAPTER 15

Interspecies Reunion

"Give your heart but not into each other's keeping.
For only the hand of life can contain your heart."
—unknown
(Taken from a bookmark bought in South Africa)

EEE!!! HELP ME! TRAPPED!— a high pitch voice cried some-
—where underwater.

"What was that?!" Dolphi thought as he heard the voice. It
sounded as if a child was drowning. Dolphi swam out further to try
and find the source of the noise. He soon came upon what looked
like a gigantic net cutting off his path. When he got closer to the
nets, he could see something moving in it. It was a dolphin and its
head was caught in a hole of the net! It was jerking around trying to
free itself. "Oh no!" Dolphi thought. He swam over to the trapped
dolphin. He put his fingers in the hole where the dolphin's head
was caught and tried to pull it open. He couldn't get it open wide
enough, so he pushed the dolphin's snout with his foot to help with
getting it free. With a firm push, the dolphin suddenly broke out of
the net! Dolphi swam up to the surface and stayed buoyant with his
head out of the water. He saw the dolphin taking a breath and going back under. The dolphin's head then poked out of the water and
faced Dolphi. They observed each other in curiosity. Dolphi did not
swim away from the dolphin and the dolphin did not swim away
from Dolphi either. Dolphi reached out and touched the dolphin's
head.

"Are you okay?" Dolphi asked. The dolphin made a sound and Dolphi suddenly heard a voice inside his head. —THANKS— said the dolphin.

Dolphi jerked backwards in surprise. It seemed the dolphin had talked to him.

"What the... ?" Dolphi thought as he could not believe his ears.

—WHAT ARE YOU?— asked the dolphin. —PREDATOR? FRIEND?—

"What?" Dolphi asked. The voice he heard sounded female. He turned his head and thought, "how can this dolphin talk?" He then faced the dolphin again. "Okay, how can I explain this to you? I'm a strange creature. I'm half and half of two species. How is it that I can understand what you're saying?"

—YOU MEAN YOU DON'T KNOW?— asked the dolphin.

"Know what?"

—WE COMMUNICATE WITH EACH OTHER AND WE UNDERSTAND EACH OTHER. ME CURIOUS OF LAND CREATURES, ME LIKE GRAY FRIENDS, ME LIKE YOU.—

"Glad to hear it," said Dolphi. "How can I hear you so clearly?"

—SOUND WE MAKE— the dolphin said in a point form language. —WE TALK WITH SOUND THAT LAND CREATURES HEAR. MAKES CREATURES OF LAND SMILE—

"Those 'creatures of land' are humans."

—HUE-MANS? WHAT HUE-MANS CALL US?—

"Oh, what we call you creatures? We call you things... you are a... dolphin."

—DAUL-FUN? WHY THEY CALL US THAT?—

"I don't know. Humans nickname other creatures."

—WHAT FOR?—

"So that we can... identify them when we see them. I used to be human, now I'm this form."

—ODD... SAY, CAN YOU LEAP OUT OF WATER AND FLY?—

"Yeah," Dolphi smiled. "Watch me." Dolphi swam under water. He then leaped into the air, did a somersault and landed back in the water. Observing, the dolphin also swam under water, jumped into the air and did the same thing Dolphi did.

—YOU GOOD— said the dolphin.

"So are you," Dolphi replied. "What is your name?"

—WHAT'S NAME?—

"Uh… something you would call yourself to identify yourself to others."

—LIKE, DAUL-FUN?— the dolphin asked. Dolphi then put his hand on his face and shook his head. "No, no, no, no, no. I'm talking about different individuals. It's in our human nature. I mean, I'm not human any more but… it's probably hard to explain to a creature like you."

—I SEE WHAT YOU MEAN— said the dolphin.

"You are female by the way, right?"

—YES, FEMALE, AND WHAT WAS YOUR NAME, HAF-AN-HAF?—

Dolphi was puzzled. "Huh…? Oh! No, no, no! 'Half and half' is not my name. It's Dolphi. By the way, when you hear humans speaking to you, you understand them full well don't you?"

—YES, MOST OFTEN—

"Well, here's something for you," said Dolphi. "Humans can hear you dolphins, but they don't know what you are saying. When you speak, you make some cute noise instead of plain English. But in this situation, we understand each other."

—ENGL-ISH? WHAT'S THAT? ME DON'T KNOW—

"You're not talking to me then?" Dolphi asked puzzled again. "Then how?" The female dolphin was silent, unsure of what to say. "Okay, I guess it must be something different. Gee, wouldn't scientists like to hear about this."

—ME KNOW NOT WHAT YOU'RE SAYING, BUT YOU VERY SMART—

"Thanks. I'd like to hear about what you have been doing lately." The dolphin was silent again. She tilted her head as if she felt depressed. She then said, —ME REMEMBER THE MORNING BEFORE. ME WAS WEAK NEAR LAND. HUMANS TAKE ME TO STRANGE CAVE. BEFORE, ME FELT PAIN IN HEAD AND IN TAIL. LOST SIGHT, SIGHT SOON CAME BACK. PAIN IN HEAD GONE, BUT STILL WEAK. SOON RECOVERED. SUDDEN PAIN IN FIN ON BACK, THEN SENT BACK TO SEA. PAIN STILL IN FIN. THAT'S IT—

Dolphi tried to understand as much of what the dolphin was trying to tell him.

"I'd like to see your dorsal fin," Dolphi said. The dolphin moved with her back beside Dolphi. He saw a tag on the back of her fin. It said, 'M.R.I.L 037'. "Hey…" Dolphi said remembering something. "You were the dolphin I had seen with a blood loss problem! Now I know what you are talking about! There was a bright light that shot out of you, bounced all over the room and went into one of our computers."

—OUR WHAT?— the dolphin asked.

"Never mind," said Dolphi. "I want to ask you, do you remember anything at all about when you first had that pain in your head?"

—WELL, MANY, MANY NIGHTS AGO, ME SAW A LARGE, STRANGE ROCK FLOATING ABOVE THE WATER. STRANGE BECAUSE ROCK DON'T FLOAT. ANYWAY, ROCK HAD STRANGE GLOWING LIGHT INSIDE. ME GOT CURIOUS AND SWAM UP TO ROCK. SUDDENLY, LIGHT SHOOTS OUT OF ROCK, LIGHT… HITS ME, AND… — The dolphin was silent. Dolphi knew that dolphin's faces could not show human emotion, but the dolphin was acting like it was afraid.

"And then it entered your head," Dolphi said, "you are taken to the facility and that light enters that computer. How strange. Say, can you take me to that 'strange rock'?"

—ME CANNOT REMEMBER WHERE IT IS— the dolphin said. —CAN ME ASK YOU A FAVOR?—

"Yes, what can I do for you?" Dolphi asked.

—CAN YOU HELP ME REMOVE THE THING THAT BRINGS PAIN TO MY BACK? ME HAVE RUBBED IT IN THE SAND, BUT PAIN IS STILL THERE—

"You mean remove the tag? I don't think I can do that. It's procedure at the facility to keep track of you."

—TRACK ME?— the dolphin's voice sounded angry. —ME IN PAIN AND COULD BARELY REST LAST NIGHT. WON'T YOU PLEASE HELP ME?—

"I…" Dolphi then remembered that he had been fired from the M.R.I.L. Besides, he also felt sorry for the dolphin after all she had been though. "Very well," he said. He tried to pull apart the tag, but it didn't break. He then put his mouth over it and bit into it. After some struggle, the tag managed to break off. It began to sink, so Dolphi jumped over the net and swam down to retrieve the object. As he swam back up with it in hand, he saw the dolphin was looking at him. She made clicking noises at him and then stopped.

When Dolphi reached the surface, the dolphin was backing away from him.

"What is wrong?" Dolphi asked. "Aren't you going to thank me?"

The dolphin was very nervous. —ME SAW SOMETHING IN YOUR HEAD. SOMETHING PRETTY, BUT ALSO DISTURB-ING—

"My head?"

—ME USED UNIQUE ABILITY TO SEE INTO YOUR BODY AND FELT SOMETHING IN YOUR HEAD ME NEVER FELT BEFORE—

Dolphi felt concerned. "What did it feel like?"

—ME FELT SOMETHING COLD LIKE WATER AROUND US AND HOT LIKE… LIKE SOMETHING—

"Like fire?" Dolphi asked.

—FIRE? ME NOT KNOW WHAT THAT IS EITHER, BUT WHAT IS IN YOUR HEAD IS A MYSTERY TO ME—

"My goodness. I will have to find out what it is sometime. So, do you have any friends or family out there?" asked Dolphi.

—ME NOT WANT TO TALK ABOUT IT. ME NOT SURE ABOUT WHERE THEY ARE EITHER—

"Okay," said Dolphi. "I think you should move along now because I should too. It was so nice to talk to you. Please take care of yourself out there."

—OKAY. BYE! THANKS FOR SAVING ME AND GETTING RID OF PAIN ON MY BACK!—

"You're welcome! Good bye!" The dolphin swam away giving one last leap in the air and was soon out of sight.

"Cute," Dolphi thought, "I can hear what other dolphins say…" He sighed and went back over the net and headed in the direction of shore. Talking to a dolphin and understanding what it was saying felt a lot more interesting to Dolphi than doing lots of paperwork at the office. He felt very privileged to see a dolphin, especially in the wild, but understanding their language, was unusual. He felt like this was an incredible breakthrough in science. He did however feel upset about what had happened to him at the M.R.I.L, but had he not been mutated, he would never have saved Regan, his mother and the female dolphin. He did feel good in this watery world he was swimming in. He was beginning to feel things he never felt as a human being before. He felt like he couldn't decide which would be best for him; to stay as he is, or find a way to be human again. He knew two things however, he had to find his family and explain things to them. And secondly, when he got the chance, *if* he got the chance, he would get revenge against the man who had committed this crazy experiment on him.

* * *

In the meantime, Mike had been explaining the situation with the murders and the mutant sharks at the M.R.I.L.

"I know it sounds crazy," Mike said, "but our father's missing and our mother is still at the facility.

"Sweet Jaysus," the cop said, listening to the story. "I'll call for backup and head over to that place as soon as possible."

"No!" Mike said. "We almost got killed by some tough creatures. I'm serious. I don't think it would be a good idea to go in there with a few officers. It would be best if the big guns were brought in, like the S.W.A.T or something." The cop scratched his chin for a moment. He did find Mike's story a little hard to believe. "Well…" the officer said, "I wouldn't know for sure if we can arrange somethin' like that, but you three better come with me." The boys got in the police car and drove off.

"By the way, my name's Bob," he said. "We're goin' down to the station to sort things out. Afterwards, we'll arrange a hotel for you three to stay at and we'll notify you if we find anything about your mother or this dolphin-like person that a couple of guys had claimed to have seen."

"Thank you, officer," said Mike.

CHAPTER 16

Unforeseen Outcome

"As experience widens, one begins to see
how much upon a level all human things are."
—Dr. Joseph P. Farrell

B EFORE DOLPHI RETURNED to the shore, he looked around to make sure the coast was clear on the beach. Luckily, there was nobody around. He left the water, went into the bushes and went back to his hiding place. He soon heard rustling in the bushes behind him. When he turned around, he saw someone a few feet away facing him. Dolphi gasped and fell backwards into the pond. He then realized it was Regan. "You scared me!" Dolphi said, taking a deep breath.

"Sorry," Regan replied. "I was just wondering where you were. I thought you might be bored, so I got you a ball." Regan showed Dolphi a red and white beach ball. Dolphi didn't know whether to laugh or punch Regan's lights out. "Are you trying to be funny?" Dolphi asked. Regan laughed a little. "Maybe. Do you want to pway wif me?"

"I beg your pardon?"

"I said, do you want to pway wif me, you adorable, pwayful Dolfy creature?"

Dolphi held his stomach and began laughing through his teeth. "You crazy old man! What the hell are you saying?" he still laughed.

"I'm baby talking to you, man," said Regan. "You know, trainers do it with their dolphins."

Dolphi calmed down and said, "I'm not a baby, you know. Come to think of it, dolphins are not always children. That baby talking might get old for them. You should speak normally to dolphins, especially to me. I'm 39 years old."

"If you say so," said Regan. "I was just trying to sound friend-ly."

"It's okay," said Dolphi, "I'm sure dolphins have feelings too. You know, you're a very nice guy. I'm starting to like you. Do you think you can give me a ride home?"

"I would love to," said Regan, "but unfortunately, my car is in the auto-shop right now." He then sighed and muttered, "it's been in that place for 2 damn years... "

"Do you have your cell phone here with you?" asked Dolphi.

"Yes," Regan replied. Dolphi gave Regan his telephone number and he dialed it on his phone. A moment later, Regan said, "there's no answer, man. The answering machine just kicked in, so would you like to leave a message?"

Dolphi began to think about it. It wasn't a good sign that his family didn't answer the phone. He wondered if they were look-ing for him. He thought about heading back to the M.R.I.L, but the police were looking for him and traffic was heavy. He then thought about heading there by the ocean. However, it would be a very long swim and even if he did get there, he would have absolutely no idea what he would be up against if Mr. Jem had been doing more muta-tions. He suddenly wondered if his family had been captured and had been turned into mutant animals as well!

"Oh my god!" Dolphi cried out.

"What's wrong?" Regan asked feeling concerned.

Dolphi was silent for a moment and then said, "I'm sorry for that outburst. I was just hoping that my family isn't in any danger. Anyway, perhaps you could help me call them again later. I'd prefer to talk to one of my family members in person. I'll just rest here in the bushes and hope that alligator doesn't come back. I have been swimming for a while and I'm tired."

"Did you catch any fish out there?" Regan asked.

"No, and I don't know if I can catch fish with my own mouth like normal dolphins do. Maybe I'll try to do that after I rest for a few minutes. Oh, and by the way, I noticed there was a large net out there in the water."

Regan suddenly remembered that there were things he hadn't told Dolphi before.

"Oh, yeah," Regan thought. "That net's out there to prevent sharks from swimming in and attacking people."

"And it almost killed a dolphin in the process," Dolphi added. "Her head was stuck in one of the openings and she was very lucky that I was there just in the nick of time."

"My god, that's awful," Regan said. "I was told that the net wouldn't allow anything to get caught in it."

"Do you know why the net is in that particular location?" Dolphi asked.

"Now I remember what I should have told you earlier," Regan smiled. "I forgot to mention that the beach you were on, is a private beach."

"Oh, so I was trespassing."

"Not exactly. I let you go onto the beach because I wanted to reward you for saving my life. You can still go back to the water if you wish."

"I'll just catch a nice rest."

"Very well," said Regan. "I'll see you later, Dolfy." Dolphi immediately reacted to the mispronunciation of his name. "No, no, no, the last letter in my name is an 'eye' sound, fool. D-O-L-P-H-I, 'eye!' 'eye!' 'eye!'"

"Okay, sorry!" Regan said laughing a little.

"It's okay. It's just that 'Dolfy' sounds too cute a name for me. I think I'll take that beach ball and see if my dolphin antics do anything to it."

"Alright," Regan passed the ball. "Bye!" He then walked away.

Dolphi lay down in his spot and began resting while letting the sounds of the waves splashing on shore act as a lullaby. He lay there with his eyes shut, but he didn't fall asleep for a while.

Time passed and when Dolphi opened his eyes, he saw it was late in the afternoon. He felt hungry again. Now was the time to see if he could catch his own fish and then continue on the path home when it became dark. He got up and picked up the beach ball. He threw it up into the air and then hit it with his snout when it came down. He bounced it several times and then put it back down. The ball made him remember another object. He had put the keychain picture of his family down when he went to save Regan. He retraced his steps and eventually found it. He set the beach ball and the picture next to each other so he could find it later. He then left his spot and went down to the water. He swam through the water quickly, looking around for anything that looked edible. He also decided to check out the nets once again in case any more dolphins had got stuck. Luckily, there were no problems. He continued past the net and had to be careful not to go out too far or he would get lost.

He soon noticed a whole school of small fish swimming by him.

"Hmm…" Dolphi thought. "How am I going to get those things?" He then remembered something he should have realized when he first became a mutant dolphin. That dolphin he saved had used her 'unique ability' to see inside him. That ability was echolocation, the dolphin's navigation system. Dolphi knew that dolphins used echolocation for finding food. Unfortunately, he didn't know how to use it. He should have asked the female dolphin. He stared at the fish for a moment wondering what to do. He went up to take a breath, went down and yelled, "go echolocation!" Nothing had happened. "Buzz." Nothing. "Go-go gadget, echolocation!" Still nothing. "Kapwing! Go! Sonar! Dolphin sonar, go!" He began nodding his head around, but he didn't notice anything different. He closed his eyes and groaned, feeling he couldn't do it. Suddenly, he saw the skeletons of the school of fish while his eyes were shut. "Whoa!" Dolphi thought. He then tried it again with some clicking noises. He saw the fish's bodies twitch, probably from his clicking. The fish shimmered with a whitish color when he used his echolocation. He then swam up as close as he could get and made a loud dolphin cry. Some fish twitched rapidly and then stopped moving. Dolphi swam up to them and started eating them. They were delicious, but he had to be careful not to take in any salt water. So he closed his mouth over one fish, filtered out as much water as he could and swallowed it. Dolphi ate until his tummy was full. He then decided to head back to the shore.

When he went up on the beach, he looked to the right and saw two guys running towards him. Behind them, there was a woman running after them. Dolphi saw a purse in one of their hands. When they got closer to Dolphi, he realized what was going on. Those men must have stolen that lady's purse! He saw a large rock which he could hide behind. He also saw a small stone at his webbed feet. When the men approached, Dolphi picked up the stone and threw it at the blonde haired man in front. It hit his head and he fell down, moaning in pain. The other man who had brown hair, was holding the purse. He stopped to see what had just happened to his partner. The woman came running up and tried to take the purse out of the man's hands. She was knocked to the ground in the process. The brown haired man then began wrestling with her.

"No!" she yelled. "Stop!"

"Why are you even trying to get your stuff back? You know we're going to get away with it," the brown haired man snarled.

"Did you hear what she just said, you punk?!" Dolphi shouted. The blonde haired man slowly got up and looked at Dolphi while still rubbing his head. The two men had big, strong, muscled bodies and they wore bathing suits. "Did you throw that rock at me?!" the blonde punk yelled. When the other guy turned to face Dolphi, he stopped wrestling the woman. "What the hell do we have here?!" he asked.

"That's not important," said Dolphi. "What's important is that you better give her back her purse and run away before I rough you up."

"I don't think so," the blonde punk said. "You asked for it, you fishy freak!" He ran at Dolphi. Dolphi threw a punch at him, but the punk ducked and he kicked Dolphi right in the groin. Dolphi screamed and fell to the ground. He looked up and saw the punk had taken out a switchblade. He was about to stab Dolphi, but Dolphi grabbed the punk's hand and tried to move it away from him. The blade however, cut the right side of his face. Dolphi screamed again and quickly got to his feet. Still holding onto the punk's hand, he threw him to the ground. Dolphi forced the switchblade out of his hand and grabbed it. Dolphi jumped on him and slashed the left side of his face. "You like that, huh?!" Dolphi yelled in anger and pain. The other punk who had the purse then dropped it and ran in to help his partner. He kicked Dolphi off him and helped his partner up. They both then started to kick Dolphi while he was lying on the ground.

"Stop it!" the woman screamed. "Stop beating him up! Leave him alone!" But they kept going. When Dolphi stopped moving, they faced the woman. "Well," the blonde punk said, wiping the blood off his face from the cut, "looks like your hero wasn't able to stop us." Suddenly, there was white colored electricity forming on Dolphi's head. He eyes opened and he slowly stood up. The two punks turned around and faced him. Dolphi looked zombie-like. He felt like he couldn't control himself. He then said, "you better... get away... before... "

"Still want more?" the blonde haired punk asked, about to step forward.

"Wait," his partner said as he put his hand out. "Let me finish him off." He ran at Dolphi, yelling with a readied fist. As he was about to punch him, Dolphi caught the man's fist with his left hand and then grabbed the man's throat with his right. As he was grabbed, the man choked with a horrified look on his face. Dolphi brought him close to his face, took a deep breath, closed his eyes and then made a loud scream that sounded like clicking.

Suddenly, there was a loud popping noise and Dolphi stopped. Another scream then followed.

"Oh... my... GOD!!!" the other man yelled. He ran away as quickly as he could. Dolphi didn't know what he had done just now, but it wasn't a pretty sight. He stood there breathing heavily for a minute. He then collapsed on his knees, fell flat on his face and lay silent.

CHAPTER 17

Caring Souls

"The cure for all ills and wrongs, the cares, the sorrows and the crimes of humanity, all lie in the one word 'love.' It is the divine vitality that everywhere produces and restores life."
—American Activist Lydia M. Child

D OLPHI FELT WATER around him as he slowly came to. He groaned in pain. He then felt some water trickling on his head. He turned as somebody said, "rest, rest." Dolphi recognized Regan's voice. "You're lucky to be alive."

"Where… am I?" Dolphi asked weakly.

"You're in my house," Regan replied. "You're in the bathtub right now."

"Wow," said a female voice, "I didn't think such a creature existed."

"Who's that?" asked Dolphi.

"Oh, that's my wife," said Regan. "She ran home to me, saying that a couple of thugs stole her purse and that you tried to stop them."

"Thanks for trying to save me," she said.

"You may have a scar from that cut on your face," said Regan.

Dolphi groaned in pain again. "I don't remember what happened… after those guys beat me up."

"What I saw before was sick," said Regan's wife. "I saw you scream at that guy's face and… his head exploded. It was gross. The other guy ran off."

"What did you say?" Dolphi asked as he tried to get up. He then felt his groin hurt. He also felt something cold at his groin. It was an icepack. "You received a pretty nasty kick in the nuts," said Regan.

"Ugh, I need to get up and sit down on something," Dolphi said.

"Okay." Regan and his wife helped Dolphi out of the tub and they got him onto the toilet.

"What time is it by the way?" Dolphi asked.

"It's just after nine," said Regan.

"So, what exactly are you?" Regan's wife asked. "Where did you come from?"

"I can explain," Dolphi said. "I'll tell you both everything that has happened to me since yesterday." As Dolphi was slowly recovering, he explained everything that had happened to him at the M.R.I.L. The strange energy that came out of a dolphin's head in the medical pen, the explosion in the same room, Mr. Jem luring him into a trap to mutate him, escaping from the lab, and getting through town today.

"That Mr. Jem is a real bad ass," said Regan.

"You were human before?" Regan's wife asked, "and then mutated? Freaky. I wonder how your boss did that?"

"I wish I knew," Dolphi said. "I remember him saying that the institute was a second interest for him. Maybe he was a scientist of some kind before I met him."

"By the way," said Regan, "I tried phoning your house several times earlier. There's still no answer."

"Did you leave a message on my answering machine?" asked Dolphi.

"I was going to last time, but I thought it would have sounded weird having a total stranger tell a family that their father is a fish of some kind. That would be a ninety-nine percent chance of the call turning out to be a prank."

"I don't blame you," said Dolphi, "but I do blame you for calling me a 'fish'."

"I know you are a mammal, I was just being sarcastic."

"I have a bad feeling about my family not picking up the phone. I hope they are okay." He got up and looked in the mirror. He saw a red diagonal line on the right side of his face. It had gone across his eye. "Ow," Dolphi said as he touched it, "I thought I felt something cut me."

"I'm sure it will get better," Regan said. "I'd like to ask you something. Is this what your family looks like?" He had the picture of Dolphi's family.

"That is my family, yes," said Dolphi. "My wife and my three children, and that's me... as a human."

"You're a good looking guy in this. I found it next to the beach ball I gave you. It must have been a precious item to you, so I brought it here."

"It's precious indeed. Thank you."

"I think I'll take some dental floss and tie it onto the picture to make it a necklace so you can carry it around your neck and not have to hold it in your hand all the time."

"That's a great idea." Regan got to work on it. "Uh, about before," Dolphi said to Regan's wife. "Did I hear you say that I *actually* blew somebody's head off by screaming at him?"

"Yes," she said. "Look at this." She showed him both Regan's clothes and hers which they had taken off. "You were covered with that punk's blood and some of it got on us as we carried you here. I came running to my husband after this terrifying incident and told him about what happened. When I took him to the scene, he told me he knew you and that you had saved him from an alligator earlier. Thank you for that. He didn't know what you did, but he thought it would be best if we brought you here and helped you. You were so heavy, I should add."

Dolphi suddenly felt very scared. "Oh... my... god..." He felt really bad about what he had done. He put his hands on his eyes and almost felt like crying. "I... killed... a man... I took a... human life. I didn't want to kill him. I'm so sorry, I didn't mean to do that. I don't even remember doing anything to him. I just wanted to protect you." He then put his head on the bathroom sink counter and began sobbing. Regan's wife put her hand on Dolphi's back and slowly rubbed it while saying in a soft voice, "it's okay, I understand. You did what you had to do and you at least saved me and my belongings."

"We made an anonymous phone call to the police," said Regan as he finished the makeshift necklace.

Dolphi got up, took the necklace and went for the door.

"Where are you going?" Regan asked.

"I must find my way home," said Dolphi. "I'm very worried about my family."

"Please don't feel bad about that incident, Mr. Dolphi," said Regan.

"You don't have to say 'mister', Regan. Do you have a roadmap that will show our location? It would help if I was able to see where I was going."

"Don't you want to stay for the night?"

"Thanks for the offer, but I intend on heading back home while under the cover of night."

"Okay," said Regan, "I'll go look for a map and meet you at the front door."

"Thanks." Dolphi went downstairs and waited. The foyer had a mixture of family pictures and seashells on the blue and white walls. He soon heard a squeaking noise enter the room. He turned and saw it was the old woman he had saved from falling out of her wheelchair.

"Hello, are you that guest my son brought in?"

"Uh, yes," Dolphi replied.

"Oh, you're the one who saved me!" she said excited.

"Yeah, I was… severely injured and Regan found me and helped me."

"You must be feeling better."

"Much. So, do you know what I am?"

"A dolphin that looks human. Regan told me, but I already knew since we first met. Your voice and that grey colored body of yours is extraordinary. I'd like to feel you if that's alright."

"Oh, okay." Dolphi walked up to her and she put her hand on his stomach and rubbed it. Dolphi made a series of clicking noises out of pleasure. He suddenly saw her skeleton, internal organs and the room around her shimmer a whitish color just like the fish he had hunted before.

"Ohh…" she smiled as she heard the clicks. "Could you do that one more time?" Dolphi made the clicking noises at her face again and she acted as if she was feeling something.

Regan and his wife appeared with a map and saw Dolphi with the old woman. "Oh!" Regan reacted. Dolphi turned and stepped backwards. "She wanted to feel my blubbery skin," he said.

"Okay, I just found a roadmap we can use."

"Let's see where we are and how to find my house."

"Aimy, please help my mother get ready for bed."

"Your wife's name is Aimy?" Dolphi asked. "You never told me that before."

"I guess I didn't," Regan smiled. The two went into the kitchen and laid the map out on the table. Dolphi looked for his home while Regan looked for his. They found their spots and held their fingers on them while Dolphi looked for a path to take. After a while he made up his mind.

"If I follow these roads, I should be home within a few hours. It will be a long walk, but now I have some guidance." Dolphi headed for the door.

"So, I guess this is goodbye?" Regan asked.

"We might meet again. It was nice getting to know you."

"It is nice to know you too. Live long and prosper." Dolphi laughed at the Star Trek quote and shook hands with Regan. He then walked out the door and began his journey home.

CHAPTER 18

Apprehension

"Everybody runs."
—Tom Cruise
Catchphrase from the movie: "Minority Report"

DOLPHI LEFT THE neighborhood and traveled along the side of the road. It was a warm night and he decided to stop for a moment next to a large field. He took a deep breath and exhaled slowly enjoying the warm temperature. He looked up at the night sky and saw so many stars. He heard a combination of waves splashing on the shore and traffic in the distance. He looked towards the city and saw the lights from the buildings. It looked very pretty. "Such a peaceful night," he thought. He suddenly looked behind him. "Is someone following me, or is it just my imagination? I guess I'm okay." He continued walking believing everything was alright.

As Dolphi came to a residential area, he saw blue and red flashing lights. There was a police cruiser stopped at the same side of the road Dolphi was on. There was a bright light shining around. Apparently, the officers inside were using a spotlight. Dolphi moved quickly to the other side and hid behind a tree. The light was then turned to the tree.

"Is someone there?" asked the officer in the driver's seat.

"I thought I saw something," the second officer with the spotlight said. "I guess it was just a squirrel."

Dolphi peeked behind the tree and saw the light shining elsewhere.

"Well," Dolphi thought to himself, "here I go." He tiptoed quietly along the sidewalk. He didn't notice however, that there was a broken glass bottle in his path. He started trotting a little faster. When he came to it, his right foot stepped right into the sharp glass. Dolphi suddenly screamed and fell to the ground holding his foot. The police heard the noise and shone the spotlight at Dolphi. They saw him sitting on the ground.

"What's going on?!" asked the spotlight officer.

"Hey, that guy looks like a dolphin!" the other officer said. "He matches the description of the report!" The officers got out of the vehicle and turned on their flashlights.

"Hey, you!" the first officer shouted. "Stay right there!" Dolphi felt some glass in his foot. He quickly grabbed whatever shards were in him and pulled them out. He jumped up and ran as fast as he could. "We said hold it!" the officers yelled. Dolphi turned a corner and went up another street. Every time his right foot hit the ground, he felt pain. The officers were beginning to catch up to him. As Dolphi came to the end of the street, he saw a river. He turned around and saw the officers pointing their guns at him. "Lie down on the ground with your hands above your head!" one officer shouted firmly.

"Actually," Dolphi said. "I think I would rather go swimming." He leaped over the side and plunged into the water. He used his echolocation to see where he was going. He then popped up on the other side and ran up the hill. He went through the trees and came out onto another road. He turned his head back in the direction he had come from and sighed with relief. The policemen were nowhere in sight. But as he turned around, something hit him. He fell down and felt a net with weights covering him. "What the… ?!" Dolphi yelled. "Who's there?!" He saw about six people surrounding him. Three men on each side grabbed the net and lifted Dolphi up. They carried him over to a van, threw him into the back and closed the doors.

"Please don't hurt me!" Dolphi pleaded. He saw men in white lab coats moving around him rapidly. They appeared to be scientists. They then covered his eyes with a cloth.

"Alright, we got him!" one of the scientists said.

"So, you can talk," another scientist said to Dolphi. "State your name."

"My name?" Dolphi asked nervously.

"Just answer the question."

"Okay, its Dolphi. Who are you people?"

"Let's just say we're researchers and we want to study you. Now hold still." Dolphi suddenly felt a prick in his arm and yelped.

"Where did you come from?" a scientist with a grey beard asked.

"I'm just trying to find my way... home," Dolphi said as he started feeling sleepy. They must have injected him with a tranquilizer. He groaned as he felt himself losing strength. The injection took its full effect and Dolphi fell asleep feeling very relaxed. "The subject is secure!" said the bearded scientist. "Now let's get the hell out of here!" The van drove off into the night.

CHAPTER 19

The Discovery Research Incorporated

"The voyage of discovery is not in seeking new landscapes,
but in having new eyes."
—French Author Marcel Proust

IT WAS MORNING at the Marine Research Institute Labs. Jaws, Chewer and Slice, the three mutant sharks, were hanging around in the shark den. Jaws was sitting by the side of the tank reading a book he had found in the room. It was all about sharks. Slice was in the tank swimming circles and Chewer was playing Solitaire on a computer. Slice then jumped out of the tank and said, "hey Jaws. What are you reading there?"

"I'm reading about our kind," Jaws replied.

"Interesting." Slice went over to Chewer now. "How's it going?"

"I'm bored," Chewer replied as he exited out of the program. "Do you have anything that will entertain me? You've been swimming around in that tank for over an hour and I got bored watching you. This card game is complicated and there are no other games on here. You've been doing lots of swimming, so maybe you can do some acrobatics."

"Acrobatics, huh? That gives me an idea." Slice walked back to Jaws. "Jaws," he said.

"What is it now?"

"Will you help me entertain Chewer?"

"Entertain? I'm not interested in playing games."

"Well, I want to try something with you. I was thinking… you've got a big, strong body and I'm the lightest. I want us to jump in the tank so I can get on your back and ride you like a bull while you leap out of the water as if you were bucking."

Right after Slice finished talking, Jaws made an angry growl to his face. "Okay, never mind," Slice said as he walked away. He was still thinking about the idea. Jaws returned to reading his book. "Ah, here we go," he quietly said to himself as he turned a page. "The Great White Shark. I'd like to know how many teeth this creature—"

Suddenly, there was a "YAAAH!!!" and Jaws felt someone jump on his back. He dropped his book and fell into the water. Chewer quickly went over to see what was going to happen. He saw Slice and Jaws suddenly breach out of the water. Slice was on Jaws' back. "Hey! Get off me!" Jaws yelled as he swam around trying to shake him off. He went under the water and breached again. Slice yelled out a "YEEHAW!" and Jaws shouted, "Chewer, help me!"

Chewer however, was laughing hard and was enjoying what he was seeing.

Just then, Chewer heard a noise behind him. He turned and saw it was Mr. Jem. "What's going on here?" Mr. Jem asked. Jaws suddenly breached out of the water and yelled, "get off me now or I'll slap my tail in your face!"

"Everyone get over here!" Mr. Jem shouted. Slice got off Jaws and climbed out of the tank. Jaws emerged feeling angry and humiliated.

"What's up?" Slice asked.

"I figured you guys would be bored so I have brought you a television to watch." Mr. Jem had a portable T.V in his arms. He set it down in the room and turned it on. There was an antenna on top that gave it good reception. In one of his hands, he held a glass cup with some orange juice. (No mutagen in that one!) He faced the shark mutants again. "I created another mutant this morning," he said. Everyone was surprised.

"Oh! Did you make a female shark?" Jaws asked. "You know, one we can have… fun with?"

"No…" Mr. Jem replied. "I created her while she was still asleep. I have her in the lab down the hallway. You three will stay in that lab guarding her during the week and you three shall only enter this room on weekends."

"Why?" Chewer asked.

"So none of the staff will see you. We don't want to get in trouble. Although I do suspect we'll be in trouble anyway sometime soon as I'm aware that I can't hide what I have done forever. But maybe someday, creatures like you three and my newest creation might do beneficial things for this world."

Slice turned to the T.V and saw a commercial for Swiss chocolate. It showed coco beans being ground up and chefs mixing up the liquidy chocolate in a mixing bowl. Then, it was poured out slowly into molds. At the sight of all this, Slice was drooling like crazy. "Slice," Mr. Jem asked, "what are you looking at?" He saw a big load of slobber pouring out of Slice's mouth. "Eww! That's disgusting!" Mr. Jem shouted. "Swallow or spit that out right now!" Slice spat out the saliva into the tank and turned to Mr. Jem.

"Sorry, boss," he said. "I seemed to have taken an interest in what I just saw. I would like to try some smooth, creamy, delicious chocolate…" He then started wagging his tail like a happy dog.

Mr. Jem sighed. "Okay, whatever. Now listen here, I've got the new mutant in a cage and I want to make something clear. None of you are to harm her. No biting, no punching, and make sure she's fed regularly."

Just then, the television showed a news report. Mr. Jem went over and turned the volume up. Everybody turned to the T.V.

"A man was found dead on a private beach in the Miami suburbs last night," said the anchorman. *"When investigators found the body, its head was missing. Even after a thorough search of the area, the head was nowhere to be seen. A man who had previously committed numerous thefts turned himself in to police and claimed he witnessed the murder. He had this to say to reporters…"* The camera went over to a man who's face was blurred to protect his identity. *"My partner…"* the man said sobbing. *"We stole many women's purses together… There was this creature that stopped us after we tried to get away with another purse. He grabbed my partner… and made this loud scream that blew his #@%*ing head off!"* Someone off camera then asked him, *"what did this creature look like?"*

"He looked like a dolphin... a man with the skin and head of a dolphin for god's sake!"

Mr. Jem then knew exactly what the man was talking about. "Dr. Jay..." he thought. The camera went back to the anchorman. *"If you thought that man was crazy,"* he said, *"listen to what we have in our top story. Last night, a mysterious creature was captured by a team of scientists five miles north of the murder scene we just told you about. The scientists told us it has the body of a human, but with the skin, head and dorsal fin of a dolphin, just like the purse thief in custody had described. The scientists have identified themselves as employees of the newest research facility in the United States, the Discovery Research Incorporated."*

Suddenly, Mr. Jem's eyes and mouth shot wide open. He dropped his drink and it shattered to pieces on the tiled floor.

"They are hoping to found out the origin of the creature and what capabilities it has," the anchorman said. *"Police believe that the human-like dolphin is responsible for the death of the late purse thief. We will keep you up to date as the D.R.I gives out more information."* Mr. Jem then turned the T.V off.

"Boss?" asked Slice. "You don't look so good. Was it something that guy said?"

The news report had shocked Mr. Jem, but he was now calming down. "It's nothing," he said. "I was just thinking about something... I'll clean up that broken glass later." He went to where the key to the special lab was hidden and picked it up. "I'll take you to see my latest mutant and... yes, later I will get you some... delicious chocolate."

* * *

Mike and his two brothers, Walter and Sid, were seated on a bench at the police station where they had been taken after being picked up by a police officer yesterday. They had explained to the police the day before about their mother who had been left behind at the M.R.I.L and the disappearance of their father and what may have happened to him. They also added that they might be related to the dolphin creature that police were looking for. A hotel had been found for the boys to stay at and they had been taken home to pick up some belongings and take care of their dog. When they woke up that morning in the hotel, they turned on the T.V to the news to see if there would be any mention of a mutant dolphin. Sure enough, they saw the same report Mr. Jem had seen. The police called at the hotel to pick up the boys after they heard the report that the suspect they had been looking for was in the custody of the new research facility. The boys were told to wait around until a meeting could be arranged between the police and the mutant, for the police wanted to question it about the death of the purse thief.

"So," Walter said, "our father has been found."

"I know," said Mike. "However, he wasn't found by the police, but by a group of scientists."

"I would like to know who those scientists are," said Walter. "But is it true that our father is a mutant like those sharks we encountered?"

"It must be true," Sid said. "What I don't want to believe is what was said on the news about dad killing someone. He would never do such a thing."

"We don't want to believe that either," Mike said.

"What if dad's boss has done the same mutation thing to mom?" Sid asked.

Mike felt like he would have to agree with Sid. "Then I guess our parents and our lives have been changed forever."

"What if they never release dad?" Walter asked. "What if we have to spend the rest of our lives with… foster parents?"

"… Who have nothing in common with us," added Sid.

"I hope not," said Mike. "We won't know what our parents' fate will be until we know for sure, hopefully sometime soon. Anyway, I'm going to find somebody to talk to and see if anything is being done to let us meet with our dad."

Mike got up and walked around the police station. He turned to see two officers bringing in a suspect for some crime that had been committed. Mike continued walking while he was still focused on the suspect and wasn't watching where he was going. He suddenly bumped into a female police officer.

"Hey!" she said.

"Oh! I'm very sorry, officer!" said Mike. "My fault." He then walked around her.

"Wait!" said the officer. Mike turned back towards her. "I've seen you somewhere before."

"You have?" Mike asked as he tried picturing her face. "Say... aren't you the officer who came to our house to take a robbery report two days ago?"

"At the Jay residence?" she asked.

"That's it."

The officer was surprised. "Nice to see you again. I'm very sorry about what had happened over at your house."

"Thanks for your concern," Mike said. "But right now, we're faced with a problem that's... a lot worse."

"Your parents are missing?"

"Yes, how do you know?"

"Officer Bob told me about you guys but I didn't realize it was you."

"You know him?" asked Mike. "He was talking with an accent of some kind."

"He's originally from Arkansas," said the officer.

"Look," Mike said trying to get to the point, "the news this morning said that a research facility found a human-dolphin hybrid and my brothers and I really want to see it."

"Everyone wants to see it," she said. "All of Florida's dolphin lovers are excited about it. So far, Florida is the only state that knows about this creature. The news will soon spread to other states."

"Don't you think it sounds like a Tabloid prank to everyone?" Mike asked.

"Of course," she said. "But if it was shown to the world on T.V, people would be... interested... and curious... I'd like to see it myself."

"If it," Mike said, "or *he,* actually, sees his children, he would recognize them. This might sound crazy, but I think he is my father."

The officer almost laughed. "Maybe, maybe not. You can check out the front desk to see if anything's happening."

"First I'll get my brothers and we'll go there right now." Mike went back to where his brothers were sitting and told them to follow him. When they went to the front desk, another female officer behind the desk greeted them. "May I help you? Oh, it's you three. I was about to call you to say that The Discovery Research Inc. is sending us a fax about a family picture that was found on the creature." In the back room, the boys could see a fax machine slowly spitting out a piece of paper. Someone grabbed it and took it to the front desk. When the officer at the desk looked at it and then at the boys, her eyes widened. "This has got you three and your parents on it."

"No way," Mike said. "Can we see that?" When the piece of paper was handed over and the boys looked at it, they almost couldn't believe it. "It's our Christmas portrait!" Mike said.

The officer Mike had bumped into was right behind him. "Hey, that's Dr Jay, the same man I talked to about the house robbery!" she said. "So let me get this straight. This human-dolphin creature is not from a sunken Atlantis city like I first thought, but a human being who was... mutated?"

"Now you know why we need to see him," Mike said.

The shocked officer then asked the man who brought the fax, "did they say anything else?"

"Yes, they said if we have those children, we can send over a few officers, the boys and the Police Commissioner. They would allow the boys to see it while accompanied by police and then the Commissioner will question it in connection with the death of that criminal yesterday."

Mike frowned. "I'm sure our father would never do such a horrible thing."

"That has yet to be determined," the officer at the desk said. "Also, we will send some officers to investigate the facility you boys came from and see if we can find your mother or any indication of problems."

"Okay then," Mike said, "let's just hope the officers don't get eaten in the process."

"I'll be one of the escorts for these boys," the officer with the boys said. "Oh, I forgot to introduce myself," she said to them. "I'm Officer Monica Roans. But you can just call me Officer Monica."

After a while, Monica and two other officers assembled in the lobby. The Commissioner then appeared. He was a thin man in his fifties and was dressed in a navy blue suit with a green tie. His grey and white hair was neatly combed. "Good morning, gentlemen," he said. "I understand we are to see a newly discovered creature at a newly established research facility. That's a new one I must say." His voice was a little cheery, but he was a serious man. He motioned to the boys. "Hello there lads, I am Police Commissioner

Harold Rex and I'll be interviewing this dolphin creature, as I hear it can speak plain English. Listen, you three will be permitted to see the creature first for a few minutes, but then, if you should choose to stay, behave yourselves while I'm conducting the interview."

"Alright," Mike said. "You will have our full cooperation."

Everyone went outside. Officer Monica took the boys to her cruiser. "The place where we are going is on the other side of the city," she said, "so it will take a bit of time."

"I'm very interested in finding out more about this... Discovery Research Inc.," Walter said.

* * *

The boys and company soon arrived at the research facility. "We're here," Officer Monica said. A large white building was seen out on a field located just outside of the city. It was surrounded by a chain link fence with barbed wire on top. The place almost looked like a prison. There was a guard post stationed at the entrance. Past it, there was a long road leading to the building. The guard allowed the visitors entry after confirming their identification. They drove up the road and parked in front of the steps. They all got out and went up the stairs. When they entered the building, they found themselves in a small lobby. The walls were as white as the building's exterior.

"Doesn't this place believe in color?" Sid asked trying to break the hypnotic effect it was having on everyone.

"Okay, we're in," said Walter. "Now where are we going to find dad?"

"He may be in a secure area," said Officer Monica. They approached the front desk.

"I will give each of you access passes to wear around your necks," the woman at the front desk said taking out a box. "I will buzz two of our employees to escort all of you to where we are holding the specimen." After everyone put on the access passes, two employees walked into the lobby. One of them was old and bearded and the other who was younger, was clean shaven.

"Welcome, everyone," the young employee said. "I am William and this is Bill."

Sid then laughed. "Will and Bill... Those names can easily be remembered."

"Oh, I get it," William said. "Now, while we do respect the police, we ask that everyone leave their weapons at the checkpoint beyond that door. You will have them back when you leave. Besides, the security setup won't allow anyone into the building if they're armed. It's a precaution for the safety of our staff."

Commissioner Rex thought about it. "Very well, but if something happens to us, we will have this whole place on a barbeque."

"Wow," Sid whispered to his brothers, "this guy's tough."

"Right this way," Bill said. Everyone walked through the door and found themselves in a hallway where there was a metal link barrier on the left wall. On the other side was a security office. When the group stopped at the window, they were given bins to hold their items through a slot below. They were advised to close the door after each person went through, starting with one of the facility escorts. The officers placed their items in the bins and one by one, everyone walked onto a pad with black panels on each side of the hall. A white line on the panels went from top to bottom. There was a click and the door was unlocked. After everyone was through, they were finally inside the facility.

The place was full of scientists, computers and other technological things. "So this is Discovery Research Inc..." Walter said in awe. As they were led in the direction of where Dolphi was being held, Walter asked one of the escorts, "what do the people at D.R.I do around here?"

Bill replied, "the Discovery Research Incorporated, or 'dry' as the short form pronunciation, is an organization of scientists from around the world looking for any new and interesting discoveries in nature. In the future, there will be at least one D.R.I facility in every state in America. Our main headquarters is just outside Los Angeles, California."

"I'm interested in scientific things myself," Walter said. "How come I haven't heard of this organization before?"

"D.R.I had been shut down due to the death of its founder and a police investigation of illegal research on genetics," Bill continued. "It was way before your time, son. Now, we are coming back on the right track."

The group approached an elevator. They went inside and went

down. When the doors opened, they saw an enormous room of busy staff moving all over the place. "Everybody is working hard trying to find out about this creature," William said. "Let's head over here to see an interesting item." They walked over to a work station. William picked up an item out of a box. "We found this on the dolphin creature." He looked at it and glanced at the boys. "It's definitely you three. The mutant hybrid claims he knows the children in this picture." He showed it to the boys. They recognized it right away.

"We think this dolphin creature is our father," Mike said.

"Interesting," William said. "How could something like this have happened?"

"Is our dad even human?" asked Walter. "Are you guys sure he's a mutant dolphin hybrid?"

"We did blood tests," William said. "His blood has the same DNA structure as a human, but it's modified with dolphin DNA and by... uh... something else. We're trying to identify it."

"I see," said Mike. "About that picture, can we have it back? It's probably of no use to you anymore."

"Sure, no problem," William replied as he gave the small picture to Mike who put it in his pocket.

"Let's head to the back where the specimen is being held," said Bill.

"I don't mean to be rude," Mike said, "but we would appreciate it if you didn't call him a specimen. It makes it sound like he's more of a prisoner."

"Okay, sorry," Bill replied. "I can also tell you boys one thing. If he *is* your father, he doesn't look anything like the man in the picture." The boys were silent. "Let's move on now."

On one wall up above, it said in big letters as Walter had spoken them.

"DRI: discovering wonders, researching new life, showing the world the best of the extraordinary." Just then, a screeching noise filled the whole area. A man's voice was heard over the loudspeaker. *"Welcome to another day at the DRI,"* said the voice. *"Please stand and recite the motto."* Everyone in the place stopped moving and stopped answering phone calls. The area, once filled with the incessant noises of people chattering, became silent. Everyone sitting down in chairs immediately rose to their feet. All activities ceased. A loud chant filled the whole room. "DRI: discovering wonders, researching new life, showing the world the best of the extraordinary!" everyone shouted in unison. Even the group's escorts were standing still and reciting the motto as well. The loudspeaker came on again. *"Today, something new has been discovered, a creature that is half the species of a man and half the species of a dolphin. Recite!"*

"DISCOVERING WONDERS!" yelled everyone.

"Research is being done on the creature right now. Recite!"

"RESEARCHING NEW LIFE!"

"A creature that will inspire those who are curious about what is in this vast world! Recite!"

"SHOWING THE WORLD THE BEST OF THE EXTRAORDINARY!"

"That is all," the man on the loudspeaker said. *"Please return to your duties."* Everyone then went on with what they were doing."

"Whoa," thought Sid.

"Seems militaristic," said Mike.

"Somehow, I like it," said Walter. "Everyone's so cooperative. Whose idea was that, I wonder?"

"Our CEO (Chief Executive Officer) made that up," Bill said. "Alright, now. We have the creature in a room behind those doors." Everyone walked over to what looked like a major bank vault door. "We don't have him chained up," Bill said. "Instead, he is in a tank filled with water for him to swim around. We do however, have a collar on him that would give an electric shock in case he tried to escape from the tank or attack our staff. But so far, he's harmless and is cooperating very well."

"I hope you're right," Mike and Commissioner Rex accidentally said in unison. They then glanced at each other feeling a bit surprised.

Bill then cleared his throat and said, "alright everyone, this is the moment you have all been waiting for. We've prepared a special introduction for all of you. Open the door!" he called. Someone pushed a few buttons and the door opened. When the group looked inside, there was a blanket covering the tank viewing window. They walked inside. Bill then started to act like a circus ring announcer. "This creature is half-human and half-dolphin. He's got the acrobatic ability of Flipper and can speak plain English like the dolphin on SeaQuest. What's his name again? Darwin, that's it." He began to climb up a ladder and stand on a platform. "Now," he continued, "allow me to introduce the incredible, the unbelievable..." He then bent down and whispered into the tank, "what's your name again?"

"Dolphi," the mutant dolphin said.

"Yes, but is that it? Is there a title that will make you stand out better?"

"Alright then, how about... The Mutant Dolphin?"

"'The Mutant Dolphin?' That's not very flashy."

"Hurry up!" the Police Commissioner shouted. "We can't bear the suspense much longer!"

"As I was saying," Bill said to the group, "I present to you, the incredible, the unbelievable, Dolphi: The... Dolphin... Man!"

The curtain dropped and everyone's eyes widened as they saw the half-human dolphin mutant floating in the tank. As the man climbed down, Dolphi shouted, "hey! I said, 'Dolphi: The Mutant Dolphin!' Hey!"

"Just go see the people near the door," Bill said.

Dolphi sighed, went under the water and swam down to where the visitors were. They looked blurry from under water. He then swam up and tried to look over the edge. Before he could see them, he got a shock from the security collar. "Ow! I think it would be better if they came up on the platform where I can see them more clearly!" Dolphi said.

"Alright then," William said. "You kids can go up." The boys hurried over to the ladder and climbed it."

"He just called him the same name I wanted to call my own dolphin someday!" Sid told his brothers. When they reached the top, Dolphi poked his head out and looked at the boys. Suddenly, his eyes widened, he gasped loudly and swam backwards, covering his heart and breathed heavily. He almost couldn't speak. He recognized his children, but they still didn't know if he was their father. "My..." Dolphi tried to speak. "My... SONS!!!"

The boys also felt like they couldn't speak. Mike then said, "if... if you *are* our father, then identify us and our interests or hobbies."

Dolphi swam up to the boys, took a deep breath and said to Mike, "you are Mike Stanley Jay and you are taking Tae-Kwon-Do. You are Walter Benjamin Jay and you're a science lover who is working on a device to disguise or camouflage people. You are

Sid Mathew Jay who wants to be a dolphin trainer someday and name his dolphin, Dolphi." Dolphi was about to cry and so were his children. "And your mother's name is Jennifer..." The boys quickly bent down and tried to hug their father. Instead, they fell into the tank, tightly hugged their father that they have been trying to find and began crying.

"Hey," Bill called, "you're not supposed to do that!"

"Shut up," William said as he nudged his partner with his elbow, "these kids are upset, so just let them be for a few minutes. This is making me a little upset as well."

"It *is* you!" Mike cried. "What happened to you, dad?"

"I'm very sorry, boys," Dolphi said. "My boss has done something terrible to me." He then looked around. "Say, where is your mother? Is she here?"

"I don't know how to say this," Mike said, "but Walter, Sid, mom and I tried to find you at your work place when you didn't come home. We found this suspicious lab inside the M.R.I.L."

"These boys might be telling something interesting," Commissioner Rex said to the officers.

"We found some interesting information on one of the computers in that room," Mike continued. Suddenly, your boss appeared in the door with these mutant sharks that tried to kill us."

"What?" asked Dolphi. "You mean... other mutants were created as well? So he must be going further with his goddamn experiments... But what about your mother? No..." he thought with worry. "Did she get killed by those sharks?!"

"No!" Mike quickly answered. "She fainted at the sight of them and we managed to escape. We couldn't save her, those things were huge and we couldn't get her out of there. We had no choice. However, I think your boss wanted to keep her alive. There may be a good chance that she is still alive and... that your boss has turned her into something... like you."

Dolphi felt like he would have to accept that possibility. "I wouldn't be surprised..." he said. "I think you boys should get back on the platform right now. But Sid, I want you to swim out to the middle of this tank. I've got something that will cheer you up." Mike and Walter got out and Sid swam into position. Dolphi then swam under Sid, grabbed his feet and lifted him up into the air as if two dolphins were pushing an individual up with their snouts.

"Yahoo!" Sid shouted. They then came crashing down. Dolphi then used his hands to push Sid through the water by his feet so that he was standing up and flying on the water's surface. They went around the tank and when Dolphi approached the platform, Sid jumped off. He laughed and everyone in the room clapped. "Thank you so much, dad!" Sid smiled. "So, your name is Dolphi?"

"Yes," Dolphi replied. "When I became a mutant, I was thinking of you and that clever name. So, where are you boys staying, at home or a hotel?"

"We were sent to a hotel yesterday and we spent the night there," said Mike, "but not before we were taken back home to get some things and feed Squall. Guess what our hotel is called, The Dolphin's Lagoon Inn. It's located just outside of the city near the highway that leads to the Keys. The street's called Dilton Blvd."

"That sounds nice..." said Dolphi. Mike noticed the scar on Dolphi's face.

"What happened to your face?" asked Mike.

"I kind of... got in a fight yesterday with some purse-stealing beach punks, as I tried to protect a woman whose purse got stolen."

"And that's what I'm here to talk to you about!" Commissioner Rex called out.

"The police want to talk to me?" Dolphi asked.

"The news said you killed a guy," Mike said. "Surely you didn't do it."

"You kids must come down now. I need to question him," Commissioner Rex said.

"Okay, we'll be right down!" Mike replied. "One more thing, dad," he asked. "How did you come to be here?"

"I don't know, really," Dolphi replied. "I'm still trying to picture the face of that bearded guy..." He suddenly remembered seeing his face inside a house from the backyards he had been jumping through. "Hey! The bearded guy who was just up here! I saw you in that house when I came out of your swimming pool! So it was you who snitched on me!"

Bill then clapped his hands. "Looks like you finally figured me out. Sorry, but what I did was necessary. Now, I think it's time for the police to see you."

"Kisses, boys," Dolphi said. The boys bent down and kissed Dolphi on the tip of his snout. "I'll be alright, kids," Dolphi added.

"Good luck, dad," Mike said.

"Glad to see you're okay," Walter said.

"I love you, daddy," Sid said lastly.

The boys climbed down the ladder and the police began climbing up. "I think we need some towels," said Walter.

CHAPTER 20

Questioned by the Authorities

"Not everything that is faced can be changed,
but nothing can be changed until it is faced."
—American Author James A. Baldwin

COMMISSIONER REX AND the three police officers stood on the platform staring at Dolphi. Dolphi stared back wondering what kind of questions he was about to be asked.

"I would like to know where you were and what you were doing yesterday," Rex asked.

"Is this about that dead guy?" Dolphi asked.

"Yes it is."

"I can explain everything."

"Yeah? Well don't splash me in the process or your name's mud."

Dolphi told about his mutation and how he ended up at the beach. As for his children, they were listening down below.

"You also broke into a seafood restaurant and stole some fish," Rex said.

"I needed to eat, for crying out loud," Dolphi said. "I later learned to catch fish on my own using my echolocation. When I got back to the shore..." He then explained about the theft that was in progress and how he tried to protect the woman. "I goofed up and they jumped me. I got beaten until I was unconscious and then... I don't remember what happened after that. The next thing I knew, I was being cared for by a couple of humans; one was the woman I tried to protect. She told me I blew the man's head off, but I'm telling the truth, I did not murder that man."

"If not you," Rex said, "then who did, an alter ego? Because I do not buy that nonsense unless you have a history of mental illness."

"When I was a human," Dolphi said, "I never had a problem with mental illness. I feel different since my mutation, but not in a murderous way. I was unconscious when this death occurred."

"Now, that woman said you 'blew his head off'," Rex said. "The other perpetrator, the one we have in custody, who witnessed you, said you made a loud noise. You yelled so loud, you ruptured every blood vessel and caused the whole head to explode in one gory mess."

"That's preposterous," Dolphi said. "To yell that loud, would cause permanent damage to my voice box. I should be mute, and yet here I am, talking to you with no pain in my throat at all. I don't understand." Commissioner Rex sighed and said nothing. "Look, if I *did* kill that man, does that make me a murderer who must rot in a cell for a decade or two? Because I wouldn't hurt anybody for any reason unless my life or the life of one of my family, was in danger and I had to defend myself or protect them. You saw how I was with my children, I love my family."

After another moment of silence, Rex said, "well, that dead guy was wanted on many counts of theft and even for the armed robbery of a jewelry store. We've been on the lookout for the 'Jewelry Bandits' as they called themselves, for quite a while."

"That title rings a bell," Dolphi said. "I think I saw a news report of them once. There was security camera footage of them in action, but I hardly saw their faces and wouldn't have recognized them. Huh, does this mean I don't get a reward?"

"It would have been better to bring him in alive," Rex said, "and besides, we usually reward humans, not mutated dolphins. The surviving criminal had turned himself in probably because you not only scared him good, but also *scarred* him good as well. He said he cut your face, but you managed to cut him back."

"*Without* intending to kill him," Dolphi added.

"Alright, I've heard enough," Rex said. "We won't press charges on you, but you're not Free Willy yet. Something must be done with you. This place can't hold you forever, so I'll request that this place contact a government agency that specializes in creatures like you.

I mean, I'm not talking about mutants, but you can be classified as a marine mammal."

"Excuse me, Commissioner," Officer Monica said. "I'd like to ask him a few questions myself while you make the contact."

"Very well, Roans," he replied, "but don't let me catch either of you three playing with him." He then climbed down the ladder.

"So," Monica said to Dolphi, "you are the man I spoke to about your house robbery. Your real name is Steele Jay, right?"

"Yes," Dolphi replied. "I remember you. I'm like this because of my boss at the Marine Research Institute Labs. My boys told me that he's made more mutants like myself. You know what I would suggest? You guys should arrange a S.W.A.T team to storm the whole place. The facility's President, Mr. Jem is definitely up to no good. I also think his closest subordinates are the ones who broke into my house."

"We'll see what we can do," Monica said.

"You've got great talent," one of the other officers said.

"I think you can haul in a lot of dough at a marine park and enter history as an amazing entertainer," the third officer said.

"Watch your tongue," Dolphi said. "I'm not a circus clown. In fact, I'm a marine mammal veterinarian. And by the way, where are your guns?"

"We had to leave them at a security checkpoint as a precaution," Monica said.

"You know," Dolphi said, "I wasn't nervous about this questioning. I would have been if I was handcuffed behind my back and sitting on a bench where everyone would stare at me. I'd feel like a criminal. But this setup is comfortable and humane. Why can't more people have this kind of treatment?"

One of the other officers with a shaved head sarcastically said, "because you're a new creature, a new discovery, you're… cutting edge science and the ones we usually take care of are vile criminals who deserve to be punished, not pampered."

"Right, I knew that," Dolphi said.

"You know, you're kind of cute," Monica said.

"Aww… thank you," Dolphi smiled. "It's not everyday you get to encounter a dolphin that can talk, right?"

"Nope," she said. "But I wonder what would happen if you interacted with a non-mutant dolphin?"

"That's already been done," Dolphi replied. "I met one when I was swimming out in the ocean."

"And?"

Dolphi thought to himself and then said, "it's a secret."

Commissioner Rex down below called up to them, "okay then, an agency has already responded to the report and they're sending a representative to make a decision about what to do with the creature."

"And what agency are we talking about?" Dolphi called. "Oh wait, don't answer! I think I know exactly what he's talking about. He must be referring to the agency that deals with marine mammals like myself, the National Marine Fisheries Service (NMFS) of the National Oceanic and Atmospheric Administration. (NOAA)"

"That's right, mutant," Rex replied. "You're quite intelligent. I'm impressed. Maybe this agent will do something wise with you. The agency said the agent will arrive by helicopter in fifteen minutes. Officers, you and the children will return to the lobby. I will join you soon after I finish up some business."

"Okay," Monica said. "Well, goodbye," she said to Dolphi. The officers climbed down the ladder. Dolphi swam down to the tank's glass wall facing the room's entrance. He waved goodbye to his children and they waved back. Dolphi then swam to the surface, breached out of the water as if saying goodbye and swam to the other side of the tank.

The boys had tears in their eyes once again as they silently left the room. The young facility escort, William, took the group back to the lobby. The officers had their weapons returned to them at the checkpoint and everyone returned their facility passes.

Everyone including William, waited in the lobby for the Commissioner to return. The boys sat on the lobby's comfy leather chairs in silence. After a while, they heard a helicopter approach.

The front doors opened and a man wearing a suit and tie walked in with two bodyguards. They all had something that looked like hearing aids on their ears. They looked like they came right out of the 'Men in Black' movie. They passed by Officer Monica and the boys as if they weren't even there and walked over to the front desk. The agent showed his badge and identified himself as Agent Simcoe of the NMFS. The receptionist gave the three men access passes and William led them through the door into the facility.

Soon after, Commissioner Rex appeared.

"Alright then," he said. "Our business here has been concluded. Now it's up to the Fisheries Service to decide what happens to our fishy friend."

"Sir," Monica said. "I just want to say that 'mammalian' would be the politically correct word to use."

"Understood," he replied. He then turned to the boys who looked very sad. "Cheer up, boys," he said. "That creature is out of my hands now. Maybe he'll end up in an aquarium or some place public where you can see him."

"… maybe," Mike said calmly. "Let's just head back to our hotel and try to get some rest."

* * *

Officer Monica drove the boys down the highway leading to their hotel. The boys were very quiet during the ride. Suddenly, Monica's police radio was calling for her.

"6FL19, please respond," a female voice said.

Monica picked up her radio. "This is 6FL19," she said.

"Do you have the three children who reported their parents missing?"

"I do," Monica said.

"The officers' investigation of the Marine Research Institute Labs has been concluded. They haven't found anything that's worth investigating with the exception of a hole in the facility's wall that was blown out two days ago by unknown persons. The facility's president is aware of the disappearance of Jennifer and Steele Jay and believes that the unidentified attackers may have kidnapped them and are terrorizing the facility. We will have units watching the outside of the facility tomorrow to ensure the safety of the staff."

"What?" Mike asked disappointed. "That wasn't the response we were hoping for!"

Monica then responded over the radio, "6FL19 to Base, I would like to confirm that the children's father has been found."

"Ten-four," the radio replied.

"Over and out," Monica said. She then put the speaker down.

"They didn't find mom or the big mutant sharks?" Mike asked.

"I guess not," she replied. "You still insist you saw mutant sharks at that M.R.I.L facility?"

"Of course," Mike replied. "You saw a mutant dolphin, right? I think that Mr. Jem is covering things up. If we only had video taped evidence of our encounter. Wait a minute," he wondered, "there's bound to be a security office where surveillance cameras record things. I don't think the officers looked there from the sound of things. If somebody gets hold of tapes showing the last two days, maybe the sharks and what happened to our parents would be on them and that would make the Police Commissioner call a S.W.A.T team to take action."

Officer Monica thought about it. "Does your dad have any friends at work?" she asked.

"Well," Mike said, "he did mention his best friend at work was a man named Henry Guy, but we've never met him."

"Alright then," she said. "I'll call the facility tomorrow, ask for him and see if maybe he can do anything."

They finally arrived at the Dolphin's Lagoon Inn. The boys got out of the cruiser. Monica got out and said, "you know, I have to admit that I was on the verge of tears as you kids played with that dolphin and waved goodbye to him."

"Thanks, Monica," Mike smiled.

"I'm very glad that we got to know you," Walter said.

"I hope daddy will be alright," Sid said.

"I'm sure that such an extraordinary creature won't be carelessly abused, and we will continue to look for your mother," Monica said. "Well, good-bye boys. I should head back to the station and start working on another interesting case. We are trying to pinpoint what caused a mysterious thirty second blackout that occurred through-out all of North America a couple of days ago." She then got back in her cruiser and drove away.

* * *

Dolphi was waiting for the agent to arrive and decide his fate. Time had passed and nobody came to see him. He was told that the agent was in the room right now, but wouldn't meet or speak to him. Dolphi decided to do some spins and acrobatics underwa-ter. He didn't know where the agent was, but he swam around the tank waving his hand. After a little more time had passed, Dolphi was called up to the platform. He was ordered to put his body onto a specially designed stretcher. Dolphi knew he had no choice, so he had to comply. As he lay on the stretcher, they deactivated the 'invisible fence' parameter around the tank. He was then given an injection. Dolphi soon realized it was a tranquilizer, for he began to feel drowsy. He then passed out.

CHAPTER 21

A Monster Called 'Reality'

"There is no ignorance; there is knowledge."
—tenet from the Jedi code (Star Wars)

DOLPHI SLOWLY REAWAKENED after being knocked out by the tranquilizer and found himself in total darkness. He felt himself submerged in cold sea water with his blowhole just above the surface. He felt something around his wrists and ankles that prevented him from moving. He lifted his head above the water and heard the waves crashing up onto shore. He realized he was outside in the fresh air. He saw the last glimpse of light from the sunset disappear beyond the chain link fence off to his side.

"Where am I?" he wondered.

Suddenly, he heard a ghostly voice speak to him. —HEL-LOOOOO?—.

Dolphi gasped and suddenly felt more awake. He tried to turn to see who was talking to him, but he couldn't move. "Who's there?" Dolphi asked. "What place is this?"

—A PLACE YOU CAN'T GO ANYWHERE— said the voice. —A MAN COMES WITH FOOD, I AM HUNGRY, BUT MAN WILL NOT FEED ME—

"Just a minute," Dolphi said, "I can't move." He felt clamps holding him down. He tried to force them off his hands and ankles. "EERGH!!!" Dolphi growled as he ripped the clamps on his wrists off their foundation. He then pulled hard on the clamps restricting his ankles easily breaking them with his new strength. "There," he said, "free at last."

—NOOOOO… — the voice said, —NOT FREE. NOT FREE FROM HERE, CAN'T SWIM ANYWHERE ELSE—

Dolphi turned around to see a male, bottlenose dolphin staring at him.

"Hello there, dolphin," he said. He looked around to see where he was. He could see high fences surrounding him in a rectangular shape. He saw stairs going from a platform at the water's edge down into the water. He swam over to the stairs and felt an underwater path he could step on. He then realized what he was in.

"Of all the places they could have put me!" Dolphi said out loud. "It just had to be a $wim-with-the-dolphins facility! I'm in captivity!"

—THAT'S IT— said the dolphin. —WE ARE IN CAPTIVITY AND THERE IS NO WAY OUT FOR US— Dolphi sat on the stairs with most of his body still in the water.

"Is there anything about this place that you can tell me?" he asked the dolphin.

—ME WAS NOT HERE BEFORE. ME WAS OUT IN THE OCEAN MANY NIGHTS AGO WITH MY FAMILY. THEN, ME SAW MAN APPROACH US ON LARGE WOODEN BEASTS—

"Wooden beasts?" Dolphi asked. "You mean boats?"

—IF THAT'S WHAT YOU CALL THEIR TRANSPORTATION, THEN YES—

Dolphi continued to listen carefully to the dolphin's story. —MAN LURED ME AND MY FAMILY INTO COVE AND TRAPPED US WITH LARGE, WHITE, STRONG SEAWEED—

"I'm sorry?" Dolphi asked. "Oh, you must mean a large net."

—YES— the dolphin continued. —ME WAS FRIGHTENED AND SCARED. ME AND FAMILY COULD NOT ESCAPE. MAN RUSHED AT US AND PULLED ME AWAY FROM MY FAMILY. ME STRUGGLED HARD, BUT GOT PULLED INTO 'BOAT' AS YOU CALL IT. NOW, ME HAVE FOUND MYSELF HERE IN THIS LITTLE PLACE. ME DON'T UNDERSTAND. MAN IS SUCH A STRANGE CREATURE. ME SHOW KINDNESS TO THEM, BUT THEY SHOW NO KINDNESS TO ME. RIGHT NOW, ME ALWAYS GETTING HAND SIGNALS FROM A MAN HERE WHO HAS FOOD IN HAND. MAN IS TELLING

ME TO JUMP. ME JUMP WITHOUT FEELING LIKE DOING IT AND ME DID IT POORLY. MAN YELLS AND PUTS FOOD IN BUCKET AND GIVES ME SAME SIGNAL. ME STILL VERY SENSITIVE FROM CAPTURE. ME TRY TO DO TRICK AGAIN, BUT ME SO HUNGRY. ME DID THE TRICK WRONG AGAIN. ME GET NO FOOD AGAIN. MAN THEN WALKS AWAY SAYING, "I COME BACK LATER WHEN YOU CO-OPERATE!" ME SHOUT TO MAN, "ME SO HUNGRY!" BUT MAN LISTENS NOT. LATER, MAN RETURNS WITH FISH. ME TIRED AND WEAK... ME NEED FOOD. MAN GIVES ME SAME SIGNAL FROM BEFORE. ME THEN PUT ALL MY STRENGTH INTO MYSELF AND LEAP OUT OF WATER. ME DIVE INTO WATER AND... ME HIT THE BOTTOM WITH THE FRONT OF MY MOUTH. PAINFUL. I HEAR WHISTLE SOUND AND I RETURN TO MAN. MAN FINALLY GIVES FISH TO ME TO EAT, BUT ME STILL... HUNGRY... —

Hearing the dolphin's experience made Dolphi feel appalled. It sounded like the dolphin was talking about a dolphin trainer who wasn't feeding him very well. When the dolphin mentioned hitting the bottom after doing a jump, that had to have meant that the water level was shallow.

—ME... SO... HUN... GRYYYYYY... — the dolphin moaned.

"That's sounds terrible..." Dolphi said, thinking about what the dolphin was telling him.

—WHY DID MAN PUT ME THROUGH SO MUCH PAIN?— the dolphin asked. —ME NEVER DID ANYTHING TO MAN. MAN DON'T SEEM TO UNDERSTAND ME. ME SO SAD AND AFRAID. ME MISSES FAMILY SO MUCH... —

Dolphi then swam up to the dolphin and hugged him. "Are you hungry now?" Dolphi asked.

—YES... — the dolphin said. —TERRIBLE PAIN. EVEN IF YOU LOOK STRANGE, YOU CARE FOR ME. YOUR UNDERSTANDING IS HEALING MY PAIN. THANK YOU... FOR SHOWING ME... KINDNESS... —

Dolphi then looked at the dolphin's body. He could almost see the outline of its rib cage. "Oh my god..." Dolphi said feeling concerned. "You are so emaciated! That man you told me about... did this to you?" He felt something was very wrong. "I am hungry too.

If only..." Dolphi looked around for a way out. He went up the stairs and onto the platform. He then walked up another set of stairs leading to a walkway. He walked along it and faced the chain-link door. He tried opening it, but it was locked. He could see a padlock on the door.

Dolphi suddenly heard footsteps coming from straight ahead. He saw a flashlight shining around. The shadowy figure came closer to Dolphi. Dolphi then ran back the way he came and jumped back into the water feet first. Before his head was about to go under, he hit the bottom. He felt a bit shocked as he didn't expect the water to be so shallow. He stood silent and motionless as the light came closer. As the person approached the fenced wall, the flashlight was pointed down into the water at Dolphi's face. Dolphi, with only his head sticking out of the water, shut his eyes tight. The light was on him for a few seconds and then the light went to the door. When Dolphi opened his eyes, he could see the figure standing at the door with something else in his hands. —IS HE BACK?— the dolphin asked.

"Shh..." Dolphi whispered. He watched as the individual broke the door open with what looked like a pair of wire cutters. The door opened and the individual came walking along the dock. Dolphi moved far off to the side as the mysterious figure came down onto the platform. The figure jumped into the water, waded up to a fence and started cutting a hole. Dolphi then realized that this person was an animal right's activist. Dolphi continued to watch silently as the man was already making a fine hole in the fence. —WHAT GOES ON?— asked the dolphin.

"Maybe we're being saved," Dolphi whispered in his quietest voice. The flashlight shone at Dolphi and his dolphin friend again. This time, Dolphi went under the water completely. It was pitch black underwater, but when Dolphi used his echolocation, he could see the fence and the skeleton of the figure in a hazy white color. "My echolocation!" thought Dolphi. "I forgot about that!" He performed it on the dolphin and he could see its skeleton and inner organs. To Dolphi, seeing those things was freaky, but something about them freaked him out even more. From what he saw, the dolphin's skeleton looked frail and he could see something inside its stomach. They were ulcers caused by stress. Dolphi then looked at the ocean floor of the enclosure. There were bits and pieces of garbage that people must have dropped in the pen while they visited. There were candy wrappers, hair bands, plastic bags and even coins. Something about the water also tasted funny to Dolphi. He swam to the fence opposite the activist and used his echolocation to see onto the other side. He saw a pipe slowly spewing something liquidy out. Suddenly, to Dolphi's horror, he realized that was a sewer outlet!

Dolphi then popped his head out of the water and saw that the activist had made a hole large enough for the dolphin to escape. He was now standing on the platform. "You should go," Dolphi whispered to the dolphin.

—ME... CAN'T— the dolphin moaned, —ME SO HUNGRY...—

"Hmm..." Dolphi thought. "I'll think of something. I'll see if I can find a fish house. Wait here." Dolphi felt very bad for the dolphin. He could not believe the pain the dolphin had endured and the conditions it was in. One thing was for sure, Dolphi was not going to live in that polluted water.

Dolphi swam over to the platform. "Excuse me," he said calmly to the activist. The activist turned and gasped in shock, thinking he had been caught. The flashlight beamed at Dolphi. "I do not wish you any harm," Dolphi said as he raised his hands out of the water in an assuring gesture. "Do you understand?"

"... Yes," said the activist. "Whatever you are, I guess you can leave anytime you wish. But what about the other dolphin?"

"He's very weak from hunger, he needs some food and then he'll go." Dolphi hopped up onto the platform. The activist was a man. He shone his flashlight at Dolphi's full body. "Wow... !" exclaimed the man.

"You've got a lot of guts coming here, trespassing and vandalizing the facility," Dolphi said. "Did you come here for me?"

"I noticed they were introducing a new dolphin to this godforsaken death pit next to a sewer outlet. You must be 'Dolphi the Dolphin Man' as the sign here advertised."

"You know, there is so much garbage on the bottom from people who have been here in the past," Dolphi said. "I just arrived here and I haven't encountered any visitors other than you. How come nobody reported the sewer thing? Surely somebody could have noticed."

"Wait a minute," the man said, "what's that around your neck?"

Dolphi touched his neck and realized that special 'invisible fence' collar was still on him.

"Something to prevent me from running away," Dolphi said feeling a little angry. "An electric collar that will shock me if I cross the perimeter."

"Unbelievable..." the activist said.

"Who are you?" Dolphi asked. Before the man was about to speak, a bright light filled the whole place. Light bulbs everywhere lit up and now, Dolphi could see everything. "Who's there?!" someone yelled. Dolphi fell back into the water and returned to where he had been clamped down. He lay with his hands and feet in the now broken clamps to make it look like he was still held down. As people ran into the enclosure, Dolphi could see they were security guards. The one who shouted was the security chief. "Don't try to run, intruder!" the chief yelled. "Drop your wire cutters and come on up here!" The activist was wearing a black wetsuit with a hood on. He did as the guards asked him and walked up to the land with his hands above his head. He was grabbed and pushed away from the enclosure and then surrounded. The security chief faced the activist. "You have no right to be here!" he said.

"You have no right to be holding these dolphins against their will!" the activist said back.

"You activists are fanatical, crazy, trouble makers," the chief said. "Leave now and you'll save yourself some trouble, or face dire consequences."

Dolphi swam out of his spot and climbed onto the platform while the guards were distracted by the activist. He grabbed the wire cutters that had been left behind and ran up the stairs to the dock. He saw the guards surrounding the activist. He just stood there without saying a word.

"I said leave or you'll be sorry!" the chief shouted.

"Not without the dolphins," the activist said as he slowly walked up to the security chief, "not without justice..." He then put his face right up to the chief and said, "... and not without my wire cutters!"

That did it. The security chief shoved the man hard and he fell to the ground. "Teach this extremist a lesson!" he ordered his men. They began kicking and beating the activist up.

"I don't want to fight!" he shouted.

"You're the one who asked for it, you intruding bastard!" one of the guards said. Dolphi ran towards the entrance. There were four guards around the activist. Two of them were attacking him. Dolphi could not believe this! Those guys were beating a man up for trying to help a suffering dolphin! He couldn't stand for this and without thinking, he ran through the door that was broken open and felt the collar zap him. He fell to the ground growling in pain.

The security chief turned around. "Hey, look who's trying to escape!" he said to his men. Dolphi moved back into the pen to stop the electrocution. "Stay in your pen if you want the pain to stop," the chief told Dolphi. Dolphi was face down on the dock. He quickly used the wire cutters on the collar. "I wouldn't do that," the chief warned. As Dolphi cut into the material, he was electrocuted again. He dropped the wire cutters, grabbed the collar and pulled on the material where the cut was made. Dolphi pulled hard, but the material was very strong and the collar shocked him even more. "You are only making this harder on yourself, mutant!" the chief said mockingly.

Dolphi was very angry. He then pulled the collar with all his strength and yelled really loud. The collar then broke off and the electrocution stopped.

The chief sighed and said, "I told you… NOT TO DO THAT!!!" He then rushed at Dolphi who was on his hands and knees, weak from the pain and kicked him in the chest. Dolphi fell and rolled onto his back. The chief then tried to press his foot down on Dolphi's neck, but Dolphi grabbed it and tried to move it away.

"How does the strength of a third-degree black belt feel?" he asked Dolphi. Dolphi then rolled back and quickly put his foot into the man's stomach. He then rolled forward, still holding the man's foot and threw him over his head and slammed him face down onto the dock. Dolphi then grabbed the collar, jumped on the man's back and put it around his neck. "How does dolphin power and justice for the animals in this cesspool feel?!" Dolphi yelled as the collar shocked the man. He then grabbed the man's head and slammed it hard into the dock, knocking him out.

The guards who were beating up the activist stopped and faced Dolphi.

"I'll give all of you one chance," Dolphi said as calmly as possible, "go home and you won't get hurt." Dolphi did not approve of senseless fighting and wanted to be diplomatic to his enemies no matter what the situation. His offer to the guards was short, simple and strong, but they replied with hostility.

"Never!" one guard said. "We have a loyalty to the Navy and to our homeland; the United States of America!" The guards must have seen Dolphi's outward appearance as animal and not human.

"Don't make me fillet you shrimps!" Dolphi warned. The guard who spoke to Dolphi then rushed at him. Dolphi grabbed him and tossed him into the enclosure's chain link fence behind himself. Another guard rushed at Dolphi and tried to punch him, but Dolphi dodged it, grabbed the guard's shirt, picked him up with one hand and rammed his snout into the guard's stomach three times.

"Behind you!" the activist shouted. Dolphi turned and saw the guard he just threw down running at him. He quickly threw the guard he was holding like a projectile at the other guard knocking him down. Dolphi turned to see the two remaining guards attacking the activist again, probably because he had warned Dolphi. Dolphi ran over and grabbed the two guards. He slammed their bodies together and threw them over onto the fallen guards to try and pile them up. The two guards tried to get up as quickly as possible.

This was complete insanity to Dolphi. He wanted this to end. He felt angry and aggressive. Those feelings triggered something inside him. "Oh..." Dolphi groaned, "my head..." Dolphi could feel pain in his head as the two guards were about to run at him. Dolphi faced the two guards and then let out a loud yell. The guards suddenly got swept off their feet and catapulted into the enclosure fence, knocking them out as they hit the ground. Dolphi rubbed his head.

"What happened?" he thought. "That felt familiar... "

The activist slowly got up off the ground. Dolphi walked up to him. "Are you okay?" Dolphi asked.

"I think so," the man said as he dusted himself off. "Thanks for saving me. How did you do that, that yell that sent them flying?"

"I don't know," Dolphi said. "But somehow, I don't think that's the secret power of the dolphin."

"Say, are you the one who killed a criminal as the news reported earlier?"

"Well, the police spoke to me about that and I persuaded them that I did not knowingly murder that man. Whatever I did just now was not my fault. You believe me, right?"

"I suppose so. You helped me and I owe you for that. Although it would have been better if they were fought with passive resistance."

"You mean civil disobedience?"

"Yes. Break a law that's unjust and when the authorities confront you, you do nothing to them but try to be their friend. Any violence is their own."

"That sounds crazy," Dolphi said.

"True, but Mahatma Ghandi proved it worked and so did Martin Luther King Jr."

"Those guards acted more fanatical than you," Dolphi said. "I'd like to find out what the hell is wrong with this whole place. Those guys mentioned the Navy. Why?"

The activist sighed and said, "allow me to explain. In the 1970's Congress passed an Act that was supposed to protect marine mammals from human harm, but it didn't. The Act was given to the Department of Commerce and—"

"They let one of their agencies enforce it," Dolphi concluded, "the NMFS of NOAA."

"That's right," the activist said, "how did you know?"

"I was once human. I was a marine mammal veterinarian working at the Marine Research Institute Labs and an experiment turned me into this. It's too long a story to go into right now. Now, what about the Navy that one of the guards mentioned?"

"You want to know something interesting?" the activist asked. "The NMFS unanimously approved the Navy to use marine mammals for whatever reasons they choose. Like, for example, retrieving defective submarine torpedoes that are resting on the bottom which are likely to explode and 'keeping out enemy submarines' as they say. These guys state that, "any means to safeguard our defense is justified". That's true, but that's their belief. They only care about their judgment, their judgment only and that to listen to the advice of others, even their own citizens, is wrong to them. It seems my suspicions are correct, that somehow, the Navy is connected to this place. It makes me so mad. Amusement parks, $wim-with-the-dolphin facilities, whatever we're using dolphins for, they are dying in captivity all for the sake of big business disguised as what this enormous industry calls 'Scientific Research'. This industry even helps organize a dolphin slaughter in Japan called 'drive fisheries'. They cut off the dolphins with nets, push them into a bay and then people club or slash the animals to death. Some of the animals are not slaughtered. Some get diverted elsewhere and then a bunch of dolphin trainers select the animals they want to train and they don't even care about the animals that are dying. I heard that some people right here in America organized those events."

Dolphi was almost speechless. "I had no idea... such things were happening. I grew up wanting to stop dolphins getting caught in fishermen's nets and drowning, but I had no idea about these brutal things! How could all that have gone unnoticed?"

"I don't know," the activist said. "I wish we all knew. Perhaps people are afraid, very afraid of the truth. They must see the truth as some kind of monster; a monster called 'reality'."

"You know, you sound like the-man-who-knew-too-much," Dolphi said.

"Yes, and I want to learn even more. So there you have it. Thanks to some careless decisions, all the marine mammals in the ocean have been handed over to a government agency that favours big business on a nice big silver platter."

Dolphi growled in disgust. "Well, thanks for rescuing me anyway. By the way, is there a fish house here?"

"Yes," the activist said as he pointed. "That brown door with the light above."

"Okay, you should get going now," Dolphi said. "I'll get the dolphin out of here. Oh, and I think you will need those." He ran over to the wire cutters, picked them up and then returned them to the man. "One more thing," Dolphi asked, "what's our location? Where are we?"

"Key West," the activist replied. "Cheers!" he said as he went back the way he came. The man turned a corner and then disappeared.

"... Key West?!" Dolphi thought. "I have to go through all the Keys to reach my children? Great..." He suddenly remembered something. "The dolphin!"

Dolphi walked towards the fish house. He reached the door and turned the handle and as he mostly expected, it was locked. A sign on the door said, 'Fish house. Keep door closed at all times'. Dolphi backed up and ran into the door shoulder first and it burst open. He walked inside and found a light switch. The room lit up and he saw a kitchen-like environment. He looked around for stuff the dolphin could eat. He noticed a freezer that opened like a treasure chest. Inside, he could see cloudy water with a bunch of dead fish that looked thawed out. "Eww…" he thought.

He then noticed a letter on a table next to the freezer. It was addressed to the Animal and Plant Health Inspection Service (APHIS). It was entitled, 'Facility Status'. Curious, he opened it and read the contents. The letter had today's date on it and this is what Dolphi read:

'APHIS officials,

Dolphin World's report: We have recently received a new male bottlenose dolphin (tursiops truncatus), but it is nothing like we have ever seen before. I shall explain this species to the inspectors on their next visit.

For facility status, the animal's environment is connected to the ocean and is surrounded by a thirty (30) foot high chain link fence. It goes out to sea from the shore for fifty (50) feet and is thirty (30) feet wide. The depth of the enclosure measures about ten (10) feet deep and construction has done no damage to the natural environment.

For the fish house, fish is well stored and is sprayed to remove infections and harmful bacteria. However, a problem has arisen. Our only refrigeration unit died a few days ago and we lack the funds to replace the unit because we had to spend a great deal of money to purchase the creature as specified by the Marine Mammal Protection Act. We are hoping the new addition to our facility will attract more visitors to help us afford to pay for a new unit. Hopefully, the food will remain edible long enough for the animals to survive until a new fridge arrives. This concludes my report.

Sincerely, Dennis Glack,
President of Dolphin World.

Dolphi was furious at some of the things mentioned and other things not. "Ten feet deep," he thought, "a freezer that has been dead several days and no mention of the sewer outlet?!" He then crumpled the letter into a small ball and tossed it onto the ground. "Anyway, I should get that poor soul some food. Then, I'll investigate this place further." He grabbed a bucket that was nearby and filled it with fish. As he went out and back in the direction of the pen, he ate some of the fish himself. "This doesn't taste very good," Dolphi thought, "I hope this will be enough for the dolphin and is okay to eat."

He returned to the pen and he saw the dolphin swimming around in a circle. Dolphi ran down and hopped into the water. "I have your food, my friend," Dolphi said. The dolphin swam up to Dolphi and Dolphi began to put fish into the dolphin's mouth. After feeding him a dozen, the dolphin felt relieved. —THANK YOU VERY MUCH— he said.

"You should leave this hellhole now," said Dolphi. "You do not want this to happen to you ever again. I wish you the best of luck."

—ME WILL NEVER FORGET YOU AND YOUR KIND-NESS— the dolphin said.

—FAREWELL.— He swam through the hole that the activist had made and disappeared into the night.

Dolphi was very shaken by the facility's corruption. He also realized that in all his years as a veterinarian for marine mammals, this was the first time he had managed to help one in captivity. In the past, he would take a report of the animals but was able to do very little for them. It hadn't occurred to him that keeping the animals in captivity was wrong. He hadn't realized that many dolphins were living in appalling conditions.

He left the water and went out of the enclosure. There was something very fishy about this facility and he was going to find out without anyone interfering. Finding his children was important to him, but that would have to wait. Tonight, his passion for dolphins had been struck by a bolt of lightning and he wanted to investigate this facility with a clear mind. If there were any other people around, he would ask them what he should have asked in the days before. It was time to ask questions.

CHAPTER 22

Truths and Lies

"Truthful words are not beautiful;
Beautiful words are not truthful.
Good words are not persuasive;
persuasive words are not good."
—Lao Tzu

D OLPHI EXPLORED THE facility to see if he could find anything else suspicious about the place, for he loved exploring and he wanted to find out why the facility staff was hostile and why the dolphin was mistreated. He came up to a small structure that said on its doors, 'Storage, Employees Only.' The doors were also locked.

"I guess I have to ram into doors once again," Dolphi thought. He then ran at the doors and exploded into them. These doors were a little stronger than those in the fish house, so they opened only partially. Dolphi then charged again and this time, the doors opened fully. He searched the walls for a light switch, but was unable to find one. He then used his echolocation as another method. He saw lots of pen equipment such as platform floats, stretchers and so on. He saw a light switch on another wall, so he headed over and turned it on. The room lit up and he looked around trying to find anything out of place. So far, everything seemed normal. He used his sonar again all around the room to see if anything was being hidden from view. When he scanned a group of large boats stacked vertically against a wall, he thought he saw what looked like the outline of a stairway going down. He walked over to the boats and tried to push them aside. They were extremely heavy and difficult to move, but Dolphi kept pushing with all his might. The boats inched away with every push. As he finally pushed the boats a few feet over, he stopped to catch his breath.

He looked at the wall and scanned it with his sonar. He definitely saw a staircase. He rubbed his hands around the wall trying to feel for an outline of a door. He then felt a small hole where his fingers could fit and pulled on it. It didn't open, so Dolphi immediately rammed it shoulder first. However, the door wasn't locked, so it sprung open inwards and Dolphi tumbled down the stairs. He stopped on a landing of the staircase. He got up and rubbed his side.

"Ow… I guess I didn't think of *pushing* on the door."

He went down the other half of the stairs and found total darkness at first, but scanning with his sonar he saw a light bulb with a pull string. He went over and pulled it. The room lit up and he saw several green, camouflaged, tarpaulins covering unknown items underneath. Dolphi was about to find out what was being hidden.

He yanked off one tarp and saw unusual items. They looked like stuff that a dolphin would bite onto and hold. On the end of one item, there was something that looked like it could grab large objects. He then spotted a small device that had a switch on it. When he pressed it, he suddenly felt a myriad of vibrations come out of it and felt his head tingle. When he shut his eyes, he saw a barrage of white and nothing else. He turned the device off and the vibrations stopped.

"This must be an underwater pinger used to summon the animals," he thought. As he searched through more strange items, he picked up another one that was meant to be held by the mouth. It had a camera on the front. He then studied the item all over and saw something written on it. It said, 'Property of US Navy'.

"Oh my god…" Dolphi thought confused. "They are hiding this stuff underneath an ordinary dolphin facility and are… secretly training dolphins to be used for the Navy? I was put here to be part of such a program? Those guards I just knocked out must all work for the Navy. I think this stuff should be seen out in the open in the parking lot." Dolphi lay out the tarp, put as many items as he could on it and then folded it up into a giant sack. He felt he could carry it with one hand, so he uncovered another bunch of items and went through the same procedure. Dolphi had no idea what most of the tools and gimmicks were, but whatever was being hidden, needed to be exposed. He certainly did not want to use any of those things and he had no intention of serving the Navy and retrieving a defective torpedo or some other explosive that could go off in his face.

He carried the giant bags up the stairs and squeezed his way through the door. He then left the storage room and headed back to where he had fought the security guards. They were regaining consciousness.

"Attention everyone!" Dolphi shouted. The men slowly looked up at Dolphi. "You have messed with the wrong dolphin! I have discovered a dirty little secret in this facility and you are all responsible for hiding it from the public! I am going to expose what I have in these bags outside the facility! If I find out that the items have been hidden once again, I won't go easy on you if I see you next time! Now dust yourselves off and go home to your mommies!" After what Dolphi had done to them, he struck fear in their minds and they all hurried away as quickly as they could. They ran in the direction of a building that looked like the entrance.

Dolphi began to walk towards the building with the bags in his hands. As he approached the doors, he suddenly felt someone jump on him. Dolphi dropped the bags and struggled to get the person off. He quickly slammed his back into a nearby wall. The unknown person detached from Dolphi and fell to the ground. Dolphi turned around and saw a man in a wetsuit. The man moaned a little and then looked up at Dolphi. When he saw Dolphi's body, he crawled backwards into the wall and stopped. The man had a goatee beard and appeared to be in his forties.

"Hey," Dolphi said to the man, "are you a dolphin trainer?"

"Y… yes I am," the man replied nervously.

"Why did you attack me?"

"I saw what you did to the guards!"

"Judging from their actions, Glack's staff were a bunch of hard asses."

"How do you know about Glack?" asked the trainer.

"That doesn't matter," Dolphi said. "I'd like to know what you are doing here at this time."

"I… heard about a new addition to this place and I was eager to see him. You must be Dolphi the Dolphin Man."

"I'm not called The Dolphin... look, how long have you been working here?"

"I have been working with dolphins for ten years and I transferred here to Dolphin World not long ago. Tell me, do you like Pogo's home?"

"Pogo?" Dolphi asked. "Oh, that must be the name of the dolphin I met."

"It is," the trainer replied. "And my name is Jordan Sinclair. I have been training my adorable Pogo all week."

"Okay... has he been working well with you?" Dolphi asked.

"He's been a little tricky, but I've learned that if you are patient with new animals, you get to know each other better and relationships build. This dolphin likes his lagoon sanctuary and we have gotten along well."

"Has he been fed well?"

"What are you trying to find out?" Jordan asked.

"Just trying to build a relationship with you," Dolphi replied almost sarcastically.

"Say," Jordon asked looking behind Dolphi, "what are in those bags?"

After glancing at them, Dolphi turned and stared into the trainer's eyes. "I have been conducting a little investigation into this facility and I have found out that things here are not what they seem to be. Now, have you noticed anything strange about this facility?"

"No, I haven't," Jordan said.

"What about the dolphin's food? Has it been refrigerated well?"

"Well, we keep our food supply for the animals nice and healthy—"

"In a freezer that has been broken for days?!" Dolphi asked strictly.

"What?"

"I helped myself to some of the fish from the only refrigeration unit in this place and all the food's gone off! Did you not notice that?"

"Well..." Jordan said nervously, "yes, but things were in a bit of a tizzy. There was a bit of an argument about what to do with the facility's struggling budget; the cost to replace the freezer for instance."

"And so *I* was purchased over the dolphin's health and food supply?!" Dolphi angrily asked.

"I didn't know!" Jordan said feeling a bit frightened. "Don't yell, please."

"I think I know what you were doing to that dolphin of yours. You wouldn't feed him if he didn't do a trick or if he did a trick incorrectly. 'Pogo' as you call him, told me that."

"He... *talked* to you?" asked the trainer.

"Not talked," said Dolphi, "he communicated with me and somehow, I could understand him. Now, about the way you trained him..."

"That training is ordinary," Jordan said. "It's the only way we dolphin trainers can help the dolphin go through a simple, harmless process that—"

Dolphi pointed a finger at the trainer and accusingly said, "you people trapped a family of dolphins in a bay, surrounded them with large nets, took one of them from its family, put it in a filthy cage and made it do tricks for food against its will just for your own selfish entertainment!"

"No," Jordan denied, "that's not true! I—"

"Pogo even told me how you just picked up the food and walked away leaving him hungry because he couldn't satisfy you!"

"But we take good care of him!"

"You're a lousy liar," Dolphi said bitterly, "and you're pathetic. Do you think that animal appreciated what you did to him? Were you going to put me through the same thing? Give me some answers!"

"Look, I wasn't involved in the collection of Pogo, okay?" Jordan said. "I do know that a representative from some agency arrived earlier today with an unusual species of dolphin, you. They said that you could be a risk to people, so you were placed in security. I guess Mr. Glack had bought you. I didn't get to see you, and security measures were put in place. I just came back here and I was planning on seeing you for the first time. That's when the lights came on and there was fighting. I just hid in this corner and waited for the action to stop. I saw some guy run by, but I didn't stop him."

"Let me tell you something," Dolphi said. "When I was in that enclosure, I saw garbage at the bottom *and* I saw a nearby sewer outlet that's poisoning the poor dolphin! I found & read a letter saying that the water's depth is ten feet, but when I stood up in the water, it was only half that depth; enough for the dolphin to hit the bottom after doing a jump."

The dolphin trainer didn't say a word. Dolphi felt very angry about the whole facility's expertise or rather lack of expertise. "So," Dolphi said, "you can do anything you want to a dolphin, such as starving it of food to make it hungry to force it to do silly things and not get in trouble for it? The poor dolphin gets emaciated, rots in bad water and nothing gets done about it?"

"W… What are you saying?!" Jordan nervously asked, not understanding.

"Did Pogo have to go through all that bull in the name of amusement?!" Dolphi was getting angry thinking about how man could be so cruel to dolphins and not get in trouble.

"I don't know what you are talking about!" Jordan said. Dolphi then grabbed the man by the back, picked him up and slammed him face first into the wall. Jordan groaned loudly in pain. "That dolphin was dying in those conditions, you idiot!" Dolphi yelled. "That is why that intruder was here! He was trying to help that poor animal and your people were beating him up! What is this facility planning to do with dolphins, what were they planning to do with Pogo," Dolphi then pushed the man harder into the wall and said, "and what were they planning to do with ME?!"

"I… I can't help you," the trainer yelled, "I just work here! I don't know what is going on! I don't make policy!" Dolphi then dropped the trainer and he lay moaning against the wall. "God, please don't hurt me!" he begged.

"You guys are lying to the public about the health and conditions of the animals here. You are a big fat disgrace!"

"Please, no more!" Jordan cried.

"Did you know about the sewer? Did you?!" The trainer still sobbed. "Answer me!" Dolphi yelled.

"YES! YES!" Jordan replied desperately. "Oh god…" As Jordan sobbed, Dolphi was silent. The trainer was overwhelmed with sorrow and Dolphi felt very upset too. "I don't know why the sewer's there!" Jordan said through his sobs. "All I know is that I noticed it a few days after I started working here! I did go to Mr. Glack about it, but he insisted it wouldn't be a serious problem to the animal's health! We can't move the facility elsewhere because it's too expensive!"

"Why can't you just tell the truth to people about what is going on?" Dolphi asked calmly.

"I... I can't do that!" Jordan said through his sobs. "I wouldn't see my favorite animal in the whole wide world again if I told people about the corruption!"

"Corruption huh?" asked Dolphi. "Is something scaring you?"

"Jesus, did you have to hurt me... ?" Jordan asked. "I don't like fighting and whatever you are, does scare me a little."

"I mean, when you become a dolphin trainer," said Dolphi, "you must have been given an order to lie to people about the dark side of dolphin captivity but I'm pretty sure lying to people isn't in your job description. You're probably afraid that if you told the public about the horrible things that have been happening to dolphins in captivity, your boss would kick you out, fire you and take away your relationship with dolphins not just for giving the facility a bad image, but for mutiny as well. Does that sound far fetched?"

"That... is none of your business," said Jordan.

Dolphi then cleared his throat.

"I mean," the trainer said, "I had absolutely no idea. I was just following orders."

"Following orders..." Dolphi thought in disgust. "Being ordered to lie about the corruption... You are told to lie to people... and children, to disguise a gulag for dolphins."

"N... no," Jordan said, "you're wrong! This isn't a gulag, it's a beautiful place where a dolphin swims in his beautiful lagoon."

"Lagoon..." thought Dolphi, "Instead of *captivity*, you use *that* word."

"No way," Jordan denied, "it's the exact same thing!"

"Enough already," Dolphi said, feeling he couldn't be any more angry. This man was clearly weak minded and couldn't think for himself. Unknown to Dolphi, somebody was behind him. "Listen, stop crying and look at me," Dolphi said as he put his hand on the trainer's chin and lifted it up. Jordan had noticed the security chief a dozen feet behind Dolphi crouched down and slowly creeping up behind him, but Jordan said nothing.

"This is your dolphin buddy talking to you," Dolphi continued. "If you love dolphins with all your heart, then you will listen to this one. You have absolutely no idea what you are involved in and you don't even know what you are saying. Those tarps with stuff in them are loaded with equipment for dolphins and other marine life that are being used in US Navy operations." Jordan looked confused. "Those guards that ran away were probably working for the Navy."

"What?" Jordan asked baffled. "They never told me that. They said they were part of the facility."

"That stuff behind me was being hidden behind a bunch of boats that concealed a passage going down inside the storage shed. If you don't believe me, you can go in there and go down the hidden passage and see for yourself. You'll find things that say 'property of US Navy' on them." Jordan didn't know what to say. The chief continued to creep up on Dolphi. He had a combat knife in his hand.

"You want to know what I think?" Dolphi asked Jordan. "I think you are being used by your bosses, especially Glack. He probably doesn't even care about you or the dolphins you train, with the exception of all the money the animals haul in. He must have been denying you the right to speak your mind freely. So please, please help me so I can help you."

"Help me?" Jordan asked sniffing.

"Yes, Jordan," Dolphi said. "If anybody here is going to respect your thoughts and feelings, then the only one here, is me. Let's help each other. What do you say?"

Jordan was thinking hard to himself. He thought about Dolphi's offer and the chief who was about to sneak right up behind Dolphi and either jam the knife into him or slash his throat. The chief raised the knife up and was prepared to stab Dolphi. Jordan loved dolphins and this one had made him aware of how things really were. The chief was about to kill Dolphi... and Jordan was not about to let that happen!

"Behind you!" Jordan shouted. Dolphi quickly turned and saw the chief about to stab him. He quickly grabbed the hand and stopped the blade from stabbing him just inches away from his face. The chief had blood on his face from when Dolphi had slammed his face into the ground, breaking his nose in the process. The chief was seething with anger. Dolphi was also angry as he tried to get the knife away from him. He jerked the arm that was holding the knife off to the side and twisted it. The chief's arm broke and he yelled out in pain. He dropped the knife and Dolphi pushed him hard onto the ground. The chief was growling and yelling loudly in pain as he held his broken arm with the other. Dolphi walked up to the fallen chief and said, "did you know that I don't know any martial arts?"

"You goddamn mutant!" the chief yelled in agony. "I'm authorized to kill you, should you get out of hand! Agh!"

"I'm sorry for that," Dolphi said. "I never wanted to fight you, but the hospitality that you Navy guys are offering me here, is unbelievably pathetic!"

"Yes, I do work for the Navy," the chief replied, "and when they find out about this, the entire fleet will come after you and put you on a MEAT HOOK!" He moaned in pain again.

"I don't understand," Dolphi said. "Why do you have to be so abusive to me and dolphins?"

"The animals are expendable commodities for science and research!" the chief said. "It's not abuse, but justified defense for my country!"

"You know something," Dolphi said as he bent down to him, "this is my country too. I may be a mutant dolphin, but I'm no animal, I'm a human being turned Frankenstein's Monster." Dolphi got up and walked over to Jordan.

"Huh…" the chief said at what Dolphi told him. He then took his unbroken arm and reached for something on his waist. "If that's the case… then die, monster!"

He sat up and suddenly pulled out a gun from his holster that Dolphi had not noticed before.

"DON'T!" Jordan yelled as he covered his ears. A gunshot suddenly fired, but Dolphi didn't feel anything. Dolphi stood completely still, wondering if he had been hit. After a moment of complete stillness, he slowly turned his head around and saw the chief sitting on the ground. However, the chief didn't move and his eyes and mouth were open and still. There was blood slowly oozing from his chest. Dolphi had not been shot, the chief had. He dropped his gun, fell backwards and lay silent.

"Who's there?!" Dolphi yelled. He immediately used his sonar to see if he could see who had shot the chief. There was a building on the other side of the fence. Up on a balcony, he saw a skeletal image starting to move. "Hey!" Dolphi shouted. The figure suddenly jumped off the balcony. From what Dolphi saw, the skeleton looked human, but it had a long tail bone and its head looked reptilian. Dolphi tried to jump the fence, but it was too high. He thought about going after whoever or whatever that was, but he probably would have lost him. Suddenly, Dolphi remembered back to when he saw a suspicious figure in a bank truck fleeing the police, back to when he saw a suspicious figure running out of the Marine Research Institute Labs after an explosion. "Was that a half-human reptilian mutant?" Dolphi thought. "Somehow, I don't think Mr. Jem created those things that attacked the M.R.I.L. But where did they come from? Are they operating alone?" He then turned to see the fallen chief lying motionless. He put his fingers on the man's neck. The dolphin trainer slowly walked up to the body. Dolphi looked up and said, "he's dead."

"Oh god..." Jordan whispered in horror.

"Don't look at the body," Dolphi said. "Let's just head back to where we were." As the two went back over to the wall where they had been talking, Dolphi looked at Jordan. "It would appear as if somebody, or some*thing* rather, has saved my life. But I doubt that my savior is coming down here to see me."

"What are we going to do?" Jordan asked nervously.

"I don't know," Dolphi said, "but you are a witness to that killing, so if you told police about it—"

"I can't, I'm so scared!" Jordan said.

Dolphi sighed. "I don't know what else to do about this. For now, let's just try not to think about it. Let's talk about dolphins."

"Okay," Jordan said. "I guess this is it for me. I'm no longer a dolphin trainer. I have been following orders blindly and I feel like such a fool."

"Why did you become a trainer in the first place?" Dolphi asked.

The question made Jordan ponder. "I suppose it was a way for me to be with the creatures that I loved since I was a little boy. I saw dolphins for the very first time at the Miami Seaquarium. The animal's intelligence and friendliness was a big motivator for me. I knew about their destruction from us humans; pollution and fishermen netting and so on. At the time, I thought that if I became a dolphin trainer, I could do something to ensure their survival."

"Not what you hoped it would be, huh? Weren't quite living the dream you wanted?" Dolphi asked.

"Perhaps not."

"How do you suppose you will help dolphins now?" Dolphi asked.

"Maybe I'll spread the message that there is corruption in the dolphin captivity world. Perhaps dolphins do not belong in captivity… and neither do you."

"Yes," Dolphi said.

"God, I feel so stupid…" Jordan said miserably as he thought about what he had been doing to dolphins he worked with in the past as well as what he had done to the dolphin named Pogo. He began crying again.

Dolphi then wiped the trainer's tears. "It's okay, Jordan," Dolphi said calmly.

"I'm upset because I feel everything I worked for was in vain," Jordan said. "I still want to be with the animals. Think about all the people those animals have inspired. Think of all the people they *will* inspire. Think about all the things research has found out and *will* find out about them, everything we've accomplished together and everything we *will*—"

"I get the point," Dolphi said. "I know they are important creatures, but such research does not have to be cruel. I know you didn't mean to be cruel to the animals, but then again, how was anyone supposed to know?"

"Maybe our dedication to the animals in the beginning came at a big cost. Did I hear you say you used to be a human?"

"It's a long story," said Dolphi, "I know it's been very hard for you tonight, but you are beginning to understand the world of truths and lies now. I would also like to apologize for roughing you up a bit. I had to knock a little sense into you because you were being really naïve."

"Your apology is accepted," Jordan said. "I'm also sorry for jumping on you like that."

"Back at you," Dolphi smiled.

"Oh, I think it is time for me to apologize to Pogo and get him out of here."

"That's already been done," Dolphi said. "Pogo has been freed by that animal activist who was here. Your dolphin is back in the wild now. The actions of that activist may have been crazy, but he got me thinking differently. I am familiar with people who protested against using dolphins for the Navy, but at the time, I didn't take it seriously. I used to be a veterinarian for marine mammals when I was human, but now, I'm having second thoughts about my job. I don't think all of my questions that I asked in the past were being answered by the dolphin facility owners. I've never met Dennis Glack, this facility's president before, but I had met one guy who accused me of telling him how to do his job. I was just asking questions and giving suggestions that made strong points."

"Interesting," Jordan said. "My boss told me once that there are some nosey vets out there and he mentioned one of them was a guy named Seal Jay or something."

Dolphi frowned a little. "*Steele* Jay?" he asked.

"Of course," Jordan said, "that's what I meant. Do you know him?"

This was interesting to Dolphi. Other dolphin facilities seemed to know who he was. He was beginning to suspect there was a major conspiracy going on, but wasn't exactly sure what it was.

"He's nobody important," Dolphi said. "I should get going now. I've got to find loved ones, but I need a vehicle and roadmap to find them."

"They wouldn't happen to be walking, talking dolphins like yourself?"

"No and I hope not."

"Okay, no problem," Jordan said. "You can borrow my vehicle. Follow me."

Dolphi followed Jordan around a corner to where a group of lockers were located. Jordan turned his lock's dial and opened the lock. He opened the small door and took out a car key. "It's a brown car out in the parking lot," he said as he handed it to Dolphi. "Go through the building where we met and you will find yourself in the front entrance and gift store. Go out the other door and you're free from this place."

"Thank you very much," Dolphi said. "I will abandon your car on Dilton Blvd. near a place called the Dolphin's Lagoon Inn. I'm sure that you will find it there tomorrow. But now, we should get out of here."

"I'm going to pack up a few things and then... I'll call the police and tell them what happened with that dead guy," Jordan said.

"What will you tell them?"

"I'll think of something. So, I guess this is goodbye?"

"Yeah, maybe we will meet again someday," Dolphi said. He then made a series of clicking noises at the ex-dolphin trainer. Jordan smiled and the two of them hugged each other.

"Goodnight, Jordan," Dolphi said.

"Goodnight, Dolphi the Dolphin Man."

Dolphi suddenly felt that the title he had been given made very good sense to him now.

As Dolphi walked away, he was almost on the verge of tears himself. He felt justice had been done here tonight, with the exception of the security chief being killed. He went back to where he had the tarpaulins full of stuff and got them into their bag forms again. He went over to the doors of the building he was told about and opened them. He felt a new resolve for the animals in captivity. From now on, he would be fighting for truth and justice.

CHAPTER 23

Night of the Racer X

"The speed of the leader is the speed of the gang."
—American businesswoman Mary Kay Ash

A S DOLPHI ENTERED the building the former dolphin trainer had told him about, he saw the lights were off. The lights that were on outside helped him see a light switch. He went over to it and flicked it up. As the lights went on, he saw the room was full of shirts, hats, travel mugs, etc. The shirts had pictures of dolphins swimming in a beautiful coral reef. "So, they like to put on a pretty face for tourists," Dolphi thought. "If only people could see those creatures in *those* environments and not in small pens where they can't explore or do much." He noticed there was an unfinished banner of what looked like Dolphi smiling and waving his hand. The words were already written out and they said, 'See man and dolphin like you've never seen them before!'

"What are these people teaching other people *about* dolphins, that it's okay to keep them in captivity and mock them? I mean, seriously, I can't make my face look *that* happy and how can I be happy in such a filthy… god, I'm talking to myself again." He then saw a nice looking plush dolphin toy that really caught his eye. He picked it up and studied it. "Hmm… maybe Sid would like this," he thought. He looked around the shop again and thought about the other employees. "Well, I made one employee think differently tonight, but everyone else who works here is unaffected. With this Navy stuff outside and visible to the public's eyes, maybe the other staff will think differently." As he was about to go out the door, he saw some cool shirts with flowers and palm trees on them. He decided to take a light blue one that he seemed to like and tried it on. There was a mirror where he could see how it looked on him. He took an extra large size, but it was too small for him to do up the buttons. Even so, it looked good on him with part of his chest and stomach exposed. He knew that he was stealing, but it didn't matter in this situation. It was now time for him to leave.

He turned off the lights and went out the front doors to the parking lot. He saw only one car out in the lot; the brown car he was about to borrow. But first, Dolphi had to set up the stuff. He spread all the pieces of equipment out all over the lot. As for the tarps, he saw the facility's billboard sign. It said, 'Dolphin World, where dreams become reality!' There was a spotlight shinning on it to make it visible at night. Dolphi noticed a ladder he could climb up. He went up and decided to hang the tarp below the sign where the spotlight could make it out. The tarp didn't say anything, but perhaps people would take notice at the camouflage color. He went back down and put the other tarp just on the driveway entrance. As he looked back at the front entrance, he could see a sign on top of the building saying, 'Dolphi the Dolphin Man: new, different, the next best thing! Only at Dolphin World!'

"I don't want to waste any more time trying to vandalize the signs," Dolphi thought. "I've already done enough here. Now, I can get back to finding my children."

He went over to the car and used the key to unlock it. He got inside and turned on the lights. He searched the glove compartment and found a roadmap.

"Now, how am I going to find where my boys are? They said they were staying at the Dolphin's Lagoon Inn, but where is Dilton Blvd?" He picked up the roadmap and began looking through it to find out where that street was. "Let's see now... Dilton... there it is, it turns off on the highway just near South Miami. It will be a long drive, but I'm going to find my boys, take them home and go after that accursed boss of mine." Dolphi started the car and left the parking lot. The time was just after 7:00 PM according to the car's digital clock. He realized he couldn't sit back in his seat very well. "Damn dorsal fin," he thought, "I can't sit back comfortably." The dolphin facility was soon out of sight and Dolphi began the long journey to find his children.

* * *

That night, the three mutant sharks at the M.R.I.L, Jaws, Chewer and Slice were in the secret room where Dolphi was mutated, eating chocolate that Mr. Jem had bought for Slice. Jaws and Chewer decided to try some too and found that they loved it. They were standing on the ground near the pool.

"Mmm!" Slice hummed as he was pouring a bottle of chocolate syrup meant for ice cream into his mouth. "This stuff tastes soooo good!"

"Yeah, you made a wise choice!" Chewer said.

"It would be wise not to eat too much of it or we will get fat," Jaws said.

"I know," Slice said.

"Could you pass me that syrup?" Jaws asked.

"Sure." Slice handed it over. Jaws turned his back and unscrewed the lid.

"You know," Jaws said, "earlier today, that was pretty funny about how you rode my back like that."

"Yeah, I'm glad you enjoyed that."

"That was hilarious," Chewer said.

"So," Jaws said, "I have a good idea too. I've always wanted to know what a chocolate covered SHARK WOULD LOOK LIKE!" Jaws quickly turned and squeezed the bottle making the syrup splash onto Slice's stomach. "AH!" Slice shouted. As Jaws continued to squeeze out the syrup, Slice grabbed the bottle and tried to direct the syrup onto Jaws. "Oh, you are so dead!" Slice said to Jaws. Chewer chuckled to himself. "Chewer," Slice said, "get this turkey off of me!"

"He's not a turkey, he's a shark," Chewer laughed. Slice then put his hand in some of the syrup and tossed it at Chewer. It hit him and that made him react. He rushed at the two and they all began wrestling. They fell down and rolled around in the chocolaty mess laughing and growling. They were having the time of their lives. Suddenly, Slice stopped wrestling and the expression on his face changed. "Wait a minute!" he said. "Stop! Stop!" As the other two let go of each other, Slice sat up and looked at his chocolate soaked buddies.

"What's wrong?" Jaws asked.

"I was just thinking... Do you guys remember... doing something like this before? Did we ever have such a playful wrestling match at one time?"

Jaws and Chewer understood what Slice was talking about. "Yeah," Jaws said. "I feel like we did do something like that before, but I don't have any memory of what happened."

"Neither do I," Chewer said.

"Maybe it's because we're tired," Slice said. "We should go to sleep."

"Yeah, I feel tired too," Chewer said.

"You know," Slice said, "I had trouble sleeping last night. I think I would sleep better if I was cuddling with somebody."

"Oooo, that's nasty!" Chewer said.

"No, no, no," Slice said, "I'm not being gross. I meant, lying in someone's arms. There's absolutely no need to do what I think you meant, I was thinking about just... snuggling next to someone... in companionship."

"Why don't you snuggle with that female mutant in that under-water cage?" Jaws asked.

"Are you kidding? One: she's not our species and two: I don't think she is going to cooperate with any of us." Slice then sighed and said, "oh, forget it. It was just a suggestion." He then hopped in the pool and washed the chocolate off his body. He turned to see the female mutant in her cage. She stared silently at Slice with her hands on the bars. Her cage was actually a shark cage that was locked. The top of it was a few feet out of the water so she could breathe. Slice waved at her and got out of the pool. He walked over to a large glass container lying horizontally on its side. It looked like a large fish tank. There were three of them that were full of water. Each of them had spongy material on the bottom. They acted as beds where the sharks could sleep while breathing in the water through their gills. The three mutant sharks had both the ability to breathe under water and breathe the air around them. However, their mutated lungs were only their secondary form of respiration. Their primary form of respiration required them to take water into their gills to prevent them suffocating from hydro deficiency. Their gills were located just above the base of their necks off to each side.

Slice crawled into one of the special beds, closed his eyes and lay quietly hoping to fall asleep and wake up to another day.

Jaws and Chewer thought about what Slice had said as they also washed the chocolate off of them in the pool. When they got out, they saw Slice in the tank with his tail hanging over the side. Since Slice was a thresher shark, the top of his tail fin was much longer than the bottom. Jaws slowly walked over to Slice's bed and decided to put his hand on Slice's tail. As he slowly stroked it, Slice began to wag his tail slowly. He then smiled and hummed. Jaws felt like he was beginning to understand what Slice was talking about. It felt good to make someone happy. Chewer was also beginning to feel that they were developing a special bond with each other. "Let's go to sleep," Chewer said. The two other sharks then crawled into their watery beds and closed their eyes. They soon fell asleep thinking about what they were going to do tomorrow.

* * *

Dolphi seemed to be driving down an endless, black road. He was all alone and there were hardly any other cars driving past him. Whatever the speed limit on the side of the road said, he would do EXACTLY what it said. The last thing he needed was to be pulled over by the police. He had just driven past Marathon and crossed the bridge to the next key. "I'm glad that I'm not living back at my old home in Tallahassee," he thought.

Dolphi remembered back to when he was growing up when he was human. He was born and raised in the state capitol of Tallahassee. Dolphi loved his mother and father very much and they loved him too. In the summer, he and his family went up to a cottage that they owned on Lake Iamonia, north-east of the city. The bay was pretty and when he saw it for the first time, he accidentally mistook it for the ocean. After graduating from marine biology at University, he moved down to Miami to find his dream of helping dolphins. He loved dolphins when he was growing up, but he never ever thought that he would eventually become one in a way.

He then started thinking about his wife who was still missing.

"Jennifer…" Dolphi thought, "could Mr. Jem have already mutated you? Oh honey… I hope you are alright… "

After two more hours of driving, Dolphi stopped at a dark and secluded spot in Islamorada. He needed to urinate in the bushes. He then felt his stomach growl. "What a perfect time to get hungry," he thought. "Where am I going to find food?" He got back in the car and drove on.

He soon spotted a restaurant that looked like it was closing up. "I'm going to see if I can sneak in and get some food because I'm not going to go out in the ocean and look for it myself, I might not find anything and it would take up too much time." He pulled into the parking lot of the restaurant and searched for a back door. The coast was clear so far and he found the back door of the kitchen. Dolphi then realized that history was repeating itself. He had done this once before and he got spotted. This time, he wasn't going to make any mistakes. He jumped up to a window to see if anyone was inside. The lights were still on. He noticed a chef inside about to take a bag of garbage out. Dolphi hid behind one of the garbage bins. The man came out, he threw the bag into the waste bin and went back inside. Dolphi didn't know if he should sneak inside like before, so he went into the bin and retrieved the bag. He hoped there would be something good to salvage. He opened it and saw there was lots of rice and meat spread around. It almost made him sick. He picked out whatever didn't look like it had something gross on it and put it in his mouth. It didn't taste too bad, but Dolphi felt that eating out of the trash was hurting his pride. "Oh, what the hey," Dolphi thought, "I might as well go in and see if anything's good." He opened the door and peeked into the kitchen. The chef who took out the trash was in the room facing the other way. Dolphi snuck very quietly over to a bunch of plastic flaps covering the entrance of a back room. He pushed his way through them where he saw bins full of water and plenty of active fish. He quickly helped himself to a handful, gulped them down, and took another handful. But suddenly, some of the fish escaped his grasp and fell on the floor. The noise caught the attention of the chef. Dolphi quickly hid behind a box that was against the wall next to the plastic flaps.

"Is that you, Doug?" the chef asked. As he walked into the room, he saw fish flopping on the floor. As he walked over to pick up the fish, Dolphi crept across the room and got out as quickly as he could. The chef turned but didn't see anyone. He then turned back to the fish he held. "Looks like you tried to escape from me," the chef said to the fish as he put them back in the bin.

Dolphi quickly ran back to his car and jumped in. He drove off and continued on the path to the Inn. As he went over the bridge, he saw the Theater of the Sea off to his right. It was another facility that had dolphins. "I can't help all the dolphins," Dolphi thought. "I better stay focused on what's important to me now."

It had reached midnight when Dolphi passed Key Largo, the last of the keys before coming up to the bridge that took him to the mainland. The next town Dolphi would come across would be Princeton.

Dolphi was ten miles from the town when suddenly, he looked in the rear view mirror and saw two cars coming up behind him. The cars were traveling at a faster than normal speed. They were next to each other on both lanes. It looked like the vehicle on Dolphi's lane was trying to get past the other guy, but he wasn't slowing down! Dolphi quickly tried to pull over, but both he and the other car spun out as they tried not to hit each other. Dolphi nearly had a heart attack as his car stopped spinning. The other car up in the opposite lane continued driving. Dolphi turned to see that the car that nearly hit him from behind was facing the other way. The driver of the car suddenly got out and slammed his door shut. He put his hands on the hood of the car and shook his head.

Dolphi got out of his car and ran up to the guy. He grabbed him, turned him around and put the guy's back onto the hood. "You goddamn fool!" Dolphi yelled. "What were you thinking?!" The man was speechless as he saw Dolphi's face. When Dolphi looked at the car, he saw a blue vehicle with outrageous designs on it. Underneath the car, there was a neon blue light that made a cool effect on the road. Then it came to Dolphi, that the car was designed for street racing. Dolphi looked back at the man and saw he was wearing punk-like clothes.

"My god, you look like you're only in your late teens..." Dolphi said. "What were you and the other car doing?"

"We were... racing," the man nervously said.

"Street racing you mean. What for?"

"... For cash. Are you that guy I heard about on the news?"

"Yeah, that's me," Dolphi said. "What's your name?"

"I'm not telling unless you tell me yours."

"Very well, it's Dolphi."

"Paul, a.k.a 'Bad Blue'."

"You've been listening to too much gangster rap music," Dolphi said. "Tell me where that other guy's heading."

"He's going to the finish line at Princeton. We started at Florida City."

"Yeah, well I'm going to Princeton as well and then on from there."

"There's going to be a huge crowd up there. I just lost five hundred bucks now and my opponent will be getting all the glory."

"I'm going to get in my car and follow you there," Dolphi said. "Now get in your car and let's go."

Dolphi got back into his car and they drove along to where the race was going to end.

* * *

There was an enormous group of people and rad looking vehicles up ahead as Dolphi and the street racer approached the town. The people were cheering and gathering around a red car. That was the other car that drove on after Dolphi nearly got aced in their illegal race. There were too many people to drive past. Lots of people had their own sexy vehicles around and some were wearing punk-like clothing. There were girls who wore short-shorts and had their shirts tied up to expose their midriffs.

The driver of the red car then got out. He wore a white tank-top and had blonde hair greased and combed to make him look really suave. Bad Blue rolled down the passenger side window and signaled Dolphi to roll down his window. "Look," Blue said, "I've got to give him my money, then I'll see if I can get you through."

"Who's your opponent?" Dolphi asked.

"Dragon Fire, a street racing champion." Blue drove up to the crowd and got out. Dragon Fire then approached Blue. "Looks like I won thanks to that civilian that cut you off."

"Just take your money," Blue said as he handed the five hundred dollars over. Dragon then walked back to his car, counting the money. There was a young lady who walked up to Dragon with a pitcher of water. "I've got another prize for you," she said. She then dumped the pitcher of water on the front of her shirt.

"Oh for god's sake!" Dolphi thought as he rolled his eyes back.

"Hey, somebody wants to get through, so could everyone move out of the way?" Blue asked the crowd of people.

Just before the people began to move, Dragon then said, "wait a minute! Stay put!" He then went back over to Blue. "This is four hundred, where's the other hundred?"

"That's all I got, man."

"You're lying, hand it over!"

Dolphi watched what was happening from a distance. He suddenly saw Dragon move onto Blue and push him to the ground. Dolphi then drove up to the scene.

"Come on, hand it over!" Dragon yelled. He forced his hand into Blue's pocket and pulled out the hundred dollar bill. Dolphi then got out of the car went up to the racer and pushed him away. "Leave him alone, tough guy!" Dolphi said. Everyone then backed up and exclaimed at Dolphi's appearance. "Well, well," Dragon said, "what do we have here Blue, your mascot?"

"Leave him out of this, I just want to get through," Dolphi said.

"That's too bad, this is where the last race is held and the road is being prepared for this occasion. The race starts here, goes through the town of Goulds and ends at Perrine."

"And after that is South Miami where I'm heading," Dolphi said. "I really don't want any trouble, mister Fire Breathing Dragon."

"Dragon Fire!" he corrected.

"By the way," Dolphi asked, "isn't tomorrow a school day for a lot of you?" The people let out a loud, "Wooo!!!" at Dolphi's comment. Dragon then tried to throw a punch at Dolphi, but Dolphi grabbed his fist and squeezed it hard, but not too hard as the man was showing pain. Dolphi let go and the man moved back. Suddenly, he pulled out something and pointed it at Dolphi. Everyone gasped and moved back as they saw it was a gun! "Don't mess with me, fish stick!" Dragon shouted.

"Whoa, there!" Dolphi said as he put his hands in front of him. "Put that thing away, you don't want to hurt anybody." After a moment, Dragon put the gun away.

Someone then walked out of the crowd. It was the race organizer. "Listen up everyone! All the preparations are in place! The

road is clear for racing and the crowd at the other end is ready...
what the hell?" he said noticing Dolphi.

"Don't mind him," Dragon said, "He's here for the race."

"What?" Dolphi asked not understanding.

"I'm going to challenge this creature. He'll be taking Blue's
car."

"But I'm not a racer!" Dolphi said.

"Hey, you want to get through? You either go back the way you
came, or participate in this."

"But I don't have any money and Blue's all cleaned out." Dolphi
then noticed an ATM on one side of a building. "Surely the cops
would have taken notice of this illegal and dangerous racing."

"Oh, don't worry about the cops," Dragon laughed. "They've
been taken care of, thanks to a few bribes."

"I'll be right back," Dolphi said. He then walked towards the
building with the ATM. As Dolphi walked by one of the girls, she
was checking him out. She then slapped her hand on Dolphi's bottom. Dolphi stopped, widened his eyes and slowly turned around.
The girl giggled. Dolphi had an embarrassed look on his face as he
continued over to the ATM. There, he noticed a stone garbage can.
With his strength, he lifted it off the ground, ran at the ATM and
threw the stone garbage can at it. The machine exploded and cash
began to spew out. Dolphi gathered a thousand dollars and put some
extra cash for himself in his shirt pockets. People suddenly began
to run up to the cash that was all over the ground and scrambled to
collect as much as they could.

Dolphi went back to Dragon Fire and Bad Blue. "Alright then,"
Dolphi said. "I've got money now. I'll be racing for... one thousand
dollars." The crowd went, "Ooh!"

"If I win this, you hand over your five hundred plus what you
just took from Bad Blue."

Dragon grinned at the bet. He turned to the crowd. "Very well,
one thousand is what we will race for!" The crowd cheered.

"Alright then," the race organizer said. "Hand me your bets."
Dolphi and Dragon handed the money over and the organizer
hopped in his car and drove off.

Dolphi went back to the car he had borrowed and took out the
plush dolphin toy he got from the Dolphin World store. He didn't
want to forget that. As he went back, he heard people say, "you're

that Dolphin Man I heard about, right?" and "way to go, dolphin dude!" and "you go splash that Dragon and extinguish his fiery breath!"

Blue then asked Dolphi, "hey, are you sure you want to do this? He's a very good driver."

"What other choice do I have?" Dolphi asked.

"I'll be coming with you then. I better teach you how to work my kind of vehicle."

The cars had ten minutes to get into position. In that time, Blue explained the car's features to Dolphi.

"Okay then," Dolphi said, "it's just like a normal car, except its more complex and has… what did you say the booster was?"

"Three cans of NAS," Blue replied.

"NAS?! That stuff is dangerous!"

"I know, but it's vital for getting the lead on someone. Both Dragon and I have used one can so far."

Outside, somebody shouted out, "its time to race!" and others repeated the same thing as everyone moved out of the way.

"Here we go," Blue said. Dragon was positioned on Dolphi's left. He gave Dolphi a nod, but he did not understand. "Nod him back," Blue said, "it makes you cool and fearless." Dolphi did that and then one of those girls like the one who poured water on herself, walked in front of the cars and held up a pink colored scarf. "Start revving," Blue said.

The girl then threw the scarf down and the race was on.

Dolphi put the car in 'drive', the wheels screeched, and they were off.

The car's speed got faster and Dolphi felt very nervous traveling at such a speed. "So," Dolphi asked Blue, "how long have you been doing this street racing?"

"Just a couple of years," he replied.

"Oh great," Dolphi thought, "I've just been caught up in a street race with an amateur who's trying to beat a champion."

"Hey!" Blue said angrily. "Don't underestimate me! Two years is a long time and I'm a fast learner!"

"Whatever you say," Dolphi said.

"Just keep your eyes on the road."

Dragon's car was just ahead. He was going pretty fast and Dolphi was praying that there weren't going to be any other cars in the way. "Speed up!" Blue said, "we're losing him!"

"I'm trying!" Dolphi said. Dolphi went into the next gear and began to catch up. When Dragon saw this, he used his nitro boost. He shot off like a rocket.

"Damn!" Blue said. "He'll be at Goulds in a minute! I better use my booster as well." Blue quickly pressed a button and before Dolphi was about to tell him not to press it, his speed shot up to a frightening 150 mph. "Jesus!" Dolphi cried as he felt the adrenaline rush through him.

When Dolphi entered Goulds, there were a few cars around. Luckily, he was still on the divided highway. Dolphi dodged the cars that were in front of him, still keeping his sights on Dragon Fire.

"Next time, don't touch the damn booster unless I say so!" Dolphi shouted.

"Relax!" Blue said. "I just don't want this to be a runaway for him!"

The racers soon passed through the town and continued on the road to Perrine. There were a few more cars on the road now. It was only a matter of dodging them. Some of them honked their horns in anger.

"From where we are," Blue said, "the finish line at Perrine should be twenty minutes from now. We should try to catch up to Dragon Fire."

"I should never have gotten in this car!" Dolphi said. "This is not my race."

"I know, but you are doing very well so far."

When Dragon found a clear lane with no cars in his sight, he activated his last nitro boost and took off.

"We better find a clear lane and boost up to him!" Blue said.

"No," Dolphi said. "He used up his last boost and we still have one left. We should save it for when we really need it."

Dolphi got into a clear lane and put the pedal to the metal. Up ahead, there were two semi-trucks blocking Dragon's path. He had to slow down and figure out a way to get by them.

"Look!" Dolphi said. "He's blocked!" As he came up to Dragon, they were both in two different lanes next to each other with two different trucks in front of them. "I wonder how we are going to get by these guys?" Blue asked. Suddenly, the road split into three lanes. At that moment, Dragon made a break for the lane off to his left.

"Go to that new left lane!" Blue said. Before Dolphi could get through, the left truck moved into the left lane, leaving the center lane open. Through that lane, Dolphi could see Dragon up ahead. As Dolphi tried to move through the middle lane, Dragon saw what was happening and quickly slowed down, preventing Dolphi from getting out.

"He's boxing us in!" Dolphi exclaimed.

"No!" Blue shouted. "Now what? We're almost there!"

Dolphi was trying to figure out what to do. "How badly do you want to win this race?" he asked Blue.

"A lot," he said. "I've always wanted to prove myself and this is something I'm very good at, even though I know its illegal and dangerous. I need the money anyway."

"Okay then," Dolphi said, "prepare to show some intimidation." Dolphi slowed down a little.

"What are you doing?!" Blue asked.

"You'll see," Dolphi said. Up ahead, Dragon wondered what his opponent was doing.

"Where's the nitro button?" Dolphi asked.

"It's right here," Blue pointed.

"Push it."

"What?"

"I said push it!"

Blue took a deep breath and pushed the yellow button. Dolphi's speed shot up and he roared up between the trucks.

"What the?" Dragon thought as he saw the car coming through at a fast speed. Dolphi wasn't slowing down. Dragon knew the car was about to crash into him, so he tried to speed up. However, at the breakneck speed Dolphi was going, it was too late for Dragon. As he tried to turn left, Dolphi nicked the rear-right corner of the red car with the front-left of his car. The effect sent Dragon almost head on into the lane barrier, spinning him around to come to a stop facing one of the oncoming semi-trucks. There was a screeching of brakes as the truck tried to avoid hitting him. The truck missed the red car by inches and slowly came to a halt. Dolphi kept on driving.

Blue was overjoyed. "WOO HOO!!!" he cheered. "Eat our dust!" he called behind himself in the direction of Dragon's immobilized car. They soon arrived at Perrine where a cheering crowd awaited them.

Dolphi stopped the car as the people surrounded them. When he and Blue got out, everyone was surprised at Dolphi's form.

"Hey, it's the Dolphin Man from the news!" one of the people shouted. Other people began to get excited at the sight of Dolphi. He just grinned and raised his arms in victory.

Blue ran up to Dolphi and charged into him with a big hug.

"What is your name?" one of the people from the crowd called to Dolphi.

"I am Dolphi!"

People then began to chant Dolphi's name. Dolphi then picked up Blue and had him sit on his shoulder.

"Yeah!" Blue shouted as he raised both arms in the air.

Just then, Dragon Fire drove up to the group and stopped. The front of his vehicle was quite smashed. Dolphi put Blue down and thought that there was going to be trouble. Dragon emerged with a bruise on his head. He looked frustrated, but he wasn't reaching for his gun. As he walked up to Dolphi and Blue, the crowd went silent.

Dragon then said with a grin, "heh, you've got guts. What a crazy way to lose. And just think, I almost had you."

"You're a good racer too," Dolphi replied. "But I couldn't have done it without Bad Blue here." The crowd cheered again.

The race organizer then came up to Dolphi. "I'm quite impressed that you beat Dragon Fire," he said. He then handed the money over to Dolphi. Dolphi counted a thousand dollars and handed it over to Blue.

"You deserve this money," Dolphi said.

"Thanks a lot, man," Blue smiled.

The race organizer then headed back to his car. He had a police scanner in his car to detect police radio transmissions. Suddenly, he heard a transmission say, *"attention all units, we have received reports of drivers participating in an exhibition of speed, possibly a street race. Suspects were last seen racing through Goulds and are heading for Perrine..."*

At that moment, the organizer shouted to everyone, "Hey! We

have cops coming for us! Cops are coming! Get the hell out of here!"

Everyone then scrambled for their vehicles and took off as quickly as they could. The crowd seemed to dissolve into thin air.

Dolphi got back in Blue's car and Blue got in the passenger seat.

"I better get out of here quickly," Dolphi said. "I'm heading for the Dolphin's Lagoon Inn located somewhere in the South Miami area." Dolphi quickly drove off, dodging the fleeing cars.

"That was a sweet race," Blue said. "I ought to have you in future races."

"Hey, I was just lucky," Dolphi grinned. "I'm just going to drop myself off at my destination and hope I don't get involved in anything like that again." He quickly got on the highway and drove on to South Miami. "Keep your eyes open for a street called Dilton Blvd." Dolphi said to Blue.

"No problem."

Dolphi now had a clear path to the Inn. "I'm coming, boys," he thought. "After I get you three, I am going to do whatever it takes to find my wife and make my boss sorry as hell."

CHAPTER 24

Reunited at Last

"Success is dependent on effort."
—Sophocles

"THERE'S DILTON BLVD!" the street racer who called himself, 'Bad Blue' said to Dolphi.

Dolphi turned off onto the road and scanned for the Inn he was looking for. He soon spotted a tall sign with a neon blue dolphin on it. It said, 'Dolphin's Lagoon Inn'.

"Finally," Dolphi said, "I've made it." He drove into the parking lot and got out, taking his plush dolphin toy with him.

"So, do you want me to stay or should I drive off?" Blue asked Dolphi.

"Can that car hold five people?" Dolphi asked.

"It's only meant to seat two people. Why do you ask?"

"I've got three boys who are staying here and I need to get them and take them back to my house."

"You mean, you're not from the ocean?"

"Nah, I was a human who got injected with something that turned me into this."

"I see. Well, if you squeezed yourself and your kids inside, it would be uncomfortable, but I think it would work."

Dolphi faced the building. "This shouldn't take too long," he said. "Just wait here."

"Okay," Blue said.

The Inn was three stories tall. The only problem now, was finding out which room his children were in. He walked towards the building's front entrance. He pulled on one of the doors, but found it was locked. He saw that the doors required a key card to open the electronic lock. Dolphi took a deep breath and made a fist. He pulled his arm back and punched the glass as hard as he could. The glass burst into pieces and a hole was made large enough for Dolphi to get his hand inside and open the door. He was glad his arm wasn't scratched in the process.

Dolphi went inside and found himself in the lobby. The floor had red carpeting and plants in large marble pots. Up ahead, Dolphi could see a pair of elevators. As he went forward, a door opened and someone ran out towards Dolphi. "Who's there?!" yelled a man in a hotel uniform. He stopped as he saw Dolphi's appearance. He started to walk back a little and then ran towards the front desk and the phone. Dolphi ran at the man, grabbed him and lifted him up with one hand. "Don't even think of calling the police!" Dolphi said firmly. "I don't want to hurt you, I'm just here to pick up a few people I know and then leave. Where is your check-in list?"

"It's... it's the brown book behind the counter!" he said nervously. Dolphi then let go of the man and jumped over the counter. He found the book and began searching through it. He soon found the name of his boys in room 315 on the 3rd floor. Dolphi then jumped back over. "Sorry for the glass I broke," Dolphi said, "now go home."

"Okay, whatever you say," the man said. "I never thought I'd see a dolphin breaking into the Dolphin's Lagoon Inn!" He then ran out the doors and into the parking lot. Dolphi went up to one of the elevators, pushed a button and waited. Suddenly, Dolphi heard popping noises from outside. He turned and saw the hotel employee lying motionless on the ground outside. At the same time, Dolphi saw Bad Blue's car taking off. "No!" Dolphi shouted. "Don't go, Blue!"

The elevator door opened. Not knowing what to do, Dolphi ran inside and madly pushed the button for the third floor. The doors closed. Dolphi sat on the floor and held the toy tightly in his arms. "Oh man..." Dolphi whimpered nervously. "Did that man just get gunned down by someone?" The elevator door opened and Dolphi slowly got up.

He looked up and down the hall. There was no one in sight. He began searching for the room. "315 is the room I'm looking for," Dolphi thought. "Let's see now… room 315… 315… 31… there it is!" He knocked on the door and waited. The door soon opened and out stepped Mike.

"Do you have any idea what time it is?!" Mike asked rubbing his eyes.

"Yes," Dolphi replied, "time to see your father once again."

"Dad!" Mike gasped.

Dolphi ran into the room. "Walter, Sid?" he asked. "Daddy's back!" He saw the two boys sleeping in separate beds. They slowly opened their eyes and saw Dolphi. "… Dad?" Sid asked half asleep. "Oh god, please don't tell me I'm dreaming!" They got out of bed and all three went to hug Dolphi. "Dad!" said Walter, "I'm so glad to see you're alright!"

"How did you escape from that Discovery place?" Sid asked.

"It doesn't matter," said Dolphi, "I finally found you boys and I'm glad you are all okay… "

"Dad?" Mike asked concerned. "You look a little pale. What happened?" Dolphi sat down on the bed. "Oh man…" Dolphi said, getting his thoughts together. "I think someone out in the parking lot just got murdered."

"What?!" asked Mike.

"I wasn't imagining it," said Dolphi. "We have to get out of here. I had a vehicle ready to pick me up, but the gunshots must have scared him off. I hope he got away safely."

Dolphi had finally found his boys, but little did he know, the ones who murdered the man outside were already in the elevator and on the way up to the floor Dolphi was on. In other words, getting out was not going to be easy. Somebody stepped out of the elevator and looked down the hall. When they saw the floor number highlighted on the elevator down in the lobby, they assumed that Dolphi was on the third floor.

"He's not here, but he's probably in one of these rooms," said a man with a Russian accent. "We are going to search all of them. Men, I want you to start looking right now."

"Yes, Colonel," his men said.

Dolphi was feeling very tired.

"Daddy?" asked Sid. "What's wrong?"

"I'm okay, Sid," said Dolphi, "I just need water. I'm drying up and I need to rehydrate."

"I know what to do," said Mike. "We have a bathtub with a shower head." Mike ran into the bathroom and turned on the water.

"I'm glad I made it here... in time," said Dolphi as he went into the bathroom. He took off his shirt, crawled into the bathtub and lay on his stomach.

"Ahh..." Dolphi gave a relaxing sigh as the water sprinkled onto him. "That's better. I had a long, boring and tiring drive to get to here. Actually, not *all* of it was boring. But right now, this is so comfortable. I could just fall asleep right here... "

Just then, Walter heard footsteps thumping outside their door. He peeked through the little glass peephole in the door and saw people in soldier's uniforms.

"Dad!" Walter said as he ran into the bathroom. "There are... soldiers of some kind outside in the hall! They have big guns and... purple colored uniforms!"

"So much for being subtle..." Dolphi thought. "Could they be after me?"

"I've never seen such people before," Walter said. "I'm going to call the police right away." He ran over to the phone next to the bed and picked it up. When he put the receiver next to his ear, there was no dial tone. He pushed buttons, but nothing happened. He ran back to the bathroom. "The phone's dead," Walter said. "Dad, do you remember being followed by anyone?"

"Not that I know of," Dolphi replied.

Suddenly, there was banging on the door. "Hey," a voice shouted from outside, "open up in there! We are looking for something that is hiding on this floor somewhere."

"Uh oh!" said Mike. "Walter, what are we going to do? How are we going to elude these guys?"

"Perhaps my new invention can help," Walter said as he ran back into the room.

"Now's not the time to play with toys, Walter," Dolphi said.

The pounding at the door came again. "Open this door now!" the person shouted.

"Okay, I'm coming!" Mike said running for the door.

Walter then returned to the bathroom with a box, a wire coming out of it and a clear plastic suit attached to the wire. He then shut the bathroom door and locked it. Mike opened the door to the hallway and saw a soldier wearing a purple camouflaged uniform.

"Sorry to disturb you, we are looking for a suspect that is in this hotel somewhere," the soldier said.

Mike was nervous. "Say, aren't you guys a little old for trick-or-treating?"

The soldier then shoved Mike aside and walked into the room pointing his weapon around. "Who are you guys?" asked Sid.

"That's not important," said the soldier. He then began to search the balcony.

Back in the bathroom, Dolphi got out of the tub.

"This is not a toy, dad," Walter said. "It hasn't been tested yet, but this is the only shot we've got at hiding you."

Dolphi dried himself off with a towel to get rid of the drips and got the suit on. His snout had gotten in the way when he tried to put the hood on, so he pulled his snout close to his chest. Walter then pushed a button.

"Where are you?!" the soldier asked as he came back into the room from the balcony.

Dolphi looked at himself. "It didn't work," he said.

"Damn it," thought Walter. He began to hit the device trying to get it to work.

The soldier then said, "I have to check your bathroom as well."

"Not now," said Mike, "my brother could be naked in there." The soldier walked passed Mike and Walter could hear the door handle turning. Walter had locked it, but the soldier was about to kick it open.

"Who exactly are you searching for?" Mike asked. "If we could help... "

"You don't need to know anything," the soldier replied. "Now, whoever is behind that door, open up!"

Dolphi looked at the device. He pushed a red button. Some lights on the box then lit up.

"Oh, I knew that," Walter said. He pushed one of the buttons again and this time, it worked. At the same time, the soldier kicked the bathroom door and it flew open. He saw Walter standing next to a person, or rather a projection of a person. The soldier looked around the bathroom. Dolphi just held his breath and hoped that he wasn't going to be discovered. After the soldier looked behind the shower curtain, he left the room.

"This room is clear," the soldier said as he moved out into the hallway.

"He didn't see me," Dolphi said. "What happened?" He turned to look in the mirror. He saw himself in his human form again.

"I'm human again," he said, "… almost."

Walter, who had the device held behind Dolphi's back, turned it off and Dolphi returned back to his mutated state.

"I've been working on a special invention that disguises anyone by making him look like something else," said Walter, "I call it, the Disguiser."

Dolphi took off the hood. "That was unbelievable!" he said. "But I looked like a painting."

"I know, it's not perfected yet," Walter replied.

Dolphi then turned back to the mirror and gazed at his face. "It's been a while since I last looked at myself." He was looking at his eyes. "My eyes still look human. Some people's eyes are blue, some green, but mine are black."

Mike and Sid walked into the bathroom. "What exactly are you saying?" Walter asked.

"I have become something different, but I also feel like I've become someone else in the process. I don't feel like I'm Dr. Steele Monroe Jay anymore. I'm not the person I used to be."

"You *are* different," Mike said, "but you are still our father."

"Yes, you're right," Dolphi said. "What bothers me is how we are going to live the rest of our lives. I have no job so how am I going to provide for the family now?"

"I know what you are talking about, dad," Mike said. "But right now, we should worry about getting out of here. We still have to find mom. She's probably still at the Marine Research Institute Labs."

"Of course," Dolphi said. "Tell me, Walter, how does that invention work?"

"I put a photo of you into a slot in this box," said Walter. "It works as a projection around different areas of the suit. You need a picture of the person to copy, so you can't just change into whoever you please."

"I think you'll grow up to be an amazing inventor," Dolphi said. "Come on, boys, let's go."

The boys got out their clothes, took off their pajamas and put on some shorts and t-shirts. They then packed their clothing in their backpacks. Dolphi put his shirt back on.

"Is the hall clear?" Dolphi asked Mike. "Are they gone?"

As Mike opened the door and peeked out, he could still see the soldiers searching the rooms, some hotel guests even stood out in the hallway feeling frustrated.

"The staircase is guarded and the elevator is up the hallway," Mike said to Dolphi.

Dolphi tucked his head into his chest and covered himself with the special plastic suit. Walter activated the Disguiser to hide Dolphi's form. He then put his invention away in his bag still leaving the wire out and stuck close to Dolphi.

"I almost forgot!" Dolphi realized, grabbing the plush dolphin toy. This is for you Sid."

"Wow!" Sid smiled. "Where did you get it?"

"I'll tell you later. Okay kids, let's go. We'll make a break for it at the elevator." They walked over to the door and went out of the room.

There were soldiers standing at every door. Hotel guests in their nightgowns were arguing with the soldiers for disturbing their sleep.

Dolphi and his boys walked quickly up the hall towards the elevator. There was a soldier standing in front of it, but Dolphi quickly pressed the button as he came in reach.

"Hey!" the soldier said. "No one's allowed to leave until we find our suspect."

Mike observed three letters on the soldier's uniform. "M-A-C?" he asked. "What does that stand for?"

"None of your business," the soldier replied, "now go back to your room or I'll call the Colonel."

Dolphi was still waiting for the elevator to pop up. Suddenly, the projection on Dolphi's suit began to flicker.

"What's going on here?" the soldier asked. The picture then shut off and Dolphi's form was visible again.

"Uh oh!" Dolphi said. Knowing the disguise had failed on him, he quickly got the hood off his head.

The soldier then reacted. "I found him!" he yelled. "By the elevator!"

The soldier was about to point his gun at Dolphi and fire, but Dolphi quickly grabbed it and rammed his snout into the man's face. The gun fell to the floor and Dolphi grabbed the man by his shirt and tossed him in the direction of a group of soldiers who were about to move onto Dolphi. Dolphi grabbed the gun.

The Colonel of the soldiers came out of a nearby room and saw Dolphi. "Stop!" he yelled as he reached for his pistol. Just then, the elevator doors finally opened, the boys ran into it first, but before Dolphi was able to run in, the Colonel fired his gun and a bullet hit Dolphi in his left arm.

Dolphi fell backwards onto the floor of the elevator and screamed in pain.

"No!" Mike yelled. He quickly mashed the button to close the doors. As they closed, Mike pressed the button for the lobby.

"He just went down the elevator!" the Colonel yelled to his men. "Proceed to the lobby immediately!"

CHAPTER 25

A Message From the Future

*"If there were no God,
it would be necessary to invent him."*
—Voltaire

"DAD! YOU'VE BEEN shot!" Walter said as he quickly removed the plastic suit from Dolphi. Looking at where the bullet hit him, Dolphi growled in pain. There was a little bit of blood coming out of his arm. "I'm alright," Dolphi said. "It was only one small bullet and my blubbery skin plus the suit cushioned it a little, but it still hurts like hell."

"Sorry about the disguise failing," Walter said. "It uses a lot of battery power, so I guess the batteries died on you."

The elevator had just drifted down past the second floor. The next stop was the lobby. Dolphi wondered if there were soldiers guarding the doors down there. Just as the elevator was slowly coming to a stop, Dolphi used his echolocation on the doors and saw two human skeletons on the other side. He also saw the shape of guns in their hands; the same kind that he had taken off the soldier on the third floor.

"Hide the gun," Dolphi said to his boys. "I've got to hide somehow."

The doors opened and there were two soldiers standing outside. They turned around and saw only the boys.

"Return to your room, kids," one of the soldiers said.

"Uh…" Mike thought. "We were just looking for a drink."

"No one is leaving until we find the suspect," said the other soldier. "Return to your rooms now." The soldiers walked into the elevator. As they entered, the first soldier felt something drip onto his cheek. He touched his cheek and then looked at his hand to see what it was. When he realized it was blood, Dolphi dropped from above and landed in between the soldiers. He punched the one on the left and kicked the one on the right in their faces. They fell to the ground and lay unconscious. Mike pulled out the gun that he had hidden behind him and ran out of the elevator. He pointed it around to see if there were any other soldiers around.

"Mike, give me that!" Dolphi shouted as he snatched the gun out of Mike's hands. "Don't go risking your life!"

"Sorry!" Mike said. "Let's just head out the door quickly!"

Dolphi turned around and used his echolocation on the doors leading to the stairways. He saw soldiers about to come out of the doors.

"Hide behind the counter! Now!" Dolphi shouted as he grabbed all three of his boys and rushed towards the desk. The boys jumped over and hid. The soldiers suddenly rushed into the lobby.

"There he is!" a soldier shouted. Dolphi ran over to a plant in a large marble pot on the other side of the room. He fired the gun at the soldiers just as he hid behind the pot. A few of them went down, but just as Dolphi hit the ground, the soldiers fired their weapons. The bullets began tearing up the plant and pot as a frightened Dolphi scrunched tightly against the disintegrating marble. He contemplated going home, crawling into bed and pretending none of all the things he had been through as a mutant dolphin had ever happened.

"I've got to help dad," Mike said to his brothers.

"We can't let those guys see us," Walter said. "We must stay out of sight."

Just then, the Colonel showed up in the lobby. "Cease fire!" he yelled. The bullets stopped and it was quiet.

"Who are you people and what do you want from me?!" Dolphi yelled.

The Colonel looked at the two fallen men. "If you have a weapon, throw it away," he said to Dolphi. Dolphi got up and slowly walked out of his hiding spot. He held the gun by the front end. He then tossed it behind the counter to where his boys were hiding.

"Okay, I give up," Dolphi said as he held his wounded arm with his other hand. "If you're going to kill me, you could at least tell me about yourselves and what this is all about?"

The Colonel thought about it. His respectable uniform was also a purple color. There were a few medals of decoration on the left side of his chest. On his head, he wore an officer's cap. "Well… I guess I should explain things to you. We are from a possible future. Our mission is to obtain a weapon that is in this time period."

"Wait," Dolphi said, "time period? Possible future? Does this mean you're not from around here?"

"Ah yes, you're probably baffled about what I'm talking about. But first, the weapon. We have tracked a powerful energy source to this location. That power is coming…" He then took out something that looked like a Star Trek tricorder and looked at it. He then pointed it at Dolphi. "… directly from you," the Colonel finished.

"Who are you?" Dolphi asked.

"My name's not important," the Colonel replied. "We have been tracking several energy bursts over the last few days. The first burst was detected at a research facility last Friday, the twenty-third of this month."

Dolphi then remembered what had happened on that day. "The energy thing from that dolphin I was treating!" he said. "This bright light came out of a dolphin and entered a computer. I think it's still there—" Suddenly, Dolphi remembered what that female dolphin he encountered near Regan's residence told him when she explained that there was something in his head that made her nervous.

"The weapon moved, however," the Colonel said. "The next burst was detected at a beach just outside a residence that became a murder scene the next day."

Dolphi remembered the purse thief that he indirectly killed.

"Finally," the Colonel said, "after losing the signal for a while, we caught the last burst way down south."

Dolphi remembered the dolphin facility incident.

"We monitored it moving north and coming closer to our current position, so we followed it up to here."

Dolphi was stunned. "No… this can't be! The enigma… is inside my head?!"

"Oh!" the Colonel said. "*That's* what people called it the first time it was discovered! You don't know what it is, do you?"

"No, I don't," Dolphi said. "You said you were from a future. Does this mean you traveled back through time or something?"

"Yes, you could say that."

"How?"

"With help from what is in your head."

"I see," Dolphi thought. "so, are there any laser guns where you're from?"

"Get real," the Colonel replied.

"This enigma, is it from the future?"

"I don't know. You see, we come from a dark future where man is at war with your kind."

"War?" Dolphi asked confused. "My kind?"

"Yes."

Dolphi remembered dreaming about a war. "Somehow, I don't think you're the good guys here," he said.

"That's were you're wrong, Dolphi."

"How did you know my name?"

"I read about you in pages of history. You were the first mutant to be created."

"If you are here to prevent mutants from existing," Dolphi said, "then go after a man named—"

"That's not what we came here to do," the Colonel said. "We are not the only ones who went back through time, though. A group of mysterious mutants used our time travel machine before we were about to. They are trying to hinder our plans."

"Wait a minute!" Dolphi said. He then thought about the car chase he got caught up in on his way to work, the attack at the Marine Research Institute Labs and then the sniper shot that killed the security chief at Dolphin World, the facility he escaped from. "Those mysterious mutants that you are speaking of, they wouldn't happen to be... dinosaurs by any chance, would they?"

Suddenly, the Colonel's eyes widened and he began scratching his chin. "Interesting," he thought. "To tell you the truth... I wouldn't know for sure. I'd have to see them to believe it."

"That's why they attacked my workplace," Dolphi said as things started coming together. "They, the mystery mutants I mean, were trying to destroy a computer that the enigma had bounced into. I guess they failed. I wonder if they know the enigma is inside me? So far, they have been helping me, but for what purpose?"

"So they can save their pathetic species, that's what!" the Colonel said.

"And you are after the weapon in my head so you can wipe them out," Dolphi said.

"So we can control them and keep them in check," the Colonel corrected. "You see, when mutants first appeared, they were used as servants for human purposes. But later on, mutants started developing self-awareness due to their human intelligence. They wanted to be 'independent' and 'free from human control', but humans wouldn't accept that, and neither do we!"

"So mutants revolted?" Dolphi asked.

"By George, he's got it!" the Colonel smiled.

"Were they of animal or human origins?"

"That information is top secret. With the weapon in our control, we can stop a disaster from happening."

"And does killing me help?"

"We weren't trying to kill you; we were trying to incapacitate you."

Dolphi looked at the plant he hid behind. It looked unrecognizable from the gunfire. "Is that what you guys call... oh right, I fired first."

"Do you remember why you killed that man on the beach?" the Colonel asked. "You were under an extreme amount of pressure. High stress levels and strong emotions cause the 'enigma' as you call it, to be active. It fills the one wielding it with a force that gives them supernatural abilities. The potential of the weapon is virtually limitless."

"I understand," Dolphi said. "Let me ask you, did you guys really have to come after me in such a public place? There are a lot of hotel guests that have witnessed you guys."

"Don't worry about them," the Colonel said, "we are rigging the place with explosives as we speak."

Dolphi gasped. "What?!"

"When we are through with getting the weapon, all witnesses will be eliminated and we will vanish without a trace."

"That man out in the parking lot," Dolphi said, "you killed an innocent man who didn't do anything!"

"I cannot take chances," the Colonel said. "He could have gone to the police and interfered with our operation."

"What about that car that drove off? You better not have killed him!"

"Maybe, maybe not," the Colonel said. "Anyway, like I said, we are here to obtain the great power you possess so we can control the future mutants. If we don't, we could be looking at a catastrophe worse than nine-eleven."

Dolphi was baffled. "What the hell is nine-eleven?"

A brief look of surprise appeared on the Colonel's face. "Oh, its 1999, right? Forget it. I've said enough. Let's get this over with."

"Well then," Dolphi said, "if I'm going to be taken by you, I'm not going down without a fight!"

"First, let's get the weapon stimulated," the Colonel said as he took something out of his pocket. It was an oval shaped device as big as his palm. He then pressed a button.

Dolphi suddenly felt an enormous headache coming on. The device must have done something to cause the enigma to react. There was a bright light emanating from Dolphi's head. He dropped on his knees and held his head, growling in pain. He then collapsed on the floor.

Behind the counter, Mike and his brothers were watching what was happening.

"At last!" the Colonel said. "We have been waiting for this day for too long!"

Dolphi suddenly opened his eyes and slowly rose to his feet. He had a different look in his eyes. He looked at his hands as if he had never seen them before. He grabbed his shirt by his sides and ripped it off. The shreds fell to the floor and Dolphi was naked. The look on his face was very calm. He then looked up at the soldiers. "I am... alive," Dolphi said. The Colonel and his soldiers knelt down on one knee as if they were worshiping Dolphi.

The boys were very confused at what was happening.

The Colonel then said, "great being, please tell us who or what you are."

"I am part light and part energy," Dolphi said. "I come from a distant place off this planet. I am known as... Cyber-soul. I have been monitoring this fascinating creature. He has strong spirit."

"You have been very eager for this opportunity, I take it?" the Colonel asked as he smiled.

"What does it mean to you?"

"You are here now, and you will do great things when you are in our control."

"Nobody controls me and nobody owns me either," said the enigma called Cyber-soul.

"Tell us," said the Colonel, "how did you find yourself in the body of this mutant?"

"I crashed into the Atlantic Ocean after I entered this planet's atmosphere not long ago," Cyber-soul said. "After drifting for quite a while, I found my opportunity. An intelligent animal known as a dolphin, was in the area. I made myself glow in my rock form. It curiously wandered up to me and that was when I struck. I transferred myself to its brain as it was the only suitable environment for me. I was now being carried around..." The mysterious Cyber-soul then explained about ending up at the Marine Research Institute Labs, getting into one of the computers and then ending up in Dolphi's head.

"Ah, fascinating story," said the Colonel. "I could learn a lot from you. Now, it's time to shut you down and extract you."

Mike saw that the Colonel was about to raise the device he held and push another button. When Dolphi had thrown the gun over the counter, Mike had grabbed it and kept it close to him. He didn't know what was going to happen when the Colonel pressed the button, but he couldn't just hide there and let those soldiers take his father away.

"No!" Mike yelled as he stood up. He quickly pointed the gun at the device the Colonel held and fired. The bullets hit the device and it exploded into pieces. The Colonel fell backwards as one of the bullets hit his hand.

The Cyber-soul possessed Dolphi dropped to his knees. "NOOOO!!!" he yelled as he fell on his hands and bowed his head down.

"You idiot!" the Colonel yelled at Mike. "Open fire!" he ordered his men. Mike quickly ducked behind the counter. As the hail of bullets went flying, Dolphi looked up and saw the soldiers tearing up the counter. He could hear the frantic cries of his boys, afraid of the gunfire.

"They're shooting at my boys... !" Dolphi thought. He then stood up. "How dare... you shoot at... MY CHILDREN!" he yelled with unruly anger. One of the soldiers then reached for something on his belt. It was a grenade!

"Fire in the hole!" the soldier shouted. The bullets stopped and the soldier pulled the pin. Dolphi ran towards the counter. The grenade was thrown, and Dolphi jumped up just as it crossed his path. He grabbed it in midair, threw it back at the soldiers while still in the air, and then just as he landed behind the counter, the grenade rolled into the center of the group of soldiers.

"Grenade!" a soldier yelled. Just before they were about to run, there was a loud explosion.

As the room became quiet, Dolphi got up and looked around. There were soldiers lying everywhere. He saw the Colonel struggling to crawl away. Dolphi walked up to him and turned him around so he could face him. The Colonel was a real mess. He was bleeding in several places where the shrapnel hit him.

"Don't... worry," the Colonel gasped, "there will be... other opportunities. You will... hear from us... again." The Colonel then fell silent.

Dolphi sighed at the entire scene. He then felt the bullet wound in his arm hurt again. "Ow, I need to have this wound taken care of," Dolphi said. "Hey... I don't remember taking my shirt off."

Dolphi's children came out from behind the counter. Mike saw the torn shirt nearby. He went over to it and picked up one of the pieces. He then noticed the money that had fallen out. Dolphi walked over to Mike.

"Wow, where did that money come from?" Mike asked as he used the torn shirt as a bandage around Dolphi's arm.

"Nowhere important," Dolphi said. "Just a little bit of bacon to bring home."

"Daddy, are you all right?" Sid asked.

"Just fine," Dolphi said as Mike tied the knot in the bandage.

"Dad," Walter asked, "what happened with you a moment ago? You started talking about how you were from a far away planet or something."

"I did?" Dolphi asked confused.

"Yes," Walter replied, "you said your name was, what was it again? Cyber-soul."

Dolphi was even more confused. "I don't remember saying anything like that. That guy pushed a button, I got knocked out, and then I woke up and saw those guys were shooting at you."

"Well then, thanks to a clean shot by Mike, he destroyed the device and freed you from that guy's control," said Walter.

"I know you said not to risk my life," Mike said, "but—"

"It's okay," Dolphi replied. "Sid, try not to look at the bodies."

"What bodies?" Sid asked.

"I'm talking about the ones that are all over the…" When Dolphi looked around, all the bodies, including the Colonel's, were gone. "… place?" he ended his sentence. "Where did they all go? That's very strange."

"Let's just get out of here, dad," Mike said.

"Wait, not yet. I have a feeling that I've forgotten about something. The Colonel said that his men planted something around this place." Dolphi suddenly remembered what he was told. "Oh my god! The building has been rigged with… !"

Just then, the red and blue flashing lights of a police cruiser appeared out in the parking lot.

CHAPTER 26

A Race Against Time

"Courage is knowing what not to fear."
—Plato

THE POLICE OFFICER in the parking lot got out of the cruiser and examined the body on the ground. The officer then headed over to the entrance of the Inn and saw Dolphi and his boys inside. As the officer entered the building, the boys recognized who it was.

"Hey, you're Officer… Monica!" Mike said surprised.

"Hey there," she replied. She then looked at Dolphi. "Oh my goodness, it's you! What has happened here?" she asked as she saw the room had been wrecked by gunfire and grenade shrapnel. "Did you have something to do with this?" she asked Dolphi in a serious manner.

"The dead guy outside and what happened here, can wait," Dolphi said. "Right now, we have a bigger problem; there are explosive devices planted around the building and we have to find them quickly!"

"How do you know there are explosives?" she asked in a controlled voice.

"A bunch of people who were after me, told me they were going to eliminate anyone who had witnessed them after they were through with me."

"And those people killed that man and shot the place up?" Monica asked.

"Yes."

"Then where are they?"

"I wish I could explain," Dolphi said, "if their bodies were still lying all over this room... "

"If there *are* explosives, do you know where they are?"

"No, but I might be able to—"

Suddenly, the door to the stairway opened and out ran a man wearing the same colored uniform as the soldiers that had confronted Dolphi. As soon as the soldier saw Dolphi, he went for his gun.

Monica went for her gun as well. "Freeze!" she shouted. The soldier already had his gun out and it was much bigger than hers. She and the boys quickly ducked for cover as the bullets roared pass them. Dolphi ran over to another plant with a marble pot. This time, he grabbed it and lifted it up. It was quite heavy, but Dolphi tossed the whole thing at the soldier. There was a loud crash and a growl of pain. When the soldier stopped moving, everyone walked over to see what had happened. The heavy pot had crushed the soldier to death. Suddenly, there was a strange whitish glow surrounding the soldier's body. He faded and then disappeared. No one could believe their eyes.

"Well, at least I can tell you that the people that were responsible for the carnage here, looked like that soldier," Dolphi said.

"I have no idea... what to make of this at all," Monica said almost speechless.

Dolphi noticed something on the ground where the soldier had been. He picked it up and studied it. He could see a time showing five minutes that was counting down. "We have less than five minutes before this place blows!" Dolphi said, horrified.

"There's no time to call a bomb squad!" Monica said. "We have to evacuate everyone!"

"I don't think people are going to be very comfortable with a corpse lying out in the parking lot," Dolphi said. "I better start trying to find the bombs before it's too late!"

Dolphi ran over to the door where the soldier came from and went into the stairway.

"Where to start looking?" Dolphi thought constantly. When he closed his eyes, he saw a small pulsating light. He began to follow it as he went into the basement. When he went through the door and found himself in the boiler room, he tracked the pulse behind a heater. He then opened his eyes and saw a suspicious device with a display matrix on it saying there were four bombs active in the building. Dolphi found one of them, but he didn't know how to disarm it. "Damn that sapper!" Dolphi thought. He carefully picked it up and quickly ran back up the stairs to the lobby.

"I found something!" Dolphi said as he laid the bomb on the ground in front of his children and Officer Monica.

"How do we disarm this thing?" Sid asked. There were three different colored wires.

"Red, blue or green?" Walter asked. "Which one should be cut?" The bomb was square, had a black color and was the same size as a basketball.

"I haven't been trained for bomb disposal," Monica said.

"I better go find the others," Dolphi said. He closed his eyes again and went past the stairway to the hallway that housed the first floor rooms. He hurried up and down, trying to pick up any pulses that were similar to the one he had already found. There wasn't anything down the left hall, so he went down the other way. Sure enough, he saw a pulse coming from one of the rooms.

"Anybody in there?!" Dolphi asked. When he got no answer, he grabbed the handle and rammed himself into the door. The room was empty. Dolphi tracked the pulse underneath a bed. When he saw the second bomb, he grabbed it and ran out of the room and back to the lobby.

"Less than three minutes remaining!" Dolphi said. "What should we do?"

"If it's too risky to cut the correct wire," Monica replied, "then we should get these things to a safe, open area and let them detonate."

"Then do that with these two and I'll find the rest," Dolphi said.

"Dad," Sid tapped Dolphi, "I found this key card behind the receptionist's desk. It's a master key for all the doors."

"Thanks," Dolphi said as he took the key and ran for the stairway. He proceeded to the second floor and entered the hallway. Using his sonar once again, he ran up and down the hall scanning for bombs. When he picked up a pulse, he opened his eyes to see it was coming from a restroom — the ladies restroom. Dolphi didn't care that he was a man; he just ran in and looked around. He then noticed the bomb was under a toilet and someone was using the stall.

"Excuse me," Dolphi said.

"Hey!" the woman angrily replied. "Get out!"

"Listen, I don't mean to alarm you, but there is a bomb underneath your toilet!"

When the woman looked, she shrieked and ran out of the stall. When she saw Dolphi, she shrieked again. Dolphi ran into the stall and grabbed the bomb. He then charged out and scanned for the last bomb. He didn't find any other pulses on the floor, but there were people out in the hall that had heard the gunfire and grenade explosion from below and wondered what was going on. The people gasped as they saw the mutant dolphin run past them.

Dolphi had only two minutes remaining. He decided to head up to the third floor where he had found his children to see if the last bomb was there. When he entered the hall, he saw lots of people who had heard the gunshot that the Colonel had fired into Dolphi's arm. When the people saw Dolphi, they gasped with curiosity. But when somebody saw the bomb he held, a man shouted, "he's got a bomb!"

Everyone then panicked. When Dolphi closed his eyes to use his echolocation, the shouting from people had filled the whole hallway with a white barrage of light. Dolphi could not see where the final bomb was hiding!

"Everyone just calm down so I can find a bomb that is on this floor somewhere!" Dolphi shouted. Nobody listened however. Dolphi decided to run over to each door, open them and peek inside using his sonar to see if the pulsating light from the bomb was in there without interference from the noise. Some of the doors were locked, so Dolphi used the master key to open them and repeat the same process.

He finally found the pulse he was searching for, but it had cost him a whole minute to find it. He now had one minute remaining. He entered the room and saw an elderly Japanese man and woman standing and holding each other, not knowing what was going on. When they saw Dolphi, their eyes widened and they knelt down. The man softly said only one word, "merman…" and the couple bowed. Dolphi smiled for a second and then looked around the room for the bomb. He saw the pulse emitting from the closet. He opened it and grabbed the last bomb. He quickly ran for the door, but turned around for a second and bowed to the couple before leaving.

Dolphi quickly ran towards the stairway. Fifty seconds remained. He arrived back on the first floor. Forty seconds remained. He dashed down the hall that led to a back door and ran outside. Thirty seconds remained. There was a bank that dropped down onto a small, sandy beach. Dolphi jumped down and ran into the water. Twenty seconds remained. He swam away from the Inn as fast as he could. In the water, it was pitch black, but when Dolphi used his sonar, he was able to see the ocean floor and everything around him. He realized that his echolocation worked much better underwater than on land. Ten seconds remained. Dolphi let go of the bombs and swam back to the shore as quickly as possible. Five, four, three, two, one. There was a loud explosion and Dolphi felt the shock wave hit him from behind. It produced a blinding light to his sonar ability and the noise was shattering to his ears. He stopped and covered his ears as it really hurt.

Dolphi got out of the water. People had moved out onto their balconies as they heard the explosion. Dolphi felt like he had had enough for the night. He walked back towards the building. People stared at him as he went inside. He walked back towards the lobby and then headed out the front entrance. He saw Officer Monica and his children walking towards him.

"Dad!" the boys called. "You're okay!"

Dolphi saw smoke coming from a field. "I see you got the other bombs out of the way."

"You're a very brave dolphin," Monica said.

"And lucky too," Dolphi replied.

"And I thought vigilantes were no good."

"Me? A vigilante?"

"Never mind." Monica turned to look at the body in the parking lot.

"He ran away after he saw me enter the building," Dolphi said. "The group of soldiers that attacked the building, like that guy you saw, had taken him out before entering."

"Ah-ha! So it was *you* who broke in!" Monica said.

"The door was locked and I had to get in there to find my children," Dolphi said. "*And* prevent the place from being blown up."

"Say, Monica," Mike asked, "how did you know we were in trouble? The phones wouldn't work."

"My radio said that there was a break-in at this place after your dolphin father tripped the silent alarm," she explained. "Because I knew you three were staying here and that I was close to this place, I took the call and headed on over. I was about to respond to a call about an illegal street race that had occurred recently."

Dolphi turned away from Monica and rolled his eyes in a furtive manner. He noticed smoke coming from another direction. It was coming from further up the road. Dolphi started walking towards it.

"Where are you going?" Walter asked.

Dolphi began jogging and as he got closer, he saw it was a car on fire.

"No…" Dolphi thought in horror. The car was becoming familiar as he ran towards it. "NO!" he yelled. "BLUE!" He then stumbled onto his knees and stared at the burning wreck. It was the street racer's car alright. The soldiers *had* done away with him.

The boys ran over to Dolphi. "Oh god," Mike said. "Did you know the person in that vehicle?"

Dolphi continued staring at the wreck and then bowed his head down. "He was so young…" he said sadly.

Monica drove over in her car and stopped. She got out with a concerned look on her face as she saw the fire and Dolphi feeling very upset. She went for her radio.

"Any available units, this is 6FL19. I have responded to the call of a break-in at the Dolphin's Lagoon Inn on Dilton Blvd. I have found a murdered man out in the parking lot and a vehicle that's ablaze just further up the road. Occupant of vehicle may have been inside. Any available units please respond, over."

The boys put their hands on Dolphi's shoulders. "I put the money you had inside my backpack," Mike said. "Come on, dad, let's go home."

"But backup is on its way," Monica said. "We should stay and explain the situation."

"And how are we going to explain that a group of unknown soldiers appeared out of nowhere and then vanished into thin air after they died for god's sake?!" Dolphi angrily asked. After that, he then sighed. "If I stay here, the situation is going to get even more complicated and I could be sent back to that horrible place I was sent to after I last saw my boys in that research facility."

"What place was that?" Sid asked.

"… Never mind," Dolphi said.

Monica began to think about it.

"We really want to get back home," Mike said.

After a moment, Monica made up her mind. "Okay," she said. "I'm not sure what's going on either. Let's head to your residence and we'll see if we can understand anything."

Everyone got in the cruiser and drove off. The boys sat in the back with Dolphi lying partially on the floor at their feet. Dolphi had his head in Sid's lap so that his head could be stroked by his dolphin loving son.

Dolphi had finally found his children and he was going home with them at last. Then, the only thing he still had to do was to head back over to his work place, find his wife and then deal with Mr. Jem. But not tonight.

"Goodbye… Paul…" Dolphi whispered as Monica drove onto the highway in the direction of home.

CHAPTER 27

Shelter

"Learn from yesterday, live for today, hope for tomorrow.
The important thing is not to stop questioning."
—Albert Einstein

OFFICER MONICA DROVE Dolphi and his children back to their home in North Miami. Since she had been at their house before, she knew where to go. Everyone in the back of the vehicle was almost asleep, as it was very late. When Monica came to a stop, the boys opened their eyes and saw their house. They yawned as they got out, helping their half asleep father. They walked up to the house and Mike unlocked the door. They went into the dark house and turned on the lights.

As the house lit up, there was a horrifying sight. Everything was trashed. Their house had been broken into before, but this was even worse.

"This isn't what the place looked like when we left!" Mike said shocked.

"Not again…" Dolphi moaned.

"Another break-in," Monica thought shaking her head. "And at the same house."

"I don't want to deal with this right now," Dolphi yawned. "Let the cop handle this, kids. It's way past your bedtime anyway."

"I'll report it in the morning," Monica said. Suddenly, there was a scraping noise coming from the kitchen. Out came an excited black and white border collie to greet his family in the usual manner;

jumping and barking and tail wagging madly. It was Squall, the Jay family's dog. He sniffed at the mutant dolphin. Dolphi bent down and the dog licked his hand. Squall didn't recognize his master, but to him, Dolphi was just another guest to enter the dog's world. "Looks like you're still okay even after two break-ins," Dolphi said. "Do you know who broke in?" Squall barked, but Dolphi heard no words. "Looks like I only understand dolphins." He moaned again. "I'm so exhausted, I feel like I'll drop any second now."

"I think it would be a good idea for dad to sleep in a watery environment so he can rehydrate," said Sid. "A bathtub with soft stuff on the bottom would help."

"Good idea," Mike said.

Mike, Monica and Dolphi went into the bathroom next to Dolphi's room while Walter and Sid let the dog outside and checked his food and water before getting ready for bed. Mike got some large towels, folded them and placed them in the bottom of the bathtub to make it comfortable for Dolphi. Mike then turned on the water in the bathtub to a reasonable temperature. When the water level was right, Dolphi hopped into the tub and said, "home... at last..." He then fell forward and made a splash that got Monica and Mike a little wet. Dolphi lay face down in the tub with his blowhole just above the surface of the water. "Dad?" Mike asked. Dolphi did not respond. "Passed out cold," Mike said to Monica. They both sat down on the floor.

"It's not every day you realize your father's been turned into a half-beast creature," Mike sighed. "What kind of job is my dad going to do now? How is he going to live for the rest of his life? So many questions in this whole mess... "

"I know how you feel," said Monica. "But you know what I think about your dad?"

"What?"

"I think he's really cute." She then giggled.

"Sure," Mike rolled his eyes and laughed.

"Don't think of him as a beast," Monica said, "instead, think of him as an anthropomorphic dolphin."

"Anthro-what?"

"It means something that has human characteristics. His human body structure's the same, but he's got the skin, dorsal fin and head of a dolphin. He has no pectoral fins or tail, but I suppose the webbed hands and feet suffice for swimming… or walking. Quite interesting really."

"Yeah," Mike said. He put his hand in his pocket and pulled out the keychain picture of his family that he received during his visit to the Discovery Research Inc. and looked at his mother. "I'm still thinking about my mom," he said. "I have no idea what's happened to her, but she was left behind at my dad's workplace in a secret lab that probably nobody knows about. I, my brothers and my mom went to the M.R.I.L after our dad didn't return home after closing up for the weekend. Inside the place we came across a hall restricted to staff only that leads to some doors with whatever's inside. There was this door that my brothers and I went through after unlocking it with this key we found by accident. There was lots of weird equipment. The place was some kind of lab. We found out the lab's purpose was to create and research these… mutant animals. That's where dad first started off as that mutant dolphin thing. I don't know how he was mutated, but our mom was left behind in that place. We were attacked by mutant sharks and we ran away. Mom had fainted at the sight of them and we couldn't get her up. Now I and my brothers fear that she might be dead, or has become something like dad."

"This is so deep," Monica said concerned. "The officers that were sent to that place said they didn't find anything."

"And I suggested to you that the security tapes from the last three days be recovered, if there are any."

"I'll head on over and do that first thing tomorrow morning…" she said. She then looked at her watch. "… if I can get enough sleep that is. Yikes, it's 4:00 A.M. We better hit the sack right now."

"We?" asked Mike.

"Yep. I am going to stay and protect you kids. Your house has been broken into for the second time and I think you need someone like me to be around."

"Well… okay," said Mike. "I'll show you my parent's room." Mike put the picture on the bathtub's edge, got up and showed Monica the room.

"Thanks," she said. "I'll take care of things in the morning. Good night."

"You too," said Mike.

Mike went to his room. He saw his clothing scattered all around.

"Who would do this to us?" he thought. He got into his pajamas and crawled into bed. "Soldiers from the future?" he pondered. He then closed his eyes and tried to forget about what happened at the Inn.

In the bathroom, Dolphi opened his eyes a few minutes later and looked around. "I'm home again..." he thought recognizing the room. "I've been through so much. I could have gotten home much sooner if it was Halloween." Dolphi then noticed his key chain picture. "I'm glad most of us are back safe and sound," he thought.

He stepped out of the tub and stood there dripping. "Why do I not feel tired?" he thought. "Is it because of the water rejuvenating me or something having to do with my dolphin form? I guess it's nothing important. Dolphi walked out of the bathroom through another door that led out into the hallway. He went to the kitchen and went out the door to the backyard. Dolphi walked over to the swimming pool and looked around. The night was warm, serene and the sky was clear and full of stars. "Finally, peace and quiet," he thought. He jumped into the pool and swam around. He went into the deep end and swam up to the surface to leap gracefully out of the water. After his jump, he began to swim around the pool in a circle at a fast speed.

"In a way," Dolphi thought, "I feel like Spider-man. Only I can do whatever a *dolphin* can." He stopped and faced the house. He began to sing like a dolphin. He made beautiful sounds as he stared up at the starry sky.

The boys could hear the sounds Dolphi was making. "Cool," Mike hummed.

"You sound beautiful, dad," Walter thought.

"Just think it's a beautiful dolphin who wants to sing you to sleep and help you forget all your troubles..." Sid smiled as he snuggled in his bed.

After Dolphi made his last whistle sound, he lay there in the water.

"Man," Dolphi thought, staring at the sky. "I love doing what dolphins do. If only Jennifer was here... "

Dolphi went out of the pool and sat on the grass. The wind was blowing softly. He closed his eyes and began to meditate. After a while, he slowly fell asleep.

Dolphi started dreaming. He found himself in a field. There were no trees or buildings. It was flat for miles. On the distant horizon, he saw dark clouds forming. Then, there was lightning. There were several bolts striking down every ten seconds or so. The thunder sounded soft. It looked very peaceful.

"Thunderclouds…" Dolphi thought. Suddenly, he heard a voice he didn't recognize.

"That's not what they are…" said the voice.

"Who's there?" Dolphi asked.

"It looks beautiful from a distance," the voice continued, "but if you get closer, it will be terrifying."

"Who are you?!" asked Dolphi.

"The lightning speaks of your destiny. You want revenge against the man who created you, then go after him. I know you will. You will face your enemies head on, despite the storm."

"What storm?" Dolphi called. The voice did not respond and Dolphi could see the sky going black. He suddenly saw a lightning bolt strike very close to him. He then saw a huge mouth, with lots of sharp teeth similar to those of a shark, open and then close over him. The dream then ended.

CHAPTER 28

In the News

"The reporter is the daily prisoner of clocked facts.
On all working days, he is expected to do his best
in one swift swipe at each story."
—American Journalist Jim Bishop

DOLPHI AWOKE AFTER the strange dream and found himself lying on the grass next to his swimming pool in the backyard. The morning sun was shinning brightly on his face. "Ahh…" he sighed, "just like a beached dolphin. I wonder what that dream was all about?" He got up and washed off the soil that was stuck to his body, in the pool. He walked into the house and headed towards his bedroom. He opened the door and saw someone sleeping in his bed. A smile came on Dolphi's face. He slowly walked into the room and stood at the foot of the bed. "Honey?" Dolphi asked sweetly. Suddenly, the sleeping person sat up and pointed a gun right at him. Dolphi instantly froze and held his arms up in the air. It was Monica. She looked at him and then put her gun down. "Oh, thank god it's only you," she said. "I'm very sorry about that. I thought the housebreaker was back."

"Oh, its you," Dolphi said with a sigh of relief as he put his arms down. "You're the officer who drove us home last and who I had also seen at that DRI place."

"Dry? Oh, D.R.I. The Discovery Research Inc."

"Yes. So, what are you doing here and sleeping in my bed?"

"I'm here to protect the kids," she said. "Somebody has raided your house for the second time and I'm going to make sure it doesn't happen again."

"I see. Seeing you in bed reminded me of my wife."

"She is still missing, isn't she?" Monica asked. "Your son Mike says that she fainted in a lab and was left there."

"Oh my dear…" Dolphi said. "I hope she is alright."

"I better get up and get some breakfast," Monica said. She got out of the bed and went into the bathroom to change clothes. She dressed into her uniform and walked out of the bathroom. "Try not to worry about anything right now," she said. "It's a school day, but the boys got to sleep late last night and they've been through so much, so they should sleep in a little."

"That will be fine," Dolphi said. Monica went out of the bedroom and headed to the kitchen. "Try not to worry," Dolphi repeated in his mind. He walked out of the room and headed down towards the rooms of his boys. He started at Sid's room. He opened the door quietly and saw Sid lying peacefully in bed with the dolphin plush toy in his arms. Dolphi smiled. It made him happy. He then closed the door slowly and walked to Mike's room. He saw Mike lying in his bed, also asleep. His bed covers were not over him. Dolphi then went to Walter's bedroom. Walter slept soundly with tools and science projects strewn about his covers. Everywhere in his room, there were pieces of science lab equipment, a poster of the table of elements over his desk and another poster of Albert Einstein on the wall above his head. There were lots of books on the shelves all about science.

Dolphi then headed towards the kitchen. Monica was having some coffee.

"I see you are drinking coffee. It had been spilled onto the floor a couple of days ago, but it was swept up and we removed the hair and dirt."

"Thanks for telling me," Monica said. "I was about to spit it out halfway through your sentence."

Dolphi opened the refrigerator and saw some left over sausage on a plate covered in plastic wrap from Thursday night's dinner. He warmed it up in the microwave, took it out onto the counter, got a knife and cut it into pieces. He put a chunk in his mouth and tried to chew it. He had a hard time trying to mash it up. "Oh, right," Dolphi thought. "My teeth are made for gripping my food." He swallowed all the sausage bits that were there.

"Listen," Monica said to Dolphi, "I'm going to head over to your workplace and see if I can obtain surveillance tapes of any illegal activities that will make a S.W.A.T team take action."

"And I'm coming with you," Dolphi said.

"Remember that I'm still an officer of the law who does not tolerate vigilante activity," Monica said. "Besides, you've barely had any sleep. Let me handle this one task and then I'll come back for you."

"Okay, I'll let you go," Dolphi said, "but I'm really concerned about my wife. I hope my boss or his... *mutants* as my boys told me, haven't hurt her."

"Is that her?" Monica asked, pointing to a picture on a nearby wall.

"That is her," Dolphi said. "She is so beautiful. I love her very much."

"You've also got great children," she said.

"We have such a blessed family," Dolphi said. "But now, I feel that recent events are starting to tear this perfect family to shreds."

"Perhaps you are right," Monica sighed.

"However, I'm not going to lose anyone," Dolphi said. "I'm going back outside. Good luck with finding cold hard evidence."

"Thanks. While I'm out, be sure to spend some time with your kids. It will make everyone including yourself feel better."

"Okay, I will. But if you get eaten by a mutant," he grinned and pointed a finger, "then I'll have to go over there myself." Monica smiled. "Oh yeah, one last thing, I'd like you to check records and see what you can pull up on a James Richwood Jem. He's the president of the M.R.I.L and my boss, who mutated me in the first place."

"I'll do that," she said. "Good bye!" She then left the kitchen.

Dolphi walked back outside. He noticed the trampoline that his boys played on at times. He climbed onto it and started hopping up and down. He was glad to be home. He had gone through many things in the past two days. He felt like his life was taking a whole new direction not just because his form had been changed, but because his view on life and his opinion of things in the world was also changing. Had he not been turned into a mutant, he might never have found out about the fraudulent dolphin facility. That experience gave him a wake-up call on his love for dolphins. Dolphi jumped higher and did a back flip. He then did a somersault and spun around in the air. "This is pretty cool," Dolphi thought. "I think I'll go inside and see if anything that's happened because of me is on the news." He got off the trampoline and went back into the house and saw Mike. "You're up early, Mike," Dolphi said.

"I was just getting something to eat," Mike yawned.

"It seems we have an even bigger mess around our house," Dolphi said. "So far, it seems to be mostly clothing scattered around."

"I think you're right," Mike said. "Maybe we'll clean it up later."

"Let's see what's on the news," Dolphi said. They sat down on the couch and turned on the television. A journalist was talking about a serious incident that had happened last week, but it had nothing to do with Dolphi. Last week on the twentieth of April, three days before Dolphi's mutation, was the deadly Columbine high school shooting in Colorado. It was one of the worst high school massacres anyone had ever known. After the incident, the first pictures to be shown on the news were heart wrenching. Dolphi, his friends and family could not come up with any words to make sense of how this sort of thing could happen. Dolphi and his wife could not stop thinking about how they would have felt if they lost their children from something like that. After a couple of days of grieving, everyone tried their best to get on with their lives.

Dolphi sighed. "What a sick thing that happened to all those poor students," he said.

"Yeah," Mike frowned. "If only those two had gotten help and had never been picked on."

The program soon ended and the news began.

"This is Florida's top news story this morning. I'm Cheryl Hunt," the anchorwoman said.

"The Dolphin's Lagoon Inn, a place of peace and serenity, was shattered by a grizzly murder last night. Tom Denson has more."

The Inn had police standing around the parking lot with yellow police tape in front of the entrance doors. There was a stretcher carrying the dead employee away into an ambulance.

"A thirty-two year old man was gunned down in the parking lot sometime around 2:00 AM," Tom said. *"Police told us that inside*

the lobby, there were lots of shots fired and a possible explosion causing great damage. Guests at the building claimed they saw, believe it or not, soldiers of unknown origin oust them from their rooms, claiming to be searching for a suspicious suspect. A guest who was on the third floor is right here with me and he says he saw something else. What did you see sir?"

"*I swear, I saw this guy in a dolphin get-up,*" the man said. "*He had a bomb in his hands. A few minutes later, I heard, I mean, everyone heard, a set of explosions outside; one off the beach and another out in a nearby field.*"

"*I see,*" Tom said with a hint of confusion as he focused back to the camera. "*Police have found no evidence of any military weaponry. Also, further up the road, there was a vehicle that had been destroyed. The cause of the explosion was unknown. A thorough search of the vehicle didn't reveal any human remains...* "

Dolphi suddenly felt the words, "any human remains" echoing in his mind. "Bad Blue... !" Dolphi said startled.

"Who?" Mike asked.

Dolphi looked around. "Officer Monica has gone out, so I think I should tell you about that car..." Dolphi explained to Mike about how he got involved in a street race in order to get to South Miami. "I guess he got out of the car before it blew up. But the NAS was already depleted. I guess the soldiers opened fire on him, but he must have rolled out of the vehicle and ran. That's my best guess."

The news went back to the anchorwoman.

"*Residents and tourists in Key West have discovered a huge situation that is so bizarre, only the images can speak for themselves.*" The TV then showed firefighters spraying their hoses over a burning building at night that Dolphi recognized. "*The store of a $wim-with-the-dolphins facility called 'Dolphin World' was seen burning last night sometime before midnight. It is believed that the cause of the fire was arson. However, it's not the burning building that's a concern, it's about what has been happening at the facility. Firefighters and investigators have discovered that the parking lot was littered with equipment that you wouldn't find at your local dolphin facility.*"

The camera showed what the burnt remains of the store looked like in the morning. A man was seen with one of the pieces of equipment.

"What we have here are tools that came from the U.S Navy. This stuff is definitely authentic, their insignia is stamped right here. The structure of these items suggest that they are to be used on the dolphins. See where the snout of a dolphin is meant to bite down on? Now, there are a lot of people around here who are against the idea of dolphins being used by the Navy for lethal acts of war. Visitors to this facility have never seen anything like this or have even heard the term, 'Navy dolphins' before."

The TV went back to Cheryl Hunt. *"The store was the only burnt structure,"* she said. *"The pen where the dolphins are kept, had been vandalized and the animals are missing. There was one human casualty found inside the inferno. Police are trying to identify the man. The facility owner, Dennis Glack, could not be reached for comment. The revealing of the Navy equipment is likely to put a new face on Dolphin World and bring up tough questions at Navy conferences. And now a look at sports... "*

Dolphi turned the TV off. "That is the facility I was taken to yesterday," he said to Mike. "I didn't start that fire, however. The guy who freed me didn't start that fire either, he was already gone."

"Who do you suppose did it?" asked Mike.

Dolphi suddenly felt like he knew who it was. "... I think it was someone whose mind had been opened up just before it happened," Dolphi said.

"Was something going on over there last night?" asked Mike. Dolphi was thinking about how that dolphin trainer reacted to the truth. "... There are people who are sheltered... and naïve, Mike," Dolphi said. "They can't think or stick up for themselves, they don't want to fight, they don't want to argue or negotiate with others, they always do as they're told... and as a result, they get controlled by people who can give them what they want, such as, their very own dolphin, which they can adore. It's frightening if you think about it... They must always follow their superiors and not do anything that will double-cross them... or else..." Dolphi was silent. Mike was showing great interest in this conversation. He had never thought about this sort of thing before.

"Sounds like Nazism," said Mike. "What are you talking about, the way the staff at the facility were treating you?"

"The way they *were* going to," said Dolphi. "It all sounds like a conspiracy of some sort to me... and the law was built for it... "

"I see…" Mike said. "And what about the dolphins? You think they're being mistreated or something?"

"Mike," Dolphi said, thinking about the poor dolphin named Pogo, "I have the power to talk to dolphins. I can hear their language. This one dolphin, he told me he was brutally captured from the wild. He was taken to the facility and this trainer, who called him Pogo, was trying to train him to do acrobatic tricks for human entertainment. He didn't feed him properly when he didn't perform tricks correctly. Pogo was in shallow water, so when he leaped and dove into the water, he pretty much collided into the sandy bottom, which was littered with garbage. He was emaciated from all that and that could have been me."

"Jesus," Mike thought. "This is interesting, I think Sid should hear about this." Just as Mike was about to get up, Dolphi grabbed his arm. "No, this isn't a conversation for such a young boy. He wouldn't understand." Dolphi was silent again. Mike sat back down. "So, about the dolphin trainer," Mike asked. "He *intended* to do cruel things to that dolphin?"

Dolphi was thinking about the orders the trainer might have received and what might have happened to him if he had turned on his boss. However, Dolphi had remembered that the trainer had learned a lot during their discussion. As a result, it was concluded; the trainer was the one who set fire to the facility.

"… Dad?" Mike asked when he didn't get an answer.

"I don't think the trainer was doing those things on purpose," Dolphi said. "He just followed orders and thought what he was doing was… perfectly normal. He didn't know what he was doing but he *thought he knew* what he was doing."

"I had no idea this sort of thing was happening," Mike said with a disgusted look on his face. "How did you escape from the place anyway?"

"I had help from an activist with wire cutters," said Dolphi. "He wanted to break me and the dolphin out because we were put in a pen to clown about for humans. That also reminds me, there was a sewer outlet nearby that was slowly spewing out muck and poisoning the water and harming the dolphin's health. The activist got caught and was being attacked by some guards. I beat them up, but I hadn't intended to fight them. I just didn't want to see the guy getting beaten to a pulp. I may have kicked their butts, but I'm not Batman."

"I know you're not a super hero of any kind," said Mike.

"I also think that guy who saved me, came because he didn't like the idea of people capturing wild animals and keeping them in captivity," said Dolphi.

"Gee," Mike said. "So, what should we do about the facilities? Shut them down, all of them?"

"That's probably the best idea as dolphins don't belong in captivity," said Dolphi.

"But, that would mean people would never get so close to those animals again," said Mike. "Dolphins and humans have such a curiosity between each other."

"I know," Dolphi said. "There are lots of pros and cons about this whole thing. I don't know what's right either."

"Well, I'm glad those Dolphin World people didn't turn your life into some kind of joke," said Mike. They then hugged each other.

"Mike," Dolphi said, "please do me a favor."

"Yes?"

"Don't tell Sid."

"Okay… You should go after your boss," Mike said as they let go of each other, "… it's not right that he did this to you."

"… You're right," Dolphi said. "I'll go when Officer Monica gets back, *if* she gets back that is. She's gone to do some investigating at the M.R.I.L. I still need to relax some more before I'm ready to go." Dolphi got up and decided to go and check out the house to see what had happened in the second robbery. He started out in the basement.

He could see lots of books and things knocked over. "I don't know if we're ever going to clean up this mess," Dolphi thought. As he moved through to another room, he saw a barbell used for weightlifting. He had gotten a weightlifting system for Mike's birthday. It wasn't used very often, but Mike or one of his brothers would take a shot at it every now and then. Dolphi walked over to it and saw a 50 pound weight on each side. The total weight was 100 pounds. "I've had a tough time trying to lift that much weight," Dolphi thought. He made a fist and checked out his biceps and triceps. After his mutation, his muscles had gotten bigger. He saw a pile of weights nearby. He decided to take all the weights and attach them onto the barbell. The weight was now 400 pounds. He put his hands on the barbell and gripped hard. He then counted to three and lifted it. The weight was beginning to strain him, but Dolphi continued lifting and managed to get it up to his chest. He then positioned himself and lifted it right over his head. "... Cooooool!" Dolphi said amazed. He then returned it to the floor as gently as he could. "That wasn't too bad!" he thought. Dolphi went back upstairs and began to look around for some paper. He found a piece and a pencil and began drawing a map of the M.R.I.L. "I'll get into the front entrance..." he thought, "I'll head to that lab I got mutated in and see if I can find Jennifer... and then I'll find Mr. Jem and kick his butt. He might have bodyguards with him... sharks that are mutated like I am." He then crumpled the paper as he knew he was playing silly buggers. "Whatever."

He suddenly felt the bullet wound in his arm hurting. He headed on back to his bedroom.

He opened a drawer and looked through a bunch of nail files, cotton balls and shaving items. He found a pair of tweezers. He put a towel in his mouth to bite on for the pain. He then took the bandage off his right arm and began to try taking the bullet out. He slowly fiddled with the tweezers trying to find the bullet. He felt sharp pain when he tried moving the tool around. Dolphi bit hard and gripped the bullet. He tried to pull it out as quickly as possible. Dolphi screamed and a huge crack suddenly appeared on the mirror. The bullet came out and he immediately dropped the tweezers on the table. His arm began to bleed. He covered his bleeding arm with the towel he had been biting on. "Ow..." he groaned. "That's better." He looked at the bullet covered in blood. He then saw the bullet disappearing into dust. "What the hell?" he thought. "A lot of weird stuff has been happening ever since I became a mutant." He took out some dressing and made a firm wrapping around his arm. He looked at the cracked mirror. "The enigma..." he thought. He then remembered last night at the Inn; the place where those soldiers attacked. He wondered if the Colonel was right about what he had said about the power in his head. He then moved to a part of the mirror that wasn't cracked. "Now listen here you... Cyber... something," Dolphi said to his reflection, "if you're really in my head, come on out and speak to me." Nothing happened. "Well, what are you waiting for? You have caused me a lot of trouble!" He knocked on his head and banged his hand on the mirror. "Show me a sign that you're there!" Dolphi shouted. Still, nothing happened. He then growled and stared at himself.

He then heard someone walk into the bathroom. It was Sid. "Are you alright, dad?" Sid asked.

Dolphi sighed and turned to look at Sid. "It's alright," he said. "Daddy's only recovering from a wound he has just treated."

"Dad," Sid asked, "can we play in the swimming pool after I get some breakfast?"

"Um, sure! So, did the burglar do anything to your room?"

"No, its fine."

"Okay, what do you want for breakfast?"

"Anything that hasn't been stolen."

Dolphi went into the kitchen and looked through some cupboards. He found some pancake mix and a frying pan to make it in.

By the time Dolphi prepared the pancakes, all three of his boys were out of bed. Everyone sat down and enjoyed their meal.

"By the way," Sid said, "I noticed that a brand new bottle of chocolate syrup has gone missing. I remember you buying it recently before your mutation, dad. None of us even had a chance to take it out of its wrapper."

"Were you going to put some on your pancakes?" Dolphi asked.

"Uh-huh."

"You know you shouldn't have chocolate in the morning, it will make you sick."

"It's okay, it's not like I put it on my pancakes *every* time."

After breakfast, Sid got into his bathing suit and joined Dolphi outside. They went into the pool and began playing. Sid held Dolphi's dorsal fin and got pulled around the pool a few times. Dolphi then held Sid in his arms and breached out of the water while holding him. "This is better than SeaWorld!" Sid cheered.

The mention of SeaWorld however, got Dolphi thinking about the captivity problem. He tried not to think about it.

Mike and Walter were watching from inside the house. "This is so adorable to watch," Mike said.

"Sure is," Walter agreed. "I guess having a mutant dolphin for a father isn't *too* bad. So, where's Officer Monica?"

"She's gone to dad's workplace to find the tapes as I suggested."

"Good luck to her."

As Mike watched Dolphi and Sid playing together, he turned to Walter and asked, "wanna play with the dolphin?"

Walter smiled, "Sure. Last one in, is a rotten egg!" The two then raced to their rooms and prepared to join Dolphi in the swimming pool.

CHAPTER 29

Operation: Convince Authorities

"Punishment is justice for the unjust."
—Saint Augustine

THE MARINE RESEARCH Institute Labs were back to work. The facility was busy with people hurrying around. Inside the dolphin medical pen, Henry Guy was talking to a veterinarian. "I would also like to recommend that a study be done on this anesthesia to determine if it's safe to use on marine mammals," Henry said. "Some of our animals under this stuff didn't make it."

The veterinarian didn't seem to be impressed. "The anesthesia works just fine as far as I'm concerned," he said. "There is no reason to do what you suggested."

"But there have been studies—"

"Those studies are *my* responsibility, not yours. Now, what *I* suggest to *you*, is that you refrain from speculating about things that are not in *your* area of expertise."

"Yes, doctor," Henry said. The vet then walked off to do something else. Henry turned his head and muttered to himself, "what a jerk… I wish Dr. Jay was here." He looked around the room. He went up to a group of people and asked, "has anyone seen Dr. Jay?" Nobody said anything. They just shook their heads. "What about Jack Degrasso? Has anyone seen him?"

This time, someone said, "they didn't show up for work today. Maybe they needed an extra day off?"

"Maybe you're right," Henry said. "One more day would have worked for me."

"Who was that you were just talking with?" another man asked.

"Oh, that was just a vet from the U.S Department of Agriculture. He's here doing his annual report." He then remembered from Friday he was supposed to do something this morning. He went to the storage closet and opened the doors. The computer he was supposed to package up, was nowhere to be seen. "Now where did it go?"

He heard a voice over the loudspeaker say, *"Henry Guy, please report to the front desk."*

Henry went to the desk to find that there was a police officer standing there.

"Oh boy," Henry thought, "I hope I didn't do anything wrong." He approached the officer. "Hello, I'm Henry Guy. How may I help you, officer?"

"My name is Officer Monica Roans," she said. "Do you know a Dolph... I mean, a Dr. Jay?"

"I sure do," Henry said.

"Please come outside. I want to speak to you about something." They walked out into the parking lot. "Dr. Jay has asked me to do a favor that requires your help."

"Oh, how is he?"

Monica wasn't sure if telling him that Dr. Jay was a mutant, was a good idea. "He's alright," she said. "He could not come today. Now, have you noticed anything suspicious over the last few days?"

"Well, there was this mysterious light that caused mayhem in our medical pen area last Friday." Henry explained about the strobe of light that shot out of a dolphin they were treating. He also mentioned an attack by unknown individuals on the same day.

"I wonder if it was that 'mysterious light' that caused a brief nation-wide blackout?" Monica thought. "And the individuals that attacked, what did they look like?"

"Well, one of our staff mentioned that the suspects looked like dinosaurs with cloaks. It sounds crazy, but that's what he saw."

"What I need to speak to you about, concerns events that may have happened over the weekend," Monica said.

"The facility is not open during the weekends," Henry replied.

"Dr. Jay's family came here two days ago when he didn't come home."

Henry looked concerned. "Has he been in an accident?!"

"Uh, something did happen to him, but I told you he's okay. I need to acquire security tapes from the last three days because Dr. Jay's wife and three kids came here and only the three boys came out, so I suspect something illegal is going on."

"Really?" Henry asked surprised. "I haven't seen anyone doing anything suspicious. Although that reminds me, the two security guards who were watching the place for the weekend are nowhere to be seen. I suppose I could go inside and inquire about the tapes."

"Alright, I'll wait out here," said Monica.

Henry went back inside. He decided to find one of his friends to help him out. "Hey, Charlie-boy!" he said to a man working in the shark den. Charlie was around the same age as Henry.

"Hey, Henry," he smiled. "Need help with something?"

"Yeah, I need to get surveillance tapes from last Friday night and all of Saturday and Sunday."

"Well, the man who works in the security room is a bit of a grouch and won't just hand out tapes like candy."

"There's an officer here who really needs them. Maybe if you can help me distract the guy... "

"But I don't want to get in trouble."

"If you help me and do end up in trouble, I'll do your duties as a favor. Besides, I'm curious as to what may have happened over the weekend."

"Alright then, follow me," Charlie said as they walked out. They went into the restricted hallway and found the door with the word 'security' on it. Charlie knocked on the door and Henry hid out of view. The door opened, revealing a guy in his late forties.

"Yes, what's the problem?" he asked with a low voice. On his head, he wore a security guard's cap that said 'security chief'. Charlie pointed in a direction down the hall and said, "there's this kid causing mischief in the building..." As the security chief turned to look, Charlie snatched the cap off his head, put it on his own head and ran.

"Hey!" the security chief yelled.

"Badger, badger, mushroom, mushroom!" Charlie sang as he danced around.

Henry slipped into the room and began to search for the tapes. Each tape had a label on it. Henry soon found the tapes he needed, grabbed them and left the room quickly. Charlie was on the ground being wrestled by the man. "You stupid kid!" he yelled. "Nobody messes with Dominic Fargus!"

"Lighten up!" Charlie tried to assure him. "You need to get out and have some fun more often!"

Henry went back outside to Monica. "Here they are," he said. "Someone had to distract the security officer just so I could sneak in and get these. I hope they're worth the trouble."

"You're help is most appreciated," Monica said. "Now I just need to find out what's on these." Monica got back in her cruiser and drove off towards the police station to review the tapes and see if there was anything of interest on them. On the second floor of the building, however, someone was watching the transaction.

* * *

Monica went back to the police station. She went into a room in the back of the station and found a small television with an integrated VCR player. She popped in the first tape and began fast-forwarding to see if anything suspicious was happening. She then came across some footage where a dolphin was behaving strangely. She saw its melon glowing. Suddenly, there was static. "It really did cause the power outage," Monica thought. Suddenly, the footage changed and she saw something happening in an office. She recognized Dr. Jay as he was talking to Mr. Jem. She saw somebody with a gun fire something at Dr. Jay. Her eyes widened to see him fall down a trap door. The camera changed to show him falling into a swimming pool. What Monica saw next, made her mouth drop open. She saw Dr. Jay thrashing around in the pool, slowly changing into a mutant dolphin.

A fellow officer caught notice of the tape. "What is this that you're watching?" he asked.

"Suspicious activities at the Marine Research Institute Labs," she said. She saw Dr. Jay turned Dolphi being loaded into a tank. As she came towards the end of the first tape, she saw a strange glow hit Dolphi and enter his head. He broke out of the tank and then afterwards, threw a ladder at the camera knocking it out.

"Get the Commissioner down here right away," Monica said to the officer. As the officer moved out, Monica popped in the tape from Saturday and looked through it. It showed three men standing in the lobby talking to each other. Monica fast-forwarded the tape some more.

Police Commissioner Harold Rex entered the room and went over to Monica. "Somebody says you found something interesting, Roans," he said.

"I am looking over some security tapes from the Marine Research—"

"Some officers were already sent over there and they didn't find anything out of place," Rex said. "How did you obtain these? Did you even have a search warrant on you?"

Monica did not think about that. But even if she did have one, Mr. Jem would have been suspicious and might have done something to cover up the evidence.

Before Monica was about to say anything, an officer said, "oh my god, look what's happening!" A group of people crowded around the TV to watch four men at a dining table. Three of the men were mutating while the fourth man sat there and did nothing. The clothing of the three men was ripping apart, their skin was changing color and they were growing tails. They soon looked like mutant sharks. The only human left in the room then grabbed each one of the sharks and dragged them into his office and threw them down through a hole in the floor.

"Somebody turned those guys into animals!" an officer said.

"That was an illegal experiment of some kind!" another officer said.

Commissioner Rex was stunned. "How is this possible?"

"I don't know," Monica said. She soon saw three boys and their mother enter the facility. Monica knew right then that it was Dolphi's family. Everyone gasped when they saw the three sharks walking with a human. "I think that man is Jem, James Richwood," Monica said. "He's the president of that facility."

"Someone pull up any information on him right away," Rex said. As one of the officers left the room, Monica saw on the TV the three boys running from the mutant sharks. Their mother wasn't with them. Monica put her hand on her mouth and gasped.

"I recommend that serious action be taken at that facility," Monica suggested.

"I'll contact a S.W.A.T team right away," Rex said. Everyone around the TV then left the room. "But there's still one more tape!" Monica said. She ejected the tape that was running and put in the new one. But then she thought, "oh, I suppose I've already convinced them enough." She then got up and went to join the officers to organize a S.W.A.T team and look up Mr. Jem's information.

* * *

Dolphi and his children were lying on their towels, resting on the grass after having such a good time with each other. Dolphi got up and saw his boys were still asleep. "Wow," Dolphi thought, thinking about the amazing time he had with his children. He decided to head back into the house and go to his bedroom.

"I'll just get some sleep in my comfy bed and prepare to return to the M.R.I.L this afternoon." He went into the bed and pulled the covers over him, but left his blowhole open to allow him to breath. He lay his head down on the pillow and closed his eyes. He smiled and hummed as he felt warm, safe and relaxed. He soon went to sleep.

Dolphi found himself in a purple haze. He saw a blue circle forming. He slowly walked over to it and he could see an image inside the circle. It was like looking out a window. Dolphi could see a huge forest. The image moved over to the left and he saw a ruined city covered in creepers and other plant life. "What... happened to that city?" Dolphi wondered. He then saw a figure on a hill nearby. It was a gray colored werewolf. It was in a dog-sitting position staring out at the ruined city. It then got up on its hind legs, lifted its head up in the air and let out a loud howl. It howled for about 5 seconds and a few seconds later, another howl from elsewhere sounded. The werewolf then walked down the hill and out of sight. "A werewolf, huh?" Dolphi thought. "Looks like a very peaceful scene." He suddenly heard a telephone ring. He turned and saw a phone sitting on a marble, Ionic style, Roman column. He picked up the phone and put it up to his ear. He had lost his human ears from the mutation, but there were tiny holes the size of a pin prick that sufficed for him to hear. He then heard his own voice quickly say, "*as I learn science, I learn how earth had been built from tiny microscopic germs. Like a solar eclipse blackening a spot on the planet, a war between religion and science causes tense disagreement and controversy and in the end, petty bickering will recreate an inevitable and endless dark age that...*"

Dolphi took the phone away from his ear. The babbling was still going on. He then thought to himself, "it's a prank call. It's just nonsense that means nothing to me."

He tried to hang up the phone. However, the phone that he held in his hand had become an injection needle. It looked just like the same needle that had mutated him. It contained the same colored liquid. The babbling went on.

CHAPTER 30

Fate and Destiny

"Do not anticipate trouble or worry about
what may never happen. Keep in the sunlight."
—Benjamin Franklin

OFFICER MONICA RETURNED to Dolphi's house in mid afternoon. She went into Dolphi's bedroom and saw him sleeping
in bed. The covers were up to his waist. "Aww…" she thought,
"he looks so cute like that. I think I'll go up to him…" She slowly
walked up to Dolphi and decided to rub his back. Dolphi hummed
and rolled onto his side. Monica then stroked his stomach. "Oh,
that feels so good," he smiled. He made low squeaking noises as he
felt the soft hand rubbing across his white-ish grey tummy. It was
beginning to turn a pink-ish color.

"Dolfy?" Monica asked, pronouncing his name incorrectly.
"Wake up, Dolfy."

"Mmm… ?" Dolphi grumbled. He then opened his eyes to see
Monica. "Oh, hello. That's a nice soft hand you have."

"Thanks," Monica replied taking her hand off Dolphi's tummy.

"I had a dream while I slept."

"Really? What was it about?"

"Just something that looked like the future and…" He stopped
and began to think about his dreams. His face was all puzzled.

"What is it?" asked Monica.

"I have been having some really unusual dreams lately," replied

Dolphi. "I feel like I have been dreaming about the future, things to come, and a voice that wants me to get my boss."

"Is it something serious?" asked Monica.

"I am not exactly sure… yet," Dolphi replied. "So, did you find what you were looking for at my workplace?"

"I sure did," Monica said. "I've convinced the Commissioner to put together a S.W.A.T team that will charge the building this afternoon."

"That's great. So, did you find out anything about Mr. Jem?"

"Well, his record is pretty interesting," Monica said. "He wasn't a Jem from the beginning. He was actually born James Harland. We couldn't find any information on the Harlands, but his parents died in a car accident when he was ten. He was sent to an orphanage and was soon adopted by a Casynthia and, get this, Dr. Richard Orville Jem."

"Interesting," Dolphi said. "And what did this Dr. Jem do?"

"Here comes the interesting part," Monica said. "Dr. Jem had been involved in unauthorized, underground research on genetics. His complex was raided and shut down by the FBI in the early nineties."

Dolphi sat up. "Did they discover any mutants such as myself?"

"I don't think so. Dr. Jem's wife had died from cancer and he was trying to find a cure."

"A facility researching a cancer cure without involvement of the government…" Dolphi pondered. "What about this doctor himself? Had he been arrested?"

"He died before the raid happened. There was an accident with an experiment that left him disfigured."

"Wait a minute," Dolphi said with concern. "Disfigured? As in, mutated?"

"Something tells me the pieces are coming together," Monica said.

"Did the investigators find what it was that mutated this guy?"

"I wasn't there and the records didn't say."

"I think that guy's adopted son, my boss, had taken whatever killed him and used it on me," Dolphi said. "I think somebody took a dolphin's blood, mixed it with the stuff and then injected it into me. Anything else about my boss?"

"As a matter of fact, yes," Monica said. "He had a wife and a son not long ago."

"Had?"

"Yes, there was something puzzling about that too. His wife and son somehow... disappeared."

"Without a trace?" Dolphi asked.

"Without a trace," Monica replied.

"Where in Florida did all this happen?"

"It didn't happen in Florida," Monica replied, "it was in California."

Dolphi was confused. "How did Mr. Jem smuggle that... mutagen I wonder?"

"Probably made it look like it was apple juice or something," Monica said.

"Whatever the reason, he must be stopped," Dolphi said. He then stretched his arms out and made a nice, big yawn. Dolphi suddenly felt something go into his mouth and out. He could see Monica's head.

"Ta da!" Monica said bowing. Dolphi realized that she had stuck her head inside his mouth like a lion tamer did. "What was that for?" Dolphi asked.

"I just had to do it," Monica laughed.

"Good grief!" Dolphi said as he rolled his eyes.

"I'm sorry," Monica smiled.

Dolphi pulled the bed covers off him. Just then, Monica stopped laughing. Her eyes and mouth widened. She covered her mouth with her hands and looked away. Dolphi looked down at his body. He could see the reason why Monica was shocked. "Oh!" Dolphi gasped. "Uh... just a minute!" He went into the bathroom and searched a closet. He found a blue bathing suit made of a wetsuit material. He put it on and it fit nice and snug. He also noticed some of his other bathing suits had been stolen as well. Dolphi walked out of the bathroom. "I'm sorry about that, Officer Monica," he said. "Men get erections all the time. Because mine is retractable, I couldn't tell if it was in or not. Are you alright?"

"I'm okay," she grinned. "And you can just call me Monica."

"Okay, and you can call me Dolphi." He then saw a pile of books on the floor next to the bed. "How did all these books get here?" he wondered. He examined them. They were all on science. "These are from Walter's room," Dolphi said recognizing them.

Walter then walked into the room.

"Hello, Walter," said Dolphi.

"Hi, dad," Walter replied, "I saw you walk into my room earlier. You took most of my science books."

"I did?" Dolphi asked, "I went to your room before, but I just opened the door and saw you sleeping. I didn't take your books."

"Well, I saw you take them off to your room and I asked you what you were doing. You didn't respond. You took the books to your room, you sat on the bed and began flipping through the pages like they were kindergarten picture books."

"... Huh," Dolphi thought, "did I upset you?"

"Actually, I was rather interested. It's good to see that you're taking an interest in such things." Walter picked up one of the books and opened it to a page. "Some of this stuff is really confusing." Dolphi took the book Walter had, sat on the bed and looked at it. He then flipped to the next page. "Somehow, I have a feeling that I've seen this stuff before," Dolphi thought. He began to flip through the pages. "Yeah, this stuff is familiar."

Walter then grabbed the book and closed it. "You... actually read it just like that?" asked Walter.

"I... I did," Dolphi said. Walter then looked at the rest of the books.

"Dad," asked Walter nervously, "did you read, understand *and* memorize all those books within one hour?" Dolphi couldn't speak. He was so confused. "I see you even took out the old bible that came with the house," Walter continued. "Did you read the whole thing as well?"

"... This is... really scary," Dolphi said concerned. "I've never read any of these before and yet I'm familiar with them. Was I sleepwalking?"

"No," Walter said as he thought about something. "You were..." He thought back to when the unidentified soldiers had done something to Dolphi. He remembered his dad was talking about something he didn't remember saying. "... You were... possessed," Walter said.

Dolphi then thought to himself, "the enigma... Walter, do you recall what I said when I was... possessed?"

"Just about every word," Walter replied. He began telling Dolphi about Cyber-soul. When Walter was finished, Monica said, "I saw you floating in a tank on one of the security tapes. Something bright hit your tank and went into your head." Dolphi put his hand on his face and sighed. "Oh, my god," Dolphi said, "so *that* is how that sick dolphin became a carrier for this thing. It went into the dolphin, it went into a computer... and now... it's inside me..." He looked at Monica and then at Walter. "Walter, please go find Mike for me, I'd like to speak to him... alone."

"Uh, okay," Walter said.

As Walter and Monica left the room, Dolphi went to get out an item that he kept very well hidden.

Mike soon entered the bedroom. "You wanted to see me, dad?" Mike asked. Dolphi was sitting on the bed with a small box in his hands. "I wanted to see you alone because I don't want anybody to interfere with what I am about to show and tell you," Dolphi said. "Please sit next to me." Mike sat down on the bed with Dolphi.

"What's in the box?" Mike asked.

"I'll show you." When Dolphi opened the box, Mike saw a small handgun with shiny bullets lined up. He was shocked. "I didn't know you had that!"

"Shh, keep it down," Dolphi whispered. "My father gave this to me before I married your mother. He used it for protection from burglars and that kind of stuff. I don't like guns, but I carried on the tradition. This is something that I'd like you to have."

"Shouldn't I get this from you before I marry my future wife?" Mike asked.

"Well, consider this an early wedding present."

Mike frowned. "Are you trying to tell me something?"

Dolphi also frowned. "Listen, Mike," he said as he put his arm around Mike's shoulder, "do you remember last night when I was acting strangely in front of those soldiers, how I was talking about something called, Cyber-soul and not remembering a thing?" Mike nodded. "Well, after we had such a wonderful time in the pool and had a rest on the grass, I came back here to have a nice nap. Now, see those books there? Walter told me I took them from his room. I don't remember going in there. I made a beeline straight to my bedroom and have never left it since. So, how did I get into his bedroom, take his books and read them all without remembering a single thing?"

"You're making a point," Mike said. "You must have been sleep-walking."

"You're getting warmer," Dolphi replied.

Suddenly, the answer hit Mike. "You were… possessed by the Cyber-soul thing in your head!"

"Bingo. It took over my mind while I was asleep. That really scares me. What if I were to attack someone in this family?"

Mike glanced down at the gun. "No… you're not telling me what I think you're going to…" Mike tried to get up, but Dolphi grabbed Mike's arm. Dolphi then faced him.

"Listen to me!" Dolphi said almost desperately. "There's some-thing in my head that is not meant to be there. I have used its powers a couple of times and I ended up killing a guy I didn't mean to kill. If I get possessed again and make a move on you or one of your brothers, you have to take this gun and…" Dolphi then stopped. He sighed and bowed his head in frustration.

Mike looked like he was about to cry. "Do you think this thing is evil?" he asked calmly.

"I'm sorry, Mike," Dolphi replied. "I don't want to think of this power as evil. So far, it has done nothing serious to me. In fact, I think its been helping me. I feel fine, but I'm concerned about what it plans to do next. I promise that I won't hurt any of you, but I won't take any chances either. Just think of the gun as a safety pre-caution. I'll feel more at ease knowing that somebody will take care of me before I do serious harm to any innocents."

Mike looked up. "Alright," he said. "I'll take it." Mike closed the box and hugged Dolphi.

"Well then, now that we've gotten that over with, now that I'm relaxed and feeling better, I want to get revenge against the man who made me into this freak of science. Plus, he has my wife."

Dolphi walked out of the room and went into the kitchen where he found Monica. "Man, I need some food!" he said.

"Oh, I bought some fish on the way here," Monica said. She went to the fridge and took out a brown package. She opened it and there was a bunch of long, skinny fish packed together.

"Mmm, they look tasty," Dolphi smiled looking at the fish.

"Catch!" Monica said as she took one of the fish and threw it into the air. Dolphi opened his mouth, caught it and gulped it down.

"Good catch," said Monica.

"That was pretty funny," said Dolphi, "but I'd rather eat properly." Dolphi ate the fish one by one.

Monica then handed a glass of water to Dolphi. He only drank a little bit of it.

"I don't need much water," said Dolphi. "According to my knowledge of marine mammals, dolphins get their water from the fish they eat. That's how they survive in a world full of salty water."

"You are very smart," said Monica.

"I am a marine mammal veterinarian," Dolphi replied. "Well... used to be. Anyway, I've made my decision. I'm going back to the M.R.I.L."

"I'm sure the S.W.A.T will handle the situation just fine," Monica said.

"I'm not going to wait here," Dolphi said. "My wife is in that place somewhere and Mr. Jem might kill her if there's trouble. Did you see any mutants on the security tapes?"

"Yes, there were three guys that got turned into sharks," Monica replied.

"Sharks? Three guys? Could they be... nah."

"Do you know who the three men might be?"

"Well, they could be Mr. Jem's subordinates, but I don't really think so," Dolphi said. "Somebody shot a needle into my arm that caused my mutation. I don't know why Mr. Jem would have wanted to mutate any of them. They're his best friends and they do his dirty work for him. Now, I think I should head over to my workplace before something terrible happens. Besides, I've got a secret weapon that the S.W.A.T doesn't have."

"Cyber-soul?" Monica asked.

"No, my echolocation; a dolphin's means of sight. I can close my eyes, make some clicking noises and then I can see inside your body. I can see your skeleton, organs, everything."

"Interesting, you think you can use it to find your wife and your boss?" Monica asked.

"Maybe," Dolphi replied. "Do you not want me to go because I'll be a vigilante?"

"You could say that," Monica said.

"What do you have against vigilantes anyway?"

"Well, one reason is that they interfere with police operations."

"Do you people not trust anybody?"

"I trust my nutritionist," Monica shrugged.

"I just saved a hotel from being blown to smithereens. My abilities helped find the bombs—"

"Okay, okay, you've made your point," Monica said.

"Just think of me as a… specialist," Dolphi said. "If you're going to neutralize the threat of a powerful enemy…" He stood tall and patted his big chest. "… then you'll need all the help you can get."

"Very well," Monica replied as she stuck her hand out. "Let's go then… specialist." Dolphi then shook hands with Monica. "Ah! Not so hard!" she yelped.

"Sorry." They went over to the front door.

"Wait!" called Walter's voice. Dolphi and Monica turned and saw Walter with his Disguiser.

"I'll wait in the car," Monica said as she walked outside.

"What's up, Walter?" Dolphi asked.

"Are you leaving?" Walter asked. "If you are, then maybe you should take the Disguiser with you."

"Thanks for the offer," Dolphi said, "but… "

"You should take it," Walter interrupted. "You never know when it may come in handy. I've repaired it and put in some new batteries. I hope you will be alright over there. Watch out for mutant sharks and anything else."

"I will," Dolphi said. "I'll take that device of yours. After all, it did save my butt back there at the hotel."

"Will you be back?" asked Walter.

"Of course," Dolphi said.

"So, you want revenge against your boss?" asked Walter. "Do you intend to kill him in cold blood?"

Dolphi was silent. He then sighed and said, "I'm not sure. He'll pay for what he's done somehow. His mutation schemes will be stopped. I wouldn't want any more mutants like me being made."

Mike and Sid showed up. "You're going?" Mike asked.

"Yes," Dolphi replied. "I'm off to find your mother and settle a score."

"Oh, if you want to get into the lab where you became a mutant," Walter said, "there's this key hidden beneath a removable tile in the shark den. It's next to a computer.

"Okay, thanks," Dolphi said.

"Dad," Mike said, "let us go with you."

"Out of the question. What I'm going to do does not require you three to put your lives at risk."

"Fine," Mike replied. "Is Cyber-soul going to be a problem?"

"I will try not to lose my mind to it." He then bent down to Sid. "Sid, I won't leave that place until I find your mother. I promise."

"Good luck," Sid replied. The horn from Monica's cruiser sounded. Dolphi patted Sid's head and walked off.

The three boys stood silently in the doorway as their father walked down the pathway towards the cruiser, towards his destiny.

"I recommend that you hide in the back so that we don't attract any unnecessary attention," Monica said.

"Good idea," Dolphi said as he got in the back. "Do we have a plan for what we are going to do once we get over there?"

"The S.W.A.T team has been scheduled to storm the building soon," Monica replied.

"There are people working," Dolphi said. "I'd hate to see anybody get caught in any crossfire." They drove off down the street. "I wanted to stay home and wish that none of this had ever happened to me," Dolphi said to Monica. "But I'm stuck in this form now and whether it'd be me or the S.W.A.T that'll get Mr. Jem, he's going to pay dearly."

CHAPTER 31

Distractions

"A man either lives life as it happens to him,
meets it head-on and licks it,
or he turns his back on it and starts to wither away."
—Producer Gene Roddenberry

T HE WEATHER WAS pretty hot and Dolphi was lying on the back-
seat in Monica's cruiser. They were driving through Miami.
"How are you doing back there?" Monica asked.

"Water," Dolphi said. "I need to find some water to moisten my
skin. I curse myself for not taking a shower or a dip in the pool
before leaving."

"You need it to prevent yourself from becoming dehydrated,
right?" asked Monica. "Alright then, where to find water?"

"Do you see any secluded spots on the beach?" Dolphi asked.

"There are too many people, so unless there's a tap behind a
building somewhere… "

"Then I'll have to jump into somebody's backyard and jump in
their pool or use their garden hose," Dolphi said. Ten minutes later,
Monica drove into a parking lot and stopped the car.

"You found some place?" Dolphi asked.

"I believe so," said Monica. "I didn't mention this before, but I
see you have a bandage around your arm. Are you okay?"

"I was shot by the leader of those soldiers that attacked the Dolphin's Lagoon Inn. It's fine now," Dolphi replied. "So, where are
we?" He peeked out the window. "A liquor store?"

"There's an outdoor tap behind the building you can use," Monica said. "The coast is clear." She got out of the car and opened Dolphi's door. She had parked as close to the alleyway behind the building as possible. "I'll try not to delay," Dolphi said. Monica and Dolphi ran over to the tap.

"If anybody comes along, I'll try to block you off from view as best I can," Monica said.

"Good idea," Dolphi agreed.

* * *

At the M.R.I.L, Mr. Jem was at his desk. He had gotten off the phone with security chief Dominic Fargus who told him about the asinine behavior of Charlie. Mr. Jem had witnessed Henry giving the security tapes to a police officer, but did not mention it to Fargus. He suddenly heard a sound coming from the dining room. He got up and walked into the room to find out what was going on. "Hello?" he asked. Suddenly, a hole began to form in a wall. "Oh my god, what's going on?!" he asked. The person on the other side then exploded into the room. It was Jaws, one of Mr. Jem's mutant sharks. "WHAT ARE YOU DOING?!" Mr. Jem yelled. Slice and Chewer then came through. Each of them was wearing bathing suits that had rips in the pant legs. "Look what you just did!" Mr. Jem shouted. "You just made a hole in my wall!"

"We're making a secret passage, boss!" Jaws said. "We found these maintenance passageways behind the walls and we used our sense of smell to find you."

Mr. Jem put his hand on his face in frustration. "This isn't happening…" he said. "Please tell me you're joking."

"We can cover the hole with something and we can see each other whenever we need to," Slice said.

"Were you guys heard?" Mr. Jem asked. "Did anyone see you?"

"No, we're cool," Slice replied.

"Listen, boss," Jaws said, "we need some meat in our bellies. We can't just keep eating chocolate. Is there anything you can do for us?"

Mr. Jem then thought about something. "As a matter of fact, I think I can. But just a reminder, you should ask me before you do something like this secret passage stuff."

"Okay," Chewer said.

Slice then noticed a packet of cigarettes and a lighter on the floor next to the dining table. "Looks like I just hit the jackpot," Slice thought. He took out a cigarette, lit it and smoked it. As he exhaled, the smoke came out through his gills. Mr. Jem then knocked it out of Slice's mouth. "You can smoke if you want," Mr. Jem said, "but not here. Not in my office. I'll get you guys some food. I have an idea."

Henry was in his office doing some paperwork. He soon heard his telephone ring.

"Hello?" he asked as he picked it up.

"Henry Guy? I wish to see you in my office right away," Mr. Jem said.

" Sure, what is the reason?" Henry asked.

"You will find out when you get here," Mr. Jem replied as he hung up the phone. Henry wondered if he had been caught giving the tapes to Officer Monica. He put down the phone, left his office and headed towards Mr. Jem's office. Along the way, he caught up with two other people walking in the same direction. They looked at each other. Henry saw it was Charlie and Dominic the security chief. "Are you two going to Mr. Jem's office?" Henry asked.

"Yes," said Dominic. "He said he wanted to talk to this jackass. You are also going to see him?"

"Yeah."

"Let's go then." When they came to the door of Mr. Jem's office, Henry knocked. "Names please," said Mr. Jem's voice. Everyone said their names. "Come in," said Mr. Jem. The door opened and the men walked inside. On the floor of the office, there was a plastic sheet. On top of it were three individual chairs.

"What's with the plastic?" Henry asked.

"Please sit down, gentlemen," said Mr. Jem. Everyone got seated.

"So what is it that you wanted to talk to us about?" asked Henry.

"Mr. Fargus tells me that Charlie had harassed him today," Mr. Jem replied.

"It was no big deal," Charlie said. "I just wanted to give him some excitement."

"I didn't have anything to do with this," Henry said.

"Oh, I think you did," Mr. Jem said. "I know everything that happens around here. I saw you give something to a police officer that came by earlier. What I believe is that Charlie here, distracted Mr. Fargus while you went into his office to take some tapes."

"Ah-ha!" Dominic said with surprise. "So something *was* going on!"

"What tapes did you give this officer?" Mr. Jem asked.

"I don't know," Henry said feeling nervous. "Just a few random tapes. The police wanted them, so I had to comply with the law."

"I have mentioned to every employee in the past that if a police officer wants to do something here, then that officer must report directly to me."

"Well then," Dominic said, "now that these two will be taken care of, I should head back down and continue—" Dominic was about to get out of the chair, when Mr. Jem stood up. "Sit down, Mr. Fargus," he said. "I'm not finished yet. You see, you are also in trouble as well."

Dominic sat back down. "What did *I* do?" he asked.

"You let somebody slip by your attention," Mr. Jem replied. "So, all three of you are going to help me with something as punishment. I am thinking of painting my office, so the plastic on the ground will prevent the carpet from getting stained."

"You want us to paint?" Henry asked. Unknown to the three men, Mr. Jem's three mutant sharks were behind them. Slice was behind Charlie, Chewer was behind Dominic and Jaws was behind Henry.

"Yes," Mr. Jem replied. "I'm thinking of a particular color for my office. I don't have any paint buckets here. So, the only color that can be provided... is from you three."

Henry scoffed. "What are you talking about?"

"There's a familiar color inside each living being," Mr. Jem continued. "So the color I'm looking for... is the red of your blood."

That was the signal for the sharks. They opened their mouths and clamped down over the heads of the three humans. There was a brief scream from the shark trio's prey and then there was silence. The sharks lowered their victims onto the plastic sheet. "Keep your meals on the sheet and don't let any blood stain my floors," Mr. Jem instructed. The sharks dragged the sheet into the dining room. Mr. Jem then sighed. "What I am sacrificing to feed you three… "

"Thanks for the food, boss!" Jaws said. "*Mrrrrrrrfffffff!!!*" the sharks growled as they snacked down on their prey.

* * *

Back at the liquor store behind the alley, Dolphi gave himself a good soaking. Nobody had seen him so far. "That's better," Dolphi said as he rested his head against the wall. "Now, we can get back on track." He suddenly felt a tingling sensation in his melon. As he closed his eyes, he saw an image of people lying on the ground. There were two figures standing. He could see what looked like shotguns in their hands. "Oh, hell no!" Dolphi said.

"What's wrong?" Monica asked.

"A robbery in progress," Dolphi replied. "Right here."

"That's all we need!" she threw her arms up. "How many gunmen?"

"Two, as far as I can see," Dolphi said. "I think we should help the people inside." He saw a door. "I think we can get in this way." Dolphi tugged on the handle, but found it locked. He then pulled hard and broke it open.

"I think I should call for back-up," Monica said.

"I must not be seen by other officers," Dolphi replied. "They will think I'm one of the crooks. We can take them, let's just go in." Dolphi went inside and found himself in a backroom. There were stacks of boxes of bottles everywhere. Dolphi and Monica crept over to a door that led inside the store itself. They could hear voices.

"Give us everything in that register!" someone shouted. Dolphi opened the door slightly and saw two men in dirty street clothes. "Please don't hurt me!" the store clerk begged. One of the gunmen was almost bald, the other had red curly hair. The bald man suddenly caught notice of the open door. "Who's back there?!" he yelled. He then fired his shotgun at the door. Dolphi ducked as the bullets made holes in it. People screamed at the sound of the gun. The bald man then turned to his partner. "Sammy, find out who's back there and bring them out!"

"Okay," Sammy said as he advanced towards the backroom. As he came to the door, he kicked it open and pointed his gun around.

He didn't see anyone. "Alright, come on out," he said. As he walked around the room, Dolphi hid behind one of the stacks. "I'm not going to ask you again!" Sammy shouted. With his echolocation, Dolphi could see where Sammy was moving. Just as the gunman was about to move around the stack, Dolphi grabbed the shotgun and rammed his snout into Sammy's chest. He fell down and Monica came out of her hiding spot with her gun drawn. "I'm with Miami police, you are under arrest," she said.

Dolphi held the shotgun, but then bent it in half with his strength.

"Is the circus in town?" Sammy asked as he looked at Dolphi while being cuffed by Monica.

"Sammy?" his partner yelled. "What's going on?"

"There's this cop and some freak who's got me, Max!" Sammy shouted. Dolphi then punched him right in the face. "Don't ever call me a freak," Dolphi said. Monica then dashed out the door with her gun. "Drop your weapon!" she shouted. Max didn't obey however and fired his shotgun. He hit a shelf of bottles that exploded glass and liquid. Dolphi ran out and knelt beside Monica. "Looks like this guy won't go down without a fight," he said. He dashed over to another aisle. Max fired again breaking more bottles. Monica got up and fired a shot towards Max, but missed him. Dolphi came around the corner of the aisle where Max was hiding. He grabbed a bottle, ran towards him while he was distracted by Monica and threw it at his head. The bottle made contact, exploded and he collapsed onto the floor. "Got him!" Dolphi said. He saw something fall out of the gunman's pocket. It was just a cigarette lighter. Dolphi picked it up as Monica came over. "Well now," Dolphi said, "looks like we got the situation under—"

Suddenly, somebody rushed into the other end of the aisle with a handgun drawn. "Don't move!" the mysterious gunman shouted. "Both of you on your knees, now!"

"Just do it," Dolphi said to Monica. With his back still turned, Dolphi said to the gunman, "okay, we're kneeling, but just let me… have a drink from this bottle!" He slowly reached for one of the bottles, and twisted off its cap. He poured the liquid into his mouth. It tasted very sour, but he kept it in his mouth.

"Okay, now keep your hands where I can see them!" the gunman yelled as he got closer. He then stopped behind Dolphi. "What have you done here?" the gunman asked as he saw his fallen partner.

"Just a little work in the name of justice," Dolphi replied. "Let me tell you something," he said as he put his hand that concealed the lighter behind his head, "crime not only doesn't pay…" Dolphi rolled his eye towards the gunman and saw where he was standing. Dolphi then said, "… it burns." He flicked the lighter and then spat out the liquid; through his blowhole. The liquid hit the flame, caught fire and then hit the gunman. The man yelled in pain as his clothes caught fire. He dropped his weapon and began rolling on the ground to put the flames out. He moaned on the floor as smoke rose from his clothes. "Let's get out of here," Dolphi said to Monica.

"Okay," she said. She then went over to the customers who were lying on the ground. "It's safe. You all can get up now." Everyone got up. Dolphi grabbed the handgun from the third gunman and walked over to the store clerk. "Are you alright?" Dolphi asked.

The clerk was surprised. "I am," he said. "Say, you are 'him' aren't you?"

Dolphi nodded. "Yes. I am that dolphin guy."

Monica then came up to Dolphi. "I'm going to take these two punks with me," she said to Dolphi. She then said to the clerk, "watch that man. I'm going to call for an ambulance."

Dolphi put the gun on the counter. "Can you handle this?"

"Of course," the clerk replied.

"I'll contact some other units to handle this situation and question the remaining gunman," Monica said. "We have to get going now."

"Thank you for your help," the clerk said.

"You're welcome," Dolphi replied. He went over to the gunman named Max and picked him up by the back of his shirt with one hand. He went to the backroom and grabbed the other gunman named Sammy.

Dolphi and Monica went back to the cruiser. Dolphi opened the back and threw the two men inside. He picked up Walter's Disguiser and got in the passenger's seat. "I'm not sitting in the back with those two," Dolphi said.

"I knew you'd say that," Monica replied. She then picked up her radio. "This is 6FL19, there has been an attempted robbery at a liquor store at 37 Hanson St. Situation is under control. Three suspects were involved. I have two in custody. The third is injured and being watched by the store clerk. An ambulance is required, over."

As the radio confirmed, Monica started up the car.

"Well then," Dolphi said, "with this little distraction out of the way, *now* we can get back on track."

"I really should take these guys to the station," Monica said, "but they'll just have to come along for the ride." She then drove off in the direction of the Marine Research Institute Labs.

CHAPTER 32

The Cat (or dolphin rather) Came Back

"Delay is preferable to error."
—Thomas Jefferson

DOLPHI KEPT HIS head low as Monica continued driving. Dolphi noticed one of the liquor store gunmen in the back regaining consciousness. When Max realized he and his partner were in a police cruiser, he made a loud curse that gave Dolphi and Monica a bit of a fright. Dolphi turned to look at Max. "Keep it down, will you?" he asked. Max hadn't got a good look at Dolphi before, but now he did.

"Who's the platypus?" Max asked.

Dolphi almost laughed. "I'm a dolphin, you dork! Well, a half-human dolphin to be exact."

"What happened to our driver?" Sammy asked.

"Let's just say he's being treated for second-degree burns right now," Monica said.

"And where are we going?" Max asked. "This isn't the way to the police station."

"We'll take you there later," Monica said. "And you two have the right to remain silent by the way." She then told them the rest of their rights.

Soon, the Marine Research Institute Labs came into view. "We're here at last," Dolphi said. The parking lot was packed with cars. Dolphi's charred car was nowhere to be seen. "I don't see any sign of the S.W.A.T."

"What S.W.A.T.?" Max asked. Dolphi slapped the grill separating him from the goons. "We don't want to hear another word out of either of you, alright?" Dolphi asked. The two men then kept their mouths shut.

Monica drove into the parking lot and stopped close to the building.

"I must warn the staff inside about this raid," Dolphi said.

"But that will jeopardize the operation," Monica replied.

"I know, but the rest of the staff is innocent and have no knowledge of the mutations. The S.W.A.T. might think everyone's responsible and they could shoot somebody like my friend Henry. It's Mr. Jem and his three goons, Drake, Jack and Robert who are guilty. Let's just head inside and see what we can do."

"Alright," Monica said. They got out of the vehicle.

"There's no turning back now," Dolphi said. "It's time to go all out!"

They went inside the building. "We're in," Dolphi said. "Now, to find Mr. Jem." There were some people in the lobby who caught notice of Dolphi. Dolphi turned to the front desk. "Drake's not there," he said. "He's usually at the front desk." He turned back towards the doors to see some black S.W.A.T. vans coming into the parking lot. "They're here!" Dolphi shouted. Just then, a sound came from above. It sounded like a fire alarm. Suddenly, a giant wooden barrier fell over the front doors and other barriers fell over windows. "What is going on?!" Monica gasped. Dolphi saw that all the doors and windows were blocked off, preventing anyone from getting out or in. "Great," Dolphi thought, "when this place was constructed, someone came up with this idea that has not been needed before, the Hurricane Defense System (HDS). Boards instantly fall over all windows and doors to protect from hurricane damage. We can't get out and the S.W.A.T. can't get in."

An enormous group of people then rushed out into the lobby.

"Uh oh, looks like everyone wants out," Monica said. People ran up to the doors only to find that they were barricaded off. The entire lobby was soon packed with people. The alarm abruptly stopped ringing. People looked at Dolphi and wondered what he was.

Dolphi pushed his way to the front desk. He thought about using the loudspeaker, but he didn't want Mr. Jem to hear what he was going to say. Somebody shouted, "what's going on? There's no hur-

ricane warning at this time!" Dolphi didn't see Mr. Jem or his three
subordinates. He climbed on top of the desk so he could be seen
by everyone. "Attention all staff of the Marine Research Institute
Labs!" Dolphi shouted. Everyone turned to look at Dolphi. "I want
you all to listen to me. There is serious corruption here. Mr. Jem has
been creating mutants like myself behind your backs! He and his
closest assistants have betrayed us all. He must be stopped before
he makes any more mutant experiments like myself." People were
shocked at what Dolphi was telling them. "There's a S.W.A.T. team
outside that will deal with the situation. I would recommend that
everyone stay calm and exit the building when it is possible. Does
anybody know how to shut down the Hurricane Defense System?"

Someone shouted out, "the Hurricane Defense System control
is down in the basement. The stairway is at the very end of the
restricted hallway. There is a password to the control console, but
only Mr. Jem knows the code. The stairway is also locked and only
Mr. Jem has the key to open it. If you can turn off the system and
raise these barriers, we should get out especially if you believe that
there is danger inside this place."

Dolphi realized he couldn't see someone that he knew. "Henry Guy?" he called out. "Are you here?" Henry's voice didn't call
out.

"He did check in today," somebody said, "but it looks like he
isn't here."

"Has anyone seen Mr. Jem?" Dolphi asked. No one said anything. "Okay then. Officer Monica here will keep you company."

Dolphi stepped down and went back to Monica. "Okay," Dolphi
said to her, "here's what I'm going to do, I'm going up to find Mr.
Jem. I'm going to nab him before I get everyone out to make sure
he doesn't slip out with the crowd."

"Yes sir!" Monica replied as she saluted him. Dolphi was about
to walk away. "Wait!" said Monica. "This is for good luck."

She gave him a kiss on the tip of the snout and then nuzzled it
with her nose.

Dolphi smiled. "That was sweet," he said, feeling loved.

"I've always wanted to kiss a dolphin…" said Monica.

"I've got to get going now," Dolphi said.

"Okay."

Dolphi took off towards the offices. He went through the doors and looked around. "Doesn't look like anything has changed," he thought. Henry's office was on the first floor. Dolphi went there first and knocked on the door. "Henry? Are you in there? It's me, Dr. Jay!" There was no response. The door wasn't locked, so Dolphi went in. There was no sign of him. Dolphi had a very bad feeling. He went out and headed towards an elevator. He pushed a button and waited. The doors opened and he looked inside. It was empty. He was about to walk in, when he stopped. "I should take the stairs in case somebody stalls the elevator," he thought. He went over to the stairs and ran up them to the second floor. "I wonder how my office is," he thought. He ran over to where his office was located. He tried to open the door, but it was locked. He ran his shoulder into the door and it opened with a crash. He saw that there was nothing in his office! Everything had been cleaned out! His desk was the only thing remaining. The drawers were empty.

"Why, that jerk!" he thought clenching a fist. He left and ran over to the door of Mr. Jem's office. He looked around to see that it was very quiet. It looked too easy. He then ran into the door and bashed it open. "Where are you, you mutater?!" he yelled. He looked around and walked closer to the desk. He remembered before he was mutated how there was a trap door. He suddenly heard a click below him. He quickly jumped backwards just as the trap door opened. He lost his balance and fell on his back. "Ouch!" he yelled as he rubbed his dorsal fin. He looked at the trap door as he got up. "I must have gone down that thing and ended up at the lab. What a crazy building." He looked behind the desk to see that nobody was there also. "Come on out, where ever you are!" he yelled. He saw another door that led to somewhere else in Mr. Jem's office. He walked over quietly and opened it. There was a large room with a dining table and a bar off to the side. The place was elegant. It was almost like being in a movie star's house. He noticed some spilled liquid, three empty glasses and ripped clothing on the floor.

"What happened here?" he thought. He noticed something on the floor underneath a door. It looked like a red stain. "Hmm…" he thought, "I wonder what's in here?" He opened the door, the room was pitch black. He felt around inside for a light switch. He found it and turned it on. What he saw next, horrified him. "AHHH!!!" he screamed as he backed away, fell to the ground and covered his eyes. "OH MY GOD!!!" It was such a horrible sight for him, but he knew he had to be strong. He slowly got up and looked inside again. There were three mutilated human bodies on a sheet of plastic. Their heads were missing. "What happened here?!" he thought. The corpses were unrecognizable, but he was about to find out who they were. He bent down and looked at the shredded, blood stained clothes of the three victims and found their identity badges. One said Dominic Fargus, the second said Charlie Manning, and then he had discovered the third badge. It said, Henry Guy. Dolphi's eyes shot wide open. "… No…" he barely spoke. He felt paralyzed. Grief suddenly overcame him. He started screaming. "HENRYYYYYY!!!" He ran for the nearest garbage can, fell to his knees and vomited into it.

Dolphi knelt in front of the corpses with his head bent down. Tears covered his face. He was almost like a statue. "I'm so sorry…" he softly said to the lifeless corpses. "I wanted to stop him… before anyone got hurt…" Dolphi felt that he should have forced Monica to take him with her earlier so that he could have prevented this from happening. "Henry, Dominic and Charlie… whatever Mr. Jem has done to you, he is going to pay dearly… soon enough… I promise you this to your graves." Dolphi was so shaken by the death of his best friend, he almost forgot that he had to remove the barriers that blocked the facility. He got up and left the room. "Mr. Jem does not appear to be in here," he thought. "I wonder if Henry was killed by Mr. Jem's mutants? Monica said she saw sharks on the tapes she found."

He hurried down the stairs and went back to the lobby. The staff were still standing around at the barrier covering the door. "Has anyone seen Mr. Jem yet?" Dolphi asked. People shook their heads. Somebody then said, "no, but we're getting pretty cramped here!"

"Sorry to keep everyone waiting," Dolphi called out. "I just discovered three murdered staff in Mr. Jem's office, but I didn't find Mr. Jem himself." Everyone gasped. "I'm going to get all of you out of here." He didn't see Monica in the lobby. "Where has the officer gone?" Somebody pointed to the door of the shark den. Dolphi pushed his way through the crowd to the door. Just as he was about to go in, one of the staff asked, "wait a minute. Who are you and how do you know so much about this place?"

"There's no time to explain," Dolphi said. He went into the shark den. He saw Monica sitting at a computer.

"What are you doing?" Dolphi asked.

"I'm trying to find another way out."

"So what have you found out?"

"Nothing so far," she replied.

"I should find the console to open the doors right now."

"Good idea." Dolphi then remembered Walter telling him about the key to the secret lab. He knelt down and began to search the ground.

"What are you doing?" Monica asked.

"My son told me that he found a hidden key in this room some-where," Dolphi replied. He soon found a tile that tilted when he touched it on the side. He took it off and saw the key. He picked it up and put it away in his bathing suit pocket. He was about to leave the room when he saw a broken glass container. "What happened here?" asked Dolphi.

"I'm not sure," said Monica. "That was there when I came in." She looked at Dolphi's face with concern. "You look upset," she said. "I heard you say there were three murders."

"Yes," Dolphi replied sadly. "One of them was my friend, the one I knew best here."

"I'm very sorry," said Monica.

"This is only the beginning and I already feel sick to my stom-ach," he said, bowing his head. "There's nothing that Dr. Jay can do to stop this…" He then looked towards the door. "… but Dolphi the Dolphin Man is another story!"

He went out the door and entered the restricted hallway. He soon came across the door to the lab where he had been mutated. "That's the lab," Dolphi thought. "I'll come here later when I've finished with the doors."

He went to the very end of the hall and found the door leading to the basement. It was right next to the emergency exit that he had used to escape the facility when he first became a mutant. The door was locked. "As I expected," Dolphi thought. He then lifted his leg and kicked the door open. "I hope this door breaking doesn't be-come a habit," he added. He went through and found a flight of stairs going down. At the bottom, he found a room full of blankets. Dol-phi had never been down here before, but he knew this was a place where people could take shelter in case of a hurricane. It was very dark, so he went to a light switch and flicked it. Nothing happened however. "This looks like a job for good ol' echolocation," Dolphi said. He proceeded down the dark hall, making clicking noises. He came across several doors. He opened each door and scanned inside looking for a computer or anything that would deactivate the crazy hurricane barriers. "Mr. Jem?" Dolphi called. "You better not be hiding down here! We have unfinished business!" Dolphi did not get an answer. He continued walking and soon found himself in a room full of boxes off to the sides. He saw there was a light above a door. He walked up to it and found it was made of steel. There was also an electronic keypad next to it. Dolphi tried to ram into the door and break it down, but it wouldn't budge. "What am I going to do?" Dolphi thought. He looked at the keypad and saw something below it. There were some numbers painted on the wall.

"6483?" Dolphi thought. "I guess that must be the number." He put his finger up to the number pad and typed in the numbers he saw. Just as he pushed the enter button, he felt something cover his body. He saw the whole place turn an orange color. Suddenly, there was an explosion that threw Dolphi back. He landed on his back and slid backwards. "What the hell?!" Dolphi thought as he slowly sat up. He looked at himself. "What is this? I'm covered in some orange... Who's there? Hello? Hello?!" Nobody answered. Dolphi got off the floor. "I landed on my back, but my dorsal fin doesn't feel bent," he thought. He saw that a line had been made in the concrete ground. There were cracks alongside it. "My dorsal fin made that?" Dolphi thought. He then realized he couldn't breathe. Whatever was on him, had covered his blowhole. "I have to get this stuff off me or I'll suffocate. I can hold my breath for five minutes, but I have to think quickly." He began to feel all around his body. He put his hands together and the orange stuff on his skin began to crack. His body was soon covered in cracks and seconds later, all the orange stuff exploded and pieces scattered all over the room. Dolphi took a nice deep breath. "Whoa," he thought. He looked around again to see if anybody was there. "What was that stuff anyway? And who put that stuff on me? I can't think about it right now, I must get to that console." He saw that the explosion had blasted the door open. He went through it and saw a computer that was on. He walked up to it and sat in the chair.

"Good thing the computer wasn't damaged," Dolphi thought. He could see a message on the screen that said, 'Hurricane Defense

System: Activated'. Below that message was another message that said, 'please enter password to deactivate HDS.'

"I need a password?" Dolphi thought. "Damn..." He looked beside the keyboard and saw a little book. It said, 'Manual for Hurricane Defense System (HDS)'. Dolphi opened the book and saw diagrams for the whole thing. He flipped through the pages and when he came to the last one, he saw somebody had written in black marker, 'HDS password: 0000'. "Huh, that's not much of a password," Dolphi thought. He typed in the four zeros and was about to push Enter, when he stopped. "What if this is another trap?" he thought. He deleted the zeros and sat there thinking about it. "I've been in this situation before. I wonder if I could just close my eyes and then think about—" Suddenly, he felt a strong vibration surge through his head. He heard a female voice say, "accessing computer network array." Dolphi believed that was the computer's voice. He found himself in a virtual world. He was flying over computer circuits. He came across a shiny red ball. The computer voice said, "Hurricane Defense System password." Dolphi touched the red ball and a box for entering the digits appeared. Dolphi then wondered what to do next. "Uh... scan?" he requested.

'scanning in progress,' said the computer voice. After twenty seconds, an enormous list of letters from A to Z appeared and this is what it looked like:

A: 30% B: 0% C: 0% D: 0% E: 90% F: 0% G: 0% H: 50% I: 0% J: 0% K: 0% L: 0%

M: 0% N: 70% O: 0% P: 0% Q: 0% R: 40%-100% S: 10% T: 20%-80% U: 60% V: 0% W: 0% X: 0% Y: 0% Z: 0%

"Alright," Dolphi said. "Decipher."

'Unauthorized command,' the voice replied.

"Are you Cyber-soul?" Dolphi asked. "Identify your program please."

'I am just a voice programmed to assist the user. I have limited Reponses.'

"I guess I have to do this myself," he thought. He looked at the letters and saw many of them showed zero percent. "Bring up a... keyboard interface please," he said. The interface appeared and he counted the order of percentages and entered the letters, S... T... A... R... H... U... N... T... E... R and pushed Enter. The password was 'Starhunter' and not four zeros. Two messages appeared

and the computer voice read, 'access granted. Deactivating HDS…
' Ten seconds later, the voice displayed and read the message, 'lifting barriers.' Then it said, 'deactivation complete.'

"Alright!" Dolphi said. "Okay now, exit sys—". Suddenly, the
voice said, 'WARNING! Explosive device triggered. Device will
reach threshold in ten seconds.'

That was not good. "Get me out of here!" Dolphi yelled. There
was a flash of light and he found himself back in reality. He shook
his head and saw a time limit on the computer. It indicated that five
seconds remained. He got up out of the seat and ran out of the room
as fast as he could. Just as he went through the door, he heard and
felt an explosion that knocked him to the ground again. He landed
on his stomach and covered his head with his hands. He felt pieces
of hot debris hit his back. He quickly got up and brushed it off. He
could see that the room he came from was in flames. He realized
that he had used the power of Cyber-soul. "Have I been possessed
yet?" Dolphi thought. "I still love my children… okay, I'm fine." As
Dolphi went towards the stairs, he saw a phone on the wall. He saw
buttons that could call different areas of the building. Dolphi found
a button labeled, 'shark den' so he pushed it. There was a ring and
the call was answered. "Hello?" asked Monica's voice.

"Monica? It's Dolphi. I deactivated the barriers, so the people
should be getting out now.

"Good job!" Monica said.

"And I almost got killed doing it!" Dolphi replied. "This place is
booby trapped! Anyway, there's no sign of Mr. Jem, but I'll check
out the secret lab where I got mutated. My wife might be in there.
Check you later!" He hung up the phone and went up the stairs.
He then thought to himself, "what's a 'Starhunter' anyway?" After
reaching the top of the stairs, he went back out into the hall to find
the accursed lab.

CHAPTER 33

Enter the Mermaid

*"The past is all that's gone, the future is yet to come.
This moment is all our own, we should live this way,
just building up our day. Now is forever."*
—Eiffel 65
from the song, "Now is Forever"

DOLPHI CAME TO the door of the lab where he had been mutated. "Jennifer, my love…" he thought. "I hope you're in there."

He was about to ram the door down, when he remembered the key. He took it out of his pocket and put it in the keyhole. He turned it and slowly opened the door as he didn't know what to expect inside. He went in and froze as he saw the three mutant sharks. Luckily, they were sleeping, lying next to each other against a wall. They had their arms over each other's shoulders and their hands on their stomachs. They looked so cute like that, but Dolphi had to remember that they had tried to kill his children. When he saw the bathing suits that they were wearing, he recognized them. "Those came from my house," Dolphi thought. "So, Mr. Jem broke in for the second time." One of the three sharks snorted. They were starting to wake up! Dolphi had to hide. He went behind a group of barrels and lay quietly.

Slice woke up and saw the open door. "Guys, wake up!" he said. The other two yawned as they got up.

"The door's open," Jaws said. "Boss, are you there?" When he got no answer, he looked around the room only to see nobody was there. They walked out of the room to see if anybody was out in the hall. When all three were out, Dolphi crept up to the door and closed it behind them.

"Hey!" Chewer said as he turned back to the door. As he tried to open it, he got an electric shock from the door's security system. "Damn, we're locked out!"

"Could the mutant that we were watching have broken out?" Jaws asked.

"She would have to have broken out really quick without making a single noise in five seconds," Chewer replied. "Maybe we should find the boss. Of course, we would have to make another hole in the wall somewhere to find our secret passage."

"Alright, let's go," Jaws said as they took off.

Now that Dolphi was back in the lab, it was time to see if he could find his wife.

He looked around the room. Not too much had changed. Dolphi saw a shark cage floating at the edge of the pool. He heard a soft sound coming from it. He walked over to the cage and saw it was locked. He grabbed the lock and pulled hard. It broke off and he opened the cage's roof. Dolphi could see a dark figure in the cage underwater. The figure suddenly swam up and leaped at Dolphi. He was knocked to the ground and the figure was on top of him. It was a mutant bottlenose dolphin just like him, only it was a female.

The female mutant dolphin had her foot on Dolphi.

"Who are you?" she asked. She then took her foot off Dolphi and continued looking at him with cold eyes. She had a thin body with bracelets and beads around her wrists and neck. She was wearing a loincloth that looked like it was made from ripped clothing. She was much like Dolphi expect for one extra feature, she had a dolphin-like tail coming out from behind just like her mutant shark captors.

"Are... are you my wife?" Dolphi asked.

"I am Jelera," (Jeh-lair-ah) she said. "I do not know you."

"I'm not with those shark guys," Dolphi replied. "Give me your hand." He put his hand out, but Jelera backed off.

"You're not going to fool me!" she said.

"Do you know Mike, Sid and Walter Jay?" Dolphi asked. "They are our three boys. You were human before, and so was I!" Jelera was confused. "Is your real name... Jennifer Jay?" Dolphi asked. Jelera was thinking about what Dolphi was saying.

"... What is your name?" she asked. Dolphi got up off the floor.

"It's me," Dolphi replied, "Steele... Steele Monroe Jay!"

"S... Steele?" she asked. Dolphi nodded his head. "I... I remember!" she said. "Oh, honey... !" They hugged each other tightly. "What happened to me? What happened to you? What is going on here?"

"It's a long story," said Dolphi. "So you're a mutant dolphin as well? Now you see why I didn't come home that day."

"So, your boss is responsible for all this," Jelera said. "We are both mutants now..." She suddenly gasped. "Oh my god! Our children!!! Are they still alive?!!"

"Yes, they're fine," Dolphi replied.

"Oh, thank god!" Jelera cried as she hugged him tight. "Those three horrible monsters told me that... they ripped their limbs off, one by one, and... dunked the pieces in clam chowder!" She then burst into tears and cried hard.

"Calm down, dear," Dolphi assured her. "They are home, safe and sound, away from the schemes of Mr. Jem and just as human as when you last saw them. They told me how you brought them here to look for me after I didn't come home. They eventually found me and soon understood the situation. They were scared that you were dead, but they always believed that the sharks may have spared you after they had escaped from their jaws. Right now, it doesn't matter if you are human or not, I still love you."

"You're right," she said. "I love you too."

"So, are you okay?" Dolphi asked. "Did they hurt you in any way?"

"They were ordered to take care of me," she replied, "but I'm recovering from something that the great white shark called Jaws did to me today."

"And what was that?"

Jelera was silent for a moment. "He came splashing down from above, he quickly opened my cage, jumped in and..." She almost trembled. "How can I say this, he... he... defiled me. I'm okay right now, but... "

Dolphi's face was almost frozen. His eyes and mouth were wide open. He glanced to the door where he saw the great white shark leave. He then knelt down and covered his eyes with his right hand. "Oh… my… god…" he moaned. "He's going to pay for that!"

* * *

Back in the Shark Den, just after she got off the phone with Dolphi, Monica got out of her chair. Just before she was about to leave the room, she noticed the water in the tank swirl near where a broken container lay. It looked like somebody was in the water. Monica slowly walked over to take a closer look. She bent down to see if she could make out anything, but she couldn't due to the murky water. All of a sudden, something splashed out of the pool and landed on her. As she fell on her back, she saw a red colored mutant crab raising its claw above its head. Monica gasped and rolled away just as the crab's claw struck the ground. Monica got up and saw the crab creature stand on its hind legs. As it turned to face Monica, it started to snap its claws and walk towards her. Monica took out her gun. "Freeze!" she yelled, "Miami Police! Stay where you are!" The crab continued lumbering towards her. "Don't make me do this!" Monica yelled. In her panic, she opened fire on the crab. She fired five bullets at it, but most of them bounced off the crab's shell. It shrieked and started to snap its claws again. The door behind the crab then burst open and a S.W.A.T. unit rushed in after hearing the gunshots.

"Freeze!" the S.W.A.T. unit yelled. The crab turned around and saw the man pointing his weapon. The crab immediately jumped into the pool. The man dashed to the edge of the tank and fired his machine gun into the water in random places. He stopped firing and there was silence. He turned to Monica. "Are you alright?"

"Yes," Monica replied. "I'm with Miami—" All of a sudden, the crab breached out of the water again. It landed behind the officer. Just as he turned around, the crab drove one of its large pincers through his stomach. The man was lifted into the air and thrown behind the mutant crab. It faced Monica again and started moving toward her. Monica looked around desperately. She noticed a fire extinguisher next to her. She took it, pulled the ring out and fired the gas at the crab. It shrieked and backed off covering its face. Monica noticed the gun that the late S.W.A.T. officer had dropped. She gassed the crab again and ran towards it. She slid underneath the crab's legs and grabbed the machine gun. She then aimed and fired. The crab shrieked loudly as the bullets tore through it. It collapsed on the floor. "Wow," Monica thought. "*I did that?*"

A S.W.A.T. team then charged into the room. "Whoa!" one of the men said as he saw the dead mutant. "A man-sized crab? Now that is freaky."

"No!" another man said as he bent down and examined the deceased S.W.A.T officer. "That thing killed Ross!" He then spoke into his radio. "Commander, we have a man down! Ross was killed by a monster, repeat, a crab monster! We have a pretty hostile situation here, over!"

"*Understood,*" the Commander replied. "*Kill anything that looks like what you just saw. Over and out.*"

Monica was then helped up by the other men. "We suggest you head outside," one of them said. "We're running the show now."

* * *

Back in the lab where Dolphi found his mutated wife, he was trying to get over what had happened to her. "Of all the things..." Dolphi growled, "he better not have been HIV positive or something... and he better not have gotten you pregnant!"

"I hope not too," Jelera said. "You see, that mutant shark thing fell out of that passage up above and landed in the water. He must have been in a feeding frenzy as I saw some blood on his mouth."

"Henry..." Dolphi sighed.

"As in, your friend, Henry?!" she gasped. "I'm so sorry."

"Thank you. Anyway, what else happened after that Jaws thing entered the water?"

"Jaws sniffed the water and rushed at me still motivated by his frenzy. He was on me for about fifteen seconds before his buddies came and yanked him off me. The three of them squabbled about what had happened for a moment and then they decided to take a rest. My assaulter was rough, but he didn't injure me." Dolphi sighed again and shook his head. "Let's go into the pool," Jelera said. "I need some exercise now that I'm out of that cage. Besides, it will make you feel better."

"Alright," he said. Dolphi noticed something next to the wall where he had seen the sharks sleeping. "Say, is that a bottle of chocolate syrup?" he asked as he examined it.

"It is," Jelera replied. "I noticed those sharks seem to like chocolate."

"This is the same bottle I bought from the store last time. I think Mr. Jem broke into our house for the second time."

"Yeah, I thought I recognized the bathing suits those sharks were wearing," Jelera said. "Come, let's go swimming." They both stood next to the pool. "So who's going in first?" she asked.

"After you," Dolphi said.

"Okay, just give me a second." Dolphi suddenly felt something hit his back making him fall into the pool.

"What the… ?" Dolphi wondered as he turned around. Jelera was smiling and waving her tail up and down. It looked just like the bottom half of a whale with the tail fluke at the end. "Oh!" Dolphi grinned. "You've got something you didn't have before." Jelera then jumped into the pool and swam up to Dolphi. "That's a nice, strong tail you have," Dolphi added.

Jelera giggled. "Thanks. It's strange how *you* don't have a tail."

"Hmm… so I've noticed," he said as he glanced behind himself. "Those sharks that I saw just now have tails. Maybe it's just part of my mutation."

Jelera wrapped her arms around Dolphi and they hugged each other closely.

"Mmm…" Dolphi hummed. "What's it like to have a tail, my dear?"

"Well…" Jelera thought. "It's kind of like having… a third arm or leg. I feel lots of power in it too. I wonder if I could…" Jelera then moved her tail hard and fast. She rose out of the water and hovered just where the water's surface came to her knees. She moved backwards for a second and fell back down into the water.

Dolphi cheered. "That was very good! You know, if circumstances were different, we could be doing this for hours."

"You know," Jelera said, "after I fainted from those shark mutants when I was still a human, I went into a dream. I dreamt that I was swimming out in the ocean as a human being. I was scared and I didn't know where to go. Suddenly, there was a dolphin swimming off to my side… and I felt assured. It got closer to me and I started to reach my hand out towards it. Just as we touched hand

and pectoral fin, we started to… merge. I could see and feel the dolphin melting like a candle in a microwave. It started to ooze all over my body and seep in. Suddenly, my form began to change. I felt every single part of my body become like a dolphin's. And then, I wasn't afraid of being in the ocean anymore. It was a wonderful dream at first. A dream where… man and beast becomes… one."

"Gee…" Dolphi smiled. "Did you really dream that?"

"I sure did," Jelera replied. "However, the dream ended when I saw three enormous shark mouths open wide about to bite down on my head. I then woke up almost with heart failure and realized that, it wasn't a dream. I was actually two species as one, just like the dream I had — just like the sharks who guarded me — just like you."

Dolphi huffed. "This new form must have been difficult for you to take the first time you saw yourself." Jelera nodded. "Well, some of my dreams haven't been as interesting as yours." He looked down into the water and saw a small object. "Hold on a sec," he said. He dove down to get whatever was down there. He picked it up with his mouth and put it off to the side of the pool.

"What is it?" Jelera asked. Dolphi saw it was an injection needle. It said, 'bottlenose dolphin' on it. "It's the needle that was injected into me while I was in my boss' office," said Dolphi. "I fell down a trap door, which I almost did again today and ended up here. That's how I was mutated. My body was in so much pain. I thought I was dying."

Dolphi then heard a ringing sound. There was a phone in the room on the wall. He got out and picked it up. "Hello?" Dolphi asked.

"*Slice?*" asked a familiar voice, "*is that you? We got S.W.A.T units in the building. They're after me. I want your buddies to get up here—*"

"Mr. Jem…" Dolphi said in a stern voice, "your shark mutants are not here. This is Dolphi, better known as, Dr. Steele Monroe Jay."

"*Dr. Jay?*" Mr. Jem asked. "*Huh, good to hear from you again.*"

"You have a choice," Dolphi said, "surrender, or I'll find you myself and do exactly what you did to Henry."

"*Hey, I didn't touch him. A great white shark did.*"

"Fine, have it your way." Dolphi then hung up the phone.

Jelera got out of the pool and went up to Dolphi.

"We should get out of this place," Jelera said.

"It's not going to be that easy," Dolphi replied. "There's a S.W.A.T unit searching the building for mutants like those sharks — searching for mutants like us."

Suddenly, Dolphi heard some beeping noises in the room. He turned to see they were coming from several groups of barrels placed in different spots. He went up to one of them and saw a timer counting down from thirty seconds.

"This room is going to blow!" Dolphi yelled. "Let's get out of here!" He ran for the door, but realized it needed a huge set of numbers to open it. Dolphi could not remember the numbers and there was no time to dive into a silicon world to figure them out.

"What do we do?!" Jelera panicked. Dolphi closed his eyes and made clicking sounds. "This is no time to make music!" she screamed.

"Trust me!" Dolphi said. Using his echolocation, he was able to see a passage behind a partition wall hidden by shelves. He pushed the shelf as hard as he could and it fell over taking the wall with it. "This looks like a passage that we can go through!" Dolphi said. "Come on!"

Jelera and Dolphi went into the passage and found it was dark. "Hold my hand and let's go through quickly!" Dolphi used his echolocation again to navigate. They then heard a loud explosion and saw fire burning through the passage. It was coming right towards the two dolphins. "GET DOWN!" Dolphi yelled. They ducked as low as they could and the fire went over them.

"Good god, that was too close," Jelera said anxiously.

"Yeah," Dolphi replied. "The reason I was making those noises is that I was using my echolocation to find a way out. I can use this to see even in pitch black conditions."

"Oh, sorry about that," she replied.

"Let's press on and see if we can find a way to get to a safe place outside."

Dolphi's objective, to find his wife, had been completed. Now, only Mr. Jem remained. Dolphi however, had a strong feeling that he would run into Mr. Jem's shark men bodyguards first.

CHAPTER 34

Devil May Cry

"At times of war, we're all the losers. There's no victory."
—The Cranberries
Taken from the song, "Warchild"

DOLPHI AND HIS wife, who was now a mutant bottlenose dolphin like himself, were pushing their way through the dark corridor trying to escape. They thought about heading back to the lab to see if they could get out after the explosion destroyed it and probably blew open the door, but Dolphi believed that the room was still engulfed in flames and that the S.W.A.T would check out the explosion, even if they could get out that way.

"Hopefully, these passages will take us somewhere," Dolphi said to his wife who called herself Jelera since her mutation.

"How do you do that, that echolocation thing?" she asked.

"I'm not sure really," Dolphi replied as they turned a corner. "I find that if I close my eyes and vibrate my voice box, the noise will bounce off things and come back to me, creating a picture in my mind. There's this fatty oil in our melons, which is the front part of our heads, that picks up the vibrations."

"Let me see," she said as she tried her echolocation. She then saw the walls around her glow. "Wow!" she exclaimed with amazement.

Dolphi opened his eyes after coming across a small hole in the wall. There was a bit of light shining in. He bent down and took a peek through the hole.

"What is it?" Jelera asked.

"We're behind the walls of the shark den," Dolphi said. He kicked the wall and made a large hole. "This is the best way out as far as I can see. If the coast is clear, I can get you out the front." They went into the room and saw the dead mutant crab on the floor.

"Eww…" Jelera said, "looks like other mutants have been made as well." Next to it, there was a small puddle of blood.

"I hope that blood is not Monica's," Dolphi said.

"Who's Monica?" Jelera asked.

"She's the police officer who came to our house the day of the robbery. She helped me get here. Now, let's hurry." Dolphi opened the door to the lobby and looked around. Nobody was there, so Dolphi and Jelera ran over to the front doors and went through them. There was no sign of Monica. Suddenly, some S.W.A.T officers came out from behind some cars.

"Freeze!" they yelled as they pointed their weapons at them.

"No!" Dolphi shouted as he put his hands out. "Don't shoot us!" Too late. One of the men fired a few shots. Jelera screamed and Dolphi shut his eyes fearing that this was the end. He expected bullets to tear through him and Jelera, but instead, it never happened. "… Huh?" Dolphi wondered as he opened his eyes. He saw the bullets hanging in mid-air in front of his eyes.

"What's happening?" one of the S.W.A.T asked. The bullets then flew away around the side of the building. The officers suddenly felt their weapons trying to escape their grasp. At the same time, they felt the cars behind them nudge them a little. Their weapons then flew out of their hands and went in the same direction the bullets went. This was some kind of strange phenomenon. Two nearby S.W.A.T vans were backing into the corner. It looked like anything that was metal was being sucked behind the building's north end.

The Commander of the S.W.A.T and some other officers who also lost their weapons, came running up.

"What the hell is going on here?!" the burly Commander yelled. He saw the two vans were blocking the way.

One of the officers nudged the Commander. "Sir, permission to climb over the vehicles and see what's happening over there."

"Granted, Corporal," the Commander replied, "but be careful!"

The Corporal looked inside the trucks. "The keys are gone!" he said. He climbed over the trucks and looked at the ground on the other side. "Hey!" he shouted to the Commander. "I've got something!" He jumped down behind the trucks. "Stop!" he yelled. Dolphi, Jelera and the S.W.A.T heard a growling noise. It followed with some punching noises, a scream and a bang on the rear of one of the vans.

"Corporal?!" the Commander shouted. All he could hear was the moaning voice of the Corporal.

Dolphi faced the Commander. "I'll explain myself later," he said. "I'm going to see if I can push one of the vans so you guys can see what just happened." Dolphi went to one side of a van and wondered how he was going to move it. He opened the door and put one hand on the console and the other on the door and pushed hard. The vehicle moved only slightly. "Honey," he called, "please go around to the other side and do what I'm doing!"

Jelera went around to the passenger side door and put her hands in the same position as Dolphi's. On the count of three, they both pushed hard and the truck slowly started to move. They soon made a gap wide enough for the S.W.A.T to go through. The Corporal was lying on the ground, bleeding and groaning.

"Corporal," the Commander said as he bent down. "Corporal, can you hear me? What did you see?"

"Spiked tail..." he moaned. "a... stegosaurus... monster!" He growled loudly in pain.

"Get this man a medic!" the Commander shouted. Dolphi and Jelera saw that the poor guy had four holes in his chest.

Dolphi looked along the side of the building and didn't see anybody.

"A stegosaurus?" Dolphi thought. He recalled the explosion in the dolphin medical pen. He remembered seeing something that looked like a lizard tail leaving the room. He also recalled the car chase incident on his way to work. "Could they be the mystery mutants that the Colonel of those soldiers at the Inn had talked about?" he thought to himself.

When a medic arrived to take the wounded Corporal away, the Commander turned towards Dolphi. "Well," the Commander said as he studied Dolphi, "if you know something I don't, then tell me. What exactly are these monsters?"

"They're not monsters," Dolphi replied. "To be politically correct, they are mutant animals."

Dolphi noticed a car coming up the driveway. As it got closer he recognized it. It was the family minivan. Dolphi walked up to Jelera and pointed at the minivan. "Isn't that our car?"

"It is!" she said. "But who is driving it?"

The minivan stopped as it got close to the building. The driver got out along with two other people. Dolphi saw it was his children.

Jelera gasped and covered her heart when she saw them. The boys ran over and looked at Jelera. She looked like she was about to cry.

"… Mom?" Mike asked. "Is that you?"

"Yes it is… my babies!" Jelera cried. The boys then hugged her.

Dolphi wasn't happy though. "I ought to smack you three," he said. "I told you to stay at home."

"We wanted to see if mom was alright," Mike said. "We couldn't just sit there and do nothing. We are all in this together." The boys looked around and saw the S.W.A.T were missing something.

"Uh… where are their weapons?" asked Walter.

"I have no idea," Dolphi replied. "They got sucked away by… some kind of magnetic force." Dolphi looked around and realized that Monica wasn't anywhere to be seen. "Monica?" he called. "Monica, where are you?!"

Dolphi walked over to the S.W.A.T Commander. "There was a female police officer around here. Have you seen her?"

"Oh, she was the one who said something about you," the Commander replied. "She said not to open fire on a dolphin with two legs if we saw one."

"Which your men just so happened to fire on," Dolphi replied.

"Sorry, they can be very nervous on operations and must not take chances."

Dolphi heard a banging noise from one of the vans. He closed his eyes and let the banging sound create an image of a person inside. He ran behind the van and found the doors were locked, so he pulled hard and made them open with a bang.

"Hey!" the Commander yelled. Out of the van, stepped Monica.

"Thank you!" she said. She was handcuffed. Dolphi put his hands on the handcuffs' chain and broke it off.

"Why were you arrested?" Dolphi asked.

"I wanted to go back into the building, but they wouldn't let me," she replied. "I tried to sneak back inside, but I was caught."

Dolphi turned to the Commander. "What are you planning on doing next?"

"I just called for reinforcements after our weapons got taken," he replied. "It will take them a while to get here. He then saw a group of vans approaching. "Dammit! The media has just shown up. I have no clue what to tell them."

"Well," Dolphi said, "tell them that the facility's president is doing illegal experiments with mutation and that the staff have no knowledge of any of it."

Suddenly, the sound of glass breaking and yelling was heard from above, but further over. Two S.W.A.T officers had been thrown backwards through the windows on the second floor. One of them landed on the roof of a car while the other hit the hood of another car.

Dolphi looked up and saw the three mutant sharks. They jumped out the window and landed hard on the ground near Monica's cruiser. One of them was carrying a plastic bag with something in it. Inside the cruiser, the two gunmen from the liquor store, Max and Sammy, were startled by the sharks.

"Max, what the hell are those things?!" Sammy asked.

"Whatever they are, they're coming right at us!"

Slice and Chewer went to the rear of the vehicle and Jaws went to the front. They bent down, grabbed the vehicle and lifted it up.

"Yikes!" Sammy shouted. "I don't wanna die!"

A couple of S.W.A.T officers ran over. "Hold it right there!" they shouted. Jaws counted to three and they threw the vehicle at the two officers. They got out of the way just in time, but Sammy and Max were yelling as they were flipped upside down. The car slid across the ground for a few meters and stopped.

"Son of a..." the Commander thought as he saw the three mutants. The sharks turned to look at the Commander. He looked nice and plump and juicy, so the sharks ran at him. Without any weapons, the S.W.A.T had to run.

"Retreat!" the Commander yelled. The sharks jumped over cars and surrounded their prey in no time.

The Commander stopped and looked at each shark. "You want a

piece of me?!" he yelled. He then rushed at Slice and knocked him to the ground. Jaws and Chewer jumped on the man and sank their teeth into his body. After some thrashing around and screaming, that was the end of the S.W.A.T Commander.

Dolphi ran at the mutants with his fist raised. "Hey!" he yelled. He was about to punch Jaws, but Jaws turned and caught the fist with his hand.

"Hello," he said with a blood soaked grin. He then swung his other arm at Dolphi and sent him flying. Dolphi landed on the ground with a thud and his family came to his aid.

"I'm okay," Dolphi said as he got up. The sharks walked towards Dolphi and stopped a short distance apart. Dolphi stared at them and they stared back.

"So," Dolphi said, "what do you guys call yourselves, Fishman, Hammy and Sharky?"

"I'm Jaws," the great white said. "Our boss told us about you. We always wondered if we were ever going to see you."

"What do you have in that bag?" Dolphi asked.

"Well then," Jaws grinned, "why don't you take a look?" He tossed the bag at Dolphi. Dolphi grabbed the object inside and pulled it out. He was appalled. It was the head of Henry!

"So, you're the one who killed Henry!" he growled at Jaws.

"We just so happened to find it in our secret passage," Chewer said. "For some reason, we decided to bring it with us to intimidate anyone who gets in our way."

"You're not intimidating anybody!" Dolphi yelled. "Your killing days end here!"

"Are you going to fight us?" Jaws asked. "We outnumber you three to one, but I think I would like to face you alone, one on one."

"If that's what you want," Dolphi said, "then I accept." He lay the decapitated head down.

"Chewer, Slice," Jaws said, "watch that female dolphin, those kids and the S.W.A.T. guys to make sure they don't interfere."

A helicopter was flying overhead with a cameraman on board.

"This is Florida News from Eye in the Sky reporting," said the cameraman. "The Marine Research Institute Labs is in chaos today. There have been reports of strange creatures that are half-human and half-beast, believe it or not. Miami S.W.A.T have tried to bring the situation under control, but have failed. Right now, I see… a couple of dolphins and three sharks and several members of the S.W.A.T. unit who seem to be unarmed. It seems like a fight is about to start between one of the sharks and one of the dolphins. This looks like it's not going to be a pretty sight. I will keep you updated as I continue our live coverage."

Dolphi stared at Jaws and took tiny steps towards him. In his mind, Dolphi thought, "why do I feel like I know this guy?"

"Let's play!" Jaws shouted. Dolphi ducked a roundhouse punch, but was then tripped by Jaws' tail. Jaws was about to bite down on Dolphi, but he rolled out of the way and the shark's mouth bit into the ground. Jaws had a chunk of concrete in his mouth that crumbled away. He spat it out and grabbed Dolphi as he was getting up. Jaws punched him in the stomach and lifted him above his head. He threw him into a nearby car's windshield. A huge crack flooded the whole piece of glass. Dolphi was lying on his back on the car's hood, trying to get up. Jaws ran up to Dolphi and lifted him up a little. He then slammed his back into the hood. Dolphi kicked Jaws away and rolled off the car. Jaws went to the opposite side of the car and lifted the side of the vehicle from underneath, flipping it upside down on top of Dolphi. He then jumped on top of the vehicle and began jumping up and down on it. Jaws thought he had Dolphi, but Dolphi managed to roll away and stand up behind him. Jaws was still jumping, thinking he was squashing Dolphi.

"Uh, ahem…" Dolphi said. As Jaws turned his head, Dolphi grabbed his feet and yanked him onto his stomach. Jaws retaliated by slapping his tail left and right in Dolphi's face. Dolphi grabbed the tail and swung him into the side of another car that was next to him. Dolphi opened the car's back passenger door. As Jaws turned around, he punched through the window, missing Dolphi. Dolphi ripped off the door and used it as a shield. He pushed the door onto Jaws, but Jaws ripped the door in half with his arms. Dolphi's arms were moved away, giving Jaws an advantage. He bent down and sank his teeth into the left side of Dolphi's torso. Dolphi screamed in pain and didn't know how to get free. Jaws lifted him up with his mouth and drove Dolphi through the window of the passenger's side door of the car he was next to. Jaws brought him back out, still holding him in his mouth and began shaking him around. He then let go and Dolphi went flying out into the open parking lot.

Dolphi was beaten pretty badly. If he had been fighting Jaws as a human, he would have perished in one blow. His lay on the ground, bruised and bleeding. There were red marks on his side in the shape of the shark's jaw. He tried to get up, but felt Jaws' foot step on his back. Jaws then bent down and faced Dolphi.

"You are no match for me," Jaws said. "You know, if you had just stayed here and cooperated with the boss, things would have been easier for you and you would not have brought this pain on yourself."

Jaws suddenly felt somebody jump on him. It was Officer Monica. She began punching him in the head. "Get off me, human!" he yelled.

Chewer saw what was happening. "Slice, watch these small fry. I'll be right back." Chewer ran into the building and grabbed the soda machine.

Jaws eventually grabbed Monica and threw her off him. She was thrown into the side of a nearby van.

"Monica!" Dolphi yelled. She lay motionless on the ground. Dolphi had rolled onto his back, but Jaws put his foot on Dolphi's stomach.

"You have really pissed me off today," Jaws said.

Chewer then arrived with the soda machine. The 'out of order' sign that Dolphi had posted on it was still there. "This should finish him off," Chewer said to Jaws.

"Thanks," he replied. Chewer then laughed at Dolphi and went back towards Jelera and her children. "Stay the hell away from my family!" Dolphi screamed.

"Oh," Jaws said surprised. "Those three boys and that mutant are your family? You are so unselfish, sticking up for them. After I'm through with you, me and my buddies are going to have them for dinner tonight and will devour them, piece… by… piece."

Dolphi was seething with anger. He was breathing heavily and clutched his fist as hard as he could.

Jaws picked up the soda machine and raised it above his head. He growled as he was about to throw it down onto Dolphi's head, intending to kill him. Dolphi felt powerless. He felt that he had failed his mission. He closed his eyes and waited for all the pain to end.

Suddenly, something hit Jaws in the side of his head. He dropped the soda machine and turned to see what was going on. Dolphi opened his eyes and saw there were people throwing shoes, rocks, anything that could be used as effective projectiles. It was the staff of the M.R.I.L.

"Hey!" somebody yelled. "You want some of this?!"

"Leave him alone!" another person shouted. "How dare you beat up someone who's trying to protect some helpless children!"

Another person then threw a red brick at Jaws and said, "here's something for your sharky ass! If you're going to cause trouble here, then you are going to have to take on every single one of us!"

"Yeah," the second person said, "that dolphin is one of us! We are the Marine Research Institute Labs and we will not stand for this!"

As Jaws was getting pelted by junk, he looked up and saw the news helicopter flying overhead. He then grabbed the soda machine and with a loud yell, he tossed it hard into the air. When the pilot saw the object, he had to react. "Holy—" Before he could finish, the object hit the cockpit and the aircraft began to spiral out of control. The cameraman who was filming the action, suddenly fell out. Dolphi quickly got up and ran towards the screaming man as he was falling to his doom. Dolphi jumped up and grabbed him. He cushioned the man's fall. "Go!" Dolphi shouted. "Get out of the way!" The frightened cameraman ran over to the facility staff. The helicopter continued to fall towards to the ground. The pilot managed to jump out, hit the ground and run away. The facility staff began to run away from the helicopter.

Dolphi turned around to see Jaws was running at him with a fist raised. Dolphi ducked and dodged the punches. As the helicopter was close to hitting the ground, Jaws threw a roundhouse punch that Dolphi ducked. Jaws was repeating the tail trip move which Dolphi anticipated. He grabbed the tail and kicked Jaws onto the ground face first. Still holding the tail, Dolphi began turning and swinging Jaws around in a circle. After several turns, Dolphi let go and Jaws went flying… straight for the helicopter blades. The ends of the blades made many gouges in his back and along his tail. Jaws' skin was very tough, so he wasn't liquefied, but the blades tore through him. He screamed as loud as he could as he hit the ground. The helicopter then crashed and tore up some concrete before stopping.

Jaws was lying on his stomach, thrashing around. His back and tail had dozens of major lacerations.

Slice and Chewer were watching what was happening. "JAWS!" Slice screamed. He then turned to Jelera and the boys. "Come on," he said to Chewer, "let's tear them to pieces!"

Before they could do anything, a loud noise was heard from above.

Everyone looked up and saw a figure on the roof of the building holding something round. The sun was behind the building and nobody could make out who was up there.

A bolt of lightning suddenly shot down and hit Chewer. He fell down screaming as electricity began to fry his body. After ten seconds, the lightning stopped and Chewer's lifeless body had fire burning all over him. When everyone looked back up, the figure turned around and after the swish of what looked like a tail, he was gone.

Slice dropped to his knees in front of the flaming corpse. "NO!" he yelled. "Chewer!" He bowed his head and began sobbing.

Dolphi had caught notice of the lightning. "Wait a minute," he thought, "the orange shield that protected me, the magnetic force that took away the S.W.A.T.'s weapons, and now this; there *is* someone else at work here! And I think they're half-human and half-dinosaur." He turned to see Monica slowly regaining consciousness. He went over and helped her up. "Are you okay?" he asked her.

"Nothing I can't handle," she smiled. She wrapped her arms around Dolphi and gave him one big kiss.

"Okay, that's enough," Dolphi smiled back. "Remember I'm married." He then saw the flashes of cameras going off. There were so many flashes, it almost blinded him. There were reporters from the Miami Herald and other newspapers all shouting questions that he could not hear clearly. Right there, Dolphi knew he was on television. He just grinned, waved for a moment and then walked back towards his family. Monica kept the media back as best she could.

Dolphi looked at Slice who was still on his knees and crying. He was munching on a piece of his charred friend. "It's over, kiddo," Dolphi said. Slice looked up and growled. He then jumped at Dolphi and kicked him in the chest. Slice fell down and then lunged for Walter. Slice grabbed him and tossed him away from his family. With a swish of his tail, Slice knocked down Jelera, Mike and Sid and then jumped on Walter. He opened his mouth and was about to bite down on Walter's neck, when suddenly, he felt something sink into his own neck. He let go of Walter and backed off. He then collapsed onto the ground. As Dolphi helped Walter up, he saw a big lawn dart lodged in the shark's neck. Dolphi turned to see a familiar man running up to him. "Regan!" he said recognizing his new friend. It was definitely the man who had been attacked by the alligator that Dolphi had got rid of. "What are you doing here?" Dolphi asked him.

"I finally got my car back," Regan said. "I decided to head here to see if I could help you after what you had told me about this place before. That was quite a battle that was going on. I was watching the whole thing." He turned to look at Jelera. "Is that your wife?"

"Unfortunately, yes," Dolphi replied.

"So your wife has become just like you."

"You saved my son's life!" Jelera smiled as she ran up to him and gave him a big hug. Regan was surprised that this big beautiful dolphin woman was hugging him. Usually, it was the human who hugged the animal first. "Okay, don't crush me to death," he laughed.

"So dear," Jelera turned to Dolphi, "how do you know this man?"

"He's someone I met while I was trying to get home after I escaped from this place," he replied. "I saved his life and his wife's purse, but I don't care to remember that. Is your wife here?" he asked Regan.

"No, she didn't want to come with me."

"Dad, look!" Sid pointed. Dolphi turned and saw Jaws slowly limping towards Dolphi.

"So," Dolphi asked, "you're going to eat my family piece by piece?" He quickly ran up to him and gave him an uppercut to the lower jaw. Jaws backflipped onto his stomach. Dolphi grabbed his head and punched it into the concrete. He lifted up Jaws' head again and punched him repeatedly in his almost pointy nose. Dolphi was about to throw another punch, when the badly wounded shark raised his hand up and shouted something unexpected.

"Dr. Jay!" Jaws yelled. "Stop, Dr. Jay! It's me!"

Dolphi had a confused look on his face. He slowly lowered his fists. This mutant great white shark knew his real name.

"I suppose you're right," Jaws moaned, "I really *am* a lousy S.O.B." Dolphi then saw something he hadn't noticed before. Jaws was wearing a chain necklace that had a symbol of a shark wearing sunglasses. Dolphi had seen that before.

"No…" he thought, "could it be…? Drake?!"

"You are strong… Dr. Jay… Strong enough to beat me… I remember… everything now… Mr. Jem… put something in our drinks… to make us like this… "

"My god…" Dolphi said. He picked up Henry's head and saw his face was frozen in agony. Dolphi put his fingers on Henry's eyelids and closed them. He went back to Jaws and showed him the head. "You killed Henry," Dolphi said. "He was my best friend… in the whole world."

"It was Jaws who killed!" the shark yelled in agony from the deep gouges along his hide. "It was the shark instinct inside me! Drake Evans would never do anything like that, neither would Jack or Robert!" He bowed his head and began sobbing. Dolphi felt flashbacks of his confrontations with Drake, with Jack working in the dolphin medical pen and with Robert.

"I have never seen so much death in my whole entire life," Dolphi said, feeling a deep sorrow. He then remembered what Jelera told him about what Jaws did to her. He punched Jaws in the face and yelled, "it was you, wasn't it?! That was my WIFE you violated back in that room!"

"Sorry, sorry, SORRY!!!" Jaws yelled. "I couldn't help it! Her body looked so sexy, I got aroused! But please… listen. In the beginning, I was just like everybody else… I wanted to help Mr. Jem in any way I could from the very first time I saw him. He had nothing and Jack and Robert and I helped him. But now… I see his true nature. I want to… kill Mr. Jem for what… he has done… to us…"

"Did you rob my house?" Dolphi asked.

"It wasn't us… We were out one night and we saw suspicious activity going on at your house." Jaws explained about the mysterious burglars that he and his buddies saw and how they ended up taking something in the process. Dolphi suddenly had a hunch that it was those mystery mutants from the future.

"You guys…" Dolphi said, "you… you tried to kill Mike… and Sid… and Walter, my three children."

"Yes... I know," Jaws said. "But I told you it was this animal instinct. I tried to overcome it, but I couldn't. I would never kill you. We may have had an argument and called each other names, but you are a man who helps marine mammals and just like you saved them, you saved me. Thank the saints... for you. Since I became a mutant, somehow... just somehow... I knew you would come back here and put an end to this nightmare..." He then looked to his left to see the burning corpse of Chewer. "I see that Chewer... or Robert actually... has been taken care of. Where is Slice... I mean, Jack?"

Dolphi turned around. "He's right—" Instead of seeing the body of the thresher shark, there was a small amount of blood and the lawn dart on the ground. "Where did he go?" Dolphi asked as he looked around. Jaws then grabbed Dolphi's arm and turned him around. "Listen, I don't have much time left," Jaws said. "I will join Chewer soon. Where I will go when I die, to heaven... or to the horrific underworld, I don't know. I can't atone for what I've done... "

Dolphi looked out at the ocean. The waves were calm and the seagulls were flying around acting as if they didn't recognize the carnage. "No..." Dolphi said as he turned to Jaws, "you and your friends... will return to the ocean... along with all the life in it... Mr. Jem... will be the one who will burn in the horrific underworld!"

"Thank you..." Jaws replied. "Stop Mr. Jem from... creating any more mutants... like us... Stop him from going through with this... He's... gone mad." Dolphi was silent. "Promise to stop him... from making any more freaks like us..." said Jaws.

"I... I'm just a father who wanted to live a normal life and maybe try to make a difference for what I believe in," said Dolphi. "I'm not a superhero, I'm not even a hero in that sense. But... I promise... I will make sure he pays dearly. Tell me, has he made any more mutants?"

"I don't know," said Jaws. "But, there is something... I must tell you. It was me... who held that gun. It was me... who pulled that trigger. It was me... who shot that needle with the mutagen... into you." Dolphi felt the flashback of the injection and his painful mutation. "I'm so sorry..." Jaws sobbed. "You must really hate me for doing that, for putting you through all this... "

Dolphi thought about what the poor soul had told him. He was an innocent man who had no idea what he was involved in.

"To tell you the truth…" Dolphi said, "I don't blame you."

"Really?"

"Mr. Jem is doing all this," said Dolphi.

"Thank you… very much," Jaws sighed. "One last thing…" he said through his sobs. "Me and my buddies… we are… Mr. Jem's only friends. He's very lonely… and I must be by his side. He's… less grumpy when he has friends around. Nobody… likes him… Like I said, he was nothing in the beginning. He was so glad to find us, his best friends in the whole… wide… world… "

Just then, Jaws' eyes shot wide open. He reached his arm out to the side of Dolphi's face and with his hand, he shoved Dolphi's head off to one side as he saw something was coming right for him. A thin arrow from a spear gun suddenly plunged right through Jaws' head. Dolphi's eyes widened as he saw it go through the poor shark. Jaws' hand slowly slipped off Dolphi's face and then hit the ground. Jaws closed his eyes and tears dripped out.

Jelera, the boys, Monica and Regan all instantly looked up after the spear hit. Dolphi then looked up himself. It was Mr. Jem holding a spear gun! He was on the second floor.

"I will have absolutely no sympathy from such a weak, pathetic guinea pig!" Mr. Jem said. "Good riddance!" He then disappeared from the window.

Dolphi looked at Jaws' body. He was dead and his face looked like he was in so much pain. Hearing what Mr. Jem had said made Dolphi angry. He had never felt this upset before. He was more upset now than he was when his grandmother died. He felt like this was the strongest feeling of anger he had ever felt in his entire life. He looked down at Jaws' face. Blood was slowly seeping out from where the spear hit. Dolphi felt like he was going to collapse on the floor and cry like a baby, but he didn't. Anger had taken over. He hated Mr. Jem, he hated the pain, he even hated the form he was in. He suddenly let out a loud anguished scream. It was so loud, nearby cars rolled over, windows cracked and people were knocked down. When he stopped, he knew he was using the enigmatic powers of Cyber-soul. He turned around and saw his family and friends were nervous. Dolphi felt a little better after his overpowering yell. Without saying a word, he walked by them and entered the building.

It was time to finish this once and for all.

CHAPTER 35

What Makes a Monster
and What Makes a Man

"I have nothing to offer, but blood, tears, toil and sweat."
—Winston Churchill

THE DOOR OF the Shark Den was being dented from the other side. The door smashed open and out stepped a mutant crayfish. "Another one of Mr. Jem's experiments?" Dolphi thought. Just then, a weapon slid up to Dolphi's feet. It was a machine gun the S.W.A.T. team had been using. Dolphi turned in the direction it came from, but didn't see anyone. He quickly used his echolocation. Where he saw nothing before, he saw a human like skeleton with a reptilian skull and a long tail bone.

"Who are you?!" Dolphi yelled. "I can see you!" But when Dolphi opened his eyes, he still saw nobody. The figure must have been using some kind of invisibility trick. Dolphi thought the invisible reptile would run away, but instead, he heard it speak.

"Don't mind me," a slightly gruff voice said, "your enemy's nearby. We must not interfere. Go!"

Dolphi turned back to the shark den and saw the crayfish was almost in front of him. Its claw was about to pierce Dolphi. He quickly ducked the claw and punched it in the chest. As it fell down Dolphi picked up the weapon on the ground and aimed it at the crayfish. He pulled the trigger and fired bullets into the mutant. The recoil of the weapon made Dolphi lose his balance a little because he didn't know how to handle it. He then moved into the office corridors and saw one of the doors off to the side burst open. Several mutant piranhas ran at Dolphi. He blasted the fish while maintaining his balance this time. "Mr. Jem must have mutated every living creature in the complex," Dolphi thought. "Now, there are no piranhas in Florida, but I guess somebody bought them from a pet store." He ran over to the stairway, but saw a horde of mutants inside. Dolphi felt he couldn't blast them all, so he dashed back out and mashed the elevator button. The door opened and he went inside. He pushed the button for the second floor and started going up. Halfway through the ride, the elevator stopped. Suddenly, the roof collapsed and a mutant cockroach fell to the floor. It was almost as big as Dolphi. He shot the giant roach and white puss splattered the floor. "Yuck!" Dolphi said. He looked up through the hole and could see another giant roach on the cables. "What are *you* doing?" Dolphi asked even if he knew the roach wouldn't respond. Just then, one of the cables broke. The whole elevator shook. "Oh, hell no!" Dolphi cried out. The roach was gnawing on the cables! Dolphi put the weapon in his mouth, made a giant leap, grabbed an edge and pulled himself up onto the roof of the elevator and grabbed for his gun. He saw the roach was gnawing on the last cable. "You really don't want to do that," Dolphi said. He saw a ladder on the wall. There was a slight snap in the cable as a few threads broke. Dolphi ran and jumped on the ladder. "You crazy bug!" Dolphi yelled as he put the gun back in his mouth. Suddenly, the cable broke and both the roach and the elevator went straight down. There was a loud crash and an eerie screech. Dolphi let out a sigh of relief. He climbed up the ladder and found the door to the second floor. He got onto the door's edge and used his hands to pry the door open. He had successfully cheated death once again.

As he was heading for Mr. Jem's office, one of the office doors smashed open and a mutated mouse popped out. It was on all fours and when it turned to look at Dolphi, it made an awful squeaking noise. Dolphi still had his gun with him, so he shot the mouse with a few bullets and it went down quickly. Dolphi looked inside the office and saw that a mouse cage was completely smashed. As he went out of the office, the mutant mouse that Dolphi thought he killed, jerked its head and bit at Dolphi's left leg. He let out a grunt of pain as he fell to his knees. He turned around and shot the mouse in the head to make sure it stayed down. Dolphi looked at his leg and saw a tooth mark with blood slowly oozing out. "God damn it!" Dolphi yelled, "I really have to be more careful." He then moved on towards Mr. Jem's office with the emotional and physical pain still fresh in his mind.

When he arrived at Mr. Jem's office, he immediately charged at the door, jumped up and kicked it as hard as he could. The door broke off its hinges and hit the ground with a loud bang. Dolphi went in and saw a burnt and smokey area around the open trapdoor. "How did that happen?" Dolphi thought. "Ah, now I see. The trap door was left open and the explosion in the lab must have gone up the passage and into his office." He walked over to Mr. Jem's desk and looked behind it. He didn't see anyone. He went back to where the trap door was and turned to the door that led to the room where he had found the bodies of Henry and the other two employees. He pointed his gun steadily at the door. "Come on," Dolphi asked, "where are you, you—"

Suddenly, something hit his weapon, knocking it right out of his hands. His weapon fell down the trap door. Dolphi turned and saw somebody standing at the main office door. It was Mr. Jem showing up for the final showdown. He was holding a spear gun and had just reloaded a new spear.

Here it was, Dr. Jay in his mutant dolphin form and Mr. Jem facing each other for the first time since the experiment Mr. Jem had conducted on him a few days ago. Mr. Jem looked at Dolphi as if feeling sorry for him, but at the same time, looked at him in awe of the experiment's success. After a moment of silence, he shook his head slowly, sighed in a satisfied way and spoke his first words to the mutant dolphin's face. "… All this, because you stuck your nose into something that was none of your business."

"It's over," Dolphi said. "I saved my wife, I saved the rest of the facility staff… and now I'm seeking revenge for what you have done here."

"You really think I'm the bad guy here, don't you?" asked Mr. Jem. "Allow me to explain how I was once involved with the studies on the mutagen. My father, or should I say, the man who raised me after my real parents died in a freak car accident, had been working hard researching a cancer cure after his wife passed away." Dolphi pretended not to know anything. "He raised me into a fine, young man and he wanted me to be a part of his top secret work. Then, one day, he accidentally mistook a cup of coffee for this mutagen that was created in the process of researching a cure. The raw substance without the D.N.A. of another creature killed him. And you know what? People thought I was responsible for his poisoning! Me and my family later remembered him at his grave."

"You had family?" asked Dolphi.

"Of course. I had a wife named Sophie and a six year old son named Aaron. He had a mental disability of some kind. Anyway, I took them over to my father's laboratory, which is now a deserted old building."

"Why?" Dolphi asked.

"Why, you ask? I wanted it to be an exciting trip for Aaron. Plus, Sophie and I wanted to revisit our past. But then, it all happened so fast." Dolphi was now hearing things Officer Monica hadn't told him. "We were attacked by someone who had been part of the research team. My wife got shot trying to protect me. I picked up my son and tried to run away." Mr. Jem then started to hesitate. "I got shot in the back and I felt my son leave my arms. He went over the railing… and he fell right into a vat of chemicals! I didn't report this to the police because I didn't want to get in trouble. The killer would have been long gone and the deaths would have been pinned on me… just like my father's. My sweet Aaron is probably still lying dead in that chemical vat, damn it! My sweet Aaron…" he sighed. "He was so young… and now he's dead. How would you feel if *you* lost family?"

"As a matter of fact, I have," Dolphi replied. "I lost my grandmother a few years back. Her time was up, but even so, it was one of the worst days of my life. So to answer your question, I'd be just as upset. But I'd put it in the past and move on with life."

Mr. Jem sneered. "There's a difference between dying of old age and dying from gunshots," he said. "Old age is nature's creation, guns and bullets are mankind's creation. Human beings are the most advanced creatures on earth. We are so powerful, we take the course of life and death into our own hands. We wage wars on other countries, we create atomic bombs, we are killing the planet and yet, all of that is a fact that we are very proud of."

"Are you trying to tell me something?" Dolphi asked.

"Not really. Just wanted to point out that man is good at creating things."

Dolphi frowned. "Whatever. Your point has been noted. Now, how come you survived when your family didn't?"

"I had a small 'good book' in my back pocket," Mr. Jem replied. "It blocked the bullet. Somebody up there must have really liked me. I moved here to Florida, built the Marine Research Institute Labs and became the president of this place. However, I could never shake those painful memories out of my head. I could never 'put it in the past' as you said."

"That mutagen," Dolphi said. "You took some with you, later mixed it with dolphin blood and used it on me. There are mutants all over this building. How did you do that?"

"I just thought I'd try a vapor inhalation experiment by releasing the mutagen into the air conditioning," Mr. Jem replied. "I guess when animals come into contact with the stuff, they become mutants themselves."

"For god's sake, haven't you done enough damage already?"

"I wanted to see if my father's life's work was worth something and I think it sure was. If not a cancer cure, then a mutagen will do. If you had cancer as a human, your new form wouldn't have that."

"What about Drake, Jack and Robert?" Dolphi asked as he slowly stepped towards Mr. Jem who still had his spear gun pointed at him. "They were your best friends. When you lost everything, they helped you get back on your feet to a fresh start. And how did you repay that favor? You double-crossed them!"

"That was not the case," said Mr. Jem. "What happened was, I overheard my three subordinates talking about feeling guilty about the night you were mutated. They planned to bust you out of the little lab to prove to the authorities that there was an illegal experiment and to sell me out."

Dolphi's eyes and mouth opened a little in surprise. "Really?"

"Yeah. I mixed the mutagen with shark blood and put it in their orange juice when I called them up to celebrate this experiment's success. You know, I didn't tell them about the mutagen until the anniversary of when my family was murdered; on one beautiful twenty-third of April."

Dolphi gasped. "The same day you mutated me!"

"Shocking, isn't it? But what was shocking to me, was when I heard on the news that you were captured by an organization that my father owned when he was still alive."

Dolphi thought to himself. He then said, "the Discovery Research Incorporated?"

"Yes. So, looks like somebody revived the company. Do you know who runs the organization now?"

Dolphi shook his head.

"Never mind then."

"You tried to kill me out in the parking lot, but you ended up hitting Drake and didn't care at all."

"Drake was dying anyway, so I put him out of his misery."

"No, I'm going to put *you* out of your misery!" Dolphi shouted.

"You don't understand," Mr. Jem said.

"Yes I do. I slept on the streets, I ran around butt-naked, got confronted by police, street punks and soldiers, I got captured, I got put in a dolphin facility that was a cesspool, I got caught up in a street race… you don't know what the hell I've been through!" He walked towards Mr. Jem a little more until he was only a few feet away. "You've had your fun and now it's time to stop."

"I want to," said Mr. Jem. "I really want to, but I can't. I feel like I have started something that can be beneficial. Mankind can understand the world of animals better. Plus… I can turn mythical creatures like werewolves, minotaurs and gnolls, into a reality."

"Gnolls?"

"That's what half-human hyena hybrids are called."

"Do you think everyone will agree with the idea of these freaks of science running around?" asked Dolphi.

"There will always and I mean *always* be people who will disagree with anything," said Mr. Jem. "When I was growing up, my father taught me that science and research has to do drastic things sometimes, like the first chimpanzee that was blasted into outer space, like the first dolphins and killer whales captured from the wild and put into captivity. A little pain and sacrifice is necessary. Yeah, I suppose it all began for me when I allowed myself to believe that I could actually achieve something remarkable."

"Tell that to Henry, Dominic, Charlie and everyone else who has died because of you and your mad scientist of a father, Dr. Richard Orville Jem!" Dolphi yelled. He suddenly felt that he regretted saying that.

Mr. Jem raised his eyebrows for a second. "Don't... you..." he then put the spear gun right on Dolphi's head and yelled, "... EVER SAY HIS NAME! I eliminated expendable targets for my father's efforts. I made sure his work was not in vain. I'm stuck with this and I'm proud of it. Do you understand? I'm just doing what I was *raised* to do!"

"Yeah?" asked Dolphi. "Same with me! Enough already. Now get that thing out of my face!" Dolphi quickly snatched the spear gun and jerked it away. The spear fired, but missed Dolphi and hit the ground somewhere. Dolphi snatched the weapon out of Mr. Jem's hands and threw it away as it didn't have any spears left which made the weapon useless. It fell down the open trap door. Dolphi then grabbed Mr. Jem by the shirt.

"Let's settle this right here and right now," Dolphi said. "You have betrayed me, your friends, everyone! I'll never forgive you! I will destroy you and I will not lose to someone who is only motivated by resentment!" He threw Mr. Jem over his head and he landed near the trap door.

"Now, now," Mr. Jem said as he got up, "that's not very dolphin-like. Dolphins are supposed to be gentle creatures. Isn't that right, Dr. Jay?"

Dolphi was silent for a few seconds and then said, "on April 23rd, 1999, you mutated a marine mammal veterinarian named Dr. Steele Monroe Jay. After the mutation, Dr. Jay... was dead. Your experiment killed him... but Dolphi... the Dolphin Man... was born! I am not just a dolphin," he cracked his knuckles, "I'm a dolphin man. I *will* kill you. You know why? Because... I'm only human." Dolphi ran at Mr. Jem and tried to kick him in the stomach, but Mr. Jem caught his foot and threw him to the ground. As he rolled onto his back, Mr. Jem jumped onto Dolphi, grabbed his neck with both hands and strangled him over the trap door. Mr. Jem was a very strong man. "Did I ever tell you that I have a black belt in Karate?" Mr. Jem asked as he also had his legs on Dolphi's arms. "I guess I still have it in me."

Dolphi couldn't move. He then noticed something in one of Mr. Jem's pockets. He struggled to get his hand to the pocket and managed to pull out a small syringe that was full of an unknown substance.

"So, you say you're only human, are you?" asked Mr. Jem. "That's exactly what I said to you on this very spot."

Dolphi pulled the cap off the end of the syringe and stabbed it right into Mr. Jem's thigh and plunged the substance into him.

"What are you doing?!" Mr. Jem yelled. As the final bit of the substance went into his body, Mr. Jem let go of Dolphi and pulled out the needle. Dolphi punched him in the face and stood up. He grabbed Mr. Jem and tossed him towards a wall. A dent was made, but the man quickly got up and rushed into the dining room. Dolphi went after him and saw him go into another room. He went over and looked inside. It was a bedroom. Above the bed, was a family portrait. Dolphi saw it was Mr. Jem, his wife and his son. He looked off to the side and saw Mr. Jem touching something on a wall.

"Now it's my turn to ask you, what are *you* doing?" Dolphi asked.

Mr. Jem was shaking as the substance that Dolphi had injected into him was starting to take effect. "I'm not... telling," he said. Dolphi grabbed him and threw him out of the room. He saw a mirror nearby and tossed Mr. Jem into it. The glass exploded and the mirror's frame fell on top of him. Suddenly, Mr. Jem began screaming and thrashing around. Dolphi must have injected a mutagen and blood mixed substance into him. Mr. Jem's screaming made Dolphi remember the pain of his own mutation. Soon, Mr. Jem stopped moving and there was silence. Dolphi went back to the bedroom and picked up the family portrait and went back out. He stood there for a little while staring at the fallen mirror covering Mr. Jem and looking at the picture of the man's family. "... I've made him pay at last," Dolphi thought. "But... for some reason, I don't feel... satisfied." He then heard footsteps in the office. He put the picture on the dining table and went back out and saw his wife and children.

"Dad!" the boys shouted as they ran up to him and hugged him.

"Is everything alright?" Jelera asked. "Did you find your boss?"

"I did," said Dolphi. He walked back into the room where he had defeated him. "... Mission accomplished." Jelera faced Dolphi and together, they kissed. They then tilted their heads and they interlocked snouts. "Well," Dolphi said, "wild dolphins may not do that, but this works just as well."

"Let's go home," Jelera said, "you've earned a rest."

With the loving support of his family, Dolphi felt the emptiness leave him. "The pain is finally over," Dolphi said.

"Good work, dad," Mike said. "Now we can—" He turned and noticed the three bloody corpses in the closet. "God damn! I take it those guys were killed by the mutant sharks."

Dolphi grabbed Mike and turned him away.

"Please don't look at them, boys," Dolphi said. "What happened to them, won't happen any more."

"I know it was tough," said Walter, "but you avenged yourself."

"I love you, daddy," Sid smiled.

"How did you guys get up here?" Dolphi asked. "There were a bunch of mutants on the stairway and the elevator was broken."

"We did see some mutants," Jelera said, "but they didn't see us. We hurried by them and went up another stairway that was clear."

Dolphi then took a nice, deep breath.

Just then, there was a cackling laughing sound from the dining room. The laughing got louder. Everyone went into the room and heard the laughter coming from the fallen mirror. Mr. Jem shoved the mirror off him and the Jay family saw he was in a new form. He was a mutant moray eel! He was holding onto a broken piece of mirror, looking at his reflection. He clothes were in shreds and his green body was naked.

"Thank you," he said in a snake-like voice. "Thank you very, very much."

"For what?" Dolphi asked.

Mr. Jem slowly got up. "For... thisss," he hissed as he spread out his arms, showing his body. "You have liberated me from all doubt." He opened a door and pulled out a white pair of pants and a black belt. It was part of his Karate uniform. He began to put on the pants and tie on his belt.

"Everyone get out of here," Dolphi said to his family. "This is going to get ugly." Jelera and her children ran out of the office and stood outside the door.

"I feel... happy," Mr. Jem said. "I've never felt ssso... alive. I thank you... with all my heart... because you have opened my eyesss to a new indulgenc(sss)e..." Dolphi then ran outside the room and closed the door. He held it shut and felt a few bangs. He saw the door hinges were breaking one by one. He got pushed back as the door popped off. He lifted the door above his head and threw it at Mr. Jem, but the mutant moray eel grabbed it, broke it in half and threw the pieces to the ground. Mr. Jem then continued what he had been about to say. "… The honor of fighting for the birth and exissstenc(sss)e of a brand new form of life — for the nex(sss)t level of mutation — for the nex(sss)t level of… EVOLUTION!!!"

"Bring it on!" Dolphi yelled, "I'm ready! HAVE AT YOU!"

Dolphi ran at Mr. Jem and began throwing punches and kicks. They ended up throwing themselves into the wall, but did not go through. Mr. Jem pushed Dolphi off of him and Dolphi tried to throw a punch, but Mr. Jem ducked it, grabbed Dolphi and threw him head first through the ceiling. He popped out and landed on his feet. Mr. Jem gave Dolphi a big punch in the face while he was dizzy. A few teeth fell out of his mouth before he hit the ground. Mr. Jem's strength was frightening. Dolphi was struggling to get up, but the eel put his foot on Dolphi's neck and pressed hard.

"No!" Mike yelled as he ran into the room. He saw a spear stuck in the ground and picked it up. He ran up to Mr. Jem and stabbed the spear into his back. Mr. Jem growled and turned around. He grabbed Mike's arm and twisted it. Mike let out a cry of pain as he heard a snap. Mr. Jem then picked Mike up by his shirt. "Foolish boy," he said. He threw Mike towards the wall next to the dining room.

"Mike!" Sid yelled as he ran to him. Mr. Jem grabbed Sid and threw him away to the other wall. Sid hit the wall, but not too hard as he tumbled toward it.

"Leave my children alone!" Jelera screamed as she charged at the eel. Mr. Jem kicked her and she fell to the ground. Walter stood by his mother in a fighting position. Mr. Jem pulled the spear out of his back and dropped it. "Let usss sssee if you're ssstill confident when you lossse your youngessst child," Mr. Jem hissed. He turned to Sid and started to run at him.

"No!" Jelera and Dolphi yelled.

Sid lay against the wall not knowing what to do. Suddenly, the wall next to Sid burst open and a figure appeared. When the figure turned to see Mr. Jem was about to jump and kick Sid as hard as he could, he charged at the eel and grabbed him. It was Slice, the last of the three mutant sharks. He picked up Mr. Jem and threw him down the open trap door.

"Jack?" Dolphi asked as he rubbed his snout. "Is that you?"

"Yes," he replied. "My memory has come back." There was a small hole in the right side of the shark's neck. Three small streaks of blood slowly trickled down his neck. Slice turned to Sid. "Don't be afraid," he said as he put his arms out. "Let me take you over to your mother."

Sid got up. "You saved me. Thanks." Slice picked him up and started to walk.

Without anyone noticing, Mr. Jem's hands were visible on the trap door's edge. He crawled out, got up and ran at Slice.

"Look out!" Dolphi yelled.

Too late, Mr. Jem jumped up and kicked Slice hard in the back. He fell down and Sid rolled towards his mother.

"I sssee," Mr. Jem hissed. "Isss that all you've got?"

"Forgive me… little one," Slice said. "I tried to kill you once, but now I realize I shouldn't have."

"It's okay," Sid replied. "You'll be alright, just give me your hand." Sid and Slice tried to reach for each other's hand. Just as they were about to touch, Mr. Jem jumped up and landed with his foot on Slice's neck. A loud snap was heard and Slice lay silent.

Dolphi could tell it was over for him. "JAAAACK!!!"

"Looksss like he and hisss friendsss had sssome heart after all," Mr. Jem said. He turned to Dolphi and jumped on his back, covered his arms with his legs and put his hands over his blowhole. "Jussst acc(sss)ept your fate," Mr. Jem hissed.

Dolphi closed his eyes and tears dripped out. Mr. Jem laughed as he was cutting off Dolphi's oxygen. Dolphi felt powerful emotion fill his body. Mr. Jem laughed louder and harder. Dolphi began to growl. His growl got louder and suddenly, it triggered the power within him. He didn't mean to use it, but he had no choice. His brain within his head began to glow.

Mr. Jem felt electricity flowing through his body. He had no knowledge of what was in Dolphi's head. He couldn't take the electrocution, so he jumped off Dolphi. Dolphi then got up on his knees and put his hands on his head. "… J… Jelera…" Dolphi tried to speak. He suddenly screamed up at the ceiling. The bright light that emanated from Dolphi's head filled the room. He collapsed to the ground and the light faded. Mr. Jem stared in confusion as to what was happening. Dolphi suddenly got up, stood tall and faced Mr. Jem with a different look in his eyes.

The air vent above the room suddenly burst open and three mutant cockroaches crawled out and fell to the floor. They got up and faced Dolphi. He turned to the mutants and put his hands up in a fighting position. A cockroach ran at Dolphi. Dolphi quickly grabbed the cockroach, picked it up, lifted it high above his head and ripped it in half with sheer strength. He then threw the two pieces at each of the other two roaches and they were knocked back into a wall. Dolphi quickly ran at one of the roaches. It had a whole bunch of arms. Dolphi raised his arms into karate chop positions and chopped all the arms off in one go. Dolphi faced the third roach and punched it right through the stomach. They both collapsed onto the ground and Dolphi turned to face Mr. Jem. Mr. Jem was staring at Dolphi. He ran at Dolphi and began throwing punches. Dolphi's reflexes seemed sharp. He was blocking every move Mr. Jem was making. Dolphi grabbed the eel's arm and squeezed it tight. Mr. Jem grunted in pain.

"… I'm… fired… am I?" Dolphi asked. He threw him up into the ceiling and as he came down, the dolphin punched him in the stomach and the eel hit the ceiling again. Dolphi did it once more and then threw him off into the wall by the dining room. Mr. Jem cowered as he lay against the wall.

Dolphi turned to Mike who was also lying against the wall. He walked over and knelt beside him. "Hold still," he said.

"You…" Mike said. "You're… Cyber-soul… aren't you?"

"This will hurt for only a second, and then you will feel better." The possessed Dolphi put his hands on Mike's broken arm. He then squeezed and turned the arm. Mike screamed and breathed heavily as he felt the sharp pain for one second and then felt less of it after. Dolphi got up and went to Mr. Jem's desk. He picked it up and threw it at the large window behind it. The window shattered and the desk fell to the ground outside.

"What are you doing?" Mike asked.

Dolphi didn't answer. He punched a part of the wall next to the window and made a hole. He grabbed some wires and yanked them out. Electricity began to surge through his body, but it didn't phase him. He closed his eyes and faced the broken window. He opened his mouth and a white energy began to flow out. It formed into a large, white portal.

Mike was shocked. "Dad?! What the hell's wrong?!"

Dolphi turned his head to look at his family. "I'm sorry," he said, "I have to go. I must see places... do things... learn much. You will see this dolphin again one day. Farewell." He faced the portal and walked into it. Dolphi then vanished.

"Dad!" the boys yelled.

Mr. Jem got up. He was coughing a large amount of blood from his mouth. He looked at the boys and then at the portal. He grunted hard and ran at it. He jumped at the portal hoping he could get into it, but instead, it disappeared. Mr. Jem found himself flying through the air. He went through the window and was falling to his doom. He yelled out loud and then his cry stopped as the sound of a loud thud was heard down below.

Jelera and the boys ran over to the window. Mr. Jem was lying motionless on the ground on his back.

"Dad?!" Mike yelled looking outside. "Where are you, dad?! Are you alright?!" There was no answer. "Dad?!" he called again. There was still no reply. There was silence. Everything was very quiet. "Dad..." Mike softy said. He then noticed the armless cockroach mutant squirming around on the floor. Mike ran over to it. "You stupid monsters!" he yelled as he lifted his foot and stomped down hard on the cockroach's head. Puss spewed out. Mike then collapsed on the ground and burst into tears. Jelera went over and hugged Mike. "Dad saved us all," Mike sobbed. "This will be a day... I'll never forget."

"I'm so sorry," Jelera said. "What did you mean when you said, Cyber-soul?"

"Something in his head," Mike said through his sobs. "I'll try to explain later."

Sid knelt in front of Slice's body and stroked his head. "I forgive you," he sobbed. "Please go to heaven." Everyone went over to Sid.

"It's okay, baby," Jelera assured him.

Just then, there was a cackling sound over the loudspeaker.

"*Jay family,*" said a strange, low toned voice, "*I have just discovered that this building is rigged with explosives and a timer for them to detonate started a few minutes ago! The whole place is going to go up in flames in two minutes. If you can hear me, get your butts out of here immediately! I repeat... !*"

Sid then put his hands on Slice's eyelids and closed them. "Good-bye," he said.

"We have to hurry!" said Jelera. Everyone got up and ran out of the office.

The Day of the Dolphin Man

"If we don't change, we don't grow.
If we don't grow, we aren't really living."
—American writer Gail Sheehy

A SWARM OF mutants began exploding out of office rooms. There were mutated roaches and rats everywhere and they looked vicious. "This isn't good!" Walter shouted. The mutants covered the walkway, so getting to the stairs was impossible. The only clear path was a connecting bridge. They hurried onto it as the mutant swarm went after them. Suddenly, the bridge broke from one end and tilted down to the first floor. Jelera and the boys slid down towards the mutants. "Oh, no!" Mike shouted. Just as they were about to slide right into them, the bridge from the other end broke and it fell flat to the ground. Everyone was alright and when they saw they were on the first floor, they climbed over the railing and proceeded towards the lobby. There were more mutants up ahead.

A S.W.A.T officer was shooting mutants with his machine gun as they came near, but there were too many of them. They jumped on the man and began attacking him. The S.W.A.T officer screamed and threw his gun towards the Jay family when he saw them. The man was ripped apart in no time.

"Everyone stay close!" Jelera yelled. She picked up the machine gun as different species of mutated fish began to run at her. She had never used a gun before, but she pointed it, squeezed the trigger and began to shoot away at the mutants. Her mutated body was stronger that her human form, so she was able to handle the recoil.

"Good shooting, mom!" said Sid. The way was clear. Everyone progressed through the door and entered the lobby. As they went towards the front entrance, they saw more mutants spewing out of the other rooms. Jelera opened fire and after she heard only clicks indicating that the gun was empty, she dropped it and everyone ran out of the building. As they went outside, they saw more S.W.A.T officers with weapons in their hands. Backup had arrived.

"Don't shoot!" the boys yelled as they ran off to the side. Mutants from inside poured out of the building. "Blow them away!" yelled one of the S.W.A.T officers. All of them opened fire, shooting down mutant after mutant. Ten seconds later, an explosion occurred inside the building. The lobby blew up and mutants went flying in all directions. More explosions sounded and the building began to collapse. After a few minutes, all was quiet. Smoke, fire and crumbling building was all that remained of the Marine Research Institute labs. Everyone was breathing hard.

"We made it…" Jelera said softly.

Officer Monica noticed Jelera and the boys and ran over to them.

"Where's Dolphi?!" Monica asked with a worried look on her face. "Did he… not make it out in time?"

"We don't know," Mike said, still breathing hard. "He vanished." He turned to the burning building. "The enemy has been destroyed. The illegal mutation projects are no more."

Monica was confused. "What do you mean he 'vanished'?"

"We don't know," Mike replied in a sad voice. "It's so hard to explain."

Jelera tried to describe to Monica what had happened to Dolphi. "I feel sad that he is gone, but I feel that he will be okay. How's your arm?" she asked Mike.

"It's still hurts a bit," Mike replied, "but whatever dad did to me, he took away most of the pain."

"His arm is broken, officer," Jelera said. "Is there a doctor anywhere?" Monica pointed to an ambulance. "Come, Mike," Jelera said as she took him over to the van. There were a couple of EMS (Emergency Medical Service) people standing around.

"You two!" Jelera said.

"What the?" one of them asked as he looked at Jelera's body.

"Don't look at *me*!" she said, "help my son! His arm's broken!"

"Uh, yes ma'am," said the other man. Mike sat up on the van's edge and the two men began treating him. Jelera walked back to Walter and Sid. Suddenly, a few S.W.A.T's pointed their weapons at her.

"You!" one of them shouted. "Get on the ground!" Jelera had her hands up, and was very afraid, but Monica walked up to them.

"Lower your weapons!" she yelled. "She is with me!" After a moment, they did as Monica said and walked away.

"Thanks," Jelera replied with a sigh of relief. "I thought I was had."

"I didn't get to talk to you before," Monica replied. "So, you are Dolphi's wife?"

"Yes I am."

Inside Monica's flipped cruiser, the two gunmen from the liquor store, Max and Sammy had finally broken out through the door. The vehicle was damaged after it was tossed, so the door was weakened.

They looked at the burning building and the scattered mutants. "Damn!" Sammy said. "This is the craziest thing I've ever seen!"

"Come on, let's get out of here," Max said. As they tried to run away, they bumped into a black SUV that had pulled up beside them. The doors opened and out came a couple of officers and the Police Commissioner, Harold Rex. "Take care of these two, will you?" he asked his escorts. He noticed Officer Monica with a female mutant dolphin and two boys. He walked up to them.

"Well, well," he said with a grin. "What do we have here, Officer Roans?"

"Some brave children and a victim of illegal mutation, Commissioner," she replied.

"Are you going to arrest our mother?" Walter asked. "She saved our lives."

Rex scratched his chin and studied her body. "You don't have to worry lads," he said. "All these dead mutants and the destruction of this place are a much bigger issue right now."

"Uh, I'd like to request something," Walter said.

"No problem," Rex replied. "What is it?"

Walter turned to the body of the great white shark named Jaws.

"I would like that shark over there to have a funeral. He should be buried out at sea."

"Why?" Rex asked confused.

"He was a human until he was mutated. He was one of the staff of this facility. His name was… Drake Evans I believe. He would be at peace and so would we if that could be done."

Rex turned to look at the body. He then turned to look at the facility. He felt saddened in a way. "Very well," he said. "I'll see if the man has any family and contact them about this."

"Thank you very much," Walter replied.

The Commissioner then walked off to meet with the S.W.A.T.

Mike walked over to his family with his arm in a sling. "This feels much better," he said.

Dolphi's friend, Regan, walked up to the Jay family. "What happened to my friend?" he asked. He was then told about Dolphi's mysterious disappearance. "Oh," he frowned unhappily. "I never got the chance to say something to him. I wanted to say that his encounter with my blind mother has helped her to see again. He must have healed her somehow." He then sighed. "I have to get going now. I have your phone number, so if I should see your husband, I'll let you know, okay?"

"Thank you," Jelera replied.

"Farewell!" He then walked away towards his car and left the area.

"I have been thinking," Monica said to Jelera, "maybe you, your children and I should be friends. I'm saying that because… well, I've never known such amazing people before."

"Sure," Jelera smiled. "You're more than welcome to come by our house anytime. I think we should go home now and get some rest."

"Wait a minute," Walter said. "Where's my Disguiser thing?"

"I think it's still in my cruiser," Monica said. Walter went over to the car and saw it was inside the front seat. "Oh, my car…" Monica sighed. Walter opened the door and retrieved it. It was undamaged.

"Dad didn't even get to use it," Walter sighed.

Some white colored vehicles suddenly showed up in the parking lot. Walter looked at the van's side and saw the words, 'Discovery Research Inc.' "I guess they are here for the… mutants." He turned to Jelera. "Mom, hide! I don't think you want to be seen by those guys. Put this suit on as best you can." Jelera decided to listen to Walter and knelt behind the flipped police cruiser, putting on the suit in the process. Walter turned it on and an image of their human father was projected. Jelera's tail was sticking out of the suit, so the boys stood behind her to hide it.

The vans opened and people in white coats came out. They went by Jelera without noticing her. "You're invention works!" Jelera said underneath the suit.

"Come on," Walter said. "Let's go before the batteries die." They went towards their minivan that was parked nearby.

"Wait a minute," Jelera said. "Mike, did you drive yourself here?"

"Yeah, but it was hardly a problem," he replied. Jelera got in the driver's seat and took the suit off.

The boys glanced out at the scene. Police and S.W.A.T were scattered around talking to the media, M.R.I.L staff were talking to each other, exchanging stories about the crazy day. To Jelera and the boys, the people and the activities outside were far away, distant and muted.

Monica went up to the minivan to say goodbye.

"Well," Jelera said, "I guess we better get going officer."

"Call me Monica," she replied smiling.

The boys looked at the ruins of the M.R.I.L one last time as Jelera drove out of the parking lot and headed for home.

"I can't believe what happened to our dad," Mike said. "He just disappeared into that portal thing."

"I know," Walter said. "He said he was going somewhere. He said that we would see him again and I believe we will."

"What should we do about mom?" Sid asked. "She's a mutant who can't go out in public looking like that."

"I'm sure I'll think of something," Jelera replied. "The future's going to bring something good. I just know it."

"There has to be an explanation for all of this," said Walter. "Whatever Mr. Jem was thinking when he created those beasts, I think he ended up starting something. Those Discovery Research Inc. people may research those mutant corpses. From what we heard from a group of unknown soldiers at the hotel we were staying at, I don't know what sort of future will come. Until then, we'll just have to wait and hope to see our father once again. What our father, Dolphi, did today, was very heroic. I think he has made the future a safer one. I believe that this day belongs to him. Today is the day of the Dolphin Man."

* * *

The mystery mutants that had traveled back through time, were watching the burning building from a nearby location, but remained out of sight.

"Sir," one of them asked their leader, "what have we learned from this experience?"

"We have learned about our origin," the leader replied. "We have learned about 'our creator' and the first mutant he created. The mutant eliminated the M.A.C soldiers, our enemies, on his own and for that, we thank him. This is why we saved his life at different times in the past. I knew he would defeat 'our creator'."

"He is gone," another mystery mutant said. "And so is the enigmatic Cyber-soul. Where should we go next?"

"Wherever the dolphin shows up. We should introduce ourselves when we see him again one day."

Another mystery mutant, a female said, "a day that I'll be looking forward to." She then stared out at the burning building in silence for a moment. "By the way," she said to the leader, "there is something that 'our creator' was wrong about."

"And what is that?"

"His son is still alive."

Epilogue

FOR OVER A week, the news was displaying the scenes of the ruined Marine Research Institute Labs. The mutant bodies had been collected by the Discovery Research Inc. Dolphi was in newspapers everywhere and his image was on TV. When Dolphi screamed in anguish after the death of Jaws, people reported they could hear it from two miles away.

Mike, Sid and Walter had assemblies held at their school. They told everyone about how their father had given everything he had to stop a major disaster from getting out of hand.

The families of those that died at the M.R.I.L, including that of Drake Evans, were contacted and given the news about their loved ones. Drake's mutated great white shark body was taken out in a boat with the help of the M.R.I.L staff and was dropped off in the ocean. As his body sank beneath the waves, some people claimed that he was smiling as he was finally laid to rest. The staff eventually found employment at other research facilities.

Regan Markinson called the Jay family some time later and said he had found no signs of Dolphi, and that he was moving away. He and his wife expressed their condolences for the disappearance of the boys' father.

The boys still had to go through school, but were planning for their futures.

Mike continued his Tae Kwon-Do education and was planning on being a martial arts instructor when he was experienced enough.

Walter was planning on joining the Discovery Research Inc. The mutant incident had inspired him and he was eager to be a scientist to study the creatures.

Sid's passion for dolphins was still strong. He had disliked sharks in the beginning because they attacked dolphins, but after his last moment with the mutant thresher shark Slice, he had had a change of heart for sharks and accepted them as natural creatures of the ecosystem. Sid was looking forward to being a dolphin trainer. Unaware of the incident at Dolphin World where his father had been sent to, he would eventually take his first step into the world of the dolphin park industry.

Speaking of Dolphin World, the former dolphin trainer, Jordan Sinclair, never told anyone about his act of arson on the facility's store. He eventually joined an animal welfare group to fight against dolphin captivity. Dolphin World was shut down after a court case for unlawful treatment of animals. The Navy claimed they had no knowledge of the equipment that was stored underneath the facility and that it was not brought to their attention. The Navy got off the hook stating that whatever happened at Dolphin World does not reflect the Navy as a whole. Their dolphin program continued.

Jelera continued to take care of the boys, but something unexpected happened a few weeks after the incident at the M.R.I.L. One night, a S.W.A.T team charged the house and took Jelera away. The boys tried to stop them, but were held down. Outraged at this, the boys did everything they could to track down their dolphin mother. The police and the Discovery Research Inc. claimed not to be responsible. The children ended up living in the care of their grandparents up in Tallahassee.

Monica Roans continued working as a police officer. After hearing the news about the raid on the Jay residence and the disappearance of Jelera, she was shaken. She told the boys that she would do everything she could to find their mother.

Earlier at the police station, after Monica put in the third security tape she got from the M.R.I.L, she had walked away from it and left it playing. There was static for a long time, but suddenly, images of the three mutant sharks appeared in the secret lab where Dolphi and his wife were mutated. The surveillance camera was broken after Dolphi tossed a ladder at it, but it somehow managed to produce images that had brief blips of static. Slice was seen waking up in his makeshift water bed. *"Nooo!"* he cried. *"Don't let the chocolate monsters get me!"* The other sharks, Jaws and Chewer woke up.

"Slice, what's wrong?" Jaws asked.

"Oh," Slice sighed. *"I just had a crazy nightmare."*

"I see." After a moment, Jaws got out of his water bed and sat at the pool's edge with his legs in the water. The scenes were after they had a chocolate wrestling match.

"Is something wrong?" Slice asked. *"I'm sorry if I woke you up."*

"No, it's okay," Jaws replied. *"I was just lying in bed and was thinking about what you said earlier."*

"How funny," Chewer said, *"so was I."* They all sat next to each other beside the pool.

"I was thinking about our relationship," Jaws said. *"That rodeo riding that you did with me was pretty funny come to think of it. You're so playful, Slice."*

"Yeah, glad that you liked that. And that chocolate wrestling..." Everyone then laughed.

"Maybe you shouldn't eat chocolate before bedtime," Jaws suggested, *"as it gives you nightmares about being chased by what did you say... chocolate monsters?"* He laughed.

"It's not funny," Slice protested.

"I know. I'm thinking this could be the beginning of an interesting relationship."

"Yeah," Chewer said. *"Tonight, let's dream about all the wondrous things that we're going to do together."*

"That's a wonderful, idea," Slice said. *"We'll explore places in the ocean, maybe meet up with some normal sharks, I just can't wait for all that to begin."*

"It's a date," Jaws said. The sharks hugged each other and the video footage cackled and faded into static.

As for Dolphi, after he disappeared into the portal, he felt himself land with a thud. He felt as if he had been asleep for a very long time. He slowly woke up and looked around. The bathing suit that he had been wearing had disappeared. He found himself in a dark alleyway. The air felt cold and it was night time. He slowly walked through the alleyway towards a dark street and ended up facing a whole new adventure.

However, that's a story for another time.

Afterward

I WOULD LIKE to thank everyone very much for reading this novel. Dolphi the Dolphin Man is a project that I started in 1997 at age 13 and finished in 2005, the weekend I turned 21.

The idea of a half-human and half-dolphin creature popped into my head after watching cartoon shows in the early 90's featuring animalistic human-like creatures. One of the best examples would be the Teenage Mutant Ninja Turtles. I was one of the many people moved by a euphoric age of what was called 'turtle power'. There's a new Turtles cartoon on Saturday mornings, but I don't wake up in the early morning very often and the 'turtle power' doesn't quite feel the same. I guess things change when we grow up.

The 'Street Sharks' mentioned in chapter 13, is another cartoon show where a bunch of teenagers get turned into half-human shark men. The show didn't last very long on the air, but it was another inspiration for me.

Around 1994, I found a TV brochure listing show times for a station called YTV (Youth TeleVision). Listed at 2:30 AM from Monday to Friday was a show called Flipper. I did not know what that word meant, but I went to watch it one Friday night and found out it was the name of a dolphin in the 1960's that foiled the bad guy's plans, rescued people and saved the day. That show sparked my passion for dolphins and I've loved the animals ever since. This love for the animals eventually motivated my mother to sign me up for a sponsorship program for a dolphin at a facility in Grassy Key,

Florida called the Dolphin Research Center (DRC). I sent money annually to feed and support a dolphin by the name of Pax. In the process, I received monthly newsletters about the 'dolphin society' at the facility. I also had the opportunity on several occasions to take part in swim-with-dolphins programs. It was an exciting and moving experience for me at the time. Everything was perfect, the dolphins made me very happy and I couldn't have asked for anything sweeter... or so I thought.

One day, in the summer of 1999, I received a newsletter from the DRC that contained an article; a story that changed the way I thought about dolphins forever. It was about a former Navy dolphin by the name of Buck. The story told of how he and two other Navy dolphins by the names of Luther and Jake had been part of a program to attempt to return dolphins back into the wild after they had been in captivity. Yes, some of you may be familiar with this story, but I'll explain it to those who aren't. The article said that two of the dolphins, Buck and Luther had been released illegally back in May of 1996, had been pushed by the boats and were abandoned. The man responsible for the release was Miami native and former trainer of Flipper, Richard O' Barry. The Dolphin Research Center article mentioned that a team was sent to rescue Buck. When he was found, they claimed he was emaciated and badly injured. He was taken to the DRC where he was given around the clock treatment until his death three years later. The story and postscript of Buck had touched me deeply and I believed the things that were written. The whole story was made to look like Ric O' Barry's fault. I sent several e-mails to O' Barry under an alias criticizing his actions on the dolphins. He told me to read a book that he was releasing called "To Free a Dolphin." When I got the book, I read through it and made some horrible discoveries. What was mentioned in the DRC article that I read, wasn't a complete picture. O' Barry's story told of how he tried to free dolphins from captivity, but wasn't getting much support. The government that enforces the Marine Mammal Protection Act, the National Marine Fisheries Service (NMFS) denied O' Barry the permits to release the Navy dolphins. Motivated by time running out, he had no choice but to release the animals without government authorization. The release of Buck and Luther caused total pandemonium. The Coast Guard, Navy, SeaWorld, Dolphin Research Center and other groups were trying to find the animals. "To Free a Dolphin" contained a picture of the Navy dolphins being released while there were cameramen filming it. When O' Barry got back to the shore, an agent from the NMFS walked up to him and the cameramen and demanded the tapes without a search warrant. Without evidence that the release of the dolphins was humane and successful, the NMFS took the whole situation, twisted it around and gave everyone a false, one-sided story that caused me to hate O' Barry. After Buck was taken to the DRC, a visitor to the facility noted that Buck looked normal when the DRC stated he was emaciated, had a gash on his back and several puncture wounds. I read in O' Barry's novel about how the Fisheries Service organized the recapture of three dolphins that escaped from a private facility called the Ocean Reef Club (now shut down) and then sent the dolphins back there, no questions asked. What is interesting about this is that one: two of the dolphins were captured without permits and two: by law, any marine mammal obtained from the wild is to be held in 'public' display and not private.

The bottom line for why this government is so protective of these unique animals is because the dolphins are powerful tools of big business. In 1972, the Marine Mammal Protection Act was created to basically protect marine mammals. However, the Act ended up in the hands of the Department of Commerce who in turn gave the handling of the system to the NMFS which is a branch of the umbrella agency known as the National Oceanic and Atmospheric Administration (NOAA). The word 'commerce' means 'business' and so all over the world, dolphin parks have been opening up. Those are just some of the things mentioned in "To Free a Dolphin."

Shaken by the flawed system and by the embarrassment of harassing a man who was punished just for being the only one who did the right thing for the animals, I went into a depressive slump for a long time. I lost sleep, I gained weight and wasn't sure what to think anymore. After years of soul searching, I have emerged with new resolve. I have a dream to overhaul the entire marine mammal protection system and make sure no one who loves marine mammals ever gets deceived and manipulated like I have been ever again. In the 1930s, Canada's first female MP (Member of Parliament), Agnes MacPhail, was appalled by the conditions in penitentiaries. She was booed and jeered by the male dominated Parliament, but her courage eventually led to the reform of the entire Canadian penal system. If she could do that, then maybe I can change things too.

I have learned even more shocking things about marine mammals from watching a couple of online news reports and reading a series of news articles put together by a Florida news media known as the Sun-Sentinel. The documentation is called "Marine Attractions: Below the Surface." It explained that no one has been issued a permit to capture a dolphin from the wild in the last decade since Free Willy groups protested that marine mammals shouldn't be captured from the wild. They won and the issuing of permits stopped. So how does this big business industry keep getting dolphins? It's easy, they slip through the cracks — they take a back door — they simply find a way around the system. A video was shot in February 2004 viewing massive dolphin slaughters in Japan called Drive Fisheries. Some of the dolphins were diverted from the slaughter and were being selected by dolphin trainers. They had all the capture tools and stretchers to take the animals away to marine attractions in Japan, China, the Philippines and other countries in Asia. In the Caribbean, South America and other places outside the United States, marine parks buy dolphins from the largest exporter of the animals in the whole world, the island of Cuba. Demand for dolphins from that country is so great, clients are on a two year waiting list. According to a report by ABC News Primetime Live, in the Solomon Islands, native fishermen slaughter dolphins for their meat and teeth which is used as money. A foreign businessman had given the fishermen real money to exploit some of the dolphins in a marine attraction in Mexico as well as several attractions in the Solomon Islands. The man claimed he was 'saving' the animals from slaughter, which is absolutely bogus. The man can save the animals from butchery, but by giving the fishermen tens of thousands of American dollars for each dolphin, he is also providing a powerful incentive for the fishermen to continue killing thousands of dolphins in the most brutal way imaginable. "He's not an environmentalist," says Ric O' Barry, an advocate of OneVoice France, "he's a dolphin hunter—he's a dolphin dealer." Recently, a law has been passed in the Solomon Islands banning the capture and export of bottlenose dolphins.

These 'dolphin hunters' will not hesitate to expand their world-wide business, even if it means having rock-solid business relationships with people that animal rights and welfare organizations as well as Amnesty International, condemns — even if it means violating the trade embargo on Cuba. This revelation is very sad for me to know about.

More information on the topic of the Japanese Drive Fisheries can be found at www.savetaijidolphins.org, www.bluevoice.org and www.WDCS.org (Whale and Dolphin Conservation Society)

Overall, this is simply unacceptable and violates not only the commonly enforced laws of animal conservation and welfare, but also violates my ethical love and interests for the animals. I suspect an enormous conspiracy where dolphins are used not only as powerful tools for big business and influence, but for blackmail as well.

There is huge money to be made in swim-with-dolphin programs and more are opening every year. By the way, you may have noticed that there is a dollar sign in $wim-with-dolphins mentioned in the story. In some of them, the animals are not cared for very well, but trainers, vets, facility inspectors or anyone else involved with the dolphins do not always admit there are problems because they are afraid of losing their jobs. *"The money influences everything, including the science," said Naomi Rose, a marine mammal scientist with the Humane Society of the United States. "If you want to be a mover and shaker in the marine mammal world, you keep your mouth shut. If you're a scientist and you take a stand against captivity, you are ostracized."* [Kestin, Sally.] I am not criticizing all dolphin facilities and employees, just the businessmen who control everything from the science and research, to the way we are made to think about the animals.

In my story, I created two chapters where Dolphi finds himself in a completely corrupt dolphin facility that is secretly training dolphins for U.S Navy operations. I wrote that up because I wanted to express how grave the situation with dolphins in captivity really is. The magnitude of corruption may not be as drastic as what I wrote, but there have been places where the lack of expertise is appalling. If those chapters offend the Navy, I apologize. I respectfully state that I'm not doing this to offend anyone, but I am a person with big dreams and ideas, who wants to get it out into the world and make a difference. There are truths that need to be told and future adventures waiting for my dolphin man to start.

To sum it all up, I am not totally opposed to having some dolphin facilities for educational purposes. However, training dolphins just to do silly tricks to entertain people is not acceptable. I would like to see a day when an international body exists to oversee the care of any marine mammals in captivity.

Thank you, and may you all discover truth and justice within yourselves.

—Graham R. Lowe

References

www.bluevoice.org

www.BrainyQuote.com

Kestin, Sally. Marine Attractions: Below the Surface, Sun-Sentinel, posted May 23, 2004

O' Barry, Richard. "To Free a Dolphin" by Renaissance Books, L.A., 2000

www.savetaijidolphins.org

Whale and Dolphin Conservation Society www.WDCS.org

ABOUT THE AUTHOR

GRAHAM R. LOWE is a young man with Autism. He was born in Toronto in 1984 and grew up in the suburb of Scarborough with his parents, two brothers, two dogs and a cat. He now lives in Kettleby, Ontario with his family. Graham is close to earning a black belt in Tae Kwon Do. He is a certified scuba diver. He enjoys traveling with his family. His summers are spent on the family island on Stoney Lake, Ontario, where he water-skis and wakeboards. He enjoys playing video games. This is his first novel which he started in 1997 at the young age of 13. Graham has a passion for dolphins and a strong determination to see an end to the exploitation, mistreatment and killing of these intelligent creatures. He believes this end can be achieved through the education and enlightenment of the public.

ISBN 141209009-1

9 781412 090094